Lady Patricia

Lady Barran

Lady Patricia

by John Bryant

Published by www.lulu.com

© Copyright John Bryant 2018

LADY PATRICIA

All rights reserved.

The right of John Bryant to be identified as the author of this work has been asserted in accordance with the Copyright, Designs and Patents Act 1988.

No part of this publication may be reproduced, stored in a retrieval system, or transmitted, in any form or by any means, electronic, mechanical, photocopying, recording or otherwise, nor translated into a machine language, without the written permission of the publisher.

This is a work of fiction. Names and characters are a product of the author's imaginations and any resemblance to actual persons, living or dead, events and organisations is purely coincidental.

Condition of sale

This book is sold subject to the condition that it shall not, by way of trade or otherwise, be lent, re-sold, hired out or otherwise circulated in any form of binding or cover other than that in which it is published and without a similar condition including this condition being imposed on the subsequent purchaser.

ISBN 978-0-244-70462-9

Book formatted by www.bookformatting.co.uk.

Contents

Chapter 1 1
Chapter 2 15
Chapter 3 21
Chapter 4 27
Chapter 5 36
Chapter 6 52
Chapter 7 96
Chapter 8 125
Chapter 9 154
Chapter 10..171
Chapter 11..202
Chapter 12..215
Chapter 13..231
Chapter 14..240

Introduction

The 1970s were a significant decade in the world of animal welfare and animal rights. At the beginning of the 1970 Annual General Meeting of the Royal Society for the Prevention of Cruelty to Animals, diminutive, grey-haired pensioner and long-term member Vera Sheppard climbed onto the stage. Before anyone knew what was happening she grabbed a microphone and announced that she had discovered written evidence of a plot by bloodsports supporters to infiltrate the Society for the purpose of preventing the RSPCA campaigning against bloodsports.

The chairman of the Society's 46-strong Council turned off Vera's microphone, ordered uniformed RSPCA Inspectors to remove Vera from the stage and closed the meeting, without any business being completed. As confusion reigned, Vera was surrounded by members asking what evidence she had, and because the hall was being closed, a group of fifteen perturbed members (including the author of this book) agreed to meet at a later date to examine and discuss Vera's evidence and its significance.

A month after the AGM, the fifteen ordinary members of the RSPCA met in a North London primary school, to examine Mrs Sheppard's evidence – the most disturbing being a letter from Lord Halifax, (then) chairman of the Masters of Fox Hounds Association, calling on supporters of bloodsports to join the RSPCA and use their votes in the Society's elections for candidates who were pro-hunting or neutral on the issue. An indication of the success of the infiltration emerged when Horse and Hound magazine announced the name of the new RSPCA Council chairman before he had even been elected!

The infiltration plot had begun in the 1960s and the fifteen outraged ordinary members, including Vera Sheppard, decided to form a 'Reform Group' to counter the hunters' infiltration, and persuade the Society's Council to form a policy against bloodsports and halt the infiltration of people who kill wild animals for sport.

The battle between the Council and the Reform Group raged, especially because RSPCA members began to vote Reform Group supporters onto the Council. In 1974 the existing Council chairman persuaded the Council to agree to set up a Public Enquiry under the leading QC, Charles Sparrow. There were many open public meetings held by the Enquiry with members raising other contentious issues – such as the high numbers of animals being destroyed in the RSPCA centres.

Charles Sparrow and his team eventually produced a huge report including recommending that the entire Council should resign so that a new much smaller Council of 25 could be elected. The Enquiry also recommended that the 'Reform Group' should disband to allow peace to break out within the Society. The 'Group' immediately agreed to do so.

Charles Sparrow announced that he had received a letter from the Vice Chairman of the Council (a Conservative Member of Parliament), praising the Council Chairman and appealing to the Enquiry to allow him to retain his chairmanship. It transpired that the letter was a forgery written by the Council chairman himself! Charles Sparrow was outraged and declared that the Council chairman 'was not fit to lead a major charity like the RSPCA' and insisted on his resignation.

The new Council and its new Chairman, Dr Richard Ryder, suggested that all the Society policies should be reviewed. One of the new policies unanimously agreed by the Council was that the RSPCA opposed all hunting of wild animals with dogs for 'sport', as well as the shooting of animals and birds for 'sport'. To counter infiltration by bloodsports interests it was decided that candidates for election to the Council must declare any involvement in bloodsports.

Dr Ryder, the new Chairman of the RSPCA Council, had

famously coined the phrase, 'speciesism' suggesting that animals have 'rights' not to be abused and exploited by human beings. He and the RSPCA head of education David Paterson, came up with the idea of a two-day 'Animals' Rights Symposium' to be held at Trinity College, Cambridge in the summer of 1977. The Council approved the initiative and the RSPCA acted as host to a mixed group of two hundred theologians, philosophers, scientists, lawyers, politicians, and ordinary folk involved or interested in animal 'welfare' or 'rights'.

At the end of the two-day symposium, on August 19th 1977, one hundred and fifty attendees signed –

THE RIGHTS OF ANIMALS

Declaration Against Speciesism

"Inasmuch as we believe that there is ample evidence that many other species are capable of feeling, we condemn totally the infliction of suffering upon our brother and sister animals, and the curtailment of their enjoyment, unless it be necessary for their own individual benefit.

"We do not accept that a difference in species alone (any more than a difference in race) can justify wanton exploitation or oppression in the name of science or sport, or for food, commercial profit or other human gain.

"We believe in the evolutionary and moral kindship of all animals and we declare our belief that all sentient creatures have rights to life, liberty and the quest for happiness.

We call for the protection of these rights."

The story in this book is a work of fiction, but all the horses and ponies named were real rescued animals living in the Ferne Animal Sanctuary at the beginning of the story in October 1977. The places, towns and villages named in the story exist, but are used fictitiously. Any resemblance to people living or dead, may not be entirely coincidental!

The Ferne equines in this story.

> Lady Patricia, Patrick, Beadle, Lucky, Gregory, Silver, Rufus, Cindy, Blue, Jason, George, Smoky, Macaroni, Red, Smithy and Donald.

I am indebted to my friend and Animal Aid stalwart Richard Mountford for applying his proof-reading skills to my early error-strewn manuscript.

Chapter 1

Midnight Thursday 27th October 1977

The headlights of an old and battered Landrover pierced the blackness of a damp October night and swept along the unkempt hedgerows bordering a narrow road on Somerset's border with Devon. The vehicle dragged a small empty horsebox, rattling and creaking behind. Passing the roadside fields of the Ferne Animal Sanctuary, the driver nudged his front seat passenger and with his left hand pointed to a wooden gate, seconds before he swung the wheel, and turned left into a narrow tree-lined lane. The Landrover slowed and crept into a gravelled lay-by, tyres crunching and splashing through muddy puddles in deep wheel ruts. The engine and lights died simultaneously - exaggerating the darkness which silently closed again over the lane.

The three occupants of the vehicle sat huddled and silent for a full ten seconds as the breeze moaned softly in the avenue of trees and the clicks and bubbling of the cooling engine faded. Their eyes gradually adjusted to the grey light filtering through the branches above them as they peered out at the tarmac surface of the lane - black and wet with fallen leaves. The first to speak was the driver, Eddie Bowen, a thickset weather-beaten man in his early thirties.

'All set then?' It was more like an order than a question. His front seat companion, his older brother Rex, merely grunted in response. 'It's just gone twelve', added Eddie squinting at his watch and twisting in his seat to address the third member of the trio. 'All right Tony?'

'Yeah', came the almost whispered answer from the much

younger man in the back seat.

The two Bowen brothers had spent their lives as travellers, their home being a caravan towed around the country, their childhood education constantly disrupted, and skills largely confined to the scrap metal trade, laying tarmac drives, and odd-jobbing. They were also skilled in the arts of poaching and dealing in horses. Both had convictions for petty theft, and Rex had served a 12 month-term for stealing lead from a church roof, although for the most part their nomadic lifestyle had kept them free from the clutches of the law. Their mother had been buried twelve months ago – and the last they had seen of their father was when Eddie was fifteen and his brother eighteen. Their mother had constantly assured them that they already possessed the only inheritance they could ever expect from their father - their black unruly hair and startlingly blue, twinkling eyes.

Tony Lewis, the third occupant of the Landrover, was seventeen, and his pale, nervous face and slight stature set him strikingly apart from the two brothers. His fair hair was overgrown and flopped over one side of his right eye-brow. Eight months previously, after a series of rows with his parents and school suspensions for truancy, his stock-broker father and Conservative councillor mother found him glue-sniffing in the garden shed. Their verbal onslaught left him so humiliated, angry and miserable that in the early hours of the morning, he quietly packed a rucksack and crept out of the house, determined never to return home to the leafy suburb of Bicester in Oxfordshire.

Hitching to London he had stumbled across a group of caravans untidily parked in a large lay-by on the A41 near Aylesbury. As he walked past, Eddie Bowen and his girlfriend Lucy were preparing to leave the group of travellers and tow their caravan to Somerset to join his older brother Rex at an official travellers' site. The convivial Eddie had called out to Tony, and asked him if he wanted a lift. When Eddie told him of their Somerset destination, but asked no further questions, Tony gratefully thanked him for the offer and joined Eddie and Lucy for the trip to the west country.

At the Somerset travellers' site, Rex was far from pleased at his brother's hasty adoption of Tony. 'There'll be people looking for 'im. That could bring trouble'.

'Get away', scorned his younger brother, 'He'll probably want to go home in a few days. If he turns out to be a problem, we'll find out where he lives and contact his folks. They'd probably be happy to pay us for our community spirit,' he added with a grin, running imaginary pound notes between his thumb and forefinger.

So Tony stayed. He quickly came to admire and then adore Eddie's cavalier attitude to life, his flashing smile and devious charm. When Tony confessed to the glue-sniffing incident, Eddie had merely cuffed him on the back of the head and mocked him with the admonishment, 'What a prat!'

Later, Rex took Tony to one side, and urged him to find a phone-box and ring his parents. 'They'll be worried to death, son, 'tis only fair to tell'em you're alright.' Eventually, after more nagging from Rex, Tony did phone home, and told his parents that he was safe and well in Liverpool and that he would let them know when he was ready to return home.

From then on Tony had lived with Eddie and Rex on the travellers' site near Taunton. Eddie taught him how to catch rabbits, taught him the relative values of scrap metal and, much to Rex's annoyance, insisted on Tony accompanying him and his brother on their various nefarious 'business ventures'. Now one of Eddie's more ambitious 'business ventures' had led the three of them to a dark country lane, near Chard in Somerset in damp October.

Eddie spoke again. 'Tony, I want you to go back up the lane about twenty yards. There's a farm track on the right-hand side. Go down there for about thirty yards and you'll see a gap in the hedge on the left. Squeeze through there and you'll find another hedge on the left. Follow it along till you come to a big metal gate. Close it as quietly as you can. I don't want them nags spooked. You got that?'

It was too dark for his companions to see his face, but when Tony tried to respond, his voice betrayed his nervousness. Quickly clearing his throat, he tried to sound unconcerned about the task he had been allocated. 'Yep, no problem', he replied, and asked, 'Then what?'

Eddie had committed the entire plan to memory. 'Make your way back here to the wagon. Me and Rex will wait here for five minutes and then we'll go round the corner of the road where there's wooden gate. You can join us there and help us lift off the gate. Then I'll go in and bring out the mare and you two can put the gate back in place. Then we'll walk her back to the trailer and load her up. Understand?'

Turning round to examine Tony's pale face, Eddie continued, 'You just have to go down the lane, through the hole in the hedge and keep going 'till you come to a big metal gate. All you have to do is close it so the ponies can't get out of the field. Easy peasy! Make sure you close it quietly! I don't want the nags spooked. OK?'

'And then I'll find you by the roadside gate', queried Tony nervously.

'No, you berk! snapped Eddie, 'Me and Rex are going to dump you here and go off to the south of France!! Now bugger off down the lane. We'll see you round the corner.'

'Sure', replied Tony, and obediently opened the nearside door and stepped out onto the gravel. He tried to whisper, 'See you in a bit', but fear gripped his throat like a claw. Coughing quietly, he turned away, zipped up his black jacket and disappeared into the night.

Rex leaned back and reached over and pulled the rear door shut with a soft click. 'I hope you know what you're doing bringing that kid with us', he hissed. 'Scared shitless! Don't blame me if he cocks it up'.

'You worry too much, Rex. He'll be all right.'

'I bloody hope so!', moaned his brother.

Five minutes later Eddie and Rex were crouched in the muddy ditch next to the wooden five-bar gate that separated the Ferne Animal Sanctuary's top field from the road.

'Where the 'ell is 'e?' rasped Rex.

'He'll be here', whispered Eddie, his confidence immediately justified as a breathless Tony padded round the corner and practically threw himself into the ditch next to them.

'OK Tony?' asked Eddie.

'Yeah!', gasped Tony, 'There must be at least a dozen of 'em in there'.

'Sixteen', snapped Rex impatiently, 'At least there was last week when I counted 'em'.

Eddie cut him short. 'Keep your voices down. We're only taking one - the Connemara mare. The rest are rubbish'.

'How are you going to catch it?' asked Tony.

Eddie interrupted him impatiently.

'Look, this is a bloody animal rest home. These ponies are treated like kids - couple of peppermints and they'll follow you anywhere. Now let's get this gate off the hinges and I'll go and get a head collar on her'.

They grunted in unison as they lifted the heavy gate off its hinges – leaving it still chained and padlocked to the gate-post at the other end. Even in the gloom, Eddie's teeth flashed in a huge grin. 'Cheer up you two, we'll be on our way out of here in twenty minutes with a good four or five hundred quids' worth of pony'.

Without waiting for a response Eddie nimbly vaulted the gate and dropped into the field and moved off into the gloom, a head-collar and rope dangling from his right fist behind his back while his left hand toyed with sugar lumps and peppermints deep in his pocket.

As his shape became indistinguishable in the darkness Rex and Tony crouched in the ditch. It would be a simple matter of dragging the gate open, letting Eddie walk the mare out onto the road, and then lift the gate back onto its hinges. By the first light of the next morning, the three men and their stolen animal would be safely hidden miles away before anyone even noticed that Lady Patricia was missing.

*

Lady Patricia's front hooves squelched in the sloppy mud around the water trough. She lowered her head, flicked floating blades of grass and leaves aside with her upper lip and gulped down three long draughts of the cold water. Her thirst sated, she allowed the last mouthful to trickle through her teeth and splatter back into the trough, then carefully extricated her feet from the slimy mud and wheeled away.

Spread out around her in the murky, four-acre field, fifteen other members of her herd chomped noisily at the last of the season's grass. Through the muffled hum of the wind, the Connemara grey mare heard comforting sounds – a cough, a snort, steaming dung slapping the damp turf. Lady Patricia was the undisputed leader of this disparate collection of ponies and horses. A thoroughbred, she had known no other life other than her entire nine years within the sanctuary. Patricia's mother, when heavily pregnant, had been temporarily homed in the sanctuary when her elderly owner fell seriously ill. A year later the owner had recovered and returned to collect her mare, but 'donated' Patricia to the sanctuary in gratitude.

The sanctuary policy dictated that once within its boundaries, no horse would ever be saddled or harnessed again to bear the weight of a human. In contrast to Patricia's life, most members of her herd had spent most of their lives in the service of humans. A few had been well-loved and cared for by their previous owners, but most had known the darker side of man.

Joey, a 13.1 hands Exmoor pony was now 36 years old and had been in the sanctuary for sixteen years since his rescue from a life of being tethered on roadside verges in all weathers. Only the toughness of his moorland ancestry had enabled him to survive. He was now the oldest in Patricia's herd.

Joey's closest herd-mate was Patrick, an enormous Clydesdale of more than 17 hands and himself more than 30 years old. The gentle giant had begun life as a plough horse, was eventually replaced by a tractor and fortunately allowed to retire in the sanctuary, having spent a few years covered in brasses as an attraction at agricultural shows.

Some of the herd members were comparatively young; George, a handsome skewbald of 13.3 hands, had been retired at seven years old because of repeated lameness. Beadle, a half shire, was a draught horse that had done his share of straining at the plough, but had rebelled after being repeatedly hit around the head with a stick by his owner for losing a prestigious ploughing match. Silver was a 13.1 hands Welsh cob 30 years old. He had spent years being used and abused in a ramshackle riding school and even now the sound of children visitors to the sanctuary was enough to send him wandering off alone to the furthest field.

Of all the rescued and retired working horses given permanent sanctuary at Ferne, Lady Patricia was unique. She had never spent a moment of her life saddled or in harness. Her straight back had never borne the weight of a human being, no whip or stick had touched her hide and no metal bits and reins had dictated the direction in which she moved.

The only terrifying experience she had ever suffered had been three years previously when the sanctuary had been forced to move, lock, stock and barrel fifty miles from its previous site at the village of Berwick St John, near Shaftesbury, to its present home near Chard. A dozen local farm workers and the sanctuary staff at that time, had struggled to keep the entire herd in a yard from which the only escape was up the ramps of lorries. Patricia had whirled, bucked and shied for a full hour, managing to chivvy and provoke the more placid members of her herd into open rebellion against this outrageous intrusion into their peaceful lives.

Eventually, when the rest of the horses had been loaded, and after she had fought alone, red-eyed and screaming against the lasso around her neck, she eventually succumbed and allowed herself to be hauled into the last lorry – but not before leaving one man with scarlet rope burns on his hands, another with a fractured wrist and two more with severe bruising from her flailing hooves.

From the day she was released into the sanctuary's new fields high on the border of Somerset and Devon, Patricia tolerated no head collar, rope or harness. In a good mood she would allow staff members to run a hand down her neck, but even then only in return for a peppermint bribe.

Only Rebecca James, the new sanctuary manager's 16 year-old daughter, could persuade Patricia to stand still for a few moments at a time for her hooves to be picked out or trimmed. Even this had to be done on a quiet and windless day. A gust of wind, a slamming door or a dropped bucket would end the exercise immediately and she would career off, taking the rest of the herd with her, amidst much excitement, snorting and whinnying.

Tonight all was peaceful and still as Patricia strode away from the trough towards the centre of the field and resumed grazing. Suddenly she stopped and raised her head, a clump of grass still protruding from her teeth. She sensed a strange movement in the darkness. Ears twitched forward, nostrils flared, she strained all her senses into the gloom. She saw a figure moving slowly towards her - a faint human scent reached her nostrils, a scent she did not recognise. Now with every fibre alert, she stamped a forefoot hard into the mud and snorted. Fifteen equine heads rose and turned to gaze in her direction at the sound of the challenge.

With limbs taut ready for flight, Patricia stamped and snorted again. Now she could see the approaching man clearly, still steadily approaching. Just as she was about to bolt, she heard Eddie's voice above the breeze.

'Easy girl, easy girl', he breathed.

A step at a time, Eddie continued his seduction, 'Steady girl, good girl'.

Years of experience soothing nervous horses were serving him well. The grey mare was still tense, but responding to his soft voice, she now seemed unlikely to suddenly take flight. Eddie edged forward another step and paused. Only a couple of metres from her, he withdrew his left hand from his pocket and held out his flattened palm. The sweet peppermint scent wafted into her nostrils and she whickered softy, gently stretching her head forwards. But her front feet stayed firmly implanted and her muscles quivered.

'Come on then girl, have a little treat then', he whispered, as he slid his foot another half a metre towards the mare – his left hand outstretched so that she could now see as well as smell the tempting peppermints. Patricia began to relax and lowered her muzzle to his palm and with a flick of her lips swept the mints into her mouth.

As she loudly crunched the sweets, Eddie realised that the rest of the curious herd were gathering around him in a jostling circle.

Patricia too was aware that members of her herd were closing in, eager to muscle in on any treats that were going. She flattened her ears and swung her rump from side to side to ward them off, but Joey had scented the mints and moved in rapidly past her flank. Patricia barged him and kicked out with her hind legs, just catching chestnut mare Cindy a glancing bow and causing her to squeal and step back.

Eddie was beginning to panic. He knew that the whole venture would be totally disrupted by a melee of greedy horses unless he acted quickly. He thrust his sticky hand into his pocket and wrapped his fingers round another handful of mints.

'Come on girl, good girl,' he said, this time a little less patiently. His hand was cupped under her nose and she followed his left hand down as he lowered it to waist level. While she crunched the sweets, shuffling her rump from side to side to defend her prize, Eddie's right hand was behind his back expertly adjusting the coiled rope and separating it from the leather straps of the head-collar.

It was now or never! He had done it many times before - just a quick flick of the rope over the horse's head and grab the other end with his left hand, hold tight and exert firm downward pressure.

But he didn't know that this was a horse whose only experience of a rope had been one of terror. At the first touch of the rope behind her ears Patricia erupted into action. She squealed, threw back her head and with front hooves firmly implanted in the turf, pushed backwards like a dog fighting in a tug-o'-war for a rubber toy. 'Whoa! Whoa! Steady girl', Eddie cried as he tried to keep her head down. But Patricia's fear gave her extra strength and she threw herself upwards dragging the rope painfully through Eddie's left hand. He should have given up then. But he had never yet been beaten by a horse and besides, £400 was at stake.

With the man and horse battling amidst a score of panicking ponies, Eddie quickly grabbed again for the dangling end of the rope, but the mare now had supremacy and reared even higher, prancing on her sturdy back legs. Eddie tumbled forward off balance as Patricia danced high above him and struck out with her front hooves. A glancing blow on his cheekbone felled him and as he sprawled in the mud Patricia squealed and reared again. Still dazed, Eddie looked up and saw the hooves flashing above him. As the mare began to plunge down, Eddie threw up his arm to deflect the blows, but only succeeded in knocking her off balance so that she crashed down on him – her left knee crunching into his face, snapping his neck with an audible crack.

The mare frantically scrambled to her feet, wild-eyed and neighing in fright. She turned and galloped away from her foe, lashing out with her hind legs every few strides in case her enemy was still in pursuit. She thundered across the field towards the large metal gate that divided the field from the rest of the sanctuary's 36 acres. The rest of the herd was already bustling and bumping around her at the steel barrier that Tony had silently closed only minutes before. Patricia barged through the milling herd and steamy breath, slithering to a halt with her chest against the cold grey metal. She whinnied loudly twice and pressed against the gate, but it resisted her weight. Turning, she barged back through her anxious herd and with her tail streaming out behind, led them thundering backwards and forwards along the hedgerow.

Back at the roadside gate, Rex and Tony saw none of the drama, but from the commotion and Eddie's raised voice they realised something had gone wrong. They could hear the horses neighing and galloping at the far side of the field, but there was no sign of Eddie coming back with the grey mare. Rex gripped the top bar of the wooden gate and shouted into the wind, 'Eddie? Eddie? You all right?' Peering into the darkness, his ears strained for a reply, but none came. Rex looked at Tony's frightened face. 'Come on', he rasped, pulling the gate open a couple of feet at the hinge end and roughly pushing Tony into the field. They stumbled through the mud in the direction of Eddie's last shout and after 40 metres saw a crumpled shape on the ground. Rex threw himself down next to his brother. 'Eddie, Eddie!', he shouted – desperation in his voice as he rolled Eddie over onto his back, ripped off a glove and pressed his fingers into the side of his brother's neck. He could see from the angle of his brother's neck that there would be no pulse.

'Jesus Christ', he cursed as he slammed his fist into the mud.

'What? What?' exhorted Tony, his eyes wide open in horror.

'He's dead', Rex said quietly. 'Busted neck'.

'No, no, he can't be', said Tony, his hands raised to his face in horror, his fingers digging hard into his cheeks.

Rex beat the ground again and groaned,

'Oh Eddie, you bloody fool.'

Tony turned away, hugging his chest, his head spinning. As he became aware that he was soaked in cold sweat, the wind chilling his glistening white face, he felt his knees going weak. His stomach heaved and he vomited violently into the mud. Rex ignored him and with his ear touching Eddie's mouth, he silently prayed in vain for a hint of warm breath on his cheek, but there was none.

Tony spat and wiped his slimy lips on his sleeve and looked down again at Eddie's body – his eyes full of tears of grief and terror.

Rex picked up his glove and rose slowly. 'Nothing we can do, son. Nothing'. Tony couldn't respond. He felt faint and grabbed Rex's arm to steady himself.

'Don't you crack up on me now', Rex growled, peering threateningly into the teenager's ghostly face. But Tony was now wide-eyed, staring over Rex's shoulder at something behind him. Rex spun around – half expecting to come face to face with a person, but there, ten metres away, motionless, a ghostly white horse stood head-on, staring back at them.

'That's the one we were after', said Rex resignedly. Tony's face slowly began to screw up grotesquely, and suddenly with a terrible scream he launched himself towards the animal. He only managed five paces before Rex brought him crashing to the ground in a rugby tackle – his scream choked off by a mouthful of mud and grass, as the mare turned and disappeared into the night.

'What the hell you doing?' rasped Rex, scrabbling to his feet and hauling Tony up by the neck of his jacket.

'I'll butcher the filthy, scumbag animal', ranted Tony right into Rex's face.

'Get a grip, son, we've got to get out of here'.

'But we can't just leave Eddie here', whined the teenager.

'What do you want to do then, fetch a copper?' Rex spat scornfully.

'We'll leave him here, and the wagon. We can be back at the caravan park before dawn – get cleaned up, dump our boots and they won't be able to prove we were even here'.

Tony stared at Eddie in amazement.

'You can't leave your own brother dead in a field'.

'Don't tell me what I can't do', reacted Rex angrily. He grabbed Tony by the shoulders and stared intently into his eyes. 'He'll be found in the morning; there'll be a post-mortem and then we'll 'ave him back for a proper funeral. I'm on a suspended sentence. If I get done again I'll go down – I can't do time. I can't be locked up'.

Tony blinked back his tears and looked down again at the body of the man he had grown to admire and even love.

'Can't we carry him to the wagon and take him home?' pleaded Tony.

'No, we're leavin' the wagon. The police will find out it's Eddie's and we'll get a visit at the site. If we drive we could get stopped with a dead body covered in blood in the trailer. Do you want to be arrested on suspicion of murder?

'But, if we explain what happened surely, they'll understand', whined Tony.

'It's all right for you – you don't have a record. I tell you, I can't go to jail, I'll go crazy,' Rex said miserably. 'And what about your folks. How are they going to react when they see your picture in the papers?'

Tony couldn't think of anything else to say. They simultaneously crouched either side of the body. 'Sorry Eddie,' said Rex, as he touched the drying blood on his brother's cheek.

Tony had never known such pain. He felt as if he was in a nightmare. It crossed his mind briefly that any moment he might wake up. As he stood up, and stared down at Eddie's battered face and lifeless eyes, the constriction in his throat only permitted him to whisper two words, 'Goodbye Eddie'.

They stumbled towards the wooden gate, but after a few paces, Tony stopped. 'What now?' asked Rex.

LADY PATRICIA

'Just a minute', answered Tony, running back towards his mentor's body. He stooped, fumbled in Eddie's coat pocket and ran back towards Rex.

'What you doing?' asked Rex.

'I wanted his knife. I always liked it', he said, showing Rex the bone-handled clasp-knife in his muddy hand.

'Come on,' Rex said softly, pulling at Tony's sleeve. 'We can be back in Taunton before the police get involved. Let's go!'

They slipped through the open hinge end of the gate and stepped into the deserted road.

'Come on, for Christ' sake', shouted Rex when Tony hesitated.

In a firm voice which surprised himself, Tony said, 'Sorry Rex. I'm not coming.'

Rex exploded, 'What? What? What the bloody hell are you doing?'

'I don't know, but I'm not going with you,' said Tony quietly.

Rex started to walk away, saying, 'Well bollocks to you'.

After ten paces, Rex paused and turned back, thrusting his hand into his inside jacket pocket. He opened a wallet, took out a wedge of notes, walked back to Tony and pushed them into Tony's hand. 'There's sixty quid. Get rid of your boots and buy some more in a charity shop. With any luck you will never be traced to the scene. And if you take my advice, for Christ's sake go home – to your family. I'm off!'

'Thanks Rex', replied Tony gloomily, staring at the money stuffed in his hand, while Rex plodded away into the darkness.

Ten minutes after Rex and Tony had left the field, Lady Patricia had returned to the prone human body and stood a few yards away, pawing at the ground with her right foot. Soon the whole herd stood silently in a circle around Eddie's body – raising and lowering their heads, breathing in the scent of death.

The ceremony continued for a full five minutes until Patricia tossed back her head and emitted a long and piercing neigh. The grey mare strutted out of the circle and trotted towards the roadside gate, the rest of the herd bunching around her. The gate sagged outwards, detached at the hinge end, but still hanging by its chain and padlock from the other gate post. Patricia could see the gap between the gate and its post and began to press through to the roadside verge. Her two lieutenants, Gregory and Lucky, both heavy hunters, tried to barge through together, Lucky's shoulders forcing the gate outwards until it suddenly snapped. In seconds the herd was milling around in the road, pushing and jostling each other for the best bites of grass on the untrimmed verge opposite the gate.

Lady Patricia didn't care about the grass. She stood in the centre of the road, looking first one way and then the other. She turned once more to look back over the splintered gate into the familiar field in which a quiet and normal night had turned to terror. Neighing loudly she set off at a slow trot along the road in the direction of the A30 and the town of Chard. One by one, some reluctantly, the rest of the herd stopped chomping at the grassy verge and fell in behind her, muffled hoof beats filling the road.

Chapter 2

1.30am Friday 28th October 1977

Police Constables Rodney Humphreys and Barry Collins sat talking in the front seat of their patrol car. For twenty minutes they had been parked in a bus pull-in in Chard's main street. The A30 runs straight through the centre of the small Somerset town – well-lit by many of the shop lights as well as the street lamps.

Rodney stretched and yawned, bracing the back of his head with clasped hands. 'Well I still think you're nuts', he said, through his yawn. 'No-one should be allowed to get married until they're forty.'

His companion shuffled in his seat and leaned forward to ease the ache in his back. 'Don't you get bored with boozing, clubbing and all the rest of the nightmare of your single life?', asked Barry.

'But you're only twenty four; you don't have to get lumbered with a wife and a mortgage and two point four kids and a Yellow Labrador, well not yet anyway.'

'We won't be going in for all that for a long time!' Barry retorted. 'But if you find the right woman, why not get married?'

Rodney grimaced with mock disgust. 'Yuk!' he said, and was immediately rewarded by a cuff on the side of the head by Barry wielding his cap.

The two friends fell into silence mentally groping for a witticism with which to put down the other. It had been a quiet midweek night. Only two calls – one to a loud, but fortunately non-violent, 'domestic', and the other to a group of young men singing noisily on their way home from a stag party.

'That could be you in a couple of years' time', said Rodney, breaking the silence.

'What could?' Barry questioned.

'That domestic. I can just see you and Marcia going at it 'ammer and tongs, when…'

He was interrupted in full-flow as Barry grabbed his arm and bowed forward to peer through the windscreen.

'What the hell is that', he yelled.

Rodney squinted. 'Bloody 'ell', he exclaimed. 'It's horses!'

They both sat there mouths agape as Patricia trotted, with her head high, down the centre of the high street towards them, the rest of the herd plodding behind, eyes rolling in the unfamiliar and brightly lit surroundings.

Rodney started the engine and turned on the patrol car's headlights. 'Shit, what do we do?' he yelled.

'Pull out in front of 'em', Barry replied. 'If a lorry or something comes up the street, it'll be a blood-bath.

Rodney swung the car out into the road, forty yards in front of the approaching herd. Barry grabbed the radio as Rodney flicked on the flashing lights.

'Victor three to Victor one', Barry called excitedly.

Sergeant George Thomas's voice responded immediately. 'Victor one receiving. What's up Barry?'.

'Sarge, we've got about a dozen or more horses galloping…well trotting, down Chard High street heading east. We're in front of them. They're just going past Woolworths, over'.

There was an interminable pause. Just as Barry was about the repeat the message, George Thomas spoke again. 'Victor one to Victor three. Stay in front of them. Keep an eye on 'em and try to make sure they stay together. I'll get assistance behind you from Honiton to stop any traffic coming up behind. I'll try to get the turn-offs to Ilminster blocked so they have to stay on the A30. If we can get them out of the town we can block the Crewkerne road and usher them into a field or something. Oh and don't turn your siren on, just the blue light, understood?'

Barry confirmed that he understood, while Rodney kept

glancing in his mirror and keeping the vehicle 50 yards or so in front of the grey mare who moved gracefully along the road leading several tons of mobile horse flesh. The strange convoy travelled eerily and steadily through the sleeping town and began to climb the long gentle incline to the east of the town.

Barry was deep in thought, but suddenly his frown cleared and he spoke. 'They must be from the animal sanctuary out at Wambrook',

'Of course, that's why they're all shapes and sizes. Better tell Sarge', responded his partner.

'No, not yet. He won't appreciate it at the moment; he'll be onto Yeovil to get some assistance so we can get them off the road. Whoops', exclaimed Barry pointing through the windscreen at head lights appearing over the hill ahead.

'It's a lorry. I hope he's awake enough to see what's behind us', he added.

'It's OK', replied Rodney, 'He's put his hazard lights on'. He glanced into the rear view mirror and saw lights approaching from behind the horses that still trotted on behind the grey mare. 'Uh. oh, what's that coming up behind us, Barry?' he asked.

'It's one of ours,' replied Barry swivelling around in his seat to look out of the rear window.

The herd of horses were now out of the town and effectively sandwiched by two police cars. Patricia moved steadily onwards up the long incline, while in her tracks the herd trundled behind, heads swinging and tails flicking. At the back Silver was struggling to keep up. They had now travelled more than two miles since they had left the animal sanctuary, where the excitement of the attempted theft of Patricia had already left several of the older horses puffing and sweating.

Silver was conscious of the flashing blue lights behind him, but his stiff old legs ached in protest and the coughing that started as the herd trotted through Chard was now troubling him. Immediately in front of him, tiny Rufus kept stumbling over his winter rug that had slipped down one side, its straps flapping and threatening to trip him over. George and Cindy, both overweight, were also beginning to feel the strain and were dropping back from the rest of the herd, excited but wide-eyed and fearful in their adventure as the procession plodded onwards.

Rodney and Barry cruised slowly ahead. Their sergeant George Thomas's voice broke the silence. 'Victor one to Victor three - where are you now, what's happening?'.

Barry responded. 'Sarge, we're still heading east on the A30. We're out of the town, just passing Jordan's garage. We did have a lorry coming at us, but he pulled into the garage forecourt. And there's a police car behind the horses, so everything is OK at the moment, Sarge'.

Rodney interrupted, slowing up as he looked into his mirror. 'They've stopped'.

Barry swung round and repeated the message to his sergeant. Then another voice crackled over the radio.

'Victor one, this is Victor four. We're behind the horses, but they've stopped. We noticed a couple of them seemed to be straggling behind and now they've all stopped. Over'.

'That's Gerry Garland from Ilminster', said Rodney.

'Mmm - interesting initials in the circumstances,' commented Barry.

'What d'you mean?' asked his partner.

'One more GG on the scene', replied Rodney, smirking.

'Silly sod!' commented Barry.

'Victor two and Victor four, stay in position', came George Thomas's voice again. 'Keep the horses on the road. If any of them start trying to get through the hedges you get out and stop 'em. And don't let any of them go forward or backwards past your vehicles. You should be able to see my lights up ahead of you on the brow of the hill. I've got a gate open into a field on your right. Just let them settle for a bit, and then you need to move them up here and into the field. Got that? Over.'

Both car crews confirmed receipt of the instruction and sat, engines ticking over quietly with blue lights flashing, behind and in front of the herd that was now almost hidden in a mist of steam from the sixteen sweating animals.

Patricia had realised that the herd was beginning to break up as some struggled with the exertion. She had stopped and moved back amongst them, gently whickering and touching noses to reinforce the bonds of the herd as they milled around her. They were all nervous of the blue and yellow flashing lights that danced around in front and behind them – monotonously illuminating, then darkening the road and its bordering hedgerows and verges.

With all members of her herd once more bunched tightly together, Patricia strode through them and glowered at the police car blocking her way, its exhaust fumes filling her nostrils. She lowered her ears and advanced towards the rear of the car, but Rodney had been watching her approach and began to move forward slowly. Barry informed their sergeant that they were on the move again and the procession advanced up the road towards George Thomas's car that now straddled the carriageway to form a roadblock with its blue lights flashing and its headlights illuminating an open gateway into a field.

Rodney accelerated towards his sergeant's car and manoeuvred carefully into a position to complete the roadblock. Rodney and Barry climbed out and stood with their sergeant in a haze of flashing blue lights and yellow hazard lights as they watched the herd of horses slowly approaching.

Lady Patricia slowed to a halt twenty yards from the police vehicles. She could see the shapes of men in amongst the confusing lights, and she could clearly see the open gate illuminated by the twin white headlight beams of George Thomas's police vehicle. The herd bunched up behind and around her, uncertain of what to do. Patricia looked back to see the third car pulling across to block the road behind the herd. Beyond that on the road back to Chard, there were now a handful of cars and a lorry that had fallen in behind the police car that brought up the rear of the unlikely procession of horses and horse power.

Big Patrick and Lucky mounted the grass verge and were pressing and testing the strength of the thick thorny hedge. The herd was rapidly moving from unease to panic, bumping and barging each other as they waited for Patricia to lead them out of the trap.

Still Patricia waited as the flashing and whirling lights added to her hesitation. George Thomas could see the tension growing amongst the horses and he seized on an idea. 'Rodney', he called. 'Kill your lights. We'll just leave the headlights showing the open gate'.

Quickly the road in front of the herd was plunged into darkness, George Thomas's headlights illuminating an inviting escape into the field. After a few moments Patricia suddenly neighed and took several paces towards the open gateway. She hesitated for a few seconds, peering into the field along the stream of light from the headlights, then trotted into the field followed quickly by fifteen other horses – the last of which was little Rufus, stumbling over the edge of his coat which uselessly dragged behind him.

As the gate was slammed shut behind them, the horses stood with their tired limbs quivering, sniffing the ground of the unfamiliar pasture. Patricia was already walking steadily along the field's edge towards a water trough and soon the herd stood patiently in line waiting their turn to quench their raging thirsts in accordance with an instinctive and well-established pecking order. Soon the ball-cock was spluttering and squirting violently as it replenished the trough and by the time lowly Rufus, Silver and Jason began to drink – the rest had spread out around the field hungrily grazing.

Sergeant Thomas and the three young police officers stood silently and relieved, with their arms hanging over the gate. The sergeant glanced at his watch. It was 2.35 am.

Chapter 3

3am Friday 28th October 1977

Trevor James was dreaming. A telephone was ringing and he picked up the receiver. 'Hello', he said quietly. 'Is that you Janet? Hello. Where are you?' But there was no reply and the phone was still ringing. Then as he began to wake up, he realised that he had not yet lifted the receiver at all. He switched on the bedside lamp, squinted at the clock and reached for the phone – the image of his late wife rapidly fading from his mind.

'Hello, this is the Ferne Animal Sanctuary,'

'Mr James?' said a vaguely familiar voice.

'Yes it is'.

'Trevor, it's George Thomas, Chard police station. Sorry to wake you at this ridiculous hour Trevor, but I'm afraid you seem to have mislaid some animals'.

'Mislaid animals, what do you mean?' asked the sanctuary manager, peering again at the clock and registering that it was just after 3.00 a.m.

'Sixteen horses, Trevor, well I assume they're yours; I can't think where else they could have come from'.

The sergeant quickly appraised the manager of the situation and described the exact location of the horses. Trevor promised to meet the sergeant there in 30 minutes, put down the phone and hastily dressed.

He was aged 46, around six feet tall, slim build, with dark brown hair that had begun turning grey at the temples, as had his short beard. He and his wife Janet had been appointed three years previously to manage the sanctuary at its new home near Chard, after years working as volunteers at an animal home in Norfolk. Janet already had years of experience as a veterinary nurse in a Sheringham practice while Trevor had travelled widely as an aircraft engineer.

Their daughter Rebecca had been fourteen when they moved to Somerset – a traumatic enough experience for her losing friends and having to feel her way into a new school, but nothing compared to the devastation of the tragic and sudden death of her mother from an unsuspected cardiac abnormality, a year to the day after their arrival at the sanctuary.

For Trevor and Rebecca the past two years had been like living with a nagging physical pain – both leaned heavily on each other to cope with the heartbreak. And in a way, being responsible for the lives and welfare of a couple of hundred stray, unwanted and abused creatures, from goats to gerbils, horses to hens, parrots to ponies, and donkeys to dogs, helped mask some of their terrible grief.

Trevor laced up his boots and grabbed the sanctuary van keys from the hook on the back of the kitchen door. He considered for a moment whether he should wake his daughter, and then ran upstairs, tapped gently on Rebecca's door, pushed it open and called, 'Becky'. He heard her stir, groan and turn over. 'Becky, you don't have to get up. I've got to go out, the police have phoned to say that our horses have got out.'

His daughter turned sleepily towards him, her face illuminated from the light from the landing – her fair hair tumbling over her face. He inwardly winced; she looked more like her mother every day.

'What….horses out…where', she mumbled, shielding her blue eyes from the light.

'You don't need to get up', repeated her father. 'I just want you to know where I've gone - in case I'm out for some time'.

'OK', she grunted, turning over and burying her face in her pillow.

Her father quietly closed the door and within minutes was

driving along the same road which Eddie and Rex Bowen and Tony Smith had travelled in their Landrover little more than three hours earlier.

He briefly pulled onto the muddy verge and surveyed the splintered field gate through which the herd had broken out. He mentally noted that the gate was still fixed by its chain and padlock to the post, but that the gate hinges were off the the post at the other end. He surmised that the horses must have leaned on the gate and broken it away from the hinge end – but whatever possessed them to come out onto the road, to keep going all the way to Chard, and then continue right through the town and out the other side?

Trevor was still puzzling over the strange exodus when, fifteen minutes later, he pulled up behind Sergeant George Thomas's police car, parked alongside the gate through which Patricia and her herd had been shepherded to safety. The two men knew each other, as the sanctuary had facilities for some of the stray dogs occasionally brought to the police station by members of the public.

'Morning Trevor,' said the sergeant cheerily. 'What a palaver we've had tonight.'

'Morning George', responded Trevor as he placed his hands on the top rail of the gate and peered into the field. 'I don't understand it. It looks as if they got out by breaking down one of our gates.'

'Well at least they're off the road now. We might as well leave them there until tomorrow….or should I say today', said the sergeant looking at his watch. 'My lads have been up to the farm and told the owner that he's hosting a few more animals than he thought. He was a bit grumpy about it - says his grass will be ruined. You'll have to sort that out with him and buy him a bottle of Scotch or something. This is his name and number', said the sergeant handing, Trevor a folded slip of paper.

'I've got to work out a way to get them home,' said Trevor, slipping the paper into his back pocket. 'We'll need a whole damn fleet of horse boxes.'

'Unless you walk them home', suggested the sergeant. 'We could help you do that tomorrow night…sorry tonight', he said, again checking his watch. 'We could temporarily close the road, if you can get enough people to lead them back'.

'I'll give it some thought and ring you later, Trevor replied, and added, 'I'd better go in and have a look at them now'.

George Thomas climbed into his police car and wound down his window. 'OK, I'm off. Let us know what you want to do', he added, before starting the engine and pulling out into the road back to Chard.

Trevor climbed the gate and walked into the field. The sky was noticeably lightening as clouds moved enough to reveal the moon. He could see his horses spread out grazing around the field that he estimated to be around three acres. In the centre of the field he saw Patricia standing and staring at him. He made a clicking sound with his mouth, and walked towards her. 'Hello girl. What the hell you doing here then?'

She recognised his voice and gently nickered her recognition. Gregory and Lucky came plodding towards him, then others began to move towards the centre. He moved around the herd patting their necks and running his hands along their flanks reassuringly. He counted them as he went, and stopped at little Rufus. 'Look at the state of you, Ruffy', he muttered, pulling the coat back over the horse's back and readjusting the straps. He moved on to Silver and immediately became concerned as he could see that the old pony was shivering and that mucus dripped from his nose. Silver suddenly coughed violently and Trevor could hear him wheezing. Trevor patted him and looked into his eyes. 'You don't look too good, old boy' he said. 'We'll have to get the vet out to you pretty quick I reckon'.

He walked back to the gate, vaulted it, climbed back into his van and started the engine. He glanced at the dashboard clock. It was now nearly four a.m – time to go home and get things sorted out. As he flicked on his lights and pulled out into the road, he thought to himself, 'What the hell could have happened to make a herd of rescued horses abandon their sanctuary?'

Soon he was almost back to the sanctuary and decided to have a closer look at the broken gate. He got out and looked at the splintered gate and noticed that the back post was still intact complete with its hinges. 'That's odd', he muttered to himself. In his mind he pictured heavy horses leaning against the gate. 'The rails of the gate would break first', he surmised. 'The hinge end should stay fixed to the post'.

He picked his way over the shattered wood and stepped into the field. He peered around at the empty pasture. It was just light enough for him to see that over the other side, the shiny new metal gate was closed. He frowned. That gate was normally kept open except in the summer to close off the field for hay-making.

Then he saw a dark mound in the centre of the field and walked towards it. His first thought was that it must be a coat that had been discarded by one of the horses – sometimes that happened due to the straps breaking when a horse lay down and rolled on its back. Then he saw that the mound was no coat.

'Oh my God', he exclaimed, as he stood in the churned-up mud, staring down at the dead man lying face up, eyes open.

Trevor crouched next to the body and closed his hand around the man's wrist. The flesh was stone cold and there was not a flicker of a pulse.

Trevor ran back to his van and sped along the road to the sanctuary's main entrance. Heart thumping, he hurtled down the drive, and pulled up in the courtyard. The kitchen light was on and he could see his daughter inside in her dressing gown. She greeted him at the door, 'Everything OK dad?', she asked. 'God, you look terrible! You all right? There's tea in the pot. What's happened to the horses? Are they all right?'

'Becky, I don't know what the hell is going on. The horses broke out of the top field and travelled all the way through Chard and out onto the Crewkerne road. They're safe in a field for now, though Silver looks rough. And now I've just found a body in the top field!'

'Which one is it?' asked Rebecca – anguish etched over her face.

'No, it's not a horse, it's a man!'

His daughter gasped.

'I must ring the police,' said Trevor going out into the hall towards his office.

By the time Rebecca had poured a cup of tea and taken it to him at his desk, Trevor had already informed George Thomas of the shocking discovery. In response to the sergeant's brief questioning, Trevor confirmed that he did not recognise the dead man or have any explanation why anyone would be in the field. The sergeant had been just about to go off duty, but he knew that he was now in for a long morning after a very long night.

'Trevor, I'm going to have to get on to CID in Yeovil. Meanwhile I need to get some of my lads out there to seal off the scene. Just make sure you keep all your staff well away from the field, don't touch any gates or move anything. I'll talk to you later – and you need to start thinking about how you're going to shift those horses back.'

Trevor acknowledged the instructions and replaced the receiver. He looked up at his daughter's concerned face and picked up his cup of tea. 'You'd better get dressed, Becky', he said. 'It looks like we're going to be crawling with policemen and I'm going to need you to help me sort out the horses. And we need to tell the staff what's happening as soon as they turn out. What's the time?'

Rebecca turned her head to look at the clock out in the hall. 'It's ten to six,' she said. 'I'll get dressed and rustle us up some breakfast', she added, stepping out into the hall, leaving her father sat at his desk in deep thought, his hands clasped around the comforting warmth of his large mug of tea.

Chapter 4

6am Friday 28th October 1977

It was Bob Rayburn's twenty-fifth birthday and he was up earlier than usual – a full twenty-five minutes before his radio alarm was due to wake him at 6 a.m. He hated lying in and he was soon in his dressing gown crunching a round of toast. He put on his glasses and started fiddling with the dial of an ancient radio on the kitchen window sill. He had been a reporter for the Chard and Crewkerne Observer virtually since he finished college, and although he didn't actually dislike his lot, he was becoming pretty bored with filing copy on the humdrum events, petty crimes, minor controversies and local politics of two small market towns and their environs.

Like many local reporters he earned a little extra as a 'stringer' for a few national newspapers and had managed to place a few items in the Sun and Mirror. He often wondered whether he ought to try to get a job with a national newspaper in London, or even try his hand in regional television news in Bristol or Plymouth. After all, he often thought to himself, he was young, not bad looking, had a good education, years of experience in reporting and had a pleasant speaking voice. There was really nothing to keep him in Chard; his parents having moved to Torquay the previous year after his father had taken early retirement.

He continued to twiddle the dial on the radio as it spouted gobbledegook, whistles and snatches of music. He was trying to tune into the police radio band as he often did. The illegal eavesdropping had brought him quite a few stories over the years, but he dare not leave the radio tuned permanently into such a waveband, in case he forgot and switched it on when he had visitors. But it was such a nuisance to have to try and find the signal every time. 'Ah, there it is', he told himself and turned back to his breakfast bar where his final piece of toast and a cup of tea were getting cold.

He immediately recognised Sergeant George Thomas's voice. He knew all the local police officers and he turned up many times at road accidents, cattle stuck in ditches, house fires, punch-ups and other incidents. The officers guessed he was either being tipped off by a local copper or unlawfully listening into police messages. 'Victor one to Victor three,' said the sergeant. The radio crackled, 'Victor three receiving, Sarge'. Bob recognised PC Rodney Humphries' voice.

'Rodney, where are you now?', asked the sergeant.

'We're at the Chardstock junction on the Axminster Road, sarge. We've just pulled over a Rover without any brake lights; Barry's talking to the driver now.'

'Forget that', ordered George. 'That breakout by the horses from the sanctuary has gone a bit more serious. There is a body in the sanctuary's top field – the field that the horses escaped from. I want you out there now, tape off the gateway and the verge, and stay there till I join you. CID from Yeovil are on their way'.

Bob almost choked on the crust of his toast. He switched off the radio and turned the dial well away from the forbidden waveband. 'Gor Blimey, this could be good', he said out loud to himself. He knew the animal sanctuary well. It was always good for a heart-warming tale about a stray dog or rescued pony. Having an animal sanctuary on your patch was always a bonus, particularly as Trevor James, the manager, was very conscious of the value of publicity.

Bob swigged back his lukewarm tea and rapidly dressed, pulled on his green waterproof jacket, lifted his camera case from its hook on his back door and was soon driving his grey Renault out of Chard towards the Ferne Animal Sanctuary - on the same road, but in the opposite direction, that sixteen unaccompanied horses had travelled four hours earlier.

When he arrived at the sanctuary's top field he saw that a police car was already parked and two uniformed officers were unravelling blue and white tape across a gateway and fixing it to upright plastic stakes pushed into the soil at the edge of the grass verge. Part of the splintered and shattered gate was still hanging from the gatepost by its chain, the entrance to the field was churned up and mud was splattered across the road. PC Barry Collins groaned as he saw Bob Rayburn pulling his car into the side of the road. 'Bloody hell, he's on the ball', he muttered to his partner.

'Morning Rodney, morning Barry, what's up then', called Bob, cheerily.

'What the hell you doing out here this time of the morning,' asked Rodney.

'Oh, just happened to be passing', lied Bob.

'Well there's a coincidence', said Barry scornfully.

Bob pretended not to notice. 'What's happened here then?' he asked, gesturing at the broken gate and the blue and white tape fluttering in the breeze.

'Nothing for you', said Barry, 'Just some horses out, that's all'.

But Bob was not easily put off – particularly as he knew full well from his unlawful eavesdropping that there was a darn sight more to this story than a few horses getting out of a field. He peered into the field, where it was now light enough for him to see a dark bundle-shaped object lying on the grass.

'What's that?, he said, pointing innocently.

'You sod', said Rodney. 'You've been listening into police radio traffic'.

'Me? Never!' said the reporter, shrugging his shoulders.

Barry rapidly thought about the situation. 'Look Bob, our sergeant and the CID are on their way here now. They won't be best pleased to find the press already here. If I give you a bit of gen, will you clear off?'

Seeing the reporter was interested, he continued, 'About a dozen or more horses came out of here last night. I can tell you where you can find 'em, now, but a body has been found in this field and we don't know if or how it's connected with the horses. I suggest you go back through Chard and up the Crewkerne road. The horses are in a field on the right at the top of the hill.'

Bob was visibly shocked. 'You mean they galloped all the way up there last night on the roads?'

Barry interjected, 'Yeah, with a police escort front and back through Chard High Street!'

'Now I think you should piss off before CID arrive and ask you how you come to be on the scene', said Rodney, threateningly.

'Fair 'nuff', smiled Bob, 'I'll ring the station later for a statement, shall I?'

Without waiting for a reply, he returned to his car, took a couple of quick photographs of the scene and drove off only seconds before another police car and a grey saloon came around the corner and pulled up in line.

'D.I. Gordon Sharman', said the first man out of the saloon, not waiting for pleasantries as Sergeant Thomas closed his car door and joined him. They peered into the field. 'That the body?' asked the inspector.

'Yes sir', said constable Humphries. 'Well, we assume so sir, not that we've been to look'.

'Good', grunted the Detective Inspector, who was in his late thirties, heavily built with short dark hair and bushy moustache. The assembled men turned as a pair of headlights approached them and a grey Renault drove slowly past the scene; Barry and Rodney looked at each other, but said nothing. Sergeant George Thomas had also recognised the reporter and noticed the furtive look that passed between his two constables. He glanced questioningly at Barry, who quickly looked away.

Rodney broke in, 'Excuse me Sarge, we've had a quick look around, and just round the corner there,' he said, pointing, 'There's a Landrover and an empty horsebox in the lay-by. We don't recognise it. The engine is cold, but we thought we shouldn't look inside.'

'You did right,' said the Sergeant. 'Let's have a look. Did you take the registration number?

'Yes sarge', said Rodney, handing his note book to his Sergeant.

Detective Inspector Sharman, interrupted . 'Yes, you did right constable, and I've taken down the number of the Renault whose driver looked a bit too interested as he went by. We can't have sightseers running up and down this road. SOCO will be here any minute; I want this road closed at least 100 yards either side of this gate.'

'No problem Inspector', responded the sergeant, 'And we'll have that Landrover and horsebox taped off until we find out who it belongs to.'

He ordered Rodney to park his car across the road 100 yards to the west of the gate while he did the same with his car in the opposite direction.

Ten minutes later a large white police van arrived. With silent efficiency, four white boiler-suited officers - two men and two women - unloaded two petrol-driven generators and several boxes of equipment. Under the instructions of D.I Gordon Sharman the team erected a tent and floodlights over the body of Eddie Bowen and another set of lights around the broken gate and taped-off entrance to the field.

So far the only fact known to the police was that an unknown man had been found dead in the centre of a field which up until a few hours before had merely been the peaceful refuge of a herd of retired and rescued ill-matched equines - led by a handsome grey mare.

Meanwhile, Bob Rayburn was having a busy day. He had visited the field in which the horses had been shepherded during the night and spoken to the extremely annoyed owner of the farm. He had also taken a whole film of photographs of both the farmer and the horses, dug out his file of photographs of the animal sanctuary and staff, and had taken his films into a local 'two-hour' photographic service shop. He had telephoned a preliminary report through to newsdesks of the Sun and the Express, as well the newsrooms of BBC South West and West Country Television. Both television newsrooms expressed interest and the Sun and the Mirror asked him to keep chasing the story on their behalf.

For sanctuary manager Trevor James it was going to be a difficult and hectic day. Firstly he had to inform the chairman of the sanctuary's Trustees about the night's events. Next he explained to the sanctuary's staff that they should be prepared for police interviews, while he and Becky would be tied up all day dealing with the horses stationed nearly four miles away along the A30. He had already been phoned by local reporter Bob Rayburn, had confirmed that the sanctuary's horses had broken out, but refused to comment about the body in his top field. Then he arranged to meet the sanctuary's vet at Walter Bagg's Hollyfield farm to examine Silver, and while there, offer profuse apologies for the invasion of Ferne's horses and invite the farmer to submit a bill for the damage and inconvenience.

He also had to visit Chard police station for an interview with DI Sharman, and it was already mid-afternoon before he sat down with his daughter to try and devise a plan to get the horses back to the sanctuary. Finding several horse transporters at short notice would be impossible, and Trevor and his daughter Rebecca decided that the best option was to adopt the suggestion of Sergeant Thomas and lead the herd back at night the way they had come. But it could not be organised tonight – they would have to wait until Saturday. That would give the detectives time to complete their work at the sanctuary, allow the local police to organise the suspension of traffic for a couple of hours, and Trevor sufficient time to rustle up enough volunteers to escort the herd the three miles or so back through Chard to the sanctuary.

The first task would be take a dozen bales of good hay to the herd and make sure they were settled in their temporary refuge.

'Is that it, Becky - anything else we need to do?' asked Trevor. His daughter pondered for a few moments and suggested, 'We ought to take the sanctuary's horsebox with us, in case Silver is not well enough to travel back under his own steam', said Becky, 'And we should take a few coats over tonight with the hay in case any of them are feeling the cold,' she added.

Her father nodded in agreement. 'Yes, we'll do that this evening. You know what our problem's going to be don't you?' he said. 'Patsy! We can't lead her back with a head collar, and the rest of them won't go anywhere unless she leads them.'

LADY PATRICIA

His daughter shook her head. 'No, I don't think that will be a problem, Dad. If I walk beside her with a bucket of pony nuts, and if the side roads are blocked off so she can't wander off the main road, I'm sure she will be happy to walk back as long as we have plenty of people chivvying on the rest of them. We can put head collars on Lucky and Gregory – the others will tend to follow them anyway.'

'Yes, you're right Becky. That should work. I'll ring Sergeant Thomas and see what he thinks of the plan and then we'll get the hay and coats over to the horses'.

That Friday evening the local BBC television news led with the headline 'Mystery death as horses break out of sanctuary.' The newsreader said, 'Police are investigating a suspicious death of an unidentified man whose body was found early this morning in a field belonging to the Ferne Animal Sanctuary near the town of Chard. Around the same time sixteen horses escaped from the sanctuary in the early hours and travelled east along the A30 through the centre of Chard until police managed to divert them into a field at Holyfield Farm, half mile east of the town. Police cannot say yet whether the man's death and the escape of the horses are connected. The manager of the sanctuary, Mr Trevor James, declined to be interviewed, but did confirm by telephone that the dead man is not a member of the sanctuary's staff'.

The item included film clips of the sanctuary's main gate and entrance sign, the police road blocks, a zoom shot of the taped off gate-way and police vehicles parked nearby, as well as a few seconds of the horses grazing in a field owned by Walter Baggs of Holyfield Farm.

At exactly the same time as the broadcast, Detective Inspector Gordon Sharman sat on a desk in the incident room of Avon and Somerset Police Station in Yeovil. Behind him on the wall was a large white laminated board decorated with black felt-tip writing. Sliding off the desk the detective tapped the board with a wooden stick and addressed the group of officers sat facing him. Four were in plain clothes and two were in uniforms, including Chief Inspector John Fowler, white-haired, tall and distinguished-looking, with grey-framed glasses.

'Right, so what have we got so far?' He tapped the board. 'The dead man we now know is Eddie Bowen, a petty criminal, a traveller, whose caravan is at Dene Park, Taunton. Cause of death? The medics are still looking, but it's likely to be a broken neck. He also took a whack in the face which broke a cheekbone. SOCO tells us that although the injuries might have been caused by being stampeded over by horses, there are footprints of two other people at the scene.'

'Round the corner in a lane local officers found a Landrover and horsebox – untaxed, but the last registered owner was the brother of the deceased, Rex Bowen, who, shall we say, shared his brother's interest in other people's horses. Rex Bowen has been interviewed and says his brother took the Landrover out last night and didn't say where he was going. He says he was home all night, and so far we haven't managed to find any of his footwear to match the prints found at the scene – though they are the same size as one of the sets. The other footprints are smaller, but likely to be a man's'.

'Both sets of footprints were found around the body, and there was also a load of vomit – we don't know who's at the moment. The Landrover and horsebox are covered in fingerprints, including both the Bowens, but also those of someone else not known to us.' He paused and looked around the room. 'So, has anybody got a theory?'

D.C. Barbara Wright raised her hand. 'Sir, maybe the idea was to steal a horse, but there was an argument - some sort of fight. Bowen was knocked out and the horses got spooked and galloped over him.'

'Possible, Barbara,' responded the Detective Inspector. 'But firstly, I'm absolutely sure his brother was involved and from what we know about the pair I don't reckon they would fall out enough for his brother to do him serious harm, or cover for anyone else who did'. The room fell into silence again.

'What if the third man was not part of the gang, and waded into them to save the horses – maybe an employee of the sanctuary', offered another officer.

'I don't think so', said the D.I. 'Rex Bowen wouldn't be covering for someone that interrupted their scam, particularly if they killed his brother. Anyway, if the third person was a sanctuary employee, he wouldn't be able to hear or see anything happening in the furthest field from his bed in the middle of the night.'

There were nods from the assembled police officers, and D.I. Sharman raised his hand.

'OK.' he said. 'Unless the final post-mortem turns anything else up, we have no evidence of a crime except the attempted theft of a horse – although what horse thieves like the Bowens would want with retired old nags from an animal sanctuary, I can't imagine. They can't be worth much dead or alive.'

'Maybe, they were planning to blackmail the sanctuary for a safe return', offered another of the officers, and continued, 'Last year there was a spate of dogs being stolen, and a week later the owners would put an advert and a photograph of the dog in the local paper, offering a reward. The owners would get a phone call from someone saying they had found their dog, and the owners would hand over the reward, even though they suspected the so-called finder was the thief.'

'Possibly', mused D.I.Sharman. 'If that was the plan it was a spectacular cock-up. But on what we have so far, I reckon the most likely scenario is the Bowens and another man were attempting to steal a horse - then something went wrong, and Eddie Bowen got himself trampled when the animals panicked. The other two legged it, left the gate off its hinges and the horses were so spooked they got out onto the road and kept going.'

He looked around and saw that no-one had anything further to add. 'Well John', he said, turning to the uniformed Inspector Fowler, 'There's nothing here for us, it's all yours – assuming nothing significant comes out of the final post-mortem of course'.

'OK Gordon, I'll wrap it all up and talk to the press office now so they can put out a statement tomorrow. Thank you ladies and gentlemen....and good night,' he added over the noise of chairs scraping on the wooden floor. The station clock showed it was 5pm.

Chapter 5

Denis Chapman glanced at the clock. 5pm already. Time to start putting the Saturday newspaper to bed. Always in shirt-sleeves, short, mid-fifties, overweight and rapidly balding, his body odour became less pleasant as the day wore on – as indeed did his temper. He never felt relaxed until he knew bundles of the Sun newspaper were safely tied in string and loaded into vans. Then and only then, he would open a cabinet, haul out a bottle of whisky, summon a handful of editors and senior reporters to his smoke-filled office, and chatter and joke as if he hadn't a care in the world. Those unfortunates he summoned to join him preferred to go home or to the pub, but knew that slighting the 'Almighty Denis', executive editor of the mighty Sun newspaper could damage a career.

Senior reporters and editors began to file into his office for the normal evening procedure of completing the newspaper. 'Right', said the editor. 'Any changes to what we've already laid out?'

Heads shook amid mumbles. Chapman pointed to Sally Clark, one of his youngest and prettiest reporters. 'Sally, what about that mystery death on the animal sanctuary down in the sticks. Anything new from the stringer down there? Bob somebody or other'.

Sally nodded. 'Bob Rayburn, boss. Last I heard from him was this afternoon. He said the police were waiting for post-mortem results, and the horses that broke out were corralled in a field a few miles away.'

'Chase it up, Sally. This Bob must have contacts in the local old Bill. Get him to find out if it's a murder enquiry yet….and who the victim is. Ring him now, from here. Sally went to a desk in the corner of the room, opened her notebook in front of her and dialled a number.

With the telephone receiver clamped between her shoulder and right ear, and her left hand over her other ear to muffle the conversation from the continuing editorial meeting, she furiously scribbled shorthand notes with her right hand.

After a couple of minutes, she asked Bob Rayburn to hang on, and turned back to the centre of the room. Denis Chapman, seeing her movement, spoke, 'Yes Sally?'

'Boss, Bob says that his contact in the police says that their press office is putting out a statement tomorrow, but basically they believe that it was an attempt to steal a horse that went wrong and somehow this guy got himself trampled, and died from a broken neck. It's not being treated as a murder enquiry - apparently the victim is a known villain who deals in horses. They think there were at least two others involved – the police are still looking for them. They left a vehicle and horsebox behind near the scene apparently.'

Denis Chapman stroked his chin – deep in thought. 'Umm, not a murder then'. he said quietly. He paused, his pen hovering over a large plain pad on his desk. Then with a flourish, he scrawled some words across the pad, then a few more, before ripping off the sheet and thrusting it towards the young female reporter. 'OK then…page five…. play around with this – it's your by-line, and keep that Bob on the story, tell him 'well done''. Sally glanced at the sheet, smiled and spoke briefly on the phone, before replacing the receiver and leaving the office. At 5.20 p.m, with her notebook open on her desk she started typing up her story.

*

At exactly the same time as Sally Clark was writing up the horse story, Trevor James and his daughter Rebecca were bundling several bales of sweet hay over the gate of Walter Bagg's field at Holyfield Farm on the A30 Chard-to-Crewkerne road. As the horses eagerly snatched and tugged at the hay, the sanctuary manager and his daughter dragged the bales further out into the field, cut the strings and kicked the bales apart so that the horses were not too closely bunched. With all the bales spread out and a bunch of strings in his hand, Trevor looked around at the feeding animals. Silver was stood quietly several yards away and had made no move towards the food.

'Silver's still not right', called Trevor to his daughter who was tying a bunch of baling strings into a knot.

'What did the vet say?' asked Rebecca.

'Well it's still only half an hour since he gave him more jabs, so he might pick up a bit later, but he said that his heart sounds lumpy and his lungs rattle a bit'.

Trevor picked up a wedge of hay and took it to Silver. The old grey pony sniffed it and half-heartedly took some strands into his mouth.

'All we can do is hope that he is better tomorrow, so that we can load him into the horse-box and take him home,' said Becky. 'It's not going to be too cold tonight, and the coat should help keep him warm enough'.

They walked together through the darkness to the far hedgerow and checked that the water trough was full and that the ball-cock was properly working. 'Let's call it a day, Becky', said Trevor.

'And what a day!' replied his daughter, as they began to retrace their steps towards the gate. They picked their way through the horses and climbed over the gate. 'I've brought some chains and padlocks in the van, said Trevor. 'I'm going to chain the gate to the metal posts at both ends. I want to go to bed knowing they'll still be here in the morning'.

After securing the gates, Trevor and his daughter clambered into the front seat of the sanctuary's van. As Trevor started the engine and switched on the lights, he nodded towards the field and muttered, 'And another hectic day tomorrow getting that lot home again!' If he could have glimpsed page 5 of the Sun newspaper which was running off the presses 160 miles away in London, he would have known that 'hectic' was hardly an adequate adjective for either the next day or many days ahead.

LADY PATRICIA

1am Saturday 29th October 1977

Lady Patricia stood dozing in the centre of a line of similarly tired horses in the lee of a dense hedgerow. All of them had stiff and aching legs from the unusual exertions of the night, but had now recovered from their nervousness when first herded into the unfamiliar field that they now occupied. They had fed well on the autumn grass and the good quality hay brought to them, and had been greatly reassured by the visits of the sanctuary manager and his daughter.

Patricia's eyelids fluttered sleepily, her bottom lip hung floppily and the tip of her hind left hoof gently touched the ground, as all her weight was supported by the locked knees of her other three legs. A strange thump followed by a gasping noise, first woke and then startled her. She peered around and saw that Silver was down, neck outstretched and legs scrabbling in the mud. The rest of the horses were now also alert, beginning to shuffle and peer around in the gloom of the unfamiliar field. Silver's gasping became more high-pitched and his thrashing more violent as the massive heart attack wreaked its violent effect on his body and invaded his mind with fear. Then suddenly, inside no more than twelve seconds, it was all quiet again as life finally abandoned his body.

Patricia paced nervously backwards and forwards and the other horses began to mill as they sensed her edginess. She approached the fallen Silver, and stood over him breathing in his scent. The rest of the herd gradually plodded forwards to surround the pony's body and stood in a circle raising and lowering their heads as their senses sought to understand this latest incident in their lives. Had they been in the familiar fields of the Ferne Animal Sanctuary, all might have been well. But, on unknown ground and following the traumatic experiences the previous night, Silver's death created alarm – particularly in their leader.

The grey mare began to trot, with head and tail held high, around the perimeter of the field. The rest of the herd obediently followed her as she stopped at each of the three field gates to stare over the bars into the gloom. Eventually the herd assembled amongst the straw and churned up mud at the gate through which they had entered the field from the road in the earlier hours of that day. Patricia pressed her chest against the top bar of the gate. She hesitated as two cars flashed by towards Chard. Then a van sped past going the other way. As the lights and engine noises faded, Patricia leaned again. On her shoulder big Patrick added his weight to the pressure against the strong wooden gate. The chains strained but remained fast to the metal posts which were embedded deep in concrete. Then Beadle and Lucky joined Patricia and Patrick in the front row – exerting a pressure that no wooden gate could possibly withstand. Amidst great creaking and cracking the gate suddenly gave way and burst out onto the wide grass verge.

2am Saturday 29th October 1977

Trevor James was asleep on his sofa, fully clothed except for his boots. His daughter Rebecca was also asleep in a huge arm chair on the other side of the room. The television was on, but only emitting a flickering screen and hissing sound. Trevor's eyelids occasionally struggled to open, but his brain refused to translate the sound from the television into anything other than a comfort. The phone rang and Rebecca stirred, but determinedly refused to wake. Her father reluctantly swung his legs to the floor and walked the few paces to his office and picked up the phone. 'Bloody hell', he said looking at his watch. 'Is there no peace?'

He answered the call and instantly recognised the voice'.

'Trevor, it's George Thomas again. We've got another problem'.

'Oh no… what the hell's happened now?' groaned Trevor.

'Your horses are out on the road again, we've had a whole spate of 999 calls. We've got the A30 between Chard and Crewkerne closed, we've got two cars in ditches and a lorry embedded in a hedge. No one hurt I'm pleased to say, and as far as I know, no horses are hurt.'

'Thank God for that', said Trevor thankfully. 'How the hell did they get out? I put chains and padlocks on both ends of the gate myself…and the posts are metal ones…in concrete'.

'Well, the gate itself is smashed to bits, just like the one that was wrecked at your place. Our problem now is that we've got them hemmed in on the green at the entrance to Cricket St Thomas Wildlife Park. We asked if we could let 'em into the park, but they refused – said they didn't want 'em upsetting their animals.'

'We're on our way sergeant', said Trevor, noticing that his daughter had joined him and was staring at him wide-eyed, 'Be with you in fifteen minutes'.

Having been allowed through the police road block east of Chard, Trevor and Rebecca drove in silence along the deserted A30, climbing the long hill and past the field in which the horses had been confined in the early hours of that day. They followed the trail of dung and mud up the road towards Windwhistle Hill, and the entrance to the famous wildlife park. An extraordinary sight greeted them. As well as the whirling blue lights of half a dozen police cars and vans, there were three other cars, one bearing the logo of BBC television south west – all with their headlights trained on a strangely silent huddle of horses – bunched almost motionless in the centre of a quarter-acre lawn at the entrance of the wildlife park. Two television cameras were in use, one filming the horses, while a news reporter was speaking into the other.

As Trevor climbed out of his van, he was immediately approached by a young, dark-haired woman in glasses, and wearing a thick sheepskin coat. Under her arm she gripped a clip-board. 'Mr James?' she asked, stepping right into his path.

'That's right,' he replied.

'Jackie Johnson, BBC. Could we have a word…to camera I mean?'

'No,' grunted Trevor grumpily. 'I need to talk to the police first, if you don't mind', he added, striding past her towards Sergeant George Thomas.

'Morning Trevor,' said the sergeant. 'It's a right old pantomime. I think its Bob Rayburn who's alerted the world and his wife to this lot. He was hanging round right at the start of it all at your sanctuary gate', he added, looking in the direction of a group of half a dozen people huddled together at the roadside. Trevor followed his gaze and saw the local reporter amongst the group. Bob Rayburn returned the look and waved, but at that moment Trevor was not in the mood to return the friendly gesture.

'Right, sergeant, what are we going to do?' he asked.

'I was hoping you'd tell me,' replied the policeman.

At that moment Rebecca joined them, and touched her father's arm. 'Dad, Silver's not with them'. Trevor saw the puzzled look on the sergeant's face.

'Silver is a grey pony', he explained. 'We had the vet to him earlier, when they were in the field at Hollyfield Farm. He's got a dodgy heart. We didn't see him anywhere on the road - maybe he's still at Hollyfield. I don't like to think what's happened.'

They turned as another van pulled up amongst the throng of vehicles. 'The RSPCA's here,' said the sergeant. 'That could be helpful'.

Soon RSPCA inspectors Keith Jordan and Joe Byfleet were sat with the sanctuary manager and his daughter, together with sergeant Thomas and two police constables in a police van well away from the ears of the assembled media. They agreed that they should make an attempt to herd the horses quietly back along the road in the direction they had come. The road was already closed as far as Chard and it would not be difficult to extend the closure through and beyond the town to the point when the horses had first joined the A30 from the sanctuary.

It was to be hoped that by taking things steady the herd could be walked all the way back to the sanctuary before dawn. It would not be possible to put a head-collar onto Patricia, so Trevor and Rebecca would put head collars on Gregory and Lucky and lead them back along the road. Hopefully Patricia would be content to join them. If so, the rest would certainly follow. The route would take them back past Hollyfield Field where it seemed likely they would find Silver – probably dead.

As the group emerged from the police van, Inspector John Fowler arrived in another car. George Thomas introduced him to the sanctuary manager and quickly explained the plan of action. The inspector nodded. 'Makes sense', he said. 'Are this lot going to be a problem?' he added, pointing to the dozen or so news reporters and a camera crew milling around amongst the parked vehicles.

'We need to keep them all well back behind the horses', said Trevor. 'No doubt they'll want to get in front to get some shots of the horses coming towards them, but they'll want to use lights and flash bulbs, and that could stop them dead. It would also be a good idea if all the police flashing lights were off, too'.

The inspector authoritatively called the media representatives to him and informed them what was to happen. He quietly, but firmly, added a warning that anyone trying to get ahead of the horses or the police vehicles, using flash cameras or otherwise jeopardizing the exercise could find themselves under arrest.

A police car moved off fifty yards and stopped, facing west down the hill towards Chard, its engine ticking over. Trevor James and Rebecca were meanwhile in amongst the horses, talking reassuringly, stroking necks, patting withers and running hands along backs. Trevor slipped a head-collar onto Lucky while Rebecca did the same with Gregory, before easing the two horses out of the herd to hold them at the edge of the green.

Lucky, was a strawberry roan hunter that had once been attached to the Saddle Club at the Royal Naval Air Station, at nearby Yeovilton. When frequent lameness threatened to end his career, members of the Women's Royal Naval Service had organised a collection to purchase his freedom.

Gregory had been used for fox hunting for many years and had suffered injuries to his splint bones through being galloped too often on metalled roads. Most horses that break down from such misuse are slaughtered, but Gregory was fortunate in that his owner had a sufficiently well-developed conscience to retire him to the sanctuary. Both animals were highly placed in the pecking order of the herd and Trevor hoped that seeing her two lieutenants happily being led away, Patricia would be content to join them and lead the whole herd home.

As everyone prepared for the journey, Trevor and Rebecca held tight to Gregory and Lucky. The rest of the herd seemed relatively calm as Patricia moved steadily in and amongst them. Sergeant Thomas approached. 'We're just about ready to go', he said. 'The press and TV people will take their photographs from behind us as we move off, and then follow in their vehicles. By the way I've just had a message from the station. Walter Baggs phoned, you know the farmer down the hill where the horses were earlier. He says he's got a dead pony in his field, it must be the one you mentioned... Silver was it?'

'Oh dear', said Trevor. 'His heart must have packed up'. Rebecca heard the sergeant pass the news. 'Oh no, poor old Silver, what a shame.' Trevor put his arm around his daughter's shoulder and gave her squeeze. 'It would have been quick, Becky,' and kissed her head.'

'Right,' said the sergeant, turning away. 'You can worry about that problem when we've got this lot back safely in your sanctuary.'

He walked over to the Chief Inspector. 'We're ready to go, sir. Are you following or are you going home?'

Inspector Fowler looked around at the scene. 'I'll see you on your way, and then I think I'll go home and leave you to it. Good luck George', he added, grinning.

'Thank you sir, very kind, thank you very much sir,' replied his sergeant with a good-natured grimace.

'OK everybody', he called. 'Quiet now while we get them moving. Off you go, Trevor.'

Trevor and his daughter gave a gentle tug on the head collars and coaxed Lucky and Gregory off the grass and onto the road. 'Come on then', they called and clicking out of the sides of their mouths as they moved forward with Lucky and Gregory. Patricia watched for a few moments and strode forward to join them and gradually the entire herd began to fall in behind – the sound of their hooves changing as they moved from the squelchy mud and grass onto the tarmac. 'So far so good,' muttered Trevor to his daughter as the assembly began to shuffle and bustle along the A30. He was aware of flashing lights behind him as the photographers took their pictures, and he was glad he insisted that such pictures were not taken from in front. He glanced at his watch and noted it was now

3am. 'Should be all over by daylight', he thought to himself, and turned his mind to how he could deal with Silver's body and placate Walter Baggs for the damage to his three-acre field and the inconvenience he had suffered.

He was jolted back to the present by Rebecca's voice. 'Uh oh', she said loudly, 'Patricia's playing up'. Trevor saw that the grey mare had wandered to the side of the road. She stepped onto the grass verge and stood watching the herd striding past before turning her head to look back towards the assembled reporters, camera crew and police officers who had already begun to get into their vehicles, ready to follow the horses in convoy. Patricia tossed her head and neighed shrilly. The herd stopped immediately and began to mill around in the road. At the front, Trevor and Rebecca struggled to keep Lucky and Gregory facing forward as they tried to turn. They spoke to the two horses, trying to keep panic out of their voices as they called 'Whoa, whoa, steady now, steady, now, whoa'.

Patricia had by now turned the herd and she stood at their head, snorting and pawing the ground - facing the headlights of at least six vehicles as if they were a group of wild predators. Beyond the lights photographers were clambering back out of their vehicles eager to get pictures of the grey mare and her bustling herd of refugees facing them. Patricia neighed hysterically and Trevor cursed as Lucky tore himself from his grasp and wheeled away to barge through the herd to his leader. Gregory neighed and tried to rear, but Rebecca still held tightly to his head collar. 'Let him go Becky', shouted Trevor, 'He'll tread on you, let him go,' yelled her father, who could see his daughter was in danger of being trampled. She let go and jumped out of the way as Gregory careered after Lucky to stand with Patricia facing the lights.

In his police car, Sergeant George Thomas's brain was racing. He didn't know what to do. He got out of the car and was immediately joined by Inspector John Fowler. 'What happened George?'

'God knows!' responded the sergeant, 'But I think we're in trouble.'

As he spoke, Patricia suddenly lurched towards them, but when it looked as if she was actually charging at the headlights, she veered off to the right, back onto the Cricket St Thomas green followed closely by the herd. Now, round behind the vehicles and their dazzling lights, the horses cantered onto the road and set off east along the empty A30.

Behind them the police hastily blocked the road and ordered the media people not to try following the horses. Police airwaves buzzed as maps were consulted, and instructions sent ahead in the quest for another suitable temporary place to capture the runaway herd of horses.

Sergeant George Thomas was sitting in his car with the door open, listening to radio traffic. He saw the sanctuary manager and his daughter standing by their van, talking to reporters. He shouted, 'Trevor,' and Trevor and Rebecca, accompanied by reporters, trotted over to the police car.

'We've had a bit of luck, Trevor. Less than a mile from here on the left is a narrow road off to Chillington. It's been fenced off for road works because of subsidence apparently. The work has not started, but the part of the road which needs repair has a set of roadwork fences either side of the repair. So, as we had already closed the A30 the other side of the Chillington turn-off, we are diverting the horses off the main road to corral them in the 50 yards between the two road-work fences. There are also good fences along both sides of the road and woods on either side, so plenty of shelter from wind.'

'That sounds good George,' said Trevor. 'Can we follow on, or are you keeping the road closed?'

'I'm not opening it until I get the message that the horses are fenced in the Chillington road,' said the sergeant, 'but you can go through. I'll let them know you are on the way and I'll open the road to traffic when I know the horses are safely off the main road.'

When Trevor and Rebecca arrived in the Chillington Road, they found two RSPCA inspectors and three police officers guarding the horses. They had secured the 'Road Works' fencing across the narrow road and fixed them firmly to the roadside fences. The RSPCA inspectors said they were waiting for a small water-tanker from a local riding stables. Trevor had earlier stacked two bales of hay in his van and he and Rebecca dragged them out, cut the strings and then bundled it over the Road Works fence. Trevor also had half a dozen buckets in the van, so he put them next to the fence ready for the awaited water-tanker.

Trevor and his daughter were exhausted – as were the horses. Some of them began to eat hay while others stood dozing. The three police officers and two RSPCA inspectors sat in their vehicles guarding the wayward herd. One of RSPCA men wound down his window and called to Trevor.

'Look mate, you two look fit to drop. We're here at least all night, When the water turns up we'll fill the buckets. Why don't you go home and get a bit of rest.'

'Well if you're sure, said Trevor. 'We'd really appreciate it. It's only been a day, but it feels like a week. Thanks fellas. We'll be back tomorrow - I mean later today,' he added, looking at his watch.

He called his daughter who was watching the horses through the 'Road Works' fence. 'Come on Becky, let's go home. We'll take a look at Silver on the way. We can come back later.'

10.30am Saturday 29th October 1977

Trevor James had showered and breakfasted by 9.45 a.m and left his daughter asleep. After doing the rounds of the sanctuary and relating events to the sanctuary's staff, Trevor rang the Reverend Gerald Stockwell, chairman of the sanctuary's Trustees and reported all the details of the last two nights' events. He promised to provide the Trustees with a full written report as soon as the horses were safely back in the sanctuary. He was thankful that the Chairman offered to deal with Walter Baggs, and his claim for compensation. Trevor reminded the chairman that Silver was still at Walter Baggs' farm and would probably be collected by a local knacker company later in the day.

As he gulped down the final mouthful of his second mug of tea, the phone rang. It was press reporter Bob Rayburn. He was unusually formal.

'Mr James, its Bob Rayburn. Have you seen the Sun this morning?'

'The newspaper? No Bob, why?'

'Well, I just want you to know that I didn't know how they would use the story when I told them about the horses and the dead man and all that; I didn't dream they would make it their front page lead.'

'So what have they said?' Trevor asked, suddenly feeling extremely depressed.

'I think you'd better read it for yourself', replied the reporter, nervously. 'I just wanted to say....well...I hope you won't blame me. I only gave them the facts...only I'll probably see you later and I just thought I should explain...well I'm sorry... bye'.

The phone went dead just as a sleepy Rebecca shuffled into the kitchen.

Rebecca looked at her father, questioningly, 'Who was that?' she asked.

'Bob Rayburn,' explained her father. 'Apparently we're on the front page of the Sun – I'll get one when I go through Chard. You should get back to bed for a couple of hours at least. I'm meeting the police at elevenish to discuss how we can bring the horses home - I'll come back when we've decided what to do. If you get any media calls, just tell 'em that I'm not here and put the phone down.'

'OK, dad, replied Rebecca, yawning. 'You look like you need a good night's sleep yourself.'

Fifteen minutes later the sanctuary manager was sat in the sanctuary van, outside Smiths newsagents in Chard High Street, incredulously reading the front page of the Saturday Sun newspaper resting on the steering wheel. The huge banner headline screamed at him;

KILLER HORSES ON THE RAMPAGE!

A ghostly photograph of several of the horses in Walter Baggs' field in the dark early hours was accompanied by a smaller one of police officers and their vehicles next to the taped-off broken gate at the Ferne Animal Sanctuary. The opening lines read;

> A herd of stampeding horses trampled an unknown man to death before breaking out of an animal refuge and rampaging through the Somerset town of Chard in the early hours of yesterday morning. Police believe that the victim was killed by the horses which were later captured some four miles away on the main A30 road and penned into a field.

'Bloody gutter press,' shouted Trevor, throwing the newspaper into the passenger foot-well. He started the van and set off down the High Street and out of town on the A30 - still loudly cursing the printed press with as many foul swear words as he could muster and glad that his daughter was not in the van with him. For a hundred yards before the turn-off to Chillington, cars were parked along the main road verge. Police 'Slow', and 'No left turn' signs were set up and two unsmiling uniformed officers were athletically waving traffic to pass quickly by on the main road.

As Trevor indicated to turn left off the main road, a policeman waved him to a halt and glanced at the Ferne Animal Sanctuary signage on the side of the van. Trevor wound down his window, and the officer said, 'I assume you are Mr James, sir.' Trevor nodded, and the officer continued, 'You need to take the left turn and find somewhere to park on the roadside. I'm afraid quite a few press people have beaten you to it,' he added.

As Trevor moved forward and began to turn the wheel into the side-road, he cursed again. 'Oh bloody hell', he mouthed. In front of him there were a queue of vehicles, a bustling crowd of uniformed police, RSPCA Inspectors and media people from newspapers and television channels.

As he got out of the van, he became aware of the invasive noise from above and looked up to see a helicopter hovering high overhead.

'This is terrible,' mumbled Trevor to himself, as people started to rush towards him with cameras, microphones and note-books. It seemed as if a dozen people were calling his name and firing questions at him. 'Mr James, what do you think happened at your sanctuary.' 'Do you think you have a killer horse?' Do you know the man who was killed?' 'Mr James, what about the horse that died last night?' 'Mr James, Mr James, Mr James ......'

Trevor pushed through the crowd. 'No comment, no comment', he repeated impatiently, scowling as cameras flashed in his face. Beyond the scrum of reporters he could see the tall, white-haired figure of Inspector John Fowler and beyond him a line of police and RSPCA officers spaced out along the 'Road Works' fence which, with a similar fence 50 yards down the road, formed the horses' temporary paddock.

John Fowler saw Trevor fighting his way through the crowd and moved forward to grab Trevor's hand. 'Ah Trevor - come with me', he said guiding him out of the melee, leading him to a police car and ushering him into the rear seat. 'Sorry about the crowds', he added as he closed the door, and then went round to the other side and climbed in next to the sanctuary manager.

The Inspector reached over the front passenger seat and retrieved a bag from the foot-well. Sitting back down, he said, 'I've got a flask of hot coffee here. Fancy a cup, while we discuss our next step?'

Trevor puffed out his cheeks and exhaled through floppy loose lips. He passed the crumpled Sun newspaper to the policeman and said, 'Have you got anything stronger?'

John Fowler stared at the front page headline for a couple of seconds and commented, 'Hmm. Not very helpful!' before handing the paper back.

In the police car, the two men hatched a plan to return the horses to the Ferne Sanctuary. They agreed to abandon any idea of walking them back along the A30 and through the town of Chard. Horse transport was the only answer and Trevor would contact livestock carriers as soon as he got back to the sanctuary in the hope that they could complete the exercise the following day, Sunday. They discussed the fact that it might not be possible to find enough lorries at short notice to take the entire herd back to the sanctuary and therefore the lorries might have to make two or even three trips.

Next came the problem with the herd leader Lady Patricia. The two men decided that an effort would be made to persuade the mare to enter a horse-box, but if she failed to cooperate, a vet with a tranquiliser dart gun would need to be on hand. Inspector Fowler agreed to ensure enough police officers were available to keep the public away, and the RSPCA would be invited to have a couple of inspectors on hand. 'Can we keep the press and TV away?' asked Trevor. 'Well, we could, but in my experience they will put us under pressure for access,' replied the policeman. 'What we can do is to create a small press area safely away from the animals so they don't get in the way, and don't frighten them with flash lights.'

'And no helicopters!' said Trevor, wagging his finger at the Chief Inspector, as he exited the police car. 'And no helicopters!' agreed the Chief Inspector. Trevor James liked the calm and experienced Chief Inspector and was in a much better frame of mind driving back along the A30 than he was an hour previously.

Chapter 6

11 am Saturday 29th October 1977

Ron Walters rose from his settee and crossed the room to pick up his ringing phone. He listened for a few moments and answered, 'Yeah, I'm watching it now – it's live on BBC News – fantastic'. He listened for a moment and added 'Yeah, talk later', before replacing the receiver and resuming his place on the settee, sitting forward, watching intently, elbows on knees.

Ron was single, aged 28, and the recognised leader of the Animal Liberation Front. The letters ALF frequently decorated the walls and windows of fur shops, factory farms, hunt kennels and other establishments associated with the exploitation of animals. He had been vegan for five years having become a vegetarian a year before that, and now lived in his rented flat in Portsmouth – a flat regularly raided by the police during investigations into illegal animal rights activities. Like many animal rights activists, Ron had begun campaigning as a hunt saboteur and had moved on to protest against other forms of cruelty as he became ever more angry at the extent of exploitation of animals in the modern western world.

He was five feet eight inches tall, slim, with grey eyes and curly dark brown hair. His flat was like a shrine to animals – posters covering virtually every aspect of animal abuse plastered his walls and bundles of leaflets and papers littered the room. He spent hours every day on an old computer drafting newsletters and leaflets for distribution by the ALF – the organisation he had founded four years previously.

As the news bulletin ended, Ron pressed down the volume

button on the remote control, picked up the telephone and dialled. 'Angie, its Ron. Are you following this horse story – the breakout in Somerset?' Angie confirmed that she had been.

'Well I think we should be there', said Ron. 'We could get some interviews. It's a chance to display our new ALF banner. We can protest about the horses killed in racing, like the Grand National, the use of whips and things like that. What do you reckon?'

Angie thought for a moment. 'I agree it would be great, but by the time we got down there, it might be all over,' she added.

'True,' said Ron, 'But we could stage something outside the animal sanctuary or in the nearest town. And anyway, don't forget they are saying that someone was killed by the horses. Have you seen the Sun headline – "Killer horses," what a lot of crap! I just think while the media is highlighting horses we need to take advantage.'

'Well maybe, but it's the start of the fox hunting season this weekend, and most sabs will be out with their local hunts. I doubt whether we can get a big turn out all the way down to Somerset – at least not quickly.'

Angie Wright had been Ron's closest ally for years. They went out together for a while, then finished the relationship after a couple of rows. Now they were great friends - unencumbered by attempts to maintain romance. Angie was 23 years old and cultivated a punk image with short spiky red hair and continual experiments with dark make-up and shapeless clothes which all served to disguise her natural good looks.

Ron accepted that the timing was unfortunate, but they agreed to share the task of ringing as many animal rights contacts they could and urging them to try and get to Somerset as soon as possible. Within hours a dozen or more animal rights activists had agreed to make their way to the west country overnight in a couple of transit vans and cars. The assembly point would be the main car park in Crewkerne on the A30, nine miles from Chard.

The campaign purpose would be to publicise the cause of 'animal liberation' using their new huge banner, to argue for the freedom of horses from exploitation, and reject any argument that the horses were responsible for the death of a person that was suspected of harming or stealing one of their kind.

12.00am Saturday 29th October 1977

Police Inspector John Fowler, deep in thought, looked vacantly ahead through the windscreen of the stationary police car. Next to him in the passenger seat sat RSPCA Chief Inspector Paul Robbins and behind them in the rear passenger seat was Ferne Animal Sanctuary manager Trevor James.

'So are we all happy with the plan for tomorrow?' asked the policeman, glancing in his mirror where his eyes met those of Trevor.

'Yes Inspector,' said Trevor. 'Even if Patricia was not in the equation, it's now too far to walk them back on the roads. We've booked three livestock carriers plus a single trailer for Patricia. I'm still worried about this tranquiliser dart idea for Patricia. I've been in the field shelter when one of them has been stung by a horse-fly…they go berserk.'

'Well, the darts are pretty fast acting these days,' replied Paul Robbins, who had joined the RSPCA inspectorate from the army five years previously and rapidly risen to his present rank. 'As long as it's done while she's in amongst the rest of the herd, she might buck and shy for a few seconds, but I don't think they will be able to get out through these fences.'

'We don't expect many locals to be here, but there may be a couple of news agencies,' said John Fowler. 'My men will make sure that any public and reporters stay in the small area we've denoted from where they can watch what happens, but not get in the way.'

RSPCA Inspector Paul Robbins spoke, 'At least we're lucky with the weather. John, I assume you'll co-ordinate the operation and get some traffic control so we can get the lorries in and out?'

'No problem', replied the policeman. 'We should aim for everybody to be here and ready at midday tomorrow. We just need to let each other know if we have any problems.'

The three occupants of the police car climbed out of the car and walked towards the main road, where a handful of local villagers from Chillington were talking to local newspaper report Bob Rayburn. Inspector Fowler said, 'I don't think we'll have any problems. The animals seem settled. We'll have a couple of officers here doing shifts overnight.'

'I'll be here all night,' said sanctuary manager Trevor James, 'I'll go home in the morning for breakfast and make sure my staff are ready for the return of the horses. And I'll be back by noon.'

Inspector Fowler addressed the villagers and informed them that nothing would happen until lunchtime the next day. Local reporter Bob Rayburn asked him if there was any news about the suspects who left their dead colleague in the Ferne field, but the Inspector suggested that he should talk to the Yeovil police press office.

Trevor James was asked whether the horses were considered dangerous. He responded by saying that it was ridiculous to think that old and retired horses that were well used to visitors to the sanctuary were dangerous. 'I can assure you,' he replied, 'No horses will be destroyed because some trespasser had been trampled in the middle of the night.'

A young man, standing listening half-hidden behind the small crowd of locals, flicked a lock of hair off his forehead and slowly walked away towards the main road. He had a scowl on his face and in his coat pocket his fingers were wrapped around a bone-handled clasp knife.

Mid-day Sunday 30th October 1977

The next morning when Trevor and Rebecca arrived at the temporary corral in the narrow road just off the A30, the crowds had gone. Half a dozen uniformed police and RSPCA officers were standing around and the horses looked relaxed behind the barriers chomping away at fresh hay. Three horse transporters and a double horse trailer hitched to a Landrover were parked in a line on the A30 main road. A Ford estate car bearing the livery of BBC Television south west and the Renault of local press reporter Bob

Rayburn, were parked half on the verge behind the lorries. The sun was trying to break through the clouds and the wind had significantly dropped overnight.

Drivers lounged against vehicles, chatting, smoking and drinking tea from flask cups while uniformed officers chatted in three small groups. Trevor parked behind Bob Rayburn's Renault and alighted from the van with his daughter Rebecca.

'I'm not very happy with you, Bob,' said Trevor, as he passed the open window of the Renault.

'Yes, I'm sorry about some of the headlines', responded the reporter.

'Today's chip wrappings, you mean,' said Trevor and he and his daughter walked on towards police Inspector John Fowler who was standing next to a police car. The Inspector greeted them. 'Hello Trevor, hello Rebecca. We're just waiting for the guy with the dart gun; he should be here within twenty minutes.'

'Everything's ready at the sanctuary,' said Trevor. 'I'll be glad when this is all over'.

'Did you sort out your dead pony?' asked the inspector.

'Yes', said Trevor. 'He's being collected today by the knackers; but I had to pay £40. Once upon a time they would have paid us. Walter Baggs is still spitting blood – he's after substantial compensation for the damage to his field and his smashed gate, and, he says, for being pestered by reporters'.

'That's farmers for you, making hay while the sun shines!' commented Rebecca.

'Or in this case,' said the policeman, 'He's not going to look a gift horse in the mouth!'

'The gift horse being Silver!' added Trevor, 'Our chairman is a vicar and if he thinks Walter is trying to rip off the sanctuary he won't hesitate to remind him that it is harder for a rich man to get into heaven than to squeeze through the eye of a needle!'

The three of them shared a chuckle. John Fowler snatched a look at his watch and said 'We might as well sit in the car until the guy turns up with the gun', he said.

Unknown to any of the police officers, RSPCA inspectors and

sanctuary staff waiting patiently in the side road, only 30 yards from them, three young men and two young women were quietly observing them from within the woods alongside the horses' temporary paddock. Robin Chamberlain's transit van which had transported them to the scene from Crewkerne was parked in a lay-by in a quiet lane a quarter of a mile away. The group of five animal activists were dressed similarly in green jackets and jeans. Ron Walters peered through a fork in the tree that hid him from the road. He whispered, 'They're obviously going to load them into the lorries. What d'you think they're waiting for?'

Angie Wright whispered back. 'Don't know. Maybe they're waiting for the main road to be closed or something.'

'There's not much media here,' said Caroline Dickinson, peering through the same fork of the tree. 'Looks like just one TV crew and a couple of reporters. They've soon lost interest'.

'Maybe the police have kept them away', said Angie. 'So what are we going to do?'

Ron looked at his watch. 'Twenty to twelve. I don't know whether we'll have any more of us. A lot of sabs are out with their local Hunts. Some opening meets were yesterday and others are waiting until next week. Brian's got four or five sabs coming from Yeovil, and Iain from Bristol reckons he will be here. Clive and Jody from Dorchester said they would try to be here.'

'What are they going to do?' asked Caroline.

'I told them to just drive straight in, get their banners out and start chanting - for the media', said Ron. 'We can nip through the trees to join them.

''Ello, what's this?' said Angie. 'Someone else has arrived'.

They peered through the autumn foliage as a silver-grey saloon pulled into the road and stopped. A middle-aged man in a brown barbour jacket and dark green corduroy trousers emerged and shook hands with the police chief inspector and the sanctuary manager.

'Looks like a vet,' suggested Angie.

After a brief conversation, the man walked to the back of his car, opened the boot and lifted out a long dark-green nylon case. Handing it to the inspector, he reached back into the boot and took out a small briefcase. He slammed the boot shut, placed the briefcase on the boot and retrieved the long nylon case from the inspector.

'Jesus,' breathed Ron as the man unzipped the long case and withdrew a dark metallic object. 'It's a bloody rifle!'

'Why would they have a rifle?' said Angie.

'Maybe it's a precaution in case any of them go berserk' said Robin.. 'After all apparently a bloke's been killed'.

'From what was said on the news, it served him right', said Ron, having difficulty in keeping his voice down. 'He could have been one of those nutters who mutilate horses – in any event he certainly wasn't there because he cared about them'.

'But there's a TV camera crew there and RSPCA inspectors,' said Caroline. 'They wouldn't shoot a horse with them around'.

'You'd think not, but maybe they have to be prepared for anything,' commented Ron and immediately raised his voice, almost shouting 'Here we go!' as a white transit van suddenly swung into the narrow road.

'It's Brian's sab van from Yeovil!' yelled Angie, as police officers rushed forward, the back door of the van swung open and six people leapt out waving placards. They quickly formed a line alongside their vehicle and started chanting, 'What do we want? Animal Liberation! When do we want it? NOW!' thrusting their placards high on the shout of 'NOW!' As the BBC television crew hurriedly turned the camera away from the horses towards the activists, Ron said, 'Come on, let's join 'em.'

Inspector John Fowler cursed, 'That's all we need – the damn animal rights brigade'. He shouted to his officers. 'Keep that lot under control.' Meanwhile RSPCA chief inspector Paul Robbins shepherded his RSPCA officers into a line with the police between the demonstrators and the horse's temporary corral.

'Don't let any of these idiots anywhere near the horses,' he shouted.

From being momentarily transfixed at the sudden invasion, Trevor and Rebecca were now very worried at the reaction of the horses. The chanting had alarmed the herd and they had begun to mill around nervously within the two sets of road work fences that confined them in the 50 yards section of road.

'Come on Becky,' said Trevor. 'We need to calm the horses.'

As the sanctuary manager and his daughter ran towards the corral, Ron's group emerged from the woods and ran to join the protestors who were enthusiastically shouting the slogan, 'What do we want? Animal Liberation!' as they unfurled their five yards long 'Animal Liberation' banner.

Herd leader Lady Patricia tossed her head and trotted purposefully down the road towards the far barriers, away from all the noise and confusion. The herd was bunched restlessly behind her, but she wheeled round once more to survey the police struggling to grab the banner and prevent the demonstrators approaching the barriers.

She just couldn't decide which way to turn. She stopped and stared, ears turned forward at the scuffling and noisy tussle going on beyond the line of uniformed police and RSPCA inspectors. Facing her at the barriers, Sanctuary manager Trevor James and his daughter Rebecca began speaking to her as calmly as they could.

Suddenly, between the gaps of the moving bodies of the horses, Trevor spotted someone at the other end of the corral, 50 yards away. A man dressed in military camouflage and a balaclava had hopped over the roadside fence and was running to the centre of the 'Road Work' fence. Trevor realised that the man held what appeared to be long-handled bolt-cutters and was attempting to cut the thick wire used to attach the two sections of the Road Work fencing. Trevor shouted, 'Oi, get away from those fences. Get out of there!'

The horses were alarmed by Trevor's shouting. Patricia turned to face the other end of the corral and saw the man dragging a section of the metal 'road-works' fence towards the road side, and then running bent double to the other side, hauling the remaining section of the fence to the other side of the road, thus leaving the road wide open.

Patricia turned back and heard the activists' chanting, and their large banner flapping in the wind, as the police and RSPCA inspectors were shouting at the activists and trying to snatch their placards.

Trevor shouted to Inspector John Fowler who was busy watching his struggling officers. 'Inspector, we're losing the horses. Look.' The policeman turned and saw that the fences at the other end of the corral had been pushed away and the horses were rapidly disappearing down the open road.

Suddenly, the RSPCA inspectors, police and the demonstrators fell silent when they saw the horses escaping. They watched the camouflaged man march smartly to the centre of the corral where he stopped and stood to attention facing his silent audience. Then in a loud voice in the manner of a sergeant major, shouted 'Animal Liberation' - Mission Accomplished'. He saluted, spun on his heels, put his long-handled bolt cropper to his shoulder like a rifle, and marched smartly away down the road to follow in the footsteps of the horses.

ALF leader Ron Walters was stunned. The intention was to stage a public demonstration to publicise their animal rights cause. Everyone expected that with the number of police and RSPCA inspectors present, the horses would be loaded into the lorries and returned to the Ferne Animal Sanctuary. Ron had been content that managing to stage a demonstration at short notice, which would achieve some publicity and mean that they could witness the transfer of the horses.

He felt a hand on his shoulder and a voice said, 'Hiya Ron.' He turned to see Iain Poller, 32 year old leader of the Bristol hunt saboteurs and a founder member of the Hunt Saboteurs Association in 1963. As always he wore smart trousers, collar and tie, and polished shoes – with a spotless camouflaged jacket.

'You're a bit late Iain', responded Ron,

'I beg to differ old boy,' laughed Iain.

'What? Who the hell was that?' asked Ron, nodding in the direction of the empty corral. One of yours?'

'No, our guys are busy checking the Beaufort Hunt's artificial fox earths this weekend – it's their opening meet next week. So I took a trip to Northampton to see a mate,' he said meaningfully, putting the emphasis on 'mate'.

Ron frowned, and then laughed, 'You bugger! You mean Gary!! Was that him?'

Iain peered around. 'Not so loud. Let's get away from these coppers.'

He needn't have worried about eavesdroppers as the police were in hurried discussions with the RSPCA, the lorry drivers and Trevor James.

Inspector Fowler, said 'We can't follow the herd down the road because of the subsidence. We could finish up with a car or lorry down a big hole.'

Sergeant George Thomas yelled to his two constables, 'Rodney, Barry. Get down the A30 to Merriott and take the back way into Hinton. Well catch you up. Find the horses and let us know where they are.'

As a police cars swung east onto the A30 with sirens blaring, the horses were avoiding the village of Chillington and were half a mile along the narrow road towards the tiny village of Hinton St George. The previous day a few villagers had wandered up the road towards the A30 to see the herd of wayward horses that had suddenly become notorious celebrities.

Now the horses were about to pay a visit to the village. Unable to follow the horses down the same road because of the subsidence, a bizarre convoy set off down the A30 to find its way through the small town of Merriott and onto the opposite end of Hinton St George – a convoy consisting of three horse transporters, a trailer, two police cars, two RSPCA vans, a Ferne Animal Sanctuary van, a BBC television estate car, and two other cars.

Finding another way into the village, the activists in two transit vans found a pull-in from where they could watch proceedings. Ron had explained to the others that the 'soldier' who liberated the horses was Gary Rorke.

1.30 pm, Sunday 30th October 1977

Nora Whitehouse counted change into the outstretched hand of her friend and customer Betty Dobson. 'There you are Betty, I think you'll find that's right,' she said, as she placed a packet of biscuits, a bag of sugar, packet of tissues and a pot of blackberry jam into a plastic bag. 'Thank you dear, I'm sure it is,' answered Betty.

Both ladies were widows in their early seventies. Nora had managed the village shop alone since her husband had died three years previously. She and Betty were firm friends and stalwarts of the local Women's Institute, regulars at the local St Mark's church and dedicated fundraisers for the local branch of the RSPCA.

'See you at church later, Betty,' said Nora as her friend moved towards the shop doorway. 'I'll be there,' replied Betty, as she pulled open the door with the customary 'ping' of the doorbell. 'Oh my lord,' she exclaimed, as the shop suddenly filled with the rumbling sound of many hooves on the road. 'What is it Betty – is it the hunt? Oh dear, my cats are out.'

Nora joined Betty at the shop door, 'No, Nora, it's not the hunt – they don't hunt on Sundays. It's those horses that were penned up by the main road. What on earth have they brought them here for?' she queried as Patricia trotted past at the head of her herd, her head turned towards them – eyeing them suspiciously.

'There's no-one with them,' said Betty incredulously. 'Do you think they've escaped?'

Lady Patricia slowed to a walk and moved into the centre of the village, with the rest of the horses obediently following her - some of them sniffing the ground, while others twitched ears nervously and turning their heads in all directions anxiously looking for something familiar.

Villagers began to emerge from homes and stand in groups in the narrow village streets. Behind a farm gate, two black-and-white border collies, the hair under their stomachs spiky with wet mud, whirled in circles and barked hysterically at the unusual events. Their owner, farmer Bob Towning, came out of his workshop, wiping his oily hands, and growled at them to shut up. Both dogs instantly became silent, and grovelled at his feet as he leaned on his gate surveying the equine invasion.

The police car that had earlier sped down the A30 and through the small town of Merriott, had been driven into Hinton from the opposite end of the village where the village hall and sports field stood on the outskirts of the village. The constables had parked their car in the village hall car park and strode into the village soon to be reunited with the rest of the police and RSPCA inspectors.

Soon it seemed as if the entire village had formed a circle around the horses. The BBC news team's camera was already busy filming the scene and press reporter Bob Rayburn had hastily commandeered the red telephone box outside the village shop and was busy filing copy to the Press Association in Bristol and the Sun newspaper's London news desk.

In a huddle opposite the shop, half a dozen uniformed police and RSPCA officers were in deep discussion with the sanctuary manager, while his daughter wandered amongst the horses checking for signs of distress, lameness or injury. The only animal Rebecca was concerned about was George, the seven year old skewbald. He had originally been retired to the sanctuary due to navicular disease – a painful condition of inflammation affecting the tiny navicular bone in the horse's foot. Owners of horses with such a condition sometimes resort to neurectomy – severing the nerves to the diseased area and thereby removing all feeling in the foot. However, without the capacity to feel pain a horse can sustain severe damage to the foot from nails or stones without the horse its or owner being aware of the injuries. Retirement from work had eventually led to the problem being cured, but now, while standing, George was 'pointing' - resting his left foot by placing it a short distance in advance of the other, often a first symptom of navicular disease.

Rebecca strolled over to where her father stood in discussion with the uniformed officers.

'Everything OK Becky?' asked Trevor.

'They seem fine, although I think George is a bit lame. I hope it's not his navicular problem flaring up'.

Just then a female voice from behind the group made them turn to see Nora Whitehouse and Betty Dobson, their rosy faces wreathed in smiles as they balanced large trays upon which stood several steaming mugs and two plates of biscuits. 'Tea anybody?'

chorused the two ladies.

The members of the group uttered exclamations of appreciation and reached out for the mugs.

'Would you prefer to come into the shop and have your tea?' asked Nora.

'No, no, we don't want to bother you; but thanks very much', replied Chief Inspector Fowler.

'But if you are having a sort of meeting,' said Nora, 'you'd be much more comfortable inside'.

'Well if you're sure', said the RSPCA chief inspector Paul Robbins, sensing that the rest of the group was more than happy with the offer.

Police Inspector John Fowler looked at his watch and noted it was ten minutes to two o'clock. He called to a constable and told him that if anything happened, he would be in the shop with the RSPCA and the sanctuary manager.

Trevor James took his daughter to one side and spoke quietly to her.

'Becky, while we discuss how we get out of this mess, do you fancy wandering along the road to the animal rights people and try to find out what they're up to?'

'Should I tell them who I am?' asked his daughter.

'Oh yes, I don't see why not'.

As Trevor followed the police and RSPCA officers into the shop, Rebecca strolled the two hundred metres to the parked activists' vans.

'Hi!' said Rebecca self-consciously.

A chorus of 'Hi's replied.

'I'm Becky James. I live at the Ferne Animal Sanctuary, my father is manager'.

'Hi Becky, I'm Angie,' responded one of the girls, sliding off the bonnet of one of the vans and extending her hand. Angie introduced everyone using first names only.

Ron Walters spoke next. 'We're members of the ALF, have you heard of us?'

'Yes, of course' said Becky, which was true, although she

couldn't recall what the 'F' stood for.

'So what's happening with the horses?' asked Ron.

'I don't know yet,' said Becky truthfully, 'My father's discussing the situation with the RSPCA and the police right now. We would have had the horses on the way home by now….. if it wasn't for you lot and the bloke who removed the fences. Who was he, he looked like a soldier.'

'No idea, who he was - never seen him before,' replied Ron.

'Talking about soldiers, what's the gun for?' asked Ron abruptly.

'Gun? What gun?' asked Rebecca.

'A guy arrived with a rifle when the horses were penned in up the road,' said Angie.

'Oh, I see. He's a vet. The gun fires tranquiliser darts,' explained Becky, and she quickly explained about Patricia's background and why it had been decided that she might have to be tranquilised and taken home separately from the rest of the herd.

'And you think you have the right to fire darts into animals?' asked Ron Walters, combatively. Rebecca felt her ears burn as her anger rose.

'Look, the horses are our responsibility. What do you want us to do, shrug our shoulders and say, well, they've decided to run away from home, so why should we bother about them?' she said.

'What about their rights?' came the voice of Caroline from within a van. 'They don't want to go home – they've voted with their feet,' added the female activist.

'That's just stupid,' exploded Rebecca. 'They ran away from danger and we need to get them back to safety. These are mostly old horses; they can't just be left to wander the roads of Somerset…one of them has already died of a heart attack. And taking down the barriers and letting them charge along the road to here was completely irresponsible,' she added, conscious that her voice was getting more shrill.

'Actually, that wasn't us,' said Robin, quietly. 'We just wanted to publicise the various forms of cruelty that horses suffer, such as horse racing, circuses, bullfighting, and slaughtered for food.'

'Well, whoever moved those barriers is an idiot and should be locked up, and if you lot hadn't been shouting and flapping banners about, the horses would be home by now,' said Rebecca, spiritedly.

Caroline Dickinson, a former veterinary nurse and a veteran hunt saboteur, leaned out of a van window, and said, 'It wasn't us that made them run away from your wonderful sanctuary. If your horses liked living there so much, why don't they show any sign of wanting to go back? They're voting with their feet – for freedom.'

Rebecca reacted angrily, 'Oh don't be so stupid!' and immediately regretted it as Caroline mockingly emitted a high-pitched 'Oooh'. Rebecca stomped briskly away, red-faced and without a further word. She didn't hear Angie say, 'That was a bit mean, Cee.'

Caroline said, 'Yes, I know I was winding her up Angie, but I was just testing her out to see whether she had any concept of animal rights. I was just hoping she would say something like, *if I had my way, I would ban whips in horse racing, and I object to using them to chase wild animals, or pull heavy loads, but that's not the way it is and it's my job to give them a nice life when their working days are over.* That's the sort of thing I was waiting to hear.'

'She was too wound up for a philosophical discussion,' retorted Angie, and the group fell silent and continued to watch the events in the village.

By the time Rebecca got back to the front of the shop, her father and the police and RSPCA officers had ended their meeting and were stood in a group waiting for her. 'How'd you get on Becky?' asked her father.

'Not very well. They were just teasing me I think - suggesting that we should just let the horses free to do what they want for the rest of their lives.'

Chief Inspector Fowler interrupted. 'Did any of them admit they removed the barriers', he asked.

'One of them denied it was them,' replied Rebecca. 'But it's pretty clear they were involved. They also said they saw the vet arrive with a gun and assumed that a horse might be shot.'

'Cynical bunch, aren't they?' commented RSPCA Chief Inspector Paul Robbins.

'What's the plan, dad?' asked Rebecca. Trevor James put his arm around his daughter's shoulders. 'Same plan really. We are going to push the herd further along the road to the village hall where there is a well-fenced sports field. The villagers suggested it themselves and we've still got plenty of hay and there is water at the village hall. The idea is that we'll get the horses into the sports field first, and then bring the horse transporters and park them at the village hall. The police will take the lorry drivers home and pick them up tomorrow morning. The police will inform the villagers what's going on, and have officers on hand all night. The RSPCA will also have someone here through the night and the village hall will be open and refreshments will be available through the evening from the two volunteer ladies.'

'What about the ALF people?' asked Rebecca, glancing in the direction of the group of people still lounging around their parked Transit vans at the other end of the village.

'Inspector Fowler is going to give them a strong warning and tell them to clear off or be arrested for obstruction and anything else he can dream up,' said Trevor.

'If he gets the chance!', exclaimed Rebecca. Trevor turned and followed his daughter's gaze. The police inspector and two constables were walking up the road towards the activists, but amongst slamming of doors, revving of engines and clouds of exhaust smoke, the transit vans conducted four-point turns and sped off out of the village and back in the direction of Crewkerne.

'Let's hope we don't see them again,' said Trevor, as the three police officers paused and turned back towards the horse transporters where the frustrated drivers stood together. He looked at his watch, 2.30 p.m.

Within an hour the horses had been chivvied along the village streets with no resistance from any of the horses, including their leader Lady Patricia. The gate to the sports field next to the village hall was open and Lady Patricia hesitated for a few seconds, then led the herd into the field. As the last pony trotted through the gateway, the gate was closed by an RSPCA inspector who rapidly wrapped a heavy chain around the gate post and secured it with a padlock. Half an hour later the horse transporters were moved into place at the village hall, together with a single horse trailer.

The sun had broken through the October clouds and the village sports field was soon a hive of activity. People with their children wandered freely amongst the horses offering carrots, pony nuts, apples and mints. Nora Whitehouse and her friend Betty Dobson had set up a trestle table inside the village hall and was selling cups of tea from the Cricket Club's urn, for a twenty pence donation in the shop's RSPCA collecting box.

Nora and Betty promised faithfully that half the proceeds would be given to the Ferne Animal Sanctuary. In particular, admiring villagers gathered around big Patrick and tiny Rufus and Donald. Small children were held high to stroke Patrick's mane and neck. The BBC Regional television news team mingled amongst the crowds and in the darkening afternoon the villagers themselves took hundreds of photographs to record a memorable day in the life of Hinton St George.

*

Meanwhile three miles away in Crewkerne town car-park, animal rights activists were congregating. The two Transit vans that had ventured into Hinton St George had returned to Crewkerne and were parked next to a small white Ford van with ladders on the roof that belonged to Clive Harris who had his own window cleaning business. Clive and his partner Jody had met through the Dorchester 'CROW' group (Campaign for the Relief of Wildlife). The group began by clearing rubbish out of local ponds and hedgerows, but later moved onto sabotage hunts – particularly the South Dorset Hunt and the Courtney Tracy Otter Hunt.

On the other side of Clive's van was an old Landrover Defender which had been renovated by the Norwich Hunt sabs and was driven down to Somerset by Debbie Sawyer. Ron Walters and other group leaders were together in one van, deep in discussion. Robin Chamberlain, leader of the West Midlands group, wore a deep frown. He removed his glasses, squinted his eyes tight and rubbed his hand over his face. 'I'm not sure we can do a lot more, he said. 'I think that our demo was pretty good, but the police won't let us get away with anything else, now that Gary has made them look pretty stupid.'

Debbie Sawyer said, 'I don't know. I reckon we can milk this a bit more….' She paused, grinning. 'Whoops, sorry, non-vegan expression,' she said, as her fellow campaigners smiled. 'This is an opportunity to get people thinking about what animal rights means', she continued. 'Take that Becky, from the sanctuary. Obviously a nice person, cares for her animals, but her thought processes are, 'The horses have escaped, apparently two or three times. She thinks they have no right to taste freedom and obey their ancient instincts. No, they have to be captured and taken back home.'

Ron agreed. 'The longer the horses are on the run and in the media spotlight the more people will have them in their minds and be talking about them so we can keep raising the cruelty and exploitation issues.'

'I agree', Ron interjected. 'There's a hell of a lot of interest in these horses, it's become a real story. The Sun virtually accused them of being murderers, but the public accept that the man who was killed was up to no good. I think something is happening here. The conventional thinking is that horses are here to work for human beings. But nobody is asking, why are horses whipped in racing when it would be a criminal act to whip a dog. They clearly abandoned the animal sanctuary because they were scared by humans. Now it's human beings trying to force them to go back to the same place. Why would they trust us?'

A silver Cortina suddenly pulled up next to the van. Iain Poller and another man climbed out. Ron looked out, and shouted from inside the van, 'In here Iain! Come on in Gary.' As Gary followed Iain into the van, he received a round of applause from the others. 'Nice one Gary', said Ron, gripping Gary's hand and shaking it enthusiastically. 'When you shifted those barriers, I wondered what the hell was happening.'

Gary was older than the others – in his mid-thirties. He had enjoyed a promising career in the Royal Marines until serious injuries from a parachute jump had put an end to his service. He still sported his military hair-cut in striking contrast to the long locks and casual dress of most of his fellow male and female colleagues in the animal liberation movement.

He was rarely seen out of camouflage, and although he formed a small group of hunt saboteurs in Northampton, he usually preferred to act alone. Many Masters of Fox Hounds whose day had been ruined would often abandon the day's hunting if Gary's group was spotted in the vicinity. His favourite hunt sabotage tactic was calling the hounds away from the control of the huntsman by use of tape-recordings of hounds 'in full cry' blasted out through a loudspeaker system mounted on top of his Landrover. Hounds hearing the sound of dozens of excited hounds on the scent of a fox, could not resist ignoring all their huntsman's attempts to stop them speeding off in the direction of the noise to join in the 'chase'.

'So what happens next?' asked Gary. 'If I'm going to stay around, I need to know exactly what the mission is. According to the radio, one horse has died of a heart attack – fortunately not the fault of our people. But if any animal is harmed because of anything we do, it would inflict terrible damage on our cause.'

'I agree Gary', said Ron, looking up from scribbling on a pad. 'I'd like to make a proposal. Firstly, our mission should be to try to keep the horses in the news for as long as possible, and that allows us to keep raising issues of the human exploitation and cruelty they suffer. I phoned home and my flat-mate said I've had lots of press calls and invitations for interviews. A couple of papers have already written features on the history of humans and horses – for instance, the eight million horses killed in the first world war and statistics showing two hundred horses killed on British horse-racing courses every year.'

Angela interrupted him, 'I slipped up not asking that Becky from the sanctuary whether they are ever take in race horses for retirement. I bet they don't. I bet they are mostly sent for slaughter

LADY PATRICIA

and the owners pick up insurance money - except for the famous ones that are used as stud horses.'

Debbie interrupted, 'Ron, are you suggesting that if they manage to capture them to take them back to the sanctuary, we should continue to try and stop them?

Ron replied, 'Let's face it, eventually we won't be able to stop them. And if we do find a way, we are sure to be in real trouble with the police. That's why I advise anyone who has a binding over order, to go home.'

Robin agreed, 'Let's get everybody together and see what they think.'

Gary Rorke raised his hand. 'Before you do that, you know me. I'm going to be working on this project in my own way. Iain was great collecting me and bringing me down here from Northampton, but he's going back to Bristol tonight.'

Iain said, 'Yeah, our sabs are conducting an investigation into the Beaufort Hunt's artificial fox earths, and I need to be there over the next few days.'

Gary continued, 'I'm staying around for a while – just to watch events. Iain's going to drop me off locally. So whatever happens please don't mention my name to anybody.'

'What about transport, Gary?' asked Angie.

'I don't need it,' answered Gary. 'Iain brought me down with a lot of kit which I've hidden in a safe place.' As he pushed open the van door, he looked round to his colleagues, and added, 'Good luck everybody!'.

'And you Gary,' the others replied, beginning to exit the vehicle to stretch their limbs.

'Where's Jody and Clive?' asked Ron. 'They went shopping,' said Angela, 'Oh, and there they are. Who's that with them?' she asked quickly as Jody and Clive came struggling across the car park carrying two obviously heavy supermarket carrier bags each, with a third person carrying another bag.

As Gary and Iain climbed into the front seats of Iain's Cortina, Jody waved to them. Iain wound down his window. 'We're off Jody. I'm going home, but I'm dropping off Gary – he's staying on'.

'Oh really?' she replied. 'We've just found a new recruit. This is Tony, from Exeter.'

'Hi Tony, said Iain. 'Have fun!'

Gary waved his hand to acknowledge Tony as Iain started the engine and moved off.

'That was Iain from Bristol and Gary from Northampton', Clive told Tony, adding, 'Both legends.'

Jody dropped her two shopping bags, puffed out her cheeks and flexed her stiff back. 'Hey everybody, we've got loads of supplies, and a new campaigner!' The newcomer, in a long black coat, slight mud-stains on his knees, and fair hair flopped over his right eye. He put down his bag and tried to force a smile. He looked around at the activists and pushed his hair back from his brow..

Jody continued, brightly. 'He saw Clive's animal liberation badge and asked if could join us. He's Tony…Tony Smith from Exeter.'

Ron spoke first, 'Hi Tony, from Exeter?'

'Yes,' lied the teenager, feeling his ears burning. To avoid looking at his questioner, he wrestled his knapsack off his shoulder and placed it between his feet.

'You involved in the Exeter group, Tony?' asked Robin, his steely blue eyes scrutinising the lad.

'Group?' queried Tony.

'Hunt sabs,' interjected Ron, 'or south west ALF?'

'No, I'm not in a group,' stuttered Tony.

Clive, feeling a bit guilty at Tony's interrogation, broke in to relieve the slight tension in the atmosphere.

'No, he's not in the movement yet. He saw the horses thing on the telly – and hitched here from Exeter to see what was going on. He watched our demo this morning.'

'How old are you, Tony?' asked Ron.

'Eighteen', lied Tony.

'But not involved in animal rights?' said Robin.

Tony turned to face his new inquisitor.

'No, well not properly, yet,' he answered.

'But you *are* veggie,' quizzed Robin.

'Oh yes, of course,' lied Tony for the second time.

'You working Tony?' asked Ron.

'No, not really. But I'm not looking for work at the moment.'

'So you've got no money,'

'I've got enough,' said Tony.

'If you hang around with us, you'll have to put in the kitty for petrol and food.' replied Ron.

'Thirty quid enough to start with?' questioned Tony innocently, pulling a thin wedge of bank notes out of his back pocket.

'Wow, sure,' said Ron taking the money, a little too readily and folding it before placing it in his wallet. 'Clive, can you introduce Tony to everybody, oh and tell them all that we're having a meeting in ten minutes, here.'

Clive and Jody picked up the shopping bags to walk to Clive's white van, and gestured to Tony to accompany them.

As soon as they were out of earshot, Robin spoke quietly to Ron. 'What do you reckon about this Tony then?'

'He's a bit odd.' said Ron, 'But then aren't we all?' he added in a whisper.

'Yes, I suppose, but 'Tony Smith'? said Robin, screwing up his face.

Debbie, peering into the wing mirror of the van and combing her hair, commented, 'Funny that. Smith is probably the most common surname name in the country, but when you meet a stranger who says their name is Smith, nobody believes them!'

*

By five o'clock that Sunday evening, the original core of animal rights activists who had set out to attend the demonstration for animal liberation, had been whittled down to Ron, Robin, Angie, Caroline, Debbie, Clive, Jody and 'Gary out there somewhere,' and new recruit Tony Smith.

The two remaining Transit vans and Clive's white 'window-cleaning' Ford van had their radios tuned to local Orchard FM whose regular news bulletins were still leading with the latest news of the famous runaway horses. From these bulletins the activists learned that the horses were being confined for the night in the sports field next to the Hinton St George village hall. The bulletin added that police and RSPCA inspectors were guarding the herd in case of any further disruptive interference by animal liberation activists. Another attempt was to be made the next day, Monday morning to transport the horses back to the Ferne Animal Sanctuary near Chard..

That night, Clive and Jody drove to the village of Hinton St George and spent a couple of hours sipping lager and eating crisps in the public bar of the Lord Poulett Arms in the High Street. Tony offered to go with them, but Ron felt it better that he stayed with the main group. While Clive and Jody listened intently to the conversation buzzing around the pub about the village's equine invasion, unknown to them or anyone else, Gary Rorke was creeping quietly around the village. The sports field and the village hall were illuminated by two arc lights, powered by a petrol-driven generator chugging quietly in the village hall car park.

The horse transporters and trailer were lined up adjacent to the village hall and Gary saw a couple of RSPCA inspectors and at least one police officer wandering in and out of the village hall. The horses peacefully munched at hay or dozed contentedly, some standing, others lying with their front knees folded underneath. Patricia stood at the edge of the field facing inwards at her herd. Her weight was balanced on her three locked knee-joints, the point of her fourth hoof resting on the turf. Her eyes were half closed and covered by her long eyelashes and her bottom lip hung floppily like a piece of limp rubber.

At midnight the activists' three vans were once again parked in Crewkerne's central car park. They were discussing a plan of action for the next day with the benefit of a report from Clive and Jody following their visit to the village pub earlier that evening. They reported that a local farmer called Bob came into the pub with two collies and they heard him telling the locals that the police had asked him to park his tractor and long trailer across the Merriott

Road just past the village hall. Apparently this precaution was to ensure that the horses didn't leave the village in that direction and also to prevent any demonstrators driving into the village from the direction of Merriott.

The group concluded that the other two roads into the village would be similarly blocked by the police in the morning. They would have to leave their vans in a layby on the A30, and make their way on foot into the village. If the group were prevented from walking down the road into the village, they would have to take the fields to get near the horses where the media would be concentrated. There was general acceptance that the best they could hope for would be to get some more media publicity.

The discussion over, Ron sat in the front seat of his van with Angie, as she smoked her last roll-up cigarette of the night, exhaling out of the open window.

'You never know, Gary might have a trick or two up his sleeve,' said Ron.

'You certainly never know with him,' answered Angela, pinching out the lit end of the cigarette, chuckling as she opened a tin and added her dog-end to her collection.

In the back of Ron's transit van Tony Smith lay awake in the darkness, his back against the metal side of the vehicle. He listened to the heavy breathing of the others sleeping, but in his mind he was still picturing his mentor Eddie Bowen lying dead in the mud. A lump suddenly grew in his throat and tears filled his eyes, but he bit his lip and searched his emotions for anger to replace the pain of his grief. He blinked away his tears and listened again to the sounds of the strangers with whom he shared the van. How contemptible were these people - people who cared for animals more than people – people who cared more for a mad horse than the magical man who died under the hooves of the beast – people who were actually planning to intervene to give the horses more 'liberation' and cause more chaos.

As Tony deliberately nurtured his inner rage, in his jacket pocket his right hand closed around the bone handle of the knife he had taken from Eddie's still-warm body in the darkness of a damp field. In the darkness he gave an involuntary jerk as he imagined himself plunging the 15 cm blade deep into the throat of the grey mare.

'You all right Tony?' muttered a voice from a sleeping bag lying hard against his side.

'Yeah, fine. Sorry', he muttered back.

*

Earlier in the evening, twelve miles away in the kitchen of the old farmhouse in the centre of the Ferne Animal Sanctuary, Trevor James and his daughter sat in their kitchen drinking hot chocolate. Rebecca held the hot cup in both hands, her elbows on the table, staring unseeingly at the uncurtained window, not even aware of her own reflection.

'A penny for 'em,' said her father, noticing her faraway look.

'Uh? Oh sorry dad – miles away,'

'What's on your mind?' he persisted.

'I was just thinking, dad, why do you think Patsy keeps going in the opposite direction to home?'

'Well, I suppose whatever happened in the field gave her a real scare and her instinct was to keep travelling away from the danger.'

'So when we get her back here do you think she still going to be nervous of being here?'

'No, I'm sure she'll soon settle down and realise that the danger no longer exists,' said Trevor.

'Yes, I suppose so,' replied his daughter. 'I just wondered......'. She paused and peered into her cup. 'No, I'm sure you're right', she added.

'Come on Becky, out with it!' insisted Trevor.

'Something one of the protesters said… about allowing the horses to do what they wanted to do, to go where they wanted to. You don't think Patsy is instinctively taking the herd in a definite direction, do you?'

'No, no, that's silly. What do you mean, following some ley-line or something like that, or going back to her birthplace? No, I'm sure not. Anyway, even if she was leading the herd on some sort of equine mission, they can't be allowed to wander the countryside, getting on the roads and railways, trampling through people's gardens, trotting around towns – it's not that sort of world. Animals have to be kept in some sort of captivity - if only for their own good. That's the way it is, I'm afraid.'

'Yes of course dad. You're right, I'm just tired - not thinking straight.' She pushed her chair back and placed her empty cup in the sink. 'I'm off to bed. What time tomorrow?'

Trevor rose and placed his cup next to his daughters and ran some water into both. 'We're going for ten o'clock. Tomorrow's Monday, so hopefully it'll be pretty quiet, although, after all the publicity there's sure to be a lot of press and public hanging around. Inspector Fowler has promised to have the place crawling with police to keep everyone back and to make sure those activists don't disrupt the whole thing again. I can't wait for everything to get back to normal round here!'

'Me too. OK dad, see you in the morning.'

'Good night Becky, sleep tight,' said Trevor, as his daughter started up the stairs.

9.45am Monday 31st October 1977

Monday morning, sun shining, a cool breeze and the village of Hinton St George was waking up. A few locals were wandering towards the village hall, but the group of animal activists, as they anticipated, had been stopped by the police at the edge of the village, and were being searched by four police officers. A loudhailer was confiscated. 'Can we take our banner, just for the press?' pleaded Ron Walters.

'Let's see what's on it,' ordered Sergeant George Thomas. Angela and Robin rolled it out to reveal the slogan 'Animal Liberation – Now!'

'OK you can take it, but if you go one inch further than the police tape across the Merriott Road you will be arrested. I've only seen two press people, and one local TV team. I've told them all not to use any lights or flashes until all the horses are loaded.'

The fifteen horses were all on their feet sensing that something was happening. Lady Patricia with Lucky and Gregory on her flanks patrolled the far end of the sports field furthest away from the village hall, with the rest of the herd bunched in the centre. Next to a double horse trailer, a police mini-bus, the Ferne Animal Sanctuary van and a silver Cortina were parked. The three large lorry horse transporters stood with their ramps down.

Farmer Bob Towning, joined Nora Whitehouse and her friend Betty Dobson, leaning on the post and rail fence watching the horses in the badly poached recreation field. 'Won't be much football played on that for a week or two,' he grumbled. Nora and Betty nodded in agreement.

As requested by the police, half an hour earlier farmer, Bob Towning had parked his tractor and long-trailer across the Merriott road, 30 yards away from the village hall. The tractor and trailer now formed a barrier across the tarmac and the wide grassy verges, beyond which the thick hedgerows and roadside ditches marked the end of the village.

'Oh, 'ere we go then,' said the farmer, the sound of his voice instantly causing his two collies to start spinning after their tails in excitement, as out of the village hall marched a dozen people led by Chief Inspector John Fowler: three police constables, an RSPCA chief inspector and two trainee inspectors, plus sanctuary manager Trevor James, his daughter Rebecca, vet Richard Carrington and three lorry drivers each with an experienced animal loader.

Trevor James was in discussion with police Chief Inspector Fowler and RSPCA Inspector Paul Robbins. 'Right,' said John Fowler, 'We need to get the horse box for the grey mare right up to the edge of the green, so that she doesn't have to walk too far after she's been darted.'

'What about the protesters?' asked the vet.

'My officers in Crewkerne have reported that one of their vehicles left the town yesterday evening and made for the M5, two men in a Cortina had also left about the same time. One transit van and a small white Ford van disappeared early this morning from

Crewkerne's car park. I'm hoping they've gone back to where they came from, but my men are under strict instructions to arrest and detain anyone who interferes today.'

'Sorry sir', interrupted one of the constables, 'Sergeant Thomas radioed through to say that a few protesters arrived at the road block. He confiscated their loud-hailer, but has allowed them to stand down the road behind the police tape with their banner.'

Veterinary surgeon Richard Carrington asked, 'Can't they be arrested?'

'Difficult', said John Fowler, 'They are entitled to protest, and anyway, we don't have a spare vehicle to take them to the station, so I assume, rather than letting them creep around the woods, Sergeant Thomas has let them have their little demo under observation.'

'OK, inspector, you're the expert. Let's get this done then,' said vet Richard Carrington.

'How close do you need to be to fire the dart, Richard?' asked Trevor James.

'Ten to fifteen metres will be ideal,' replied the vet.

'And how long before she drops?' asked RSPCA inspector Robbins.

'Well, if we're lucky and I get the dosage spot on, she won't drop, but within a few minutes she should be docile enough for us to walk her into the horse box. She may need propping up with straw bales and a sling to keep her upright on the journey.'

'What if she goes down and out like a log?' asked John Fowler.

'Then we'll have to wait until she's coming round a bit before we can get her on her feet and guide her into the horse box.' said the vet.

'But meanwhile we can be loading all the others into the lorries,' said the police inspector.' He looked at his watch. 'Ten thirty. Shall we do it gentlemen?'

The group broke up and Trevor jogged over to where his daughter was chatting to a couple of RSPCA inspectors.

'It's time Becky. The vet's going to dart Patsy, now.'

'She looks nervous dad, look how Lucky and Gregory are

hanging around her.'

Trevor watched as the three herd leaders trotted around the sports field, about thirty metres in from the perimeter road. Several police officers were shepherding onlookers away from the green and ordering them to stay on the other side of the fences around the field.

When everyone was safe, everything suddenly fell eerily silent and the vet opened the gate and strode purposefully onto the field - his rifle pointing downwards. In the distance, the animal activists had spread their banner and began chanting, but they could hardly be heard above the breeze.

He walked towards Patricia who now stood, flanked by her two lieutenants, facing the rest of the herd bunched in the centre of the field. Richard Carrington had loaded his gun, and the three horses eyed the man suspiciously. When he moved within thirty metres, Patricia snorted before swinging away and trotting off, still flanked by Lucky and Gregory.

'Come on Becky, let's help the vet,' said Trevor lightly tugging his daughter's sleeve. They picked their way into the field through the clinging mud to join the vet.

'I can't get a shot into her rump with those two either side of her,' said the vet.

'We'll see if we can separate them,' responded Trevor. He and his daughter walked slowly after the trio, calling their names, but the three horses kept moving away towards the far end of the field with the rest of the herd beginning to react to the tension.

'This isn't going to work,' said the vet. 'We need more space. Why don't we open the gate so they feel less confined. I'll ask the police to move the police minibus and maybe one of the cars to block the road to the village.'

When the vehicles had been moved into place, Trevor and Rebecca wandered casually amongst the horses, handing out mints, and the herd began to follow them out of the field and into the village hall car park. Richard Carrington just wandered slowly around patiently with his gun as the horses began to investigate the grass verges of the road. Patricia, Lucky and Gregory were now separated by a few yards from the rest of the herd and were only a dozen yards from Bob Towning's tractor and trailer that blocked the road out of the village.

The trio of horses halted and Lucky and Gregory began to turn away from their leader as they saw they could go no further. Patricia stood alone, gazing across the flat bed of the trailer at the road beyond, and the vet saw his chance. He moved forward quickly, settled into a firm stance and raised his rifle. He peered along the barrel and lined up the sights on the grey mare's rump, his finger gently closing around the trigger. Then suddenly with a terrifying roar which made both him and his target jump, the tractor's engine burst into life and black smoke exploded from its exhaust. In an instant the machine lurched forward three yards and crashed into the hedgerow, its front wheels deeply embedded into the ditch, the trailer jack-knifed at a crazy angle, leaving the road completely clear.

Her heart thumping in panic at the sudden noise, Patricia could now see the escape route. She tossed her head and whinnied loudly as Lucky and Gregory returned to her side and the rest of the herd thundered in pursuit. Trevor, Rebecca and vet Richard Carrington were unable to do anything but scramble out of the way of the horses. As the herd galloped into the road through the gap behind the trailer, no-one noticed a camouflaged figure drop from the tractor cab into the ditch and clamber through the hedge into the field beyond.

Onlookers dashed from their vantage points and rushed towards the exit road in time to see the last of the horses disappearing round the first bend. Uniformed police and RSPCA officers sprinted to their vehicles as a television camera crew hurriedly bundled their equipment into their car. Chief Inspector Fowler and RSPCA inspector Paul Robbins quickly joined the veterinary surgeon, the sanctuary manager and his daughter who were grouped around the stricken tractor and trailer.

'I don't believe it!' exclaimed the policeman. 'What the hell happened?'

RSPCA Chief Inspector Paul Robbins climbed up onto the

tractor and swung open the cab door. 'Have a look at this,' he called to the group standing below him, and he held the door open for them to see into the cab. On the cab's opposite window, written in mud, were the letters 'ALF.'

'Bastards!' cursed John Fowler. 'These animal rights nutters are in big trouble,' he added, thinking at the same time, that he too would have some explaining to do.

'Oi, what about my bloody tractor?' came a voice from behind them and the group turned to see Bob Towning, stumbling towards them with his two collies at his heels, their ears down and tails between their legs as they sensed their owner's anger.

'You asked me if you could use my tractor as a road block, and now look at it,' he snapped at the police inspector. Before John Fowler could think of a response, RSPCA Chief Inspector Paul Robbins, still balanced on the step of the tractor's cab, shouted down at the farmer, 'Did you *have* to leave these in the cab?' The RSPCA man reached in and then tossed down a large bunch of keys which fell with a clunk onto the tarmac. The embarrassed farmer stooped to pick them up, and didn't react as John Fowler muttered, 'Idiot!'

As the group walked back towards where their vehicles were parked, they could see the drivers of the horse transporters and single trailer pushing up the ramps and bolting the back of the vehicles.

Trevor quickened his pace and reached the first lorry as its driver was starting his engine. 'Where are you going?' called Trevor anxiously.

'We've had enough, mate,' replied the grim-faced driver. 'We can't waste any more time – there was the cock-up yesterday and now again today. Time's money, mate.'

'Yes I know,' said Trevor, 'But you will be paid – can't you stick with us to finish the job? We can soon catch up with the horses and have another go. It's not eleven o'clock yet.'

'But, you said it would all be over by lunchtime. Even if we can catch 'em, it'll be late this afternoon before we can get them back to your place, and then we've got to clean out the lorries ready for tomorrow's jobs. Sorry mate!'

With that, the driver crashed his lorry into gear and drove off, following the other two lorries and the double horse box that was to have been Patricia's transport and had already begun to move back down the road to the village.

Rebecca, the two chief inspectors and the vet joined Trevor, who shrugged and spread his hands. 'That's it!' he said hopelessly. 'We've got no transport and no horses.'

'This is bloody ridiculous!' exclaimed police officer John Fowler, as Sergeant George Thomas and two constables joined the group at the village hall. 'George, what happened to the protesters?'

'They're gone sir. They rolled up their banner and I gave them back their loudhailer.'

'Did any of them disappear from the group? Somebody got in the tractor and crashed it into the ditch. That's how the horses got away.'

'No sir, we watched them like a hawk. They seemed resigned to the horses being taken home, and were content to chant their slogans and pose for press pictures. From where we were at the police tape we couldn't see what happened, and the activists seemed as surprised as we were.'

*

'This is bloody ridiculous, inspector,' said Chief Superintendent Brian Morgan of the Avon and Somerset Police, as he pushed back his chair, rose from his desk and walked over to the window of his first floor office at Yeovil police station.

'Yes sir,' replied John Fowler quietly.

Brian Morgan was in his very early fifties, grey-haired and with a rugged face that reflected his long experience as a senior police officer. He leaned on the window sill and peered at the busy roundabout below. He took off his glasses and pinched the bridge of his nose between the finger and thumb of his other hand, before replacing his glasses. Turning to the chief inspector he said, 'So here we are at the start of a new week and we've got a bunch of broken down old horses wandering the county after trampling some poor bugger to death, a couple of vehicles in ditches on the A30, a gang of animal rights nutters causing chaos, a farmer demanding police compensation for damage to his field and gate, another farmer demanding we pay for his damaged tractor, a village sports field looking like the Somme, a vet pacing around with a rifle like Clint Eastwood in Dirty Harry and….and the whole thing all over national TV and the papers Not only that, but we've also got at least half a dozen police officers bogged down dealing with the case….and now you tell me nobody can supply lorries to carry these nags back home!'

'That's about it sir,' replied the Chief Inspector, inwardly smiling at his senior officer's summary.

'Not quite, Chief Inspector. The other thing is that the chief constable is not amused and is on my back….and that is why I'm on yours!'

'Yes sir.'

'And now you want to borrow three or four police horse transport vehicles from Bristol, and their drivers. How much is that going to take out of the budget?'

John Fowler knew he was not expected to reply.

'Right,' said Morgan, 'Where are these horses now?'

'Near Merriott sir. Fortunately, we had temporarily closed the road at the Merriott end so when the horses got past the tractor they didn't meet any traffic coming their way. Also fortunately, the horses went off road and down a narrow dead end lane. The RSPCA boys and the sanctuary manager have arranged water and food, and there's a vet on call. Rather than trying to pen them in, we're just keeping an eye on them and keeping vehicles out of the lane.'

'So they just have to be loaded up and taken back to Chard.'

'Well, yes sir, but it is complicated by the fact that one horse, the leader of the herd, can't be handled. There is no problem with the others as long as she is out of the way and can't wind them up. Hence the vet with the dart rifle, because where she goes the others follow and it's not easy to stop them once they've got a move on – a couple of them must weigh a ton each!'

'And it was the animal rights mob that disrupted the whole exercise?' surmised the superintendent.

'Yes sir, but only on Sunday when they turned up just off the A30. We thought after that, we had them under observation. I don't know whether they even knew who pulled the barriers away or who shifted the tractor.'

'Right,' said the superintendent emphatically.

'Right, I want these animal people picked up and out of the way before there are any further attempts to get these horses onto lorries. I'll arrange with Bristol to get the lorries and drivers on standby, but not until you can assure me there will be no further interference.'

'Yes sir. The problem is that the ones that staged a protest at the first site, weren't the ones that removed the barriers, and we didn't see who shifted the tractor at Hinton St George.'

'What you're saying is that we can't arrest anybody!'

'Well we could sir, on suspicion of conspiracy, or obstruction, or something, but we wouldn't be able to hold them for long.'

'Long enough to get the job done, d'you think?'

'Yes sir, if everything was co-ordinated, but you know what these people are like. They've got access to lawyers and we could end up with protesters from all over the country demonstrating outside the station, MPs asking questions and possibly actions for false arrest.'

'Hmm, I see what you mean,' said the superintendent thoughtfully. 'OK, why don't we meet them, away from the horses. Appeal to them to allow the animals to be returned to where they belong. If they get stroppy, I'm sure we could hint that we might have to examine their driving licences, insurance, and check their vans for roadworthiness. The thought of walking home to wherever they come from might bring them to their senses'.

'It's worth a try sir, I'll get right onto it.'

'And keep me informed inspector,' said Brian Morgan as his inspector left the room.

*

It was 10.45 on Tuesday morning, the activists' two transit vans were parked back to back in an Ilminster car park, with their back doors wide open. Eleven occupants were crowded in the back of the vans, including latest 'recruit' Tony Smith. Ron Walters stood between the two vehicles so that he could talk to both groups.

'Firstly, congratulations to Gary again, for a brilliant job in shifting the tractor.'

Murmers of approval came from the activists. Ron continued, 'I can tell you, from where I was watching, when I saw that guy aim his rifle, I thought it was all over.'

'It would have been if somebody hadn't left the keys in the tractor,' said Gary. 'I thought that I was going to have to leap out the cab, stand in front of the grey mare and try to catch the dart!'

Ron continued,. 'The question is, can we keep this going? The police are bound to be much heavier from now on. I can't see them allowing us to intervene again. According to the local radio the horses are now closeted in a lane near Merriott which is only a couple of miles from Hinton St George. They are being supervised by the RSPCA and the sanctuary people. The police have put up 'No Entry' signs at both ends of the road between Hinton and Merriott. The horses are somewhere along that road. We could go back to Merriott to see what's going on - I'm doing a TV interview there anyway at midday.'

'Who's that with, Ron,' asked Angie.

'West country BBC or somebody, for their evening news bulletin'.

Gary spoke up. 'Well if we do pack it up today, it's been well worth the trip – fantastic publicity for the cause.'

'Yes,' said Ron, 'but I still think it would be great if we could find a way to keep the horses on the move for as long as possible. The grey one that leads them certainly doesn't want to be captured – it's really spooky how she goes for it when she sees the chance and how the rest just keep on following.'

'Why don't we pick up some supplies here, and then run over to Merriott and assess the situation. If we can find a way to keep the ball rolling, let's do it. If the police have got the whole thing wrapped up then we can go home and maybe sab a hunt or two on the way perhaps.'

'Well I'm off,' declared Gary pulling the van side door open. 'Oh, do you have to?' asked Angela. 'Yep, and don't forget. You haven't seen me. You know nothing about the barriers or the tractor business.'

With that he slipped out of the van and was gone.

An hour later the two transit vans trundled into the village of Merriott. After a couple of enquiries the activists found the 'Road Closed' notice and a police van parked half on the grass verge. As they approached, two uniformed officers emerged from the van and began walking towards them.

'Quick, back-up', said Ron to Angie who was driving.

'I can't, Robin's right up behind me,' said Angie, peering into her wing mirror. 'Oh it's OK he's going back'.

Both vehicles rapidly reversed, swung round and retraced their steps to Merriott where they stopped in line outside the Swan public house in Lower Street.

'Uh oh, we've got company', said Angie, as a police car and a large black saloon car pulled up alongside them.

'It's the inspector that was in charge at Hinton', said Ron. 'He's out of uniform'. The driver of the saloon car wound down his window and Ron did the same, 'Can I have a word?' asked John Fowler.

'Sure,' said Ron, immediately adding, 'Eh, what's going on?' as the police car pulled in front of his van and reversed within inches of his bumper. Simultaneously the black saloon car reversed into the space behind activist's second van, and crept forward until the car was actually touching bumpers, neatly trapping both activist's vans.

Inspector Fowler appeared at Ron's window. Ron spoke quickly as he placed his hand on the door handle, 'Angie, you talk to him, with Robin if you like. I've got to meet the TV people in the square. I'll see you later.'

Ron explained, 'Sorry, inspector, I've got a date with a reporter,' and as he hurried off he shouted, 'Angie and Robin will help you.'

Robin and Angie clambered out of the transit van and John Fowler offered his hand to them both.

'Chief inspector John Fowler.' he said.

'Angie.' the girl replied shaking his hand briefly.

'Ah yes, Ms Wright', he said, watching the girl's eyes closely for signs of any surprise that he knew her name. He was impressed to see hardly a flicker. 'Shall we go in the pub – my treat,' he said breezily.

'Not drinking and driving inspector, surely,' she mocked. 'Just a sec, I want Robin in on this, if you don't mind,' as she beckoned to the driver of the second van.

Robin clambered out and was similarly offered the inspector's hand.

'This is chief inspector Fowler,' said Angie.

'Wild,' exclaimed Robin and he and Angie exchanged grins. The inspector frowned. 'Am I missing something?' He looked questioningly from one to the other.

'No, you're all right,' said Angie. 'It's Robin's little joke. Wild...wild fowler...d'you see?'

'Ah, I see, very droll, Mr Chamberlain', and felt a stab of satisfaction as he saw the concern sweep across the young man's face at the mention of his surname.

Robin frowned at Angie, but she smiled reassuringly, 'It's all right Robin, he knows my name too. You've been talking to ARNI then, inspector!'

The policeman was not in the least surprised that such experienced activists would be aware of the computerised records filed in New Scotland Yard and known as the Animal Rights Network Index.

They found a table in the quiet corner of the pub and the policeman returned from the bar with a tray bearing two large orange juices, a pint of bitter shandy for himself and four packets of assorted crisps.

'I'll get straight to the point,' said the inspector after his first mouthful of his drink. 'We want to get these horses back safely into their sanctuary. The manager there is concerned that some of them aren't up to coping with all this excitement and exertion. We know that your group has been interfering with efforts to get them home – after all, you staged a noisy demo where the horses were confined the first time, and I don't believe it was a coincidence that while you were waving your banners, someone pulled the barriers away so the horses could escape. And at Hinton your ALF initials were smeared on the cab window of the tractor that was moved to allow the horses to escape again.'

Robin and Angie simultaneously picked up their glasses and drank. Realising neither intended to comment, the inspector continued. 'So far no-one has been seriously hurt, but they could have been…and so could the animals. If they had been, it would have been down to you and you could be facing prosecution under the Protection of Animals Act – for causing unnecessary suffering. Think about that! I accept that it is nothing to do with you that the horses got out in the first place, and we are prepared to forget everything that has happened provided there is no further interference. I still can't get my head round what your actual point is with regard to these horses and it's not my concern anyway. I just want you to know that if you don't call it a day, we will not be happy. For instance we might find a problem or two with your vans that necessitates taking them off the road. We might take a close look at your driving documents, licences, insurance certificates, etc. And if you can't produce them we might ask your local police to visit your homes and search for them. Am I making myself clear?'

He paused, took a mouthful of shandy and replaced his glass on the table. He looked from one to the other.

'Well? Cat got your tongues?'

Robin reached for a packet of crisps and pulled it open.

'Sure, we get the picture, normal police hassle,' he said inserting his fingers and pulling out a wedge of crisps. As he poked them into his mouth and began crunching them, he looking unblinkingly into the policeman's eyes.

'Look, inspector,' said Angie, picking up her glass of orange juice. 'We don't expect you to understand the animal rights philosophy – if you did you would be the first copper we've ever met who did. But our object in this has been to get people to think about the fact that human beings don't give any animals the freedom to indulge their natural instincts; they are only allowed to do what we human beings want them to do or behave as we want them to. With horses, when human beings have finished with them, they are either neglected or butchered for meat, or if they're lucky they're allowed to spend the last days of their lives in a sanctuary. Even then, as we've seen in this case, they are not safe from somebody wanting to do them harm. These horses, having escaped from the sanctuary don't seem to want to be rounded up and taken back there. So why, just for once, can't we just see where they want to go, give them an escort and food and water, and care if they need it, until we can work out what they want?'

Hear, hear,' said Robin, reaching for a second packet of crisps.

'Oh, come on,' retorted the policeman scornfully. 'Are you suggesting that we should just open all the gates, let all dogs off their leads, open all the zoo cages and let all animals go where they want? That's just stupid! The dogs would form packs and massacre sheep…and animals, such as lions and tigers, would massacre the cows…'

Robin interrupted him. 'You mean they'd do exactly what human beings do.'

'John Fowler was losing patience. 'I'm just saying…..look, I didn't come here to discuss philosophy. I just wanted to let you know that we cannot tolerate any more interference with these horses. They HAVE to go back to their owners. Good God, the owners are people who really care for animals, your allies, no less.'

'That's what they used to say about runaway slaves,' said Robin. 'They can't have freedom, they don't know what to do with it. They are best off back with their owners who can look after them and give them employment, a roof over their heads and sufficient food to survive on.'

'OK, OK', said the inspector pushing back his chair. He drained his glass and stood up. 'Please think about what I've said. You're not villains, I know that. We'd rather spend our time catching real crooks, but if you break the law, we won't hesitate to treat you like any other criminal.'

Angie reached behind her and dragged her coat off her chair. She had warmed to the inspector enough to want to end the meeting on a conciliatory note. She held the door open for him as he ducked out through the low-beamed doorway to the road.

The policeman thanked her, and when the three of them were standing on the pavement, he extended his hand,

'We appreciate the chat, inspector,' said Angie. 'I can assure you we'll discuss what you've said with the rest of the group.'

'And thanks for the drinks and crisps,' added Robin as he too took the offered his hand.

'You're welcome,' replied the inspector before stepping back to his car and climbing into his driving seat.

'Not bad for a copper, I suppose,' said Robin, grudgingly, as the inspector started his engine and drove off, quickly followed by the police car that had been parked in front of the vans. As the police vehicles disappeared, Ron Walters appeared from around the corner and joined them.

'How'd it go, Ron?' asked Robin.

Just then the pub door opened and an elderly couple emerged onto the pavement.

'Let's go somewhere more private', said Ron, reaching for the door-handle of the front van.

A few minutes later the two vans were just outside the village of Merriott and again parked back to back with the rear doors open. Ron reported the contents of his interview with local BBC television reporter Terri Clark, and Angie reported the almost identical exchanges she and Robin had had with chief inspector Fowler.

The threat of police action worried some of the activists – particularly the threat of arrests and action to deprive them of transport. They were well used to such tactics when trying to sabotage their local fox hunts, or picketing local animal research establishments, but now they were miles away from their homes. Some argued that there was little more that they could do without risking serious criminal charges, and that they should cut and run – especially as Ron's televised interview due to be shown that evening would be the culmination of unprecedented publicity for the Animal Liberation Front.

Ron was for staying on. 'We can still manage to prevent them taking the horses back, without getting arrested. We just need to be less visible and keep away from the media.'

'But we need the press to keep explaining our reasons for interference,' said Robin, 'otherwise we'll just be labelled as nutters.'

'But you've already explained it to the media, and Angie and Robin have explained it to the police,' said Caroline, who was eager to get home. She was not the only one coveting a bath, some decent food and a good night out. There was a limit to how long one could stomach sleeping in the back of van and living off cans of coke and vegetarian sandwiches and being half-suffocated with body odour and stale cigarette smoke.

Huddled in the depths of one of the vans, Tony Smith, listened to the arguments with incredulity. What sort of people were these? Were they all mad? Why all this fuss about animals?

After another forty minutes of discussion a plan of action had been agreed. Both vans would drive together to Taunton and onto the M5 motorway. They were sure that the police would be watching them and would assume they had taken John Fowler's warning and were calling off the operation. One van would indeed join the M4 and take home the Norwich group. The second van containing those who wished to try and keep the horses free would turn round at the Bridgwater junction and drive to the large town of Yeovil which is only eight miles from Merriott. They would wait there relying on the local radio to keep them informed of the progress and location of the horses, and move quickly back to the scene if there was any attempt to load them into lorries.

Ron reminded the group that Gary Rorke was still in the area. 'The fact that we are still around will keep the police occupied. It might allow Gary to continue with his sabotage.'

'He's right,' said Robin. 'Perhaps a few more of us could hide up out there.'

'No, leave that side of things to Gary. We can keep the police busy, and we can talk to the press and media'.

'OK', so who's staying and who's going?' asked Ron. 'All those staying come into this van, and all those not coming back, go in the other one'.

The activists clambered in and out of the two vans, until Ron's van contained only himself, Angie, Robin, Caroline and Tony Smith. Clive and Jody decided to return to Dorchester to check on Clive's window cleaning enquiries, but if possible they would try to join up again with the 'staying group' depending on his work load.

'What about you, Tony?' asked Ron, looking at the pale and drawn face of their latest recruit. 'You could easily hitch back to Exeter from the M5 services at Taunton.

'I'd like to stay around, if it's all right with you', replied Tony, to the surprise of everyone.

'Good on you, Tony,' said Robin, slapping the youth on the back, not noticing the scowl which briefly flashed across the newcomer's face before it quickly turned into a false smile. 'OK, so that's six for the first van and us five in this one', said Ron. He looked at his watch. 'It's just gone two, might as well get going.'

*

Trevor James and his daughter Rebecca were breaking open bales of hay and spreading it along the edges of the narrow lane. The lane was originally tarmacked but was rarely used. Grass and weeds had long crept steadily in from the edges. The hedges either side were thick and grew against a robust post and rail fence. The horses were relaxed - tugging wispy strands out of the bundles. Two RSPCA inspectors were collecting buckets of water from a trough a few yards inside the adjacent field and heaving them over the gate and pouring them into a line of further buckets. At the far end of the line of horses, Lady Patricia stood eating hay, and gazing up the lane over the backs of her herd, and beyond them she could see a police car, RSPCA van and the sanctuary van parked.

It was just gone three o'clock in the afternoon. The vet had been and gone, declaring all the horses as fit and well as could be expected. Trevor stretched his arms skywards, pushed his shoulders back and groaned at the ache in his back.

'You all right, dad?' asked his daughter.

'Yes Becky, just getting old!'

The sound of a vehicle and a slamming car door out of sight around the bend caused them to look up the lane. Chief inspector John Fowler appeared and came walking breezily towards them.

'Good news,' he called as he approached.

'We could do with some, inspector. What's happened?' said Trevor wearily.

'The animal libbers have gone. My men followed them all the way to the M5 and they've gone east. I had a chat with a couple of them earlier at the request of my chief super, and warned them that any further interference would be jumped on from a great height. It appears they've taken the hint'.

'About time!' said Trevor bitterly.

'And the super has arranged for all four of the Bristol police horse transporters to be here tomorrow morning. And a single trailer for your grey mare. The vet knows to be here with his dart gun at 10 a.m.

'No problem', replied Trevor, 'But what about the horses tonight?'

'Can we get them into this field?' said the inspector, gesturing towards the wooden gate.

'Not a chance,' said Trevor, 'Becky and I went up to the farm, but he's heard all about Walter Bagg's field being wrecked the other night. He said we could take water from his trough, but he wouldn't let us put the horses in his field.'

The inspector glanced at the horses contentedly munching hay. 'Well they seem settled enough at present. It's good that the lane is a dead end.'

'I agree inspector,' said Trevor. He gestured towards the grey mare. '…except, Patricia, seems to get edgy when she feels confined.'

LADY PATRICIA

'But dad, that could be because of things that have happened when they've been confined', interjected Rebecca. 'The first night she must have panicked at Silver dying, then the next time there was the demonstration, and this morning she was clearly nervous of the vet with the gun, then the tractor starting up – I think she just panics and looks for a way out the situation.'

'Yes, that makes sense,' said her father. 'Now that the public and press seem to have lost interest and if the animal rights people have left, maybe everything will settle down now.'

'Right, let's get a barrier organised,' said the chief inspector. 'I'm sure the RSPCA will keep someone here all night and I'll get a couple of officers to be on hand – just in case.'

Trevor spoke, 'Once I've taken Becky home and had a meal and shower, I'll come back. I can sleep in the van…just in case.'

'Me too, dad,' said his daughter, 'otherwise you'll have to come and pick me up in the morning. If we go back to the sanctuary now, we can make sure everything's OK at home, and I can make us some food and flasks for the night and breakfast tomorrow.'

Chapter 7

By 5pm the police car and the RSPCA van had been manoeuvred to form a substantial barrier across the open end of the lane. Chief inspector John Fowler had gone home earlier and Trevor and Rebecca had driven back to the animal sanctuary leaving the horses in the care of two police constables in their car and two RSPCA inspectors in their van. The horses settled down for the night – some lying down on the straw and hay spread across the lane, while others stood, dozing with their hind quarters facing into the October breeze.

At around 7pm, Patricia meandered slowly up the lane, plucking grass from the verge every few steps. Opposite her on the other side of the lane, Gregory moved at the same pace as he too snatched clumps of grass and nibbled leaves from the overgrown hedge. Patricia stopped browsing as she became aware of the low voices of men talking in the white RSPCA van and the police car parked across the lane. After a few moments she and Gregory turned and wandered back down the lane which was approximately 100 yards long.

The buckets of water were stationed about half way down the lane in front of a gate that had been fixed to the gate-post by a dozen coils of barbed wire. Gregory strolled over to a bucket and took in a long draught of water while Patricia picked her way through the herd and plodded down the darkened lane in the other direction. At the end of the lane a wooden fence stood in front of a line of mature silver birch trees bordering a copse. The grey mare turned away and walked back up the lane to where the buckets stood in front of the gate. She kicked over a couple of buckets and peered over the gate into the dark field. Her ears were pricked forward with her chest bearing onto the top bar of the gate.

Just then she detected the slight whiff of human scent and she took a step backwards from the gate. Then she saw a movement as a man suddenly appeared from behind the hedgerow and crouched only feet from her on the other side of the gate.

The grey mare snorted and stamped a challenge with her front feet – an action that instantly placed the whole herd into a state of high alert. Ignoring the horse, Gary Rorke withdrew a pair of wire cutters from the breast pocket of his camouflaged jacket and started snipping through the strands of barbed wire that fastened the gate to its post. When all the strands were cut, he replaced the tool in his pocket, carefully collected up the wire and pushed it into the depths of the hedge. With a grunt, he heaved and dragged the gate open into the field, and then quietly slipped away along the hedgerow.

Patricia hesitated, her ears twitching nervously. Big Patrick joined her, staring into the field, then Joey, Gregory, Lucky and George, their front feet all in a line as if waiting for a starting signal. The signal came with a movement from Patricia, stepping gingerly into the gateway where she paused for a few seconds looking right, then left along the hedgerow, before striking out into the grey field that stretched out in front of her. Within half a minute the whole herd had passed through the gate and were now spreading out and taking bites from the fresh grass.

Soon all the animals had moved far into the field, leaving the lane quiet and empty except for a dozen black buckets, a carpet of hay and straw, and scores of piles of sweet-smelling dung.

At 8pm, Trevor James and his daughter returned from Ferne Animal Sanctuary, entered the lane and parked their van facing the two vehicles that formed the barrier. They emerged into the darkness, each with a powerful halogen torch. Police constable Barry Collins opened his car door, stepped out and flashed his own torch at the two figures facing him.

'Good evening folks,' he said cheerfully.

'Hello constable, everything all right?' asked Trevor.

'Yes, all quiet', responded the constable.

As the two RSPCA inspectors climbed out of their van, Trevor said, 'We've got loads of hot tea and sandwiches – you're welcome to share them.'

PC Rodney Humphries, still sat in the passenger seat, spoke through the open car window, 'Very kind, Mr James, don't mind if we do. We're on 'till ten, and we've had all ours.'

'We'll just check the horses. See you in a couple of minutes then,' called Rebecca, before she and her father squeezed between the two vehicles and set off along the lane, the beams of their torches sweeping the lane and hedgerows before them.

In less than a minute the two policemen saw the beam of a torch swinging backwards and forwards erratically as the light came back towards them. Rebecca banged on the bonnet of the police van, and yelled, 'They've gone!' she blurted breathlessly as the four officers threw open their doors and climbed out into the lane.

'They've gone' she shouted again, 'through the gate into the field,' she grabbed another breath, '…but they've gone out of the field on the other side, into another lane, God knows where they are now.'

Rodney Humphries' heart sank as he realised that he was going to have to inform Sergeant Thomas of the latest event in the saga. 'Where's your father?' he asked.

'He's trying to track them down.' Rebecca sighed tearfully.

Rodney slid back into the front seat and reached for the radio.

'Victor three to Victor one.'

'Victor one, receiving. What's up Rodney?'

'We've got a problem, sarge.'

'What sort of problem?'

'I'm afraid we've lost them again, sarge.'

'Lost what?'

'The horses, sarge,' replied Rodney, nudging his partner Barry in the ribs to stop him giggling.

George Thomas didn't bother to disguise his anger. 'What the hell d'you mean, lost 'em; how the hell can you lose fifteen bloody horses? You're supposed to be watching them!'

'Somehow they've got into the next field and then apparently out the other side sarge'.

'Well you can bloody well find'em again'.

'Right you are sarge – we're onto it'.

George Thomas barked, 'I want to know exactly where you are every five minutes, understand?'

'Yes sarge,' said Rodney.

'Who's this?' muttered Barry as a torch beam jogged up the lane towards them.

'It's my dad,' said Rebecca.

'I've had a look at the gate', said Trevor into the driver's window of the police car. 'The barbed wire that was wrapped round the gate post has been cut and there are boot prints where someone has pulled the gate open, he added. 'And the gate on the other side of the field has also been opened and as far as I know whoever is doing it may have opened gates all over the place.'

'Sabotage again,' said Barry. 'I thought we were told the animal rights nutters had gone!'

'We'll go round the lanes in our van', said Trevor, 'I hope to catch up with you later. The lane's in a mess, but we'll have to leave the buckets until tomorrow'.

'That's OK', shouted Rodney, already swinging the wheel of the police car to reverse out of the lane. We'll leave the road closed signs in place.'

*

Chief inspector John Fowler dozed in his chair in front of a flickering television set that competed with the flames of gas fire to flash colours onto the cream walls of his comfortable lounge. His wife Sheila had gone to bed half an hour previously. Occasionally his eye-lids quivered enough for him to see the colours of the picture, but his brain resolutely refused to register the sounds and vision emanating from the set. He gradually became conscious of a persistent telephone ringing and forced his eyes open a fraction in the hope that the sound may have been coming from the television. He groaned, struggled unsteadily to his feet and walked out into the hall to pick up the receiver.

'Hello, John Fowler,' he mumbled.

'Good evening sir, it's George Thomas.'

'Yes, sergeant,' he said, blinking himself awake. 'What's the problem?'

'Sorry to ring you so late sir, but I thought you'd want to know....it's the horses, inspector. They're in Norton, Norton sub Hamdon, wandering round the village.'

'How the hell did they get there, sergeant?' groaned the chief inspector.

'We're not really sure yet, sir. They were nicely bottled up in a lane at Merriott, with two of my officers and two RSPCA chaps supposed to be watching over them, and somehow they got through a gate into a field, then through a series of gates, and in and out of fields and along lanes until they finished up at Norton. It looks as if the gates have all been opened deliberately.'

'What time is it sergeant,' asked the inspector, realising that he had not put his watch on after his earlier shower.

'11.10 sir,', answered the sergeant.

'Have you got it all under control George?'

'Well, we've got two constables and two RSPCA inspectors over there and of course Trevor James and his daughter.'

'OK, I'll be over in the morning – you don't need me tonight George, do you?'

'No sir, we'll cope, but there is one more thing sir,'

'Go on,' said John Fowler, knowing from the sergeant's tone that there was worse news to come.

'The first call we had that they were in Norton, was from Mrs Delia Haskins. She had half a dozen horses in her front garden – made bit of a mess of her shrubs apparently!'

'Mrs Delia Haskins?' queried the inspector, wondering why the name was familiar.

'Yes sir, wife of Jeremy Haskins, MBE, MP – sometimes referred to as Mr Angry the Member for Yeovil. Apparently she rang him – at some sort of late night sitting in the House of Commons – and he's already been onto Chief Superintendent

Morgan at home about it.'

The inspector groaned, 'They're old enemies…went to the same school apparently'.

'Yes sir, that's why I thought I'd let you know what's going on – before he gets onto you.'

'Good, I'm grateful, sergeant. I'll get over there first thing tomorrow. Thanks for letting me know.'

'You're welcome sir, see you tomorrow.'.

John Fowler replaced the receiver and stood pondering, deep in thought for a moment, until he heard a sound behind him. He turned to see his wife standing on the stairs in her dressing gown.

'What is it, John?' she asked anxiously, 'something serious?'

'Well, not really darling – not as world disasters go,' he said, grinning. 'You're not going to believe this, Sheila.'

It was midnight and lights were on in every house and cottage in the Somerset village of Norton sub Hamdon. The rambling village spread along both sides of a road running the length of the western lee of Ham Hill. Yellow light streamed from dozens of open front doors and beamed down damp paths to find people huddled in coats and slippers at their garden gates. Police vehicles with flashing lights were parked at various points along the road and people in luminous yellow jackets were standing in small groups.

RSPCA chief inspector Paul Robbins stood at the open iron gates of the village recreation ground. He watched as two ponies were shepherded by two police constables and an RSPCA inspector, through the muddy gateway into the field.

'How many more to come?' called the chief inspector.

'We think that's the last two, sir,' responded his junior officer.

'Let's get this gate closed then and do a count. There should be fifteen.'

A van drew up alongside him and the manager of the Ferne Animal Sanctuary and his daughter Rebecca climbed out of the vehicle.

'Ah, just in time, Mr James. You can come in and check that all your horses are present and correct'.

'This situation is going from bad to worse,' moaned Trevor.

At that moment, sergeant George Thomas joined them. 'Even worse than you think, Trevor!' he said jovially. 'We've got the media all over the village again; as we speak the BBC television news is interviewing the local MP's wife under arc-lights and filming the remains of her new shrubbery! Yet another perfect opportunity for her husband to stand up in Parliament and slag off the police. I can hear him now….. Mr Speaker, the Home Secretary presides over a police force that can't even keep a handful of geriatric horses under control, let alone the criminal community.. blah blah blah.'

Paul and Trevor grinned at the sergeant's excellent mimicry of the notorious Tory MP.

Trevor pulled open the metal gate as he said, 'Come on Becky, let's see how they are.'

They closed the gates behind them and walked into the field. There was just enough light to see the shapes of the horses shuffling amongst and around the swings and slides in the centre of the field. Trevor and his daughter wandered amongst the horses, counting as they went. Within a few minutes they were back at the gate and reported that all the horses were present.

'The whole field is fenced with high metal bars, so there is no way they can get out,' said the sergeant.

'But bearing in mind what's happened, we'll need a padlock and chain on this gate and a couple of guards overnight', replied the RSPCA inspector.

'I'm going to have to organise some water for them', added Trevor. 'I've got plenty of buckets in the van, I'll have to ask at one of the locals if I can use their outside tap.'

'Don't ask Mrs Haskins!' joked the sergeant.

Trevor and Paul chuckled, before the latter asked, 'What about hay, Trevor?'

'I think we can leave that until tomorrow, I'd like to give them short feed, but there's still a bit of grass in the field they can pick at – although I reckon it will be a bit of a mess by the morning.'

By two o'clock in the morning, the village was quiet again. The reporters and television crews had left, Mrs Delia Haskins was asleep, while in his London flat her Member of Parliament husband snored in his chair. On his lap was a piece of paper upon which he had scribbled a parliamentary question for the Home Secretary about the joint incompetence of the Avon and Somerset Constabulary and the world's biggest animal welfare society.

In Norton sub Hamdon's recreation ground the Ferne herd of horses rested. The only noise was the creaking of the childrens' slide that rocked precariously as Clydesdale Patrick rubbed his itchy rump on it. A police car containing two officers was parked facing, and just touching, the padlocked gates. The grey Connemara mare plodded slowly around the inside perimeter of the barred fence, while a camouflaged man crept unseen around the outside perimeter before disappearing into the night with a heavy rucksack on his back.

The next morning it was raining steadily. Those residents of Norton sub Hamdon whose houses overlooked the village's recreation ground watched from their windows as police cars and other vehicles arrived. In the back of a police mini-bus a meeting had been convened. Present were police officers chief inspector John Fowler and sergeant George Thomas, RSPCA chief inspector Paul Robbins, sanctuary manager Trevor James, veterinary surgeon Richard Carrington, plus the formidable wife of the Honourable Jeremy Haskins, MBE, MP.

The recreation field was a sea of poached mud. The children's slide leaned at a crazy angle and one of its stanchions uprooted from its base under the weight of Big Patrick's rump. The fifteen horses quietly munched on hay supplied by a local farmer, being distributed along the driest edge of the field by Rebecca James and three volunteers from the village. Four other cars were parked in the narrow road alongside the recreation field with steamed-up windows concealing two television crews and two newspaper reporters.

After completing introductions, John Fowler leaned forward with his hands clasped. 'OK, I'll begin by laying out our position. We have police horse transporters standing by to take the horses back to Chard. And this time we will ensure that there is no interference by animal rights people or anyone else. The problem is that we can't get the horse transporters up this lane – not even one at a time.'

'So we've got to get the horses out of the field and shepherd them to the lorries,' interjected Trevor James, 'which still leaves us the problem of Patricia'.

'Excuse me, but who is Patricia?' asked Delia Haskins, peeping out from under a plastic rain hat that she declined to take off because she was acutely conscious of the dramatic contrast between the colour of her dark hair and the grey of her roots. The fact that the equine invasion had caused her to cancel her hairdressing appointment did nothing to improve her irritation with the situation.

'I am sorry, Mrs Haskins,' said Trevor. 'I should explain. Patricia is the name of the grey mare who leads the herd and unfortunately they won't go anywhere without her being at the front.'

'Well, why can't you put it on a lead or something and let the others follow?' (Mrs Haskins never acknowledged that any animal could be anything other than an 'it').

'I'm afraid she's never been broken to a halter, Mrs Haskins and she refuses to be controlled in any way', replied Trevor apologetically.

'How ridiculous,' snapped the MP's wife. 'Do you mean to tell me that we have had a wild horse roaming around our village? Good Lord, they were in my garden – I could have been attacked!'

She suddenly remembered the newspaper and television news headlines and clasped her hands to her cheeks. 'Oh my God, it's the horse that killed that man isn't it,' she whimpered.

'We can't be sure about that Mrs Haskins,' struggled Trevor. 'She really has a nice temperament, unless someone tries to get a halter or a rope on her'.

'Well an animal like that should be put down, I've....', she was interrupted by vet Richard Carrington.

'I assure you Mrs Haskins that all we need to do is to get a little tranquiliser into the animal. We would have already achieved that had it not been for interference by some animal rights people who for some reason object.'

Paul Robbins joined the conversation. 'On behalf of the RSPCA, Mrs Haskins, I can confidently say that the problem will be solved and the animals taken back to their sanctuary at Chard, as soon as we can separate the herd leader from the rest of them. The only problem is that we will have to walk them back through the village to the lorries, after, that is, we can get their herd leader tranquilised and out of the recreation field.'

The lady in the plastic rain-hat rounded on him. 'No, I'm sorry, it's too dangerous. As chair of the Parish Council, I cannot agree to a pack of dangerous animals being allowed to charge around the village. We have elderly residents and young children. These horses have already killed someone and wrecked my garden, not to mention our recreation field that has been virtually destroyed. My husband is furious and intends to raise the matter in Parliament.'

The five men silently glanced at each other, each of them conscious of the power that the ridiculous woman held in her hands. Sergeant George Thomas broke the silence. 'There is another solution.' He saw immediately that he had the attention of all five of his audience. 'There is a well-fenced public footpath running alongside the recreation field. It leads up onto Ham Hill,' he continued. 'We could easily remove a section of metal fence and nudge them out onto the footpath. Even if they turned left towards the village, instead of going up the hill, it wouldn't matter because there is a turnstile at this end. There's no way a horse could get through that.'

John Fowler butted in. 'Hang on a minute. At the moment we've got the whole herd trapped in a field of less than two acres. If they get up onto Ham Hill they'll have God knows how many acres to roam about in. The Hill's got a perimeter of around three miles. How's that going to help us, George?'

'The point is sir, they'll be out of the village, and out of Mrs Haskins' hair.' (Delia Haskins flinched and snatched a glance at her reflection in the van window to check that her plastic rain hat was still in place.)

The sergeant continued, 'There's only one road running through the Ham Hill park and there are cattle grids at both ends so we won't need to worry about the horses escaping through gates….and there are plenty of quarries to choose from, where they can be corralled, if you know what I mean.' Thinking on his feet, he added, 'And the tracks and ground are all hard-standing for the lorries and our vans….and there's even a pub, the Prince of Wales!' he added over-cheerfully.

Everyone looked at the chief inspector. After a few seconds thought, he said brightly, 'Everybody happy? Trevor, Paul, George, Mrs Haskins?'

Only the latter responded. 'As long as they're out of our village chief inspector, you can do whatever you like with them. Now I really must go gentlemen.' She rose, untangling her wet umbrella from under her seat, and made her way to the minibus door which George Thomas slid open for her. The men mumbled goodbyes, as she stepped down into the lane and hurried off, as the sergeant pulled the door shut.

'Phew, I'm glad she's gone,' uttered chief inspector John Fowler.

'No doubt she'll be on the phone to hubby within a minute,' said his sergeant.

John Fowler resumed, 'Ok let's tell everyone the plan. George, can you get onto the Council and tell them we need someone out here to remove a section of the play area fence?'

He turned to Trevor and RSPCA man Paul Robbins. 'You two better go up the hill and check out the other end of the footpath, I'll get a couple of officers at each end of the road. We'll need to organise water and horse-feed and find a quarry we can keep them together in.'

George Thomas said, 'There's a quarry right next to the pub. They're bound to have an outside tap.'

'Great,' responded his chief inspector. A thought flashed across his mind. 'Does the pub get busy at this time of the year? I don't want to have problems refusing people entry at the park entrances.'

Vet Richard Carrington responded, 'I've been there a few times for a meal. It's very popular at weekends in the summer, but I don't

LADY PATRICIA

think it gets crowded at this time of the year.'

'Good', exclaimed the chief inspector, 'Let's get on with it. Let's get these horses out of this village before Mrs Haskins declares war. Then we can work out how and when we take them home.'

John Fowler took on the task of explaining the plan to the representatives of the media and appealed to them to keep clear until the animals were up on the hill.

On its news broadcast, Orchard FM dutifully notified the local radio audience, including a group of five young people lounging in a Transit van in a Yeovil supermarket car park.

'Where do you think Gary is now?' said Angie Wright, rubbing an apple on her jeans.

'He won't be far from the horses,' replied Ron Walters as Angie crunched into the fruit. 'What a guy!' he continued. 'You've got to hand it to him…getting fifteen horses out from under the noses of the police and RSPCA!'

Robin Chamberlain stretched his arms up and touched the roof of the van with his palms. 'He's a good'un all right. What do we do now? I reckon we should go out to this Ham Hill place and see what's going on.'

Angie frowned. 'We could be in trouble if we do. They could arrest us for …', she hesitated, looking for a word.

'What?' Ron interjected. 'What could they arrest us for?'

'I don't know - coppers will always find something if they want to'.

'Well, I still say we go and take a look. We have to find Gary sometime anyway, we can't just abandon him out there. What d'you reckon Tony?' he asked straining his neck around to peer at their latest recruit.

Tony Smith had just taken a gulp from a can of Coca Cola and was wiping his mouth with the back of his hand. 'Yeah, I'm for going out there,' he said.

'OK' said Ron, 'Let's have a look at the map. Where is this Ham Hill?'

They peered at their Ordnance Survey map and quickly found

the location.

'What's PH stand for?' asked Angie, pointing to the letters on the map.

'Public house!' said Robin, brightly. 'Even better, let's go!'

Half an hour later they had driven through the tiny village of Odcombe and were approaching the entrance to Ham Hill country park. It was late afternoon, gloomy, but no longer raining. Suddenly Ron braked and pulled into the verge. 'What's up?' called Robin from the depths of the van.

'A police car…and a cattle grid', replied Ron, as he noticed the road sign.

'That's OK, keep going,' said Robin. 'They can only tell us to go back.'

Ron pulled forward again and slowed to a halt just before the cattle grid, where a policeman signalled to him to stop.

'Good afternoon, sir,' said the policeman as Ron wound down his window. 'D'you mind if I ask where you are going sir?'

'Uh, to the pub, officer,' he replied.

'Not open yet, sir; not 'till 7 o'clock at this time of year, sir', droned the constable, his eyes flicking around the inside of the van.

Angie leaned across Ron and smiled at the young officer.

'But can't we get to Stoke sub Hamdon, this way?'

'You can indeed madam, but we've got a herd of lost horses under guard near the pub, and we've somewhat taken over the pub car park with horse boxes and things.' As he spoke, he squinted into the darkness of the van at the other occupants, before continuing in monotone. 'But if you stay on the road, you'll find one of my colleagues at the cattle grid the other end. He'll let you through - then it's just down the steep hill to the village.'

'Thank you, officer,' chorused Ron and Angie, as the van moved forward and rumbled over the grid.

'What d'you reckon?' said Robin, leaning forward on the back of Ron's seat. 'Did he sus us?'

'Dunno', replied Ron, glancing in his mirror and seeing the policeman get back into his car.

'Best go right through and down to the village,' said Angie. 'We can tell the copper at the other end that we are coming back to the pub later.'

Sergeant George Thomas picked up his phone and dialled a number. It rang twice before the familiar voice of Chief Inspector John Fowler responded. 'It's George Thomas, sir. I just thought you'd want to know that the animal rights people have just turned up again, on Ham Hill. Four of them in one van - registered to a Ron Walters of Portsmouth.'

'Right George. Thanks for that. Where are they now?'

'They drove right through the park and down into Stoke, but they did tell one of my officers that they were intending to go up to the pub tonight…the Prince of Wales.'

'OK George. I think we should hold a little reception for them don't you? Tell your men to wait until they are in the pub and then block their van in. As soon as they are in the bar, let me know and I'll be there. Meanwhile, try to think of something we can lift them for – take a look at their tyres and lights.'

'Yes sir, understood. Talk to you later, sir.'

At 7.34pm Ron's Transit van rumbled over the cattle grid, waved through by a caped policeman swinging a powerful torch. After a couple of hundred yards or so, the headlights picked out a sign which bore a large blue arrow pointing to the left under the words, *'Prince of Wales, Car Park 400 yards'*. Ron Walters swung the van off the road onto a tarmac track and even though he drove slowly, he couldn't prevent the van lurching from side to side as the wheels thumped into some of the many potholes. The road wound its way between several small grassy hillocks on either side. Rough gravel tracks ran off into small flat bottoms of old quarries. The red reflectors of parked cars suddenly loomed up, and then a dazzling white board bearing the hastily chalked words, *'Car Park closed, please park on left'*. Ron obeyed, and pulled in behind a line of four parked cars. He switched off the engine and the headlights. They all sat quietly in the darkness for a few seconds, staring out through the windscreen at the inviting lights of the Prince of Wales public house with its illuminated sign gently swinging in a light breeze.

'Are we going in then?' asked Robin.

'Yes, 'course we are,' replied Ron, pulling on the handle and noisily sliding back the door.

They clambered out and picked their way amongst the potholes towards the door of the pub. Ron glanced at the entrance sign, lifted the latch and leaned on the old, black studded door. It had only opened an inch or two when they heard a low whistle behind them. Robin was at the back and turned. 'It's Gary!' he whispered. Ron gently pulled the door back into place and noiselessly let the latch drop. They stepped back into the narrow road. Where an unshaven Gary stood grinning at them.

'Great to see you Gary,' said Ron.

'Fantastic!' added Angie.

'We can't talk here,' said Gary. 'Let's get in the van.'

They quickly made their way back along the road and climbed into the Transit.

'How you doing, Tony?' rasped Gary. 'Still here then.'

Tony felt his ears burn. 'Oh yeah!' he said as enthusiastically as he could.

'Good on you,' replied the former commando.

'Are you all right Gary?', asked Angie, concernedly. 'Have you eaten?'

Gary grinned, 'Yep, I used up my pack rations, but I found a store room behind the pub...unlocked. Nicked some bread rolls and biscuits and a couple of cartons of fruit juice.'

Robin laughed. 'Trust you, Gary.'

Angie continued, 'But where have you slept, in all the rain? Aren't you soaked?' She reached out and touched the sleeve of Gary's combat jacket. It was dry.

'No problem. I can always get out of the rain, and luckily it's not been cold.'

'Well, we've got to make a decision on where we go from here,' said Ron.

Gary responded. 'They've got four police horse wagons in the car park behind the pub and the plan is to load the horses in tomorrow and take them back to the Chard. The vet with the dart gun is still involved so presumably they intend to stick to the original plan of knocking out the grey mare first.'

'Where are the horses?' said Angie. 'We've not seen them.'

'They're in a sort of quarry – fenced in. They've brought in lights and a generator, food, hay and water. And there are four coppers and two RSPCA guys guarding 'em. It's only a couple hundred yards away…listen'. He wound down the van window and in the silence they could just hear the muffled chugging of a diesel driven generator.

'Where are the sanctuary people and the lorry drivers, Gary?' asked Ron.

'Gone home and coming back tomorrow for a 10 o'clock start. The press people, TV and all that lot are all coming back tomorrow as well.'

'Realistically Gary,' Angie asked, 'Is there anything else we can do?'

'Well I'm working on it, but there are problems. For instance there are cattle grids at each end of the road so even if we could get them out the quarry they can't get off the hill. The sides of the hill are too steep for the horses, especially old ones, to get down to the surrounding fields, and they can't go back down the footpath to Norton where they were last night, because its only wide enough for single file and there's a turnstile at the bottom.'

'What is this Ham Hill, anyway?' asked Angie, peering out of the window, 'Anybody know?'

Gary responded. 'Yeah, I've been reading the notice board…quite interesting really. It's now a recreation area – sort of country park run by the local Council. 2000 years ago it was an Iron Age hill fort, and it's been used for quarrying stone since the Roman times. The Normans bred rabbits here for food apparently and there is a record of someone nicking a thousand of 'em.'

'Wow, maybe the first report of the ALF,' interrupted Angie. Gary continued over the chuckles. 'In the Industrial Revolution trade unions organised picnics and outings up here.'

'Well, well,' said Robin. 'So radical animal rights is not too far out of place here then.' 'Wrong!' said Gary, 'Guess who actually owns the park. Prince Charles that well known animal rights supporter.'

'What!' said Robin. 'I thought his empire was in Cornwall'.

'Would the fact that Charlie owns the place help us get more publicity?' ventured Angie. 'We could try and stage another demo. The media is sure to be here tomorrow.'

'I don't think they'll let us get anywhere near next time.' said Ron. 'The place will be crawling with police.'

'What about you, Tony,' said Robin suddenly.

'Me?'

'Yeah, you're quiet. Any thoughts?'

Tony had plenty, but not the sort that would have impressed the five animal activists whose company he reluctantly shared.

His hands were deep in the pocket of his jacket. His fingers closed around the handle of the knife and he could feel all eyes upon him. He knew he should be showing some interest.

'Well, I don't know, really. Maybe we could hide somewhere and cause some diversion well away from the horses, something they all have to rush to….' (he began to speak more quickly as the plan evolved in his mind) '….set fire to a car or something.' He suddenly became aware of an excruciating silence.

'Are you bloody mad Tony?' burst out Angie eventually. 'Burn a car? Are you joking? D'you know what the penalty is for arson?'

Tony's neck and ears burned with embarrassment as he looked at his knees and mumbled, 'I was only trying…just thinking out loud …sorry!'

'That's all right Tony,' said Ron. 'But Angie's right, arson is out, and anyway, as Gary says, even if we got the horses out of the quarry and they all scattered, they can't get off the hill - and all we'll have done is scared 'em'.

Robin sighed, loudly. 'I don't know about you lot, but I'm desperate for a pint. Why don't we get in the warm and think about it?'

'Good for you, Robin,' said Ron. 'I'm for that'.

'You all go.' said Gary. 'I'm going to have another look

round…just for ideas. When you come out, if I'm not here, wait for me in the van. I won't be long.'

Gary had already disappeared into the darkness when Ron pushed open the door to the Prince of Wales public house. As he and his four companions squinted in the bright lights, the pub fell quiet, the eyes of a dozen or so people briefly measuring up the group of strangers. The hum of conversation almost instantly resumed as Ron motioned towards a table in an empty alcove formed by two high-backed upholstered bench seats. 'I'll get' em in,' said Ron, 'What are we having?'

They were still supping their first pints of beer and greedily plucking assorted crisps from a large bowl in the centre of the table, when the latch clicked loudly and the door swung open. Again all conversation paused for a moment. Ron and Robin had their backs to the door and didn't look round, until Angie muttered in a low voice, 'Uh Oh! Don't turn round!'

'Evening all!' came a familiar voice. 'Nice to see you again.'

As the policeman passed their alcove and strode towards the bar, 'Bloody hell,' whispered Robin, 'It's Wild Fowler.'

'Who?' asked Ron frowning.

'Chief Inspector Fowler, the copper who warned us off at Merriot. You weren't there, you were doing an interview.'

Ron's heart sank. 'It's obviously no bloody coincidence he's here, is it?' he said angrily.

John Fowler approached their table, a pint of bitter firmly grasped in his right hand.

'Now, I wonder what made me think you had all gone home? Oh, I'm sorry Mr Walters…may I call you Ron?' (and without waiting for a reply continued) 'We missed each other at Merriott… I think you were busy performing on TV,' he smiled, mockingly.

'Hello, Chief Inspector,' muttered Ron. He looked up and stared unsmilingly into the policeman eyes and added, 'I've heard a lot about you…none of it very good I'm afraid.'

'And who's this?' asked John Fowler, glancing at Tony who sat fingering a beer mat in deep concentration. None of the four seated young people responded.

'You got a name son?'

'Tony.'

'Tony who?'

'Smith'.

'Ah...Tony Smith...of course you are. And where are you from Tony Smith?' asked the inspector, quietly.

'Exeter.'

'Exeter. Well, well! Practically a local then?'

Ron felt his anger rising at the policeman's ridicule.

'Do you mind?' he rasped. 'We are just having a quiet drink. Will you go away please?'

'If you'd have gone away, I wouldn't be here, would I?' replied the inspector. 'I'm going to ask you to finish your drinks and come to Yeovil police station. I'm not arresting you, I'm asking you to come to the station to assist us with our enquiries, so to speak. You can either follow me in your van, or I can take you in. Your van will be safe here and with luck we will bring you back.' He looked from one to the other, as he took a long draught of his beer.

'What do you want to ask us about?' asked Angie.

'Oh, obstruction of the police, criminal damage to farm gates, endangering road users, possible cruelty to animals ... '

Robin jumped up and faced the policeman.

'That's crap.' he barked, eyes blazing, as the pub fell silent. 'We've not done anything except hold a demo.'

John Fowler realised that his contemptuous attitude had been a mistake and he hurriedly backed off. 'OK, OK,' he said, 'Calm down. Just come to the station and tell me that. But offences have occurred and it's clear that they revolve around attempts to keep these sanctuary horses from being returned to their home. And you have told me yourself that you think they should be given their freedom. You must see that you are suspects.'

'And if we refuse to come with you?' asked Ron.

'Then I will have to arrest you,' said the inspector, resignedly.

Ron looked at his colleagues. 'Some choice eh?'

'OK inspector, we'll come with you, but Tony here is really nothing to do with us. He just came along for the ride. He's not

LADY PATRICIA

even animal rights! We met him in Crewkerne, after the Merriott demo.'

John Fowler pondered. He looked at Tony's pale face. 'How old are you son?' he asked.

'Seventeen,' replied Tony, avoiding looking at the inspector.

John Fowler groaned inwardly. Taking in a seventeen year old could mean all sorts of problems…trouble with stressed parents, intense social workers…reams of paperwork…juvenile courts. He made up his mind.

'Right, I'll drop you off at Yeovil Junction station Tony, and you can catch a train back to Exeter. You got money for fares?'

Tony nodded, and the Inspector continued, 'And you four will come down to the station, right?'

He could see that there was still some indecision in their faces. He finished his drink, looked behind him and placed the empty glass on a neighbouring table. Leaning forward and placing his hands on the table between his audience of four activists, he said firmly, though quietly, 'Tell you what. I'm going for a pee. You make up your minds. But don't do a runner 'cause there are three coppers over there,' (he flicked his head in the direction of bar) 'and your van is jammed in tighter than a sardine,' he added with a smile and he straightened up and turned towards the door marked 'Toilets'.

'Right!' whispered Ron as the toilet door swung closed behind the inspector. 'Let's leave the van here and go with him. He obviously doesn't know about Gary and I've got spare keys. I'll lodge them on the top of the front offside wheel. Gary is bound to find 'em. They obviously want to hold us in Yeovil until they've got the horses back to the sanctuary. You never know, Gary might be able to pull off something else! And if he does, they can't hold us because we'll have the perfect alibi!'

As Robin and Angie nodded, Ron turned to Tony, 'And you'll sod off back home to Exeter then Tony?'

'Yeah, s'pose so,' replied Tony.

'Well, thanks for coming along anyway', said Robin.

'Maybe see you again Tony, at some animal rights demo or

another,' added Angie touching his arm.

'Yeah, probably,' flinched Tony, wondering what the four of them would think if they could read his mind.

A few minutes later the five of them were travelling in Inspector Fowler's car, having collected coats and bags from the Transit van. They drove in silence, Robin sat in the front seat while Angie and Caroline sat snuggled between Ron and Tony in the back. The headlights picked out their journey along the rough track from the Prince of Wales pub, onto the road through the country park and over the cattle grid. There the inspector got out briefly and told the young, shivering uniformed constable that he and his colleague at the other end of the park, could go home.

They travelled on, deep in thought. John Fowler was relieved that this whole ridiculous operation would be completed the next day and he could get back to normal duties.

Ron pondered what Gary's next move would be while Angie wondered what facilities she could expect at the police station. Robin hoped that someone had kept the cuttings of the press coverage ALF had achieved for the cause of animal liberation over the last few days. Tony was trying desperately to make up his mind whether he should find an opportunity to warn the inspector that Gary Rorke was the primary saboteur of the attempts to recapture the horses and that he was at this very moment hiding on Ham Hill. He couldn't decide whether his ambition to avenge the death of his mentor, Eddie, would be better advanced by the horses going back to the sanctuary where the terrible event occurred, or by the horses remaining on the run. If he told the inspector what he knew, the police would want him to make a signed statement and that would mean them insisting on contacting his parents and thus finding out that he was a runaway from his Oxfordshire home. That clinched his decision. If he was put on the train, he would get off at the next station and catch up with the horses again – wherever they were.

Suddenly he realised that the car was pulling up at Yeovil Junction railway station. The Inspector switched off the engine and took the keys out of the ignition. He switched on the interior light and looked at Tony in the mirror. 'Come on son, Let's get you on a train'.

While the other activists sat in the car, the inspector and Tony walked over the footbridge and down onto the deserted platform.

'There's a public phone over there, why don't you ring your folks while I sort your ticket out? I'll pay for it. What do you want, Exeter St David's or Exeter Central?'

Tony didn't even know Exeter had two stations, but replied without hesitation, 'Central'. The public pay phone was only yards from the ticket office and he could hear the inspector asking for a single to Exeter Central. Tony inserted a coin, dialled a number and after waiting for a few seconds, surreptitiously used his little finger to depress the saddle lever.

'Hello Mum, it's me', he shouted, flicking his eyes towards the ticket office where the inspector stood with his back to him. 'I'm all right. I'm at Yeovil, on my way home. I'll be back tonight. See you later.' he said as loud and brightly as he could, adding a final 'Bye, mum,' before putting the phone down.

He moved away from the phone and stood looking at the inspector's back until the policeman stood up and turned to face him, a ticket in his one hand and a receipt in the other.

'Right Tony, all fixed. There is a train due in twenty minutes and I've arranged for the staff here to see you on the train.'

Tony mumbled, 'Thanks,' as John Fowler handed him a ticket.

'OK son, I'll be on my way. Let me give you a bit of advice. If you want to campaign for animals, nothing wrong in that, but don't get yourself a criminal record, it'll haunt you all your life.'

'Yes, thank you, sir,' said Tony, unable to look the inspector in the eye, and wondering if he should now tell the policemen about Gary Rorke. His thought was truncated by the inspector's final words, 'You can get a cup of tea from a machine in the waiting room while you're waiting. OK?'

'Uh, OK thanks,' said Tony as the inspector turned and walked back towards the stairs of the footbridge.

*

The next morning was bright and sunny. On Ham Hill, in one of the many small flat-bottomed quarries with steep grass banks, Trevor James and his daughter, assisted by two uniformed RSPCA inspectors, were shaking out bales of hay. The herd of fifteen horses jostled each other as they munched the sweet-smelling top quality hay. Near the open end of the quarry four strands of white rope formed a fence at which two more RSPCA inspectors were filling large black plastic buckets with water from a small tanker attached to a Landrover.

Two hundred yards away, in the bar of the Prince of Wales public house police sergeant George Thomas, RSPCA chief inspector Paul Robbins and veterinary surgeon Richard Carrington stood looking out of the window. A female voice behind them announced, 'Coffee gentlemen?'

They responded thankfully and turned to see an attractive woman in her early thirties with shoulder-length black hair, wearing faded blue jeans and a thick brightly-coloured woollen sweater. Penny Cotton, the licensee of the public house, set down a heavy tray bearing several blue mugs, a large glass coffee pot, three jugs of milk, a bowl bristling with packets of sugar and a large white plate blanketed with a selection of biscuits.'

'There you are then,' she said, and paused as she watched them filling their cups and murmuring their appreciation.

'This is very kind of you Mrs Cotton,' said George Thomas stirring his cup.

'It's my pleasure, sergeant – but while you're here perhaps you could make a note that we have had a few odd thefts from our food store at the back. The night before last, it was a loaf of bread, oh, and a couple of cartons of fruit juice, and last night a bag of potatoes.'

'Must be a tramp,' offered Richard Carrington.

'Well, not like any tramp we've ever had here before,' she said brightly, as she turned towards the kitchen. 'Just shout if you need any more coffee,' she added as she pushed through the swing doors to the pub kitchen.

RSPCA inspector Paul Robbins took a sip from his cup, licked his lips, and asked, 'George, is John Fowler going to be here?'

'Yes, he's coming with the drivers of the horse transport,' responded the sergeant as he tore off the corner of a packet of sugar and tipped it into his cup. 'Should be here any minute.'

'Trevor James should also be here soon,' commented veterinary surgeon, Richard Carrington. 'He and his daughter are just feeding the horses. I notice a lot of media people arriving,' he added.

Paul Robbins groaned. 'We'll have a lot of public to contend with. too,' he said. 'It was all over the TV news this morning, and local radio. Ah, here's Trevor now.'

The sanctuary manager brushed hay seeds off his clothes and stamped his feet free of dust on the door step before stepping into the room.

'Morning, gentlemen,' he said breezily. 'Ah coffee, just what I need. Rebecca is still with the horses.'

'Help yourself, Trevor,' said George Thomas. 'We're just waiting for chief inspector Fowler and the drivers to turn up.'

Ten minutes later, the party was complete and Inspector John Fowler explained his plan of action.

'First, we'll have the lorries warmed up and ready to be manoeuvred into position for loading. I've got a press officer and enough constables to make sure that camera crews and press people don't interfere, and we won't let anybody get close enough to see the horses until Richard has darted the grey mare and she is nicely tucked into the small horse trailer. Once that's done they can film whatever they like.' He paused and looked at his watch. 'Right, it's ten past ten. If we're lucky, we should be out of here by eleven.'

'And we can be sure that the activists are off the scene, can we Inspector?' asked Trevor James.

The Inspector smiled, 'They had a comfortable night at the station and I left them having a hearty breakfast in the canteen. I have told them that they can have a lift out here in a police car to pick up their van, after midday'.

'And where is their van, Inspector?' asked his sergeant.

'It's......oh blimey, it isn't there, is it?' he exclaimed as he realised that he had driven past the spot at which the activists' van had been parked the previous evening and that he had not even noticed it was no longer there. 'George, find out if anyone has moved it. I hope it's not been nicked! I can just imagine the ALF people suing us for losing their van!'

Sergeant Thomas rose and left the pub. He was back within minutes.

'None of our people moved the van, sir,' he reported. 'The men guarding the horse wagons said they heard a vehicle start up and move off during the night... and of course we stood down the two officers on the cattle grids.'

'Might have been the tramp whose been nicking the food from the pub,' suggested Richard Carrington.

Inspector Fowler rose, angrily pushing back his chair so that it scraped noisily on the tile floor.

'Great! That's all we need,' he said. 'We've got animal rights people setting animals free to wander the world, and now we've got tramps nicking vans.'

'Not to mention questions in parliament!' said the sergeant.

'What?' exclaimed the inspector.

'Yes sir. I heard our esteemed local MP on Radio 4 this morning, blaming it all on the government's failure to deal with law and order.'

'Oh to hell with the lot of 'em,' retorted the chief inspector impatiently. 'Let's get this show on the road. We'll worry about the van.... and the politicians, later.'

The group emerged from the pub and split up. Vet Richard Carrington returned to his car to fetch the case in which he kept his rifle and darting equipment. Trevor James and RSPCA inspector Paul Robbins made their way along the track towards the quarry where the horses were still under the guard of, and being comforted by, Trevor's daughter Rebecca. In the lane outside the Prince of Wales pub a crowd of local people had gathered and milled around in groups. Reporters with notebooks conducted hasty interviews with anyone who would offer a comment. Television camera crews assembled equipment and lounged against cars waiting for some action. Amongst them, a police press officer, accompanied by several informed constables, attempted to inform everyone else what was due to happen.

Inspector John Fowler, his sergeant George Thomas and five drivers walked around the back of the pub to the car park where four huge, white police transporters stood lined up in two pairs. A small single horse trailer attached to a police Landrover was parked in front of the transporters.

The inspector stopped at the front of the Landrover. He turned to his officers. 'Right, I suggest you get your engines warmed up. Sergeant, you come with me and we'll make sure that all the public and press and out of the way.' He turned again to the five drivers. 'When everything's ready, sergeant Thomas will come back and lead the small trailer down the quarry to pick up the grey mare. Once she's dealt with, the sergeant will come back and lead you, one lorry at a time, to where we can load the rest of the herd. Any questions?'

'No sir,' chorused the four drivers.

'Good. OK, come on then sergeant.'

The inspector and the sergeant walked away as the drivers climbed into their vehicles and pulled their cab doors shut. The two officers had only walked five paces before they stopped dead. They looked at each other, but didn't turn round. They knew from the first turn of the starters, that something was wrong. There was a strangled 'whirr' and a 'clunk', followed by another 'clunk'. None of the five engines fired into life.

'What the hell is happening, George?' queried the inspector, finally turning on his heel to face the vehicles.

'I don't know, sir,' replied the sergeant. The drivers were now clambering back out of their cabs and dropping down onto the gravel surface. The first, a dark-haired man in blue overalls, ran round the rear of his lorry, where he dropped onto his knees and sniffed at the open end of the exhaust pipe.

Still on his knees, he yelled towards the two officers. 'I thought so sir, sabotage - potatoes!'

'What the hell do you mean, man, potatoes?'

'Potatoes rammed up the exhaust pipe, sir. Looks like it's been done to all of us,' he said gesturing towards the other lorries whose other drivers were now out examining the rear of their vehicles.

'He's right sir,' called another of the men.

'What happens now?' the inspector asked the first driver.

'The pipes will have to come off sir, and be cleaned out.'

'How long will that take, for God's sake?' whined the inspector.

'I'm not sure, sir. Not long, once we can get some tools here….maybe an hour or two,' replied the driver.

'Don't you have the tools on board?'

'We've got a basic tool kit sir, but we'll need long rods or something to push through the pipes. And of course who knows what else might have been done. We'll need to check brake pipes and fuel tanks for water or sugar before we start the engines – otherwise the engines could be wrecked.'

John Fowler pondered silently for a full seven seconds, while the group of men silently waited, all eyes on his face.

'Right,' he exclaimed decisively. 'I'm postponing everything until tomorrow. Sergeant, get the press officer over here. We'll have to make an announcement to the media and the public. We'll no doubt get another panning in the papers, but we'll just have to blame vandalism by animal rights activists. Get some mechanics here – I don't care whether they are from the police pound or local garages. And tell the RSPCA boys that the horses will have to spend another day and night in the quarry. I want you drivers to be in your vehicles all night. I'll see Mrs Cotton at the pub to see if we can arrange for use of a bathroom, and a decent dinner and coffee and stuff tonight.'

'I'm going to ring the Chief Super and ask him if he wants to hang on to the activists we've already got and question them some more. He might want to send CID out here to see if we can lift some prints from the pub food store and the lorries. This is no bloody tramp! It's another damn animal vigilante. Whoever it is has probably taken the van. What I don't know is, whether this one is part of this particular activist group, but I intend to find out!'

Later that afternoon, he had been informed by Scotland Yard that their staff on the Animal Rights Network Index suspected that the identity of the person who was sabotaging the attempts to recapture the horses could be animal activist and former marine Gary Rorke. Police had spoken to his wife in Northampton and she said that he was on one of his favourite week-long walking holidays in Cumbria.

Robin Chamberlain, Ron Walters, Angie Wright and Caroline admitted that they knew of Gary Rorke, but had not seen him since last fox hunting season. The three of them even attempted, unconvincingly, to be outraged that the police had mislaid their van and demanded unsuccessfully that they be provided with alternative transport until their van was recovered. Eventually, they were released without charge from Yeovil Police Station and the description and registration number of Ron Walters' van was circulated to all police officers in Devon, Somerset and Dorset.

By nightfall Chief Inspector John Fowler had received reports from everyone involved. The exhaust pipes of all five horse transporters had been removed, cleared of the potatoes that had clogged several feet of their lengths and replaced. No evidence of any further damage had been found by mechanics. The drivers were already in their vehicles for the evening, and there were spare constables to take over during toilet and coffee breaks at the pub. The entire car park was illuminated by powerful arc lights, and a police dog handler patrolled it every 30 minutes. The horses, well fed and watered, were also under close guard by both police and RSPCA officers. White tape strung across the open end of the shallow quarry between two RSPCA vans formed the fence, with two police cars parked outside the tapes.

Prince of Wales landlady Penny Cotton had agreed to close the pub to the public for the night and a sign to that effect had been erected at the cattle grids at each end of the road through the country park. The weather forecast was for a dry, but overcast night, followed by a dry day. The main item on the local television news featured the 'shambles' at Ham Hill, as well as recounting the previous 'bungles' and the inability of the police to control a herd of aged horses and handful of young animal activists.

Yeovil Member of Parliament Jeremy Haskins OBE MP was

interviewed on College Green outside the Houses of Parliament, demanding that the Home Secretary set up an enquiry into the affair as it was *'perfectly obvious that the Chief Constable of the Avon & Somerset Constabulary was incapable of handling the situation'*. Film of his wife in his wrecked garden and of mechanics lying under expensive police horse-transporters, completed the humiliating news broadcast, an edited version of which also featured on national news channels.

Chief Inspector John Fowler sighed as the late news item ended. He had already been carpeted by Chief Superintendent Brian Morgan, who was merely passing on the drubbing he had received from the Chief Constable, who was smarting from being attacked by Jeremy Haskins OBE MP. There had been no sign of Gary Rorke and the van, but the chief inspector felt hopeful that the sabotage of the transporters had been the last act of defiance and he had gone home to Northampton where police officers were watching for his return. John Fowler poked the remote control and the television went off with a clump. He made his way wearily upstairs to bed, where he spent a disturbed night, his dreams punctuated by the repeated image of a newspaper headline, 'Chief Inspector Sacked Over Horse Fiasco'.

Chapter 8

One hundred miles away in a leafy road in Bicester, Oxfordshire, the television was on. There would be no sleep tonight in this household. The normally ultra-dignified Conservative Councillor Mrs Edwina Smith was almost in hysterics. 'Robert, I tell you it was him,' she yelled at her husband.

'But darling, it was just a brief glimpse of a face in the crowd,' implored her husband. 'Calm down for God's sake. The neighbours will be calling the police if you don't stop yelling.'

'I am calm, Robert. I tell you I saw our son on the news. You would have seen him too if you didn't have your nose stuck in your damn newspaper. His hair was long and he looked thinner, but it was him all right.'

'OK, OK. Where was this place?'

'Somerset somewhere, a country park I think they said, something - hill. I've read a piece in yesterday's paper about this horse escape thing. It'll be in the recycling box.'

'All right darling,' her husband said, wearily pushing himself up out of his chair. 'But please don't get your hopes up too high. You know how many times we've gone on wild goose chases.'
'Yes I know, but that was because of sightings reported by other people. This time I've seen him for myself.'

A few minutes later they were both kneeling over a newspaper spread out on the floor.

'There,' said Edwina pointing to the story half way down the page. 'Horses from the Ferne Animal Sanctuary, near Chard, Somerset. She swept her finger along the print. 'Da, da,… Merriott…..police spokesman……da,da,…Yeovil. Where's your road atlas, Robert?'

'I'll get it,' said her husband clambering to his feet.

The road atlas was opened up on the floor..

'There, Yeovil….and Chard.' said Robert, dabbing his finger on the map.

'Oh, what was the name of the hill they mentioned on the news?' said Edwina, impatiently.

'I didn't notice,' said her husband, feebly.

'There,' cried Edwina, the long painted nail of her index finger almost piercing the map. 'Country park, Ham Hill,' she said excitedly, 'That's the place.'

Her husband looked at her, admiringly. 'Well done darling! What now?'

'We go down there of course, tonight!'

'Tonight?'

'Yes, tonight. The news said that the horses were being taken back to their sanctuary tomorrow. We could drive down tonight, and be there in the morning when everybody turns up. I really do have a feeling that we'll find Anthony there tomorrow.'

At 2 a.m, while Robert and Edwina Smith travelled down the A420 in their BMW towards Swindon, with two full flasks of coffee, a tupper-ware box full of sandwiches and a hastily packed suitcase full of their wayward son's clothes, an old grey and heavily-laden transit van laboured slowly up the half-mile long-steep hill from Stoke sub Hamdon to Ham Hill country park. As it crept the last few yards towards the grey bars of the cattle grid, Gary Rorke's left hand gripped the handle of the hand brake while his right hand gently slid back the driver's door. He peered into the soft light cast ahead by his side-lights, ready to yank on the brake and dive into the darkness if necessary. 'Good!' he said to himself.

The van trundled slowly over the bars with a low rumble and halted with its rear bumper only a yard past the grid. Gary switched off the lights and engine, and eased himself out onto the road. He walked round the back of the van and opened the rear doors. Inside, stacked two feet high, were six layers of rolled-up grass turfs, and on top of that several sheets of half inch thick plywood. Gary pulled

LADY PATRICIA

out the first sheet and laid it across the cattle grid, repeating the exercise with the other sheets until the grid was completely covered. Despite the outside temperature, Gary was already sweating, both from his exertions and from the adrenalin flowing freely in his veins. He grunted as he tugged at the first roll of turf, the pleasant smell of grass in his nose. Inside four minutes the cattle grid was completely carpeted with turf – like a newly laid lawn.

Gary was panting hard when he gingerly started the engine and with sidelights only, moved forward deeper into the country park. He passed the lane on the left that led to the pub and kept going until he estimated that he was in line with the quarry in which the horses were corralled about a hundred yards away behind the hillocks. A few yards further along the road, Gary swung the wheel and pulled onto a track on the right hand side, leading into a parking area formed by another old shallow quarry. He switched off the engine and the lights and sat in the darkness for a few seconds. There was no sound apart from the gentle whisper of wind.

He reached beneath the seat and pulled out a loud-hailer of the type often heard blaring from the roof of vehicles at general election campaigns. Gary wound down the front passenger's window, held the hailer outside and then wound up the window to clamp the device. In hunt saboteur circles the device would have been known as a 'gizmo' – a loud-speaker attached to a cassette player, and over which is played at full volume the sound of a pack of hounds, excitedly baying in full pursuit on a fox. When saboteurs catch up with a hunt, the 'gizmo' is turned on and the hounds find it irresistible, and instantly rush towards the sound. Few hounds will obey the call of the huntsman's horn over the sound of their kind in full cry.

Gary connected the wires to the van's cassette player, checked that the tape was fully rewound and that the volume dial was on full. He reached into the back of the van and hauled his rucksack into the front before dropping out onto the ground. He removed the key from the ignition, walked round the back of the van and locked the rear doors, before returning again to the driver's open door.

Gary paused, ears straining for any sounds of danger. He pulled out a damp cloth, and wiped the steering wheel, switches, and door handles. Finally, he swung his rucksack onto his shoulders, reached inside and still with the cloth in his hand, pressed down the 'play' button on the cassette player. The tape 'swishing' sound began as Gary closed the driver's door, locked it and pushed the keys under the front wheel. He then sprinted into the darkness just as the night exploded in a nightmarish cacophony of screaming dogs.

Trevor James leapt so violently in the front seat of his sanctuary van that he banged his head hard on the driver's mirror. He threw the door open and saw the RSPCA men and police officers rapidly climbing out of their vehicles at the tape barrier of the quarry.

'What the hell's that?' yelled a constable.

'Dogs, it's dogs!' yelled back an RSPCA inspector.

'Hounds!, It sounds like a pack of hounds,' said Trevor. 'What the hell is a pack of hounds doing out here at this time of night?'

The three police officers began to run towards the noise, powerful flash lights sweeping the way before them.

'Come on lads', said one of them, 'It sounds as if they are killing something.'

Trevor could see and hear that the horses were highly agitated behind the tapes. He knew from experience at Ferne, that whenever the local Hunt was anywhere within earshot of the sanctuary, the horses were always highly nervous and excitable.

Only a minute before, the horses were totally relaxed, now they were shuffling around in the darkness, snorting, and barging each other. Trevor heard footsteps running towards him and lights from torches flashed and danced around him.

'What's going on?' came a voice, and two of the drivers of the horse transporters trotted up to him.

'God knows,' replied Trevor. 'Sounds like a pack of hounds are free from somewhere. 'Your guys and the RSPCA boys have gone to take a look.'

'The horses look a bit spooked,' said one of the men.

'Yes, I'm going to have to go in and try to calm them down,' said Trevor. 'Why the hell do those dogs seem to be staying in one spot. I don't understand it.'

One of the drivers responded curtly, 'We'll go and have a look to see what's happening. You all right here for a bit?'

'Well as long as the horses don't try to break through the tape,' responded Trevor.

'We'll be back as soon as we know what's happening,' called back one of the drivers, as they disappeared towards the road.

Trevor ducked under the tape and moved in amongst the agitated animals. 'Easy fellas, easy now,' he crooned repeatedly as he ran a hand down Patrick's neck, smoothed Lucky's flank and scratched Gregory's nape. He could see Patricia trotting in and around the rest of the herd, her head and tail held high.

'Patsy, Patsy', he called. 'Easy girl, easy now.'

Suddenly the noise of screaming dogs stopped, leaving an almost deafening silence.

'Thank God for that,' murmured Trevor.

He was now at the far end of the corral, and he turned to push his way back through the milling herd, now rapidly settling in the silence. Suddenly he heard Patricia whinny, and again. He flashed his torch in the direction of the sound, but all he could see was the grey and dark shapes of horses. Then he thought he saw some other shape in amongst the horses.

'Becky, is that you?' he yelled, not really sure whether the shape was human or not. 'Get out of there,' he yelled again and he began to force his way through the equine throng towards the spot he saw the shape. Then he heard Patricia whinny again, and he realised that the whole herd was on the move. 'Surely they won't try to go through the tapes,' he thought, knowing that lines of flapping white ribbons are usually as efficient a barrier as a solid fence. From the position he had reached he knew that the horses had gone past the tapes and were out of the quarry. His torch merely picked out the swaying rumps of the last of the horses disappearing into the gloom.

Rebecca came rushing toward him. 'Dad, what's happened?' she yelled as Trevor was joined by breathless police and RSPCA officers.

'Someone was in with them,' he replied. He bent down and picked up the end of one of the white tapes. 'It's been cut! I knew I saw someone.'

They all set off trotting after the horses, joined by more officers. An RSPCA inspector running alongside Trevor, blurted out, 'D'you know what the pack of dogs turned out to be? A damn tape cassette and a loud speaker in an locked van. No-one with it…... .spooky or what?' he added.

'We had to force the van window to pull the wires out,' said a policeman who joined them in the pursuit.

'More animal liberation sabotage then,' said Trevor. 'What's the point? The horses can't get out of the park.'

'We'll just have to follow them and try to chivvy them back into the quarry,' said Trevor. 'There's enough of us.'

They trotted in the direction that the horses had taken, along the rough track and onto the road that runs through the country park.

'They've turned right towards Stoke,' said an RSPCA inspector, pointing at a trail of horse dung still steaming on the tarmac. The group trotted down the road following the trail in the direction of the exit from the Ham Hill country park. 'At least they can't cross a cattle grid,' said Trevor.

A hundred yards in front of the group of men, the herd had reached the cattle grid and stood bunched behind Patricia. The grey mare eyed the new turf suspiciously and lowered her head to smell the grass apparently growing out of the road. She ventured one of her front feet onto the turf. It felt firm. Wide-eyed, she moved forward, tensely, ready to spin away at any sign of danger. Nothing happened as her back feet were now on the turf carpet. She gave a low whinny and stepped briskly over the grass and onto the tarmac on the other side of the grid. The rest of the herd quickly followed and they set off at a slow trot down the hill - their way lit by the yellow street-lights of the village of Stoke-sub-Hamdon.

Only seconds later their human followers stood in shocked silence, gazing at the newly surfaced cattle grid. Some of the turfs had been kicked onto the road beyond, exposing the buff-coloured plywood underneath. More than a few of the men felt a sneaking admiration for the ingenuity of the unknown saboteurs – little realising that there was only one.

A police constable broke the silence. 'Jesus, who's going to tell the sergeant?'

*

'And what time was that, Chief Superintendent?' asked Chief Constable James Bowlingham, the query delivered almost gently.

'I got the call from Sergeant Thomas at '02.30 hours this morning, sir,' replied Brian Morgan.

'And whose van was it?'

'That's a bit embarrassing sir. It belongs to one of the animal rights members, but they were all in Yeovil police station overnight when the van disappeared. We've given the van back to its owner, Ron Walters – who is a known activist. The van was officially in our care on Ham Hill, when it was taken. We dusted it for prints, but it had been well wiped.'

'OK, so where are the horses now?'

'Tintinhull, sir, possibly further.'

The Chief Constable shifted the receiver from his right ear to his left and picked up a pen with his right hand, pulled the top off with his teeth and started scribbling notes on a pad.

'And why are they still moving?' he asked, just as gently, although Brian Morgan knew full well that his Chief Constable was internally seething.

'Apparently sir, the sergeant felt it best to keep them moving so that they don't end up…er., in anyone's….er, garden, sir.' Brian Morgan winced, inwardly cursing his choice of words, but then mouthed a silent 'phew' as the words, 'Yes, perhaps just as well,' came down the somewhat crackly phone line.

'OK Chief Superintendent. Is the RSPCA on the case?'

Brian Morgan confirmed that the animal welfare society had a team of inspectors accompanying the herd, as well as sanctuary manager Trevor James and his daughter.

'Whatever you do, keep them off the main roads, and I want you to keep police involvement to an absolute minimum. From now on let the RSPCA take the lead – after all they are the damn animal welfare people.'

'Yes sir, I'll talk direct to their chief executive tell them we are relying on them to resolve the situation. But we'll have to try and find the gang who have been sabotaging the operation sir, I don't think the RSPCA will see that as their job.'

'Fair enough', replied the chief constable. 'But our role must be limited to managing traffic and dealing with anyone interfering with the horses. It is not our job to round 'em up, guard 'em, or provide transport. I want our horse transporters and their drivers sent back to Bristol. The sanctuary people and the RSPCA can pay for all that from now on.'

'Yes sir. What about the vet? We called him in because he is licensed by the Home Office to carry a tranquiliser rifle.'

'The RSPCA can pay for him, too,' said the chief constable, wondering how much the entire business had depleted his budget so far.

'Yes sir, I'll square it all with the RSPCA chief executive and keep you informed,' said Brian Morgan.

The next words from his chief constable were delivered more slowly and not a little chillingly.

'Brian, you will be aware that I have come under considerable fire in the House of Commons over this saga. No doubt I will get some more because of what has happened during the night. I am relying on you to make sure that any further criticism is directed elsewhere. Do you understand?'

Brian Morgan responded as confidently and reassuringly as he could. 'Yes sir, exactly sir, of course', although he couldn't immediately fathom what his boss meant. 'Good night, sir'.

'Good morning, chief superintendent'.

Brian Morgan looked at his watch. It was indeed morning, just past 5 a.m.

By then, Patricia had led her herd through the picturesque villages of Tintinhull and Chilthorne Domer and were nearing the A37 main road north of Yeovil. Two hours later at the break of dawn police Chief Superintendent Brian Morgan had found a home telephone number for Mary Sheppard, chief executive of the Royal

Society for the Prevention of Cruelty to Animals, and had recounted his chief constable's instructions.

By 9.30 that morning the RSPCA chief executive had appointed Wessex Regional Manager Helen Watson to coordinate a team of four senior inspectors and two of their own veterinary staff for the purpose of resolving the continuing chaotic and complicated 'runaway horses' calamity. Two hours later the new team had arrived in Somerset and found that Lady Patricia and her herd had crossed the A37, moved through the village of Mudford, across the A359 that links Yeovil with Sparkford, and on through Sandford Orcas. Shepherded quietly by RSPCA inspectors with the help of local police and a few volunteers, the herd briefly crossed over the county border into Dorset before re-crossing into Somerset and came to a halt in the outskirts of the small town of Milborne Port.

Helen Watson with the help of the police had already made contact with the town council with a plea for temporary sanctuary for the horses, in or near the town. The animals were now tired and hungry and stood calmly behind their herd leader. A barrier made up of vehicles prevented them moving further into the town and its shopping area. Patricia stood still surveying the scene. As the news of the now famous horses began to circulate, townsfolk came rushing out of shops and offices, excited and fascinated by the sight of fifteen assorted equines standing silently in the street. Patricia recognised the voices of Trevor and Rebecca calling her and she saw them breaking bales of hay and scattering it along one edge of a large empty car park at the side of the street. Several horses snorted and whinnied as they caught the scent of the hay.

The barrier of vehicles began to move slowly forward and then stopped just past the empty car park. The red and white pole forming the gate to the car park jerked into the air, startling Patricia. The grey mare nervously watched until the pole reached its vertical position and had stopped quivering; then with a toss of her head she strode through the gap into the car park, followed by her faithful herd.

While the horses spread out and with heads down began eating the hay, Patricia chewed hers with her head held high, constantly watching what was going on in and around the car park. Rebecca wandered amongst the horses that she knew so well. She checked skewbald George and she was pleased to note that he was standing firmly on his suspect foot. She then sought out Rufus and he seemed none the worse for losing his badly fitting coat.

As far as she could see, none of the horses seemed to be having problems with their hooves, despite the miles of roads they had travelled without metal shoes. She surmised that the absence of wear on the horses' feet must have been due to the fact that much of the journey had been through fields and along grass verges. She turned to tell her father of her theory, only to see him walking away towards a group of people including uniformed RSPCA inspectors, and a few other people she didn't recognise. As she joined her father, Trevor said, 'All right Becky? They don't look too bad do they?'

'Well, George seems OK and Rufus is probably happy to lose his coat which was always half-off anyway.'

Trevor smiled, 'Well that's good news, Becky. Oh, sorry, this is Helen Watson from the RSPCA. She's heading up the RSPCA's team, now that the police have backed out.'

Helen Watson smiled and clasped Becky's hand. Becky instantly liked the look of Helen, in her mid-forties, with shoulder length dark hair, bright hazel eyes, and smart brown trousers tucked into green Wellington boots.

'Nice to meet you, Becky,' said Helen. 'Now the horses are safely off-road, we're having a meeting in a few minutes and I would value your input, then later perhaps you can introduce me to your equine family - particularly any you are worried about. We have two RSPCA vets in the team so we should be able to cope with most health problems.'

'Sure, I'd like that,' responded Rebecca. 'The horses usually have a short feed of bran and flaked maize as well as hay at this time of the year, and they may need it now that it's getting colder.'

'Don't worry about that, Becky', said Helen, 'We can get everything we need from local feed merchants, and anyway, I hope we can get them all back to your sanctuary tomorrow.'

Local people were gathering around the car park, which was enclosed by two black metal rails above a low brick wall. Soon the crowd become more animated as children began arriving in their schools' lunch-time. A grey-haired lady in a duffle-coat half-carried and half-dragged a heavy bag full of carrots to the wall, and leaned on the top railing trying to get her breath. After a few seconds she began to throw carrots to the horses, and two young girls immediately raided her bag and stood on the wall with their legs leaning against the metal rails, while they called to the horses and waved carrots.

Seeing the horses jostling each other for the treats, two female RSPCA inspectors quietly approached the girls and gently suggested that they get down from the car-park wall and stand on the ground in case they lost their balance.

RSPCA team leader Helen Watson invited Trevor, as manager of the Ferne Animal Sanctuary and thereby technically the owner of the herd, to brief the new members of the team on events so far, particularly the repeated acts of sabotage that had frustrated all attempts to resolve the situation. He reported that the car park had been empty because it was due to be re-surfaced, but that the local Council officials had agreed to an emergency police request for use of the car park as a temporary corral for the horses.

'The thing is, we can only have it for two more days,' said Paul Robbins, RSPCA Chief Inspector. 'The Council says that any longer, not only would local shops start complaining about loss of business, but the tarmac contractors would also have to re-arrange their schedule.'

'Which means we're back to organising transport to take the horses back to Chard,' said Trevor. 'The local RSPCA branch chairman has offered us his motor home for temporary accommodation for me and Becky.'

RSPCA chief inspector Paul Robbins added, 'We've had the same idea. I've got someone ringing round and any minute now we should have two small caravans arriving for us all to use meanwhile as a base. And the good folk of our local RSPCA Branch are organising provisions for us as well as the horses.'

Discussion turned to the problem of capturing and subduing Lady Patricia. 'We can't use a tranquiliser dart gun here with all the press and public standing around,' said the RSPCA's Paul Robbins. 'Anyway, is Richard Carrington still here?' he asked.

'He's gone back to his surgery in Axminster, replied Trevor. 'But we can soon get him back. I've got his home number.'

Helen Watson said, 'OK Trevor, give him a ring and see whether he has any other ideas about the tranquiliser. We don't want the locals and especially the media watching him pointing a rifle at the horses. Maybe a blow-pipe instead of a rifle to fire the dart or perhaps something in the feed. From now on the RSPCA is footing the bill for him, so we don't want him kicking his heels about the place waiting for everything to be ready.'

'The Ferne sanctuary trustees will certainly be happy to contribute considerably to the costs, too.' added Trevor defensively.

'What about the media?' Paul asked. 'There's still a lot of interest – local TV and papers are here, and that reporter bloke, Bob somebody from Chard, is still hanging around. Apparently he's reporting for the Sun and other papers.'

Helen spoke, 'Well Trevor, they're your horses so perhaps you and Becky can handle the press. After all you know this Bob Rayburn chap. The main thing is making sure we don't get any more interference from the animal rights people. So we'll have to keep a good watch tonight and ask the local police to stay alert in case we need them,' said the RSPCA team leader.

She was interrupted by the sound of diesel vehicles pulling up in the street outside the car park. 'Great, that's our accommodation sorted,' she said cheerfully, and waved to the drivers of two cars pulling two small caravans, and directed them to an area alongside the car-park wall. Behind them waited the motor-home that Trevor had been offered as a temporary accommodation.

All round the low wall and rails that formed the boundary of the car park, local people huddled like spectators at a street entertainment. A couple of teenagers inanely waved and made faces behind a TV news reporter who was bringing his lunchtime viewers up to date.

LADY PATRICIA

*

At the same time, in his office in Yeovil Police Station Inspector Brian Morgan watched the lunchtime news report and felt relief to be no longer involved in the farce. There was a knock at the door. He switched off the television and called, 'Come in'. The door partly opened and fresh face of a young female constable appeared around its edge.

'Excuse me sir, but there's someone here asking to see a senior officer'.

'What about?'

'A missing person, sir'.

'Talk to the desk sergeant, constable'.

'I tried that sir, but he thinks *you* should see them sir'.

'Oh? And why is that?'

'Because the sergeant thinks you have information about the missing person sir.'

'And what makes him think that?'

'Because apparently you might have put him on a train, sir.'

The inspector's heart sank.

'Oh no,' he moaned. 'Is it a young lad from Exeter?'

'He's seventeen sir, from Oxfordshire, not Exeter.'

'OK, I'll see them. Who are they?' sighed the inspector.

'The parents sir, Mr and Mrs Smith. The son's name is Anthony.' She snatched a look behind her before pushing her face a little further into the room and mouthed, 'Quite posh, sir!'

*

At 2pm that afternoon in a caravan stationed alongside the Milborne Port car park, a meeting of the RSPCA team and the Ferne Animal Sanctuary manager and his daughter got off to a bad start.

Opening the meeting, team leader Helen Watson introduced Tina Richards, one of the RSPCA's recent intake of trainee inspectors, who had been allocated the task of contacting local horse transporters.

Helen asked, 'Right Tina, how did you get on?'

'I'm afraid I've not been successful,' Tina said nervously. 'The first three just said they didn't have any suitable vehicles, which seemed odd, but then the fourth told me that they would like to help, but they had arrived at work to find a message on their answerphone suggesting that anyone helping to forcibly return the horses to Chard could be regarded as an enemy of animal liberation. After I'd made a few more calls it became obvious that all the local carriers have had the same message'.

'That's outrageous,' exploded Trevor. 'Have they told the police about these threats?'

'Apparently some have and others haven't. No specific threats have been made. I mean no-one has actually said they will target their vehicles or anything, but the owners are all shrugging their shoulders and saying that they just can't afford to get involved.'

'Can't blame them,' said Paul Robbins sympathetically. 'Don't forget the immobilisation of the police horse transporters at Ham Hill was well-publicised. And it certainly led to the police pulling out of the job.'

'So what are we going to do?' appealed Rebecca, looking despairingly at her father, who could only shrug his shoulders in response.

Tina Richards spoke again. 'Well I've been thinking about who else has horse transporters, and it struck me that the army might help.'

'Great idea,' said Helen to a collective murmur of approval from around the small caravan table. 'Well done Tina! I don't think threats will bother the cavalry!'

Tina rose from her seat. 'I'll get straight onto it shall I?'

Helen Watson, said, 'Yes Tina, but I will contact headquarters and ask the Chief Executive to make the initial contact. Perhaps, you could find the nearest military base with horses.'

As the young trainee left the caravan, Trevor looked around the table. 'So we're going to have to keep the herd here at least another day, then,' he said. 'I'd better make sure that we've got plenty of feed and straw. Becky, can you call Richard Carrington and tell him what's happening, and ask whether he would be available for tomorrow and maybe the next day?'

He turned to the two RSPCA veterinary surgeons, Roger Penman and Wendy Phillips and said, 'Perhaps you two could come round with me and Becky, and inspect the herd with us in case any of them are a bit worse for wear. The horses are all over the television news, so we're likely to have even bigger crowds here today. Hopefully, local bobbies will be around to watch the local yobs. I'm worried that fireworks are in the shops now for November 5th.'

The two vets reached for their coats as Helen continued, 'Right, shall we all meet here again later this evening to review progress? I'll let you know if Tina manages to find some horse transport and I suggest everybody sorts themselves out regarding food before the shops close. Hopefully there will be a chippy in the town. Oh, and keep your receipts.'

Trevor James rose and said, 'The simple fact is the horses have to be out of the car park the day after tomorrow. The Town Council has made it clear that the tarmac people will be arriving at the latest midday and they will be working all night. If we can't get transport before then, we still have to move them somewhere else.'

Helen grinned, and lifting her coat off a peg, said in mock-German accent, 'Tomorrow could be very interesting!!' Her companions chuckled, pulling on coats as they emerged into the overcast afternoon.

Trevor and Rebecca led Helen and the two vets into the car park and they wandered amongst the herd checking each and every animal including Patricia, who seemed surprisingly mellow. 'She seems friendly enough,' commented Helen.

'If you tried to put her in a halter, or even showed her one, you would see the complete opposite,' said Trevor. 'Mind you, she lets Becky pick out her hooves,'

'Well, most of the time,' said his daughter. 'Sometimes she just walks away and leaves me sprawling in the mud, but she's never kicked out.'

Rebecca led the group to George the skewbald and she

explained the history of his sesamoid injury in his right foot, and then moved onto Rufus who didn't seem to be bothered about losing his coat. All in all, everyone was satisfied at the condition of the herd – a huge relief to Trevor and Rebecca.

*

The next morning, the RSPCA team and volunteers, together with Trevor Rebecca, had just ended their health-check of Lady Patricia's herd and were enjoying a mid-morning snack of toast and coffee supplied by local RSPCA branch members. There were fewer people hugging the car-park barriers than the previous day, but one of the watchers was a lone teenager, staring at the Connemara grey mare standing quietly 20 yards away. Lady Patricia returned his stare as Tony Smith flipped his hair off his brow with his right hand and in his left hand he held a bottle of cola. He pushed his right hand deep in his pocket and fingered the knife that he had taken from his dead hero Eddie Bowen, as he laid still warm in the Ferne Animal Sanctuary's mud only days ago.

He was so haunted by the dreadful image in his mind that he was unaware of someone moving in next to him resting their arms on the top metal rail. As Tony straightened up to swig a mouthful of cola, the man next to him, without diverting his gaze from the horses, said, 'Ello mate. Fancy seeing you here.'.

Tony froze, the bottle still at his lips. Turning slowly, he found himself looking at the side of Gary Rorke's face. No words formed in Tony's mouth, but Gary solved his problem by firmly gripping Tony's sleeve with his thumb and first finger and whispering 'Come with me!'

Gary walked Tony briskly away from the town centre, still firmly gripping the teenager's sleeve. After a few minutes they turned into a quiet road of terraced and semi-detached houses. Tony was worried. He asked plaintively, 'Where are we going Gary?'

The answer came immediately, 'We're going to watch a bit of day-time TV.'

'What for?' asked Tony incredulously.

'You'll see. Anyway what are you doing here? The others told me that a copper put you on a train home.'

'Yeah, he even paid my fare, but I got off at the first stop and hitched back again.'

Gary halted, looked Tony in the face and said, 'Good for you, Tony. I'm impressed.'

Still tugging Tony's sleeve, Gary marched on. Tony felt increasingly apprehensive. Was Gary's compliment genuine? Was it possible that his link with the dramatic events at the Ferne Animal Sanctuary had been discovered?

He nervously asked again, 'Where are you taking me?'

'Right here,' said Gary, pushing open a small green garden gate of a terraced house, and pulling Tony along a flag-stone path to the front door.

Gary pressed the door bell, which instantly prompted a dog to bark. The door opened and there stood Ron Walters, leaning sideways to grip the collar of a large black Labrador with a furiously wagging tail.

'Look who I've found,' said Gary gently bundling Tony into the short hall.

'Bloody hell, it's Tony!' shouted Ron over his shoulder into the front room off the hall.

'I found him by the horses,' Gary explained. 'That copper put him on the train home, but he jumped ship at the first stop and hitched back.'

'Nice one Tony', said Ron, closing the front door. 'I didn't realise you were that keen.'

Angie appeared in the doorway, 'Hi Tony, nice to see you again. Come on through.'

'Whose house is it?' asked Tony.

'My auntie Jean's,' said Angie. 'She's in the kitchen, making us all beans on toast. Come on through. Fancy some?' she added, gently guiding him into the kitchen.

'Auntie Jean, this is Tony – our latest recruit.'

'Hello Tony, nice to meet you,' said Jean cheerfully, in her fifties, comfortably plump, in green trousers and yellow 'T' shirt sporting the slogan, 'I Love Foxes'.

'Fancy beans on toast and a cup of tea?' asked Jean. 'Or maybe a chunk of home-made vegan cake....or both?' she added enthusiastically.

Tony, suddenly remembering he had only consumed a couple of chocolate bars, and still had an empty cola bottle in his hand, blushed deeply, and responded, 'Yes please,' and smilingly repeated the answer when Jean asked, 'And sugar in your tea?'

The door-bell rang again prompting another bout of dog barking. Angie looked out the front window. 'It's Clive and Jody in their window-cleaning van. Let them in Ron.'

Ron again hung onto the dog's collar and opened the door.

'Are we in time?' asked Jody, as Ron closed the door behind the two newcomers and let go of the dog's collar as it thrashed its tail against Clive's leg.'

Clive stooped to pat the dog. 'Hello Henry. Who's a good boy then?' He rose and was surprised to see Tony. 'Hello, Tony', said Clive, 'Thought we lost you.'

'Not quite,' replied Tony, smiling as Jean placed a tray bearing a plate of steaming beans on toast and a large mug of tea in his hands.

'Blimey, Tony,' said Angie, 'That's the first time I've ever seen you smile. You should do it more, it's nice!' Tony blushed.

'Hey Tony,' shouted Ron from the front room. 'You better not be chatting up my girlfriend.' Tony blushed deeper and grinned.

'Ron leave him alone and find him a space to eat.' shouted Angie.

'Quick then Tony,' said Ron. 'The programme's just about to start.'

Seeing Tony's confusion, Ron said, 'Oh, sorry Tony, of course you don't know about it. Robin is on the Jeremy Bateson Show – it's all about the horses.'

Jeremy Bateson's signature tune blared out into the room as the activists made themselves comfortable and the screen was filled with a beaming face of the host, then panned around the audience, as always, of exactly 100 people. The weekly show was reputed to draw a television audience of up to 1.7 million viewers – depending on the issue to be debated.

As the signature tune faded, the popular host introduced the show. 'Good morning, good morning!' he enthused into the television camera, his white teeth and equally white hair gleaming. 'We have covered the issue of cruelty to animals many times on this programme. We've debated the farming of animals for meat with a passionate livestock farmer on one side and an ardent vegan on the other.'

Turning to face camera two, he continued, 'We've debated fox hunting with a huntsman ranged against a hunt saboteur. You may recall that during a debate between the Medical Research Society and the National Anti-Vivisection Society, people became so impassioned that we had to stop for an advertising break to cool things down! Today the object of our attention is horses, not just whether they should be used in horse-racing or circuses or bull-rings, but whether we should set horses free, which presumably would mean we would have to provide them with land and allow them to become wild.'

He turned back to camera one. 'You all know the story! Of course you do! You must have been asleep for the last few days if you haven't been aware of the break-out by the horses from a Somerset animal sanctuary where they have been living in retirement, and have taken to the road after what the police suspect to have been an attempt to steal a horse. The incident ended in a man's death. Attempts to get the horses back to the sanctuary have failed so far, due apparently, both to the determination of the horses not to return, plus by interference by animal rights..…well I won't say extremists, because that is for you to decide.'

The unique thing about our debate today, is that both sides clearly care about the welfare of these horses. You will hear from an officer of the RSPCA, the Royal Society for the Prevention of Cruelty to Animals, who will argue that for their own safety and welfare the horses should be recaptured and taken back to their sanctuary home. Then you will be addressed from a leading member of the Animal Liberation Front who says the horses should be given the freedom and indeed assistance to help them end being the servants of human beings.'

Turning back to camera two, Jeremy Bateson continued, 'Before we hear from them, and with the agreement of both sides, we have put together a short film to remind us of Man's long and continuing involvement with horses. I should mention that some scenes in the film may distress some viewers.'

The film began with shots of old paintings depicting ancient battles where horses died alongside their riders, speared with lances, peppered with arrows, and downed by cannon fire. The scenes changed to grainy black-and-white footage of the first World War with teams of horses heaving heavy guns through glutinous mud and glimpses of dead horses lying in ditches at the road-side.

The horror was quickly followed by scenes of people gently cantering on horses in the countryside, children riding small ponies at a Fox Hunt meet and disabled children joyfully riding on ponies at a riding school for the handicapped.

The scene changed to mounted police walking their horses sedately through London traffic, then dramatically to wild-eyed horses masked by visors and rearing under their police riders facing missiles and fireworks, hurled by rioters in an unidentified violent demonstration. This was followed by a brief shot of a bull charging and goring a horse in a Spanish bullfight and onto horse-racing footage with two horses battling neck and neck for the winning post with the crowd roaring and the flailing arms of the jockeys whipping their steeds. This faded into frantic scenes and loud music from an old western movie as horses carrying native American Indians plunged, buckled and crashed to the ground under 'fire' from wagon train pioneers.

The final scenes were of working plough horses with their proud owners being awarded rosettes for their skills, race horses and jockeys being feted by race-goers, horses galloping at speed in the surf of a sandy beach and the film faded with horses grazing in the dappled sunshine of the New Forest in Hampshire.

As the film faded, Jeremy Bateson spoke to a hushed audience, 'Well, I hope you the audience, both here and at home, will agree that the film illustrates our complex relationship with horses. Those of you familiar with the way the programme works will know that at this stage we give each of our two guests the opportunity to tell us what they think about the herd of rescued horses which we have all seen in the news, and which allegedly, with the intervention of animal rights activists, are seemingly refusing to return to the animal sanctuary from which they escaped a few days ago.'

The programme host paused, and then continued, 'The question to be debated is this. Should this wandering herd of horses be captured and, if you like, loaded into lorries and returned to their previous home, as advocated by the RSPCA and the Ferne Animal Sanctuary management, or should they be permitted, and indeed assisted, to travel and settle wherever they finally seem to want to be?'

The presenter paused again. 'Right, let's begin with the RSPCA's public relations director, Brian Boulton. He has been with the RSPCA for five years. He has won the toss and has chosen to speak first. He will be followed by Robin Chamberlain of the Animal Liberation Front. So here we go, please give them both a warm welcome.'

To enthusiastic applause, the smiling presenter turned and with a hand gesture invited the RSPCA guest to walk to a wooden lectern facing the studio audience and two cameras. Brian Boulton was in his mid-forties, well-groomed, six feet tall, with a pleasant smile and well-practised in his art of public relations – having been a highly successful insurance salesman before he answered an RSPCA advertisement and thus began a new career in one of the most well-known British charities. As the applause faded, he placed some sheets of paper on the lectern and began his speech.

'Good morning. The RSPCA says that the best place for these horses is back in the sanctuary in the care of the dedicated staff who know them and have cared for them since they were handed into the sanctuary's care. As I understand it, that is exactly where they would be now if it were not for an apparent attempt to steal one or more horses, which ended with the death of a person, and the herd breaking out of their sanctuary. They would by now be back there were it not for the temperament of the grey unbroken mare that appears to be leading the herd, and for the unhelpful interference by animal rights people, to frustrate attempts by the sanctuary, the police and our officers to get the horses back to safety. These animals are at this moment corralled in a car park in the town of Milborne Port where attempts are being made to find transport to return them to their sanctuary near Chard, and back into the care of the Ferne Animal Sanctuary, a well-respected animal welfare charity.'

Turning over a page of his notes, Brian Boulton, continued, 'The fact is, these animals are domestic animals, mostly elderly and some in need of regular veterinary care. They are not tough, fit native horses like Exmoor or New Forest ponies which can survive in the forests and moorland of Britain. The horses were happy and safe in their sanctuary until someone apparently trespassed for some criminal activity and a man perished as a result. There are other unidentified persons involved, and it is not yet known why they should target virtually valueless animals. However, it seems obvious that the actions of these night-time trespassers caused the herd to panic, and flee from the perceived danger. The fact is though, that these horses do not know that they are safer in their sanctuary than wandering the roads, disrupting traffic, breaking down fences, and damaging crops. The grey mare which is leading this small herd is unique in that she has never been broken to saddles and reins, and attempts to dart her with an anaesthetic have been thwarted by animal activists, who may be sincere, but who, in the opinion of the RSPCA, are not acting in the best interests of these animals. All that is needed is to humanely dart the leading grey mare with an anaesthetic, so that she and the rest of her herd can be transported in lorries back to the sanctuary.' He continued after turning another page.

'I believe that allowing them the freedom to wander near and far is idiotic. They are not wild animals. What happens if they suddenly stop and don't want to go any further. Is the nearest landowner or farmer expected to say, 'Oh all right, they can live on my farm forever and I will ensure they are provided with food, water and shelter and I will even pay vets' and farriers fees.'

'I don't see that happening. Most of these rescued horses are elderly – one has already died – probably from exertion the night that the horses broke out. If they are allowed to end up in a wild place like moorland or forests, they will suffer from extremes of weather and shortage of food. These are domestic animals for which we humans are responsible. Their previous owners or rescuers handed them over to the Ferne Animal Sanctuary charity to be cared for, for the rest of their lives, and the sanctuary, as owners of the whole herd, are responsible for their welfare. The sanctuary cannot wash its hands of these animals, even if they wished to. If they abandon these horses in the name of some deluded concept of freedom, the sanctuary could be prosecuted under the Abandonment of Animals Act 1960.

'The only possible solution is to take these horses back to their home. The RSPCA is committed to assist in this mission, and I can only appeal to my fellow guest and his friends to help us RSPCA officers and the sanctuary staff, to achieve that aim. Thank you.'

Led by host Jeremy Bateman the studio audience applauded loudly as the RSPCA man returned to his chair. The smiling presenter turned back to the camera, and as the applause abated, addressed his television audience.

'Well, that is the RSPCA view and Brian has made it very clear what he thinks must happen to these horses, which are at this very moment penned in a public car park in the Somerset town of Milborne Port.'

'May I now introduce Robin Chamberlain, a spokesman for the Animal Liberation Front. He has a very different view, which I'm sure is equally sincere, so please welcome Robin,' he said as he ushered his second guest forward. There was polite applause from the studio audience, but in the front room of a terraced house in Milborne Port there whoops, whistles and shouts of, 'Go for it Robin!'

Robin, strikingly tall and slim, shoulder length dark, wavy hair, rose quickly and strode to the lectern, his face not betraying his nervousness. He quietly cleared his throat, placed his hands on the top edge of the lectern and faced the audience, hoping that no-one noticed the slight tremors in his knees.

'Good morning. On behalf of the Animal Liberation Front, I submit that just once, just once, in the history of Man's exploitation of animals, we begin giving the animals some freedom of choice. The film at the beginning of this programme showed the misery, pain and brutality we humans have meted out to the kingdom of horses – as indeed we have meted out to untold generations of virtually every animal species all round the world.

'We took horses from the wild thousands of years ago and now there are no truly wild horses left on the planet. There are a few feral horses living wild, but even those are regularly rounded up and their young offspring taken from them to sell for human exploitation.

'What have we done to horses the world over? My fellow guest mentioned that the leader of this herd of horses, has not been 'broken' to harnesses or reins. The word 'broken' is highly significant. As so often with man's exploitation of animals, we have to 'break' them so that we can handle them, or as I would say, enslave them. To carry us, to haul wagons and carts, plough our fields, to transport our weapons, to race each other for our entertainment or to jump high obstacles, and to serve the human addiction to betting and even to carry people who wish to chase and kill other animals for 'sport'. We whip them, we rake their flanks with spurs, we put metal bits in their mouths so that we can steer them in the direction we want them to go. Hundreds of horses die in horse racing every year, in the name of sport and gambling. Millions of horses have been sacrificed in our stupid human wars – eight million in the first World War alone.

'In Spain and other countries we humans blindfold them and cut their vocal chords so that they cannot scream when they are barged and gored by infuriated and tortured bulls. For a lucky tiny handful of horses, we reward them with a peaceful environment at the end of their days, but for the rest it is the horrors of the slaughter house.

'We don't know what happened at the Ferne Animal Sanctuary fields that caused the herd to flee their sanctuary, but they did choose to leave. And when they have been given the choice, they have chosen to keep travelling away from the sanctuary. Yes, I admit that someone who shares our members views have interfered with attempts to recapture the horses, but we have not dictated what direction they chose take.

'I make a plea, just this once, if only as an experiment if you like, to offer this herd and their unique 'unbroken' leader the freedom to choose, if indeed they are actually choosing, to carry on their adventure with the assistance of us humans, instead of the usual domination and resistance. It would be a fascinating experiment.

'Is the herd or their leader following instinct? Do they know of their intended destination? Is it solely the fear induced by the incident at the sanctuary that is keeping these animals travelling east despite not exhibiting any fear of the other humans they are meeting?'

'Our members and supporters will be pleased to assist with monitoring the animals, carrying water and food, and helping in any way the RSPCA and the Sanctuary staff suggest, until it becomes clear that the herd is either just wandering aimlessly or has reached some particular destination where they wish to settle – and then it can be debated as to whether the herd's wishes can be granted.'

'Finally, the fact is, less than two hundred years ago, we captured and enslaved black humans, broke them to our will, and forced them to work for us. When we invaded countries such as Australia, we slaughtered thousands of the natives and even hunted them with dogs for sport. In America we violently robbed the native Indians of their land and slaughtered millions of bison. We captured black people, made them work for us – just like animals. Now we look back in shame at our treatment of people like animals. Mr Boulton can confirm that the people who created the RSPCA were also the men and women who campaigned alongside William Wilberforce for the end of human slavery.'

'The Animal Liberation Front believes that the slavery of animals, particularly those that we kill to eat, is wrong. My dream is that one day, we will end our exploitation of the other inhabitants of our earth, and, as far as possible give them the freedom and space to obey their own natural instincts and follow their own paths. We could start with this little herd of assorted horses which clearly trust the instincts of their unique, 'unbroken' leader.

Thank you for listening to our point of view.'

Robin turned and walked back to his seat in a heavily pregnant silence, but hesitatingly, a few members of the audience began to clap, and which then rapidly escalated into genuine applause.

Jeremy Bateson turned to camera 2.

Smiling, he said, 'Well, you can't say that Robin's alternative solution is not imaginative. But now we go to a break after which members of the studio audience will be able to question our two guests. At the end of the programme we will ask our 100 audience members to vote. The choices are clear. Do you support Brian's solution of capturing the horses and transporting them back to their sanctuary near Chard, or do you support Robin's appeal to allow and even assist them to find some other destination and destiny? We will see you after this short break.'

As the show's signature tune began, there was a shriek from Auntie Jean. 'Tony, you've not touched your beans. They'll be cold – like your tea!

Tony visible flinched 'Oh, I'm sorry I…was…um…'

Ron intervened, 'The word you're looking for is transfixed, Tony. I know what it's like when you first get involved in animal rights. I remember how embarrassed I was when I first learned that cows have to be made pregnant every year to produce milk, and when their calves are born they are taken away so we get the milk, and the male calves are killed for veal and the females reared on to spend their lives pregnant, to produce yet more milk. I felt such an idiot when I found that out. I'd not even thought about calves before that.'

Tony began to eat his beans on toast during the TV advert break, while Ron updated him on how the police had taken him, Angie, Caroline and Robin to Yeovil police station for the night, leaving their van outside the pub on Ham Hill. He explained how Gary had used the van to transport sheets of plywood and turf to cover the cattle grid, and created a diversion to allow the horses to escape from their quarry and move on again. Ron and Angie had the perfect alibi – a night in the police station and the embarrassed police had to transport the four of them back to Ham Hill to reclaim Ron's van.

'Here we go,' said Angie as the Jeremy Bateson show began again. Tony suddenly felt confused and annoyed with himself because he was beginning to understand the cause of the people in the room. He tried to concentrate on his food, and close his mind to the images in the film which preceded the debate. He was shocked to realise that he felt admiration for Gary's exploits and had begun feeling some affinity and pleasure from the company of his new colleagues. Throughout the rest of the programme he tried and failed to crush the confusion that both the film and Robin's arguments were influencing on his mind.

He felt a tap on his shoulder and turned to see a smiling 'Auntie' Jean with a large mug of tea. 'You all right Tony? Don't let this one get cold,' she said.

'I'm sorry', Tony replied. 'I got a bit...' Jean smiled as she placed the cup in his hands, and said, 'Yes, as Ron says...transfixed. Don't allow it to happen again,' she added with a mocking wag of her finger.

Tony thanked Jean with a grateful smile, which was noticed instantly by Angela who called out, 'There's that smile again. It's a lovely smile. I'm changing your name to Smiler Smith from now on.'

'Do you mind, Angie?' said Ron sarcastically. 'Can you stop chatting up Tony, just while we watch the programme?'

'Take no notice of him, Smiler,' replied Angie in an audible whisper. 'He's just jealous!'

Tony blushed again and was grateful for the first question from a member of Jeremy Bateson's studio audience. For the next few minutes questions were put to the two speakers. Ron was only a foot away from the screen determined to hear the questions and add his opinion to the comments from the members of the studio audience. His running commentary consisted of, 'What a prat!'...'Right on Robin,'... 'He's definitely a hunter,' and similar comments, until Angie shouted, 'Ron, we want to hear, too.'

Suddenly, there was the loud sound of a bell mimicking the end of a boxing bout, and Jeremy Bateson put up his hand and called a halt to the proceedings. 'That's the end of the debate,' he said to camera, 'at least in this studio. Now it's time for our studio audience of one hundred people to vote. Each member of the audience has three cards under their seat. One says, 'RSPCA', another says 'ALF', and a third says, 'Not Sure.' Some audible shuffling took place as members of the audience found the cards under their seats and made their choices.

The TV studio and Auntie Jean's front room fell quiet as Jeremy Bateson said,

'Firstly, those with RSPCA cards show them now and keep them up to give us the chance to count them. A few seconds later, the TV host asked for the RSPCA cards to be placed back under the audience seats, and called for the ALF cards to be raised. Finally, the 'Not Sure' cards were counted.

Jeremy Bateson faced the camera and was handed a sheet of paper by a member of the studio team. He paused and then spoke slowly, 'The votes have been cast and checked, and the results are as follows. For the RSPCA, 43 votes. For the ALF, 41 votes. Those not sure, 16 votes. Make of it what you wish. Next week, we will be examining another controversial issue and asking another audience of 100 members of the public to vote. Goodbye, and thank you for watching.'

The programme's signature tune played, accompanied by the applause of the studio audience, the camera revealed Robin and Brian shaking hands, and as the credits rolled, there was silence in Auntie Jean's front room.

The silence was broken by Ron. 'What do we make of that?'

'We lost!' said Jody.

'You gotta be joking', said Gary. 'The RSPCA is one of the most respected charities in Britain, and the best known animal welfare society in the world. The ALF is tiny, castigated in the press, accused of terrorism, and battered by politicians. Yet, our argument was only beaten by two votes! Robin was fantastic. His master stroke was to offer our services to try and discover what the horses want, and help them find it. Ron, I think you and Angie should go into town and approach the RSPCA and sanctuary people. We need to know whether they have managed to find horse transporters, and if not what are they going to do next?'

Chapter 9

That lunch-time, Trevor James, his daughter Becky and Helen Watson, the RSPCA team leader, were sat around a table in the RSPCA's caravan. The mood was sombre. Helen had explained that her assistant Tina had reported that every horse transport firm she had contacted either couldn't or wouldn't get involved. The police and even the military either couldn't or wouldn't get involved in the controversial issue.

There was a knock on the door. Helen called, 'Come in,' and RSPCA vet Roger Penman opened the door and peered around it. 'What do you want first, the good news or the bad news?' he said with a hint of a grin.

'Oh please, the good news!' Helen pleaded, holding up both her hands with fingers crossed.

'Well, today's Jeremy Bateson Show audience has voted in favour of the RSPCA's opinion that the horses should be returned to the Ferne Animal Sanctuary.

'That's great,' said Helen. 'So what's the bad news?'

Roger paused. 'The RSPCA vote was only 43 per cent and the ALF solution of allowing the horses to find their own destination was 41 per cent - with the don't knows, 16 per cent'.

'What!' exclaimed Trevor angrily. 'Where the hell do they find these people?'

Roger shrugged and said, 'Apparently, the ALF guy made a good fist of it, but I'm told that the film shown before the debate, included a lot of abuse of horses – much of it historical – ancient wars including World War one, bull fighting, Grand National casualties, circus acts, etc etc.'

LADY PATRICIA

Rebecca spoke, 'Well, what are we going to do? We have to move the horses out of the car park tomorrow morning.'

'We'll just have to find another place for them while we work things out,' said Helen.

Trevor ran his fingers through his hair. 'Becky, this might sound weird, but do you remember the day you met the activists, you wondered whether the horses were deliberately following a route, and I mentioned ley-lines and then immediately dismissed it as nonsense?'

'Yes', said his daughter, 'I remember. Do you think it is possible then?'

'No, not ley lines,' said Trevor. 'But take a look at this.' He unfolded an Ordinance Survey map and spread it on the table as everyone rose from her seats and leaned over the table.

The map covered much of east Somerset and north Dorset. Trevor held a red pencil and marked the centre of Chard. 'This is where the horses started travelling along the A30,' he said, and then traced a red line along the A30. 'About here they were stopped and pushed into a field, but later the broke out and were stopped by the police at Cricket St Thomas. We thought we could walk them back west to Chard, but that failed because Patricia refused to go back, and she turned the herd back to the east. To get the horses off the main road, the police diverted the herd off the A30 into the narrow road that leads to Chillington and Hinton St George, and we managed to use the 'Road Work' signs and fences to pen them in.

Placing the pencil at that point on the map, Trevor continued, 'Then the animal activists turned up with their demo and the mysterious guy in military uniform removed the temporary barriers and that allowed the horses to get to Hinton, where we thought we had them village hall sports field - perfect place to load them into lorries and take them back to the sanctuary.'

Trevor placed his pencil on the words Hinton St George and continued. 'Then, somebody, presumably the guy in uniform, moved the tractor and trailer that we used to block the road, and that allowed the herd to go towards Merriot, and the police managed to divert them into a dead-end lane where we blocked them in for the night. Assuming none of the horses use wire-cutters, someone, again, presumably our private soldier, opened up a gate in the night, and it seems several other gates, and the herd finished up in Norton sub Hamdon's recreation field.'

Trevor stabbed the map with his pencil, stood up and flexed his back. 'The village street was too narrow to get horse-transport into, so, under pressure from the local MPs wife we pushed them up onto Ham Hill where we corralled them in a quarry, and arranged for the police to supply horse transporters from Bristol and a single trailer for Patsy. That night the lorries were nobbled – even though the drivers slept in them. Potatoes were shoved up the exhaust pipes which resulted in the exhaust systems being removed and cleaned out ready for the following day. But again in the night, the soldier, or possibly a new gang, found a way to get the horses out of the quarry and across a cattle grid and into Stoke sub Hamdon…here,' he said stabbing his pencil on the map again.

Trevor continued, 'From there they were followed by police all over the place, and finished up here in Milborne Port, …which is where, Becky?'

'On the A30!' cried his daughter, triumphantly.

'Now then', said her father, 'Where did the horses come from three years ago?'.

'The original Ferne Animal Sanctuary, where Patricia was born!' shouted Becky, excitedly.

'Which is where, daughter of mine?'

'On the A30 just the other side of Shaftesbury!' came the reply.

'How far is that from here?' asked Helen.

'I reckon fifteen miles at the most.' said Trevor.

'But would it be possible to escort them that far?' asked Helen.

'Looking at the map, we would have to go round the lanes and B roads. The police would never let us walk them on the actual A30.'

'Is the original sanctuary still there?' queried Helen.

'The truth is, I don't know,' replied Trevor, 'But we could drive over and take a look. We could be there in half an hour – it's only a quarter to twelve. Shall the three of us do that now?' said Trevor.

'I'll stay here with the horses,' said Rebecca. 'You two go.'

LADY PATRICIA

'Well, let's put everybody in the picture', said Helen.

'We'll take the sanctuary van,' said Trevor.

Helen left the caravan to explain to her team, where and why they were going off for an hour or two.

'She's lovely, isn't she Dad?'

'Who's that, Becky?' said her father taking his car keys out of his pocket and avoiding eye contact with his daughter.

'You know full well who I'm talking about,' said Becky.

'Oh, you mean Helen, yes very nice lady,' he said quickly.

'I've seen you looking at her,' said his daughter. 'You fancy her, and if you say you don't, you're a fibber!'

Trevor blushed, just as Helen joined them, 'Who's a fibber?' asked Helen.

'Just a joke,' said Trevor, jangling his car keys and stepping towards the sanctuary van.

'Have a nice time,' cooed Rebecca mischievously as Trevor held the passenger door open and Helen slid into the front seat. Trevor walked round to the driver's door, slid into the driver's seat and deliberately kept looking to the right in the hope that Helen wouldn't notice his blushed face.

*

As the Ferne sanctuary van moved out of Milborne Port and onto the A30 going east, a blue BMW saloon entered the town from the west and pulled into the car park of the Bull Hotel. Mr Robert Smith and Mrs Edwina Smith walked into reception. Having quickly booked in for three days, they walked to the High Street and towards the car park - each with a pack of leaflets bearing the photograph of their missing son Anthony.

Back at Auntie Jean's house, the activists had agreed that following Robin's sterling performance on the Jeremy Bateson Show, Ron and Angie would approach the RSPCA and sanctuary staff and offer help with the horses in any way except transporting them back to the Ferne Animal Sanctuary.

Tony was asleep in his chair and Auntie Jean said, 'Don't wake him up. He looks exhausted. He'll be OK here.'

'Shall we go to see what's going on in the car park,' Clive asked.

'I'll stay here,' said Gary. 'No-one has seen me yet, and I think I'll keep it that way, just in case we need to take further action.'

'OK,' said Clive, You coming Jody?'

'Sure am, 'said his partner.

Ron, Angie, Clive and Jody walked into town together, and then split up when Ron and Angie moved towards the caravan which was the temporary office of the RSPCA team – leaving Clive and Jody leaning on the car park railing looking at the horses. 'They still look fine, don't they?' commented Clive. Before Jody could reply, a voice behind them said, 'Excuse me'. The pair turned to see a middle-aged, smartly dressed lady with what looked like a fist-full of small leaflets.

'I'm sorry to bother you young people, but my husband and I are trying to find our son Anthony,' she said, making a gesture towards her husband who was handing a leaflet to a person a few yards away.

Mrs Smith handed to leaflet to Jody, and said, 'We saw him on TV a couple of days ago, when he was in a crowd of people looking at these same horses. The police in Yeovil suggested we came here in case he was still interested in these horses for some reason.'

'Not that we can think of any such reason. He never showed any interest in animals,' mumbled Mr Smith as he joined his wife's side.

Jody's heart skipped a beat when she saw the photograph of their 'new recruit' Tony – younger, but undoubtedly him. Jody turned her back on the Smiths to face Clive and showed him the leaflet while narrowing her eyes as a warning to him. He glanced at her and then the leaflet and immediately handed the leaflet back to her.

'No, never seen him before,' said Clive, a little too briskly for Jody's liking.

Jody looked again at the leaflet and asked the Mr Smith, 'How long since you saw him?' she asked sympathetically.

'More than eight months ago,' answered Mrs Smith.

LADY PATRICIA

'Eight months ago. Wow!' said Clive, again a bit too loudly for Jody's liking.

Jody quickly asked, as sympathetically as she could, 'Where do you live?'

'Bicester in Oxfordshire,' replied Mr Smith.

'Any idea, why he ran away?' asked Jody.

'Bit of a family row,' said Mr Smith.

'So you're not from the west country,' probed Clive.

'No, he did ring us once to say he was in Liverpool, but he warned us not to try and find him, or he would never come home,' said Mrs Smith. 'He was only sixteen when he left. I'm so worried about him, but when we saw the TV news about these horses, we spotted him and we came straight down to Somerset.'

Jody felt sorry for the pair. Mrs Smith was trying to keep back her tears as her husband threw his arm around her shoulders and squeezed her arm.

'Let me have a few leaflets,' said Jody. 'We will keep an eye out for him.'

'Oh, you're so kind. We are staying at the Bull Hotel for a couple of days, but our home number and the Yeovil police number are on the leaflet. Thank you so much for caring,' said Mrs Smith, touching Jody's hand.

'Good luck,' called Clive, as Tony's parents moved away to distribute more leaflets.

'Well, what do you make of that?' said Clive, 'We better get back to the house and talk to Gary. Tony could drop him right in it with the police. He could tell them all about what happened on Ham Hill, and at Hinton St George. Let's see whether Ron and Angie are still talking to the RSPCA.'

They visited the RSPCA caravan and asked for the Sanctuary manager or RSPCA representative. An inspector explained that they were on an errand to try and find another temporary venue for the horses, but were expected back within a couple of hours.

'Ron and Angie have probably gone back to Auntie Jean's, or maybe their looking for a café,' said Clive. 'We'd better get back and warn Gary.'

As they half ran, half walked to Aunt Jean's house. Jody was visibly angry. 'What a little shit Tony turned out to be?' she said. 'All the lies he's told us. Lives in Exeter, vegetarian, blah, blah, interested in animal rights. Lying little turd.'

'What worries me,' said Clive. 'He told us that the police put him on a train to Exeter and he got off at the first stop and hitched all the way here. What if he is actually working for the police. Remember he had a wad of notes when we met him in Crewkerne. Ron couldn't grab the cash quickly enough. We should have been more suspicious.'

'But his mother is clearly in pieces,' said Jody. 'She said he'd left home eight months ago when he was only sixteen. The police wouldn't dare employ a kid that young. It's clear his parents don't know anything.'

'Who knows?' answered Clive. 'The government are paranoid about the animal rights movement. That's why the met police have ARNI – probably all our names and addresses are on that.'

They reached Auntie Jean's door, rang the bell, prompting Henry the Labrador into noisy action. Gary opened the door to them, 'Hi, what's the news then?' he asked.

'Not good,' said Clive, putting his finger to his lips and whispering, 'Where's Tony?'

'Helping Jean wash-up,' said Gary quietly.

'Close the door and we'll walk up the road a bit.'

As they moved a few yards away, Jody handed Gary one of the leaflets.

Gary peered at the picture, stopped dead, read the text, and stood looking from Clive to Jody with his mouth open. As they began walking again, Jody told Gary about their conversation with Tony's parents.

Gary winced, 'Jesus, he knows enough to put me inside. Damaging police vehicles, breaking and entering a pub, wrecking a tractor, driving a van without insurance, wasting police time. Let's have it out with him.'

'We need to be careful though', said Jody. 'I think you should tackle him first, Gary. Jean obviously has a soft spot for him, so you should take him for a little walk'.

They turned and walked back to the house and arrived at the gate the same time as Ron and Angie. They both looked anxious and Ron pulled a leaflet out of his back pocket and said 'Take a look at this.'

'We know', chorused Clive and Jody, displaying the same leaflets.

Gary spoke, 'Don't say anything when we go in. Act normal. I'll suggest to Tony we go into town for some chips or something. Angie, you can tell Jean what's happened after I've left with Tony.'

*

'Are you warm enough Helen?' enquired Trevor.

'Sure, I'm fine,' she replied.

'Trouble with the heater in this van, you're either sweltering or freezing, and there doesn't seem anything in between.'

'Honestly Trevor, I'm very comfortable,' insisted Helen

The A30 traffic between Milborne Port and Shaftesbury was moving well.

Trevor said, 'We go past Shaftesbury, and after a few miles we turn right toward Berwick St John. The entrance to the old Ferne estate is on the right. It'll be interesting to see what's happened to it since the sanctuary trustees were forced to move the whole caboodle down to Chard three years ago.'

'Why did they do that?' asked Helen.

'Well, apparently the Duchess of Hamilton turned her 250 acres and stately home into an animal sanctuary at the outbreak of war in 1939. She went to London and announced on the radio, that if anyone was joining the forces and couldn't keep their pets, she would arrange for their animals to spend the war at Ferne. Apparently, there were queues of people with their pets lining up to be transferred in caravans, all organised by the Duchess. Everybody thought the war would soon be over and they could reclaim their pets, but of course, it was six long years and although a few people did reclaim their animals, most of them became the sanctuary's first clients.'

Trevor continued, 'The Duchess was very much involved in the Animal Defence Society which mainly campaigned against vivisection and when she died in the 1950s her family was hit by huge death duties. Her mansion was knocked down and it was said that the demolition company's owner became a millionaire by selling the contents. Lots of the estate's cottages were left to rot as the workers lost their jobs. Then, so I understand, a huge court case ensued to settle the disputed ownership of the land. The judge bizarrely decided that the land was owned by the Animal Defence Society, but that the Ferne Animal Sanctuary was a separate entity on that land. So the Animal Defence Society ordered the Ferne Animal Sanctuary to take its animals and leave. Outrageous really, but then the animal welfare world is notorious for such bust-ups!'

'And don't I know it!' said Helen. 'The rows within the RSPCA over fox hunting went on for years because the hunters were urged by the Masters of Fox Hounds Association to join the society to stop it campaigning against bloodsports. For years there were ferocious rows between the pro-hunt and anti-hunt members at the annual general meetings which eventually led to a year-long public enquiry. The enquiry report eventually demanded that the entire Council should resign and stand again in a new election for a smaller Council - half the size of the original one of forty-six.'

'Forty six?' exclaimed Trevor, 'Struth, I would be amazed if a committee that big could agree on anything!'

'Quite,' said Helen. 'Fortunately, the newly elected Council voted for a new policy of opposition to all forms of hunting with dogs – and the hunters couldn't do anything about it. Since then it's all been peace and light – and we even organised an Animal Rights Seminar last summer with virtually every animal welfare society sending delegates and speakers on all current animal issues – even, I suspect some of the activists who have prevented you getting your horses home.'.

'Wouldn't be surprised at all!' agreed Trevor.

'So, Trevor, how did you get involved in this animal business?' asked Helen.

LADY PATRICIA

'It's a long story, Helen. I'll tell you about it on the way back. We've not far to go, next right I reckon....should be signed Berwick St John.'

Within a couple of minutes, they saw the road sign, turned right and drove for a short while past high hedges on the right. Suddenly the hedges on the right ended at a semi-circular lay-by separated from open park land by a trimmed hedge and high black wrought iron gates set between a pair of stone pillars topped with carved stone acorns. Beyond the gates, a narrow road rose gently up through park land to distant woodland. On the right-hand side of the gates was a small attractive bungalow with a tidy garden enclosed by a white picket fence.

Trevor pulled into the lay-by and parked in front of the wrought-iron gates. 'There's a light on,' he said turning off the engine and pulling on the hand-brake. 'Let's see who's in.' They emerged from the van and approached the wrought iron gates to find them firmly secured by a chain and padlock. As Trevor tested the gate with a brief shake, a short grey-haired man in a green pullover and black trousers stepped out of the bungalow and called, 'Just a minute, I'll open up.'

The man strode quickly to the gates, turned a key in the padlock, unwrapped the chain and pulled open one of the gates.

'Sorry about that,' he said. 'We have to keep them locked to stop people driving round the estate like it's a public park.'

'Not exactly the weather for picnics,' observed Trevor.

'You'd be surprised!' came the response. 'Your van will be fine where it is, but I have to lock the gate again.'

Helen felt she should provide some identification. 'I'm Helen Watson from the RSPCA and this is Trevor James, manager of the Ferne Animal Sanctuary.'

'I know who you are, said the host, 'I've been following the story on the news. My name is Joe, Joe Turner, and I work for the Animal Defence Society as a sort of caretaker and gate-keeper. Come on in, my wife put the kettle on as soon as we saw the Ferne Sanctuary sign on your van.'

Joe led Helen and Trevor into the neat bungalow where Joe's

smiling wife greeted them. 'I'm Clare,' she said. 'Have the sofa. Kettle's on, coffee or tea?'

Trevor said, 'Coffee please - two sugars for me,' and Helen said, 'Coffee would be great, but no sugar for me.' They sat down together and smiled at each other as they sank deeper into the sofa than they anticipated.

Trevor took a sip of coffee and placed his cup back onto the saucer. 'How long have you lived here Joe?' he asked.

Joe called out, 'Clare, how long have we been here?'

'Only thirty-one years,' chuckled his wife from the kitchen.

'So you were here when the Duchess lived here,' observed Trevor.

Joe replied, 'Yes, when I came out of the army after the war, we saw an advert for a married couple to act as gate-keeper and some help with the animals. The duchess herself interviewed us and gave us the job. We've been here in the lodge ever since. She was a wonderful woman. When she died, the whole village was devastated. She used to put on a huge party every Christmas in the big house for all the children of the village, and of course she was brilliant with the animals.'

Clare added, 'She wouldn't have hunting or shooting on the estate. When Churchill's government ordered landowners to have dairy herds for the war effort, she built a huge shelter for the cows, where they could go in any weather, and lie in deep straw. It's still there along with most of the farm buildings. She also built a maternity unit for the cows to calve in, and she insisted that the calves had their fill of their mother's milk before the rest went into the churns and off to the dairies. And she even had a slaughter house built, to save any of her livestock being transported to abattoirs. She used to tell everybody, 'I'm not having any of my animals killed by people I don't know.'

'What do you make of the current problem with Ferne's horses?' asked Helen.

Joe sat down at a small side table. 'Well, we've been following the story and we recognised most of the horses, didn't we Clare?' His wife agreed and Joe continued, 'It said on the telly, that the herd leader played up when attempts were made to transport the horses back to the Chard. That would be Lady Patricia. We saw her born here, you know!'

Trevor spoke, 'Well, we had a lot of trouble from animal activists as well, but we've been coming round to the idea, strange as it seems, that Patricia might instinctively be trying to bring the herd back here. Anyway, Milborne Port Town Council insists that we have to move the horses out of their car park tomorrow morning. We've not been able to find any horse transport because their owners are worried about animal rights reprisals. So we have no choice but to move them, and looking at the map we think we have a chance to supervise the herd around the lanes and minor roads in the hope that our theory about Patricia's instinctive destination is here. We know that the herd simply won't cooperate with attempts to move them in any other direction.'

Joe said, 'I would have to ask Animal Defence if they would allow that.'. He looked at his watch, and continued, 'I could ring their secretary, Jessie, and see whether she can contact the directors. Would you like to speak to her?' he asked, turning his head from Trevor to Helen.

'Perhaps it would be better from you Helen, woman to woman - so to speak,' suggested Trevor.

'OK,' responded Helen with a smile. 'What do you think of the chances Mr Turner?'

'It's Joe by the way,' replied the gate-keeper. 'Well, they do let out land for grazing and for hay sometimes, but as far as I know they have not made up their minds what to do with the estate. There was talk about setting up a new animal rescue centre coupled with a home for disabled children and even a British wildlife education centre. But nothing has happened over the last two years. Perhaps I shouldn't say this, but it was a shame they couldn't let the sanctuary stay here.'

Joe rose, and walked over to a telephone on a chest of drawers. 'I'll ring Jessie now, and see if she will speak to you Helen, but you will have to assure her that if the horses do come back here, it will only be a temporary arrangement until transport can be arranged back to Chard.'

'Sure', said Helen. 'I will emphasise that.'

Joe picked up the receiver and dialled, spoke for a couple of minutes, and then handed the phone to Helen, after which he, Trevor and Clare listened in concentrated silence.

*

'Brilliant, brilliant!' yelled Trevor as he conducted a three-point turn to leave the Ferne entrance. 'You were fantastic, Helen!' he yelled again hammering both fists on the steering wheel.

'Steady on Trevor,' replied Helen. 'We've still got to walk fifteen horses…what maybe fifteen miles, all on narrow back roads and lanes, in the hope, I repeat, the hope, that they are heading right here.'

'Oh ye of little faith, Helen,' he said. 'It was Becky that came up with the idea that Patricia was instinctively heading somewhere, and not just wandering around the countryside because they had a dreadful scare at our sanctuary. It seems that nearly half the Jeremy Bateson show's audience supported the idea of finding out whether the herd had a safe destination in the leader's memory banks. I think it's very exciting, don't you?' asked Trevor turning to see the amusement in Helen's deep hazel eyes.

'Well, your enthusiasm is very attractive, Trevor, and your daughter is also clearly open to the idea, but if we finish up in Battersea Park, don't blame me!'

'Don't be such an old cynic, Helen,' responded Trevor.

'Not so much of the 'old', thank you!' she replied haughtily, before touching his arm and smiling at him. Trevor felt his heart miss a beat and was conscious that his ears were burning.

They rode in an excruciating silence for a full ten seconds, broken when Helen asked, 'You were going to tell me how you got involved in animal work.'

'Oh yes, I was,' said Trevor, relieved that she had broken the silence. 'Well, we lived in Norfolk where I was an aircraft engineer. My wife Janet was a veterinary nurse in a big practice in

Sheringham. Ever since I was a boy, I felt a deep empathy with animals, and Janet and I used to do voluntary work at a local animal rescue centre at weekends and sometimes do a bit of fund-raising – you know, shaking tins in the town centre. As Becky got older we felt we would be happier working together for animals and we saw an advert for a couple to manage at Ferne, which had just relocated to Somerset; so we applied, got the job and I chucked in engineering and we moved down to Somerset.'

'Sounds just like Joe and Clare!' said Helen.

'But not such a happy ending,' said Trevor, staring hard at the road ahead.

'Oh?' asked Helen.

'I lost Janet a year to the day after our arrival at the sanctuary – an undiagnosed cardiac abnormality. No symptoms. Died in her sleep, just like that.'

'Oh my God, Trevor!' exclaimed Helen. 'How awful, I'm so sorry, Trevor. You poor man!'

Trevor flicked on the windscreen wipers, and instantly realised that what he thought was light drizzle on the windscreen was actually tears filling his eyes.

'Sorry, do you mind if I pull over for a minute?' he asked, and not waiting for an answer pulled into a lay-by and turned off the engine.

He reached into his jacket pocket for a tissue, and dabbed his eyes. 'I'm sorry,' he said, 'Every time I think about it, I start sniffling. Sorry!'

'You don't need to be sorry, Trevor,' Helen said softly, and Trevor saw tears were welling up in her eyes.

'Here,' Trevor said, handing Helen a fresh tissue. 'What a couple of softies we are,' he said, as they chuckled and wiped their eyes in unison.

'Right', said Trevor briskly, 'Sorry about the water-works.'

'There's no rush,' said Helen softly. 'What about your daughter? It must have been devastating losing her mother so young.'

'I don't know what I would have done without Becky,' replied Trevor. 'I tried to stay strong, but in fact she is my rock. It also helped that we had scores of animals to care for, find homes for cats and dogs, vet calls, farriers, food, deliveries – it all helped. And staff to supervise, phone calls all day, medicine rounds, meeting the public, we really didn't have time to properly grieve. That's what worries me about Becky. She seems so strong, but she was so close to her mum, I fear that sometime or another she will mentally collapse.'

Helen sighed and said, 'I can see what you mean Trevor, but often children can cope with such tragedies better than adults. I'm sure she can cope with just about everything that's been thrown at you both.'

'I do so hope you're right, Helen', said Trevor, before taking a deep breath and puffing out his cheeks in relief at the natural end of the discussion.

Trevor started the engine and pulled out onto the A30 going west.

'Right,' he said, 'Your turn. I hope you've got a happier story than me,' he laughed.

'Well, not very interesting. At college I studied public relations and politics, married David, a guy in the same fields and I even thought about trying for a Parliamentary seat. The trouble is I like bits of all the parties' policies, and don't like other bits, and being what most folk would call, an 'animal lover,' I eventually applied for a post in the RSPCA's PR department. At the interview, they asked me if I fancied being an area manager, as down here in the south west there were a lot of squabbling branches, threats of resignations – you know what it's like.'

'I can guess,' said Trevor. 'What about your husband, what does he do?'

'My ex-husband,' said Helen. We divorced after five years. He works in insurance – I can't think of anything more boring, but there's lots of perks. He wanted children and I didn't – at least not for a while.' Helen hesitated. 'We didn't really row. We still speak occasionally – we're still, well, I suppose you could say, friends, but he didn't much like my commitment to my job, sorting out problems between people he called, 'animal loving - people haters.'

So, that's my thrilling life story! David would have hated me being away for days on this sort of escapade – but I think it's great.'

They drove the rest of the way back to Milborne Port quietly digesting each other's stories.

Back at the car park they climbed out of the van feeling like conquering heroes. Helen called out to the members of the RSPCA team to come to the caravan and Trevor called Rebecca who had been busy telling members of the public the stories behind the fifteen horses ponies still calmly occupying the car park.

Helen and Trevor recounted their successful trip to the old Ferne estate, Helen's phone call to the Animal Defence Society and an agreement to accept the horses at the estate temporarily – if Patricia and her herd were actually going in that direction.

'We've also got some good news', said RSPCA vet Roger Hardy, 'The animal activists have offered to help us escort the horses on foot provided it's not into lorries back to Chard. They know we have to get the herd out of here tomorrow and they will be here at 8 o'clock in the morning. They have two vans and at least half a dozen people. They said they will go wherever the horses go.'

'No doubt they are the ones that have messed us about for the last few days,' said Trevor. 'But together with all of us, and the RSPCA volunteers, we can make this work – provided of course Patricia is actually making for her birth place at the old Ferne estate.'

Helen added, 'It's late in the day, so I suggest we all get some food and prepare for an early start tomorrow. So we've got Trevor's van and if necessary, his hired camper van. This caravan might be a problem – if we can't get a local volunteer to tow it. Must ring round for insurance for instance. We will need, short feed, hay and water or at least empty buckets we can fill on the journey. I will talk to the police about a possible route, though I suspect they want to wash their hands of us. We will try to figure out a route tonight, away from main roads.'

'What about the press?', asked Rebecca.

Helen replied, 'If they are around in the morning we'll have to tell them where we THINK we're going, and that we hope that horses agree!' Her companions greeted her summary with laughter. 'Glad we're all happy,' said Helen grinning.

Chapter 10

Gary Rorke was far from happy, but didn't show it when he said, 'Fancy a stroll, Tony? You lazy bugger, if you stay in that chair any longer, Jean will be charging you rent.'

'Leave him alone Gary. He did help with the washing up, which is more than you did!' responded Jean, wagging her finger at the former commando.

'What do you say, Tony?' Gary asked again.

'OK. I could do with a bit of fresh air', replied Tony standing up and stretching his arms before reaching for his coat

As the front door closed behind Gary and Tony, Jean noticed what she perceived as meaningful glances between those left in the room.

'What's going on?' Jean demanded.

Angie handed her aunt a leaflet. Jean quickly scanned the document and with a puzzled look on her face, peered at the young activists who were waiting to see her reaction.

'I don't understand it. What does it mean?'

Angie said, 'We don't know, auntie. Hopefully Gary will find out.'

A few yards from the house, Gary said to Tony, 'I wanted to have a chat with you Tony, without the others. There's a little communal garden up the road with a bench where we can chat.'

Tony was instantly worried, and said nothing until the pair reached a neat little garden and they sat down on a green slatted wooden bench. Without a word, Gary reached into the inside pocket of his waterproof coat, pulled out a crumpled leaflet and handed it to Tony.

The teenager looked at the picture and quickly read the text. He felt the blood drain from his cheeks as Gary simply stared him full in the face, still saying nothing. Tony looked at the leaflet again, and remained silent.

'OK Tony,' said Gary, 'What I want to know, is this. Have you had any conversations with the police about our actions over the past few days?'

'No, no, I promise, honest.'

'What about the copper who took you to the station and put you on the train. You told us that he paid your fare.'

'That was true, but all he did was warn me not to get a criminal record.'

'So what about this?' asked Gary, taking the leaflet out Tony's hand. 'You've never been involved in animal rights have you?'

'No,' said Tony miserably.

'You realise that you could cause us problems with the law – particularly me', Gary said emphatically. 'The police don't know that I have even been involved behind the scenes in this campaign. None of the others would tell anybody, but why should I believe that you wouldn't?'

Tony bent forward, looked down at his feet for a few seconds, and then straightened up. Looking into Gary's eyes he blurted out, 'Because, I would be in worse trouble with the law than you,' he said emotionally. 'What I'm going to tell you is the absolute truth, and you will see that I am not in any position to betray you.'

Gary was intrigued. 'OK, Tony, start with why you ran away from home eight months ago.....and don't give me any bullshit,' said Gary.

Tony began explaining his troubles at school and rows with his parents culminating in them finding him glue-sniffing in the garden shed. As his story flooded out he began to feel relief, but then became emotional as he told how he met the Bowen brothers and how Eddie treated him like a son, with endless humour and teasing – in stark difference to the grumpy impatience and awkward silences of his real father.

Tony hardly paused before telling of Eddie's plan to steal a horse from a sanctuary and how he and Rex waited by the gate, when suddenly it all went wrong. Tony's eyes welled up with tears, and he started talking more rapidly as he recounted how he and Rex heard Eddie shouting and a horse neighing while the other horses began thundering round the field in panic. Tony's throat began to close and he could hardly get the words out to describe how he and Rex found Eddie dead in the field and how the 'white horse' stood only a few yards away from Eddie's body.

'I was in a state Gary, I was puking everywhere and Rex had to stop me attacking the horse. It's the one that everybody says is the leader of the herd,' added Tony.

'OK Tony, take a break a minute,' said Gary. 'Here', he added, handing Tony a tissue. 'Sort yourself out.'

Tony blinked his tears away and blew his nose, before Gary asked, 'You OK to carry on?' Tony nodded. 'So what happened to this Rex?'

'He wanted to leave the Landrover and horse-box there. He reckoned we could get back to the travellers' site across country on foot and we could say we were there all night.'

'What?' interjected Gary, 'Leaving his brother dead in a field?'

'That's what I said,' said Tony, 'But Rex said he couldn't face jail again. I think he had a bad time last time he was locked up. I got the impression that he was roughed up by some of the prisoners and wardens looked the other way. Anyway, I didn't want to go back with him, but he gave me some money and we split up.'

'But what I don't understand, is why you are here, with us?' asked Gary.

Tony slipped his hand into his jacket pocket and withdrew the bone-handled knife that he had taken from Eddie's pocket as he laid dead in the mud.

'You won't like this,' Tony whispered, handing the knife to Gary.

'Try me,' growled Gary, opening up the clasp knife and taking a quick look round in case anyone was near.

'I wanted to kill the horse that killed Eddie,' he said.

'Jesus, Tony. Are you telling me that you hitched up with us in the hope that you would get a chance to kill a bloody horse?'

'I know, but I didn't know what I was doing, I thought you were all crazy.'

'Looking back, I realised that Eddie couldn't give a monkey's about me, he just thought I might be useful in some way. But I worshipped him and when he was killed I went mad. And at first I thought you were all stupid and I just couldn't get my head round about how you felt about animals.'

'But I gradually realised that you all saw me as a friend. I've never really had any friends at school. I've never had contact with animals, 'cause neither of my parents wanted pets. I gradually became to feel happy in your company, and when we watched the film and Robin on TV I suddenly understood how you all felt, and what you were campaigning for.'

Tony paused. 'I know that I've lied to you and pretending to be vegetarian and all that, but I have changed. You've all been great to me and I feel really guilty. But all I can do is apologise.'

Gary looked at the knife that Tony had handed him, and opened it to reveal the blade. 'When I was in the military, I was taught how to kill people with a knife. Do you reckon you could kill a horse with it?'

'Not now, but when Eddie was lying there in the mud, I was out of my mind, and I just ran at the horse, and Rex brought me down with a rugby tackle. So yes, looking back I wouldn't have got anywhere near the horse, but yes, I hated that horse more than I hated anything in my life. Now of course I'm ashamed of what I might have done and for lying to you all.'

Tony and Gary sat in silence for a several seconds and Gary closed the knife, and offered it back to Tony, who immediately put his hands up in desperation and said, 'No, I don't want it. You need to keep it because it is proof that I was in that field helping to steal a horse. You could take the knife to Rex who would confirm that it was his brother's knife and that would be proof that I was involved on that night.'

Gary was deep in thought turning the knife over and over in his hands. Suddenly he stood up - making Tony jump. He strode to the pavement, looked along the road and walked a few yards to a gutter and dropped the knife between the grill into the darkness. They both heard the 'plop'.

'Why did you do that, Gary?' asked Tony, his face a picture of confusion. Gary sat down on the bench, flashed a mischievous grin at Tony and joked, 'It had to go mate. The handle is bone – not vegan!'

Tony blurted out, 'But it was proof....' Gary still enjoying his 'vegan' joke, interrupted him. 'I don't need any proof. I believe every word you've told me. Now we ought to go back to Jean's. I won't tell them anything about what happened before you joined us. But, you have to go home to your parents. Jody and Clive have spoken to them and they are staying at the Bull Hotel in the town. Apparently your mum was in tears when she was handing out the leaflets. As far as I'm concerned you had family problems and you ran away to sort yourself out. I'll suggest to Jody and Clive that they to take you to the hotel and they can verify that you have been, what's the phrase? - trying to find yourself, and joined our animal rights campaign. '

Tony laughed and said, 'I dread to think what my dad will say about that!'

'Don't worry about that. If they came all the way down here to look for you, they care all right,' insisted Gary.

Tony nodded. 'I know that, but I will never be able to tell them or anybody else about what happened at the sanctuary.'

'We've all got secrets, Tony. You just shove them to the back of your brain – like a scene in a film or page in a book until they eventually fade.'

Gary rose from the bench, offered Tony his hand and hauled him to his feet. They walked in comfortable silence back to Jean's house.

*

When Gary and Tony walked into Jean's front room, they found that Robin and Caroline had returned from London following

Robin's impressive appearance on the Jeremy Bateson Show. The pair had obviously been put in the picture regarding Tony's parents' eight-month search and their distribution of leaflets, and there was an awkward silence as the activists wondered what had transpired between the former marine and the runaway teenager.

Gary immediately said, 'Right, Tony and me have had a chat. He would like Clive and Jody to take him as soon as possible to the Bull Inn to be reunited with his parents. When he gets back to his home, he'd like to contact us to see if there is a sab group in his area he can join. He's had a tough time, but he's an OK guy, and I'm sure we will see him again as an animal rights campaigner.'

Jean made everybody jump by clapping ferociously and in tangible relief everybody else joined in the applause.

'Well done, Gary.' whispered Ron as he manoeuvred past him to shake Tony's hand and hand him a card with his phone number.

'I'll put the kettle on,' said a delighted Jean.

Tony stood up, red-faced, and was close to tears as the room fell silent. 'I don't really know what to say. I'm sorry I've not been straight with you, and I couldn't have complained if you just chucked me out. All I can say is that you have changed my life. You have given me a cause that I can fight for. I'm dreading meeting my parents, because I gave them such as bad time, but I will be able to tell them that I have made a lot of friends with really good people. Thank you all so much, and especially you, Gary.'

An hour later, Tony, Clive and Jody walked in the reception area of the Bull hotel. The receptionist put a call through to Mr and Mrs Smith's room and in seconds a hysterical and weeping Mrs Smith came hurtling down the carpeted stairs, and literally threw herself at her son. Her husband felt more than a little embarrassment at the commotion, but as his wife relinquished her embrace of his only son, probably for the first time in his life, he threw his arms around Tony, and muttered a sincere, 'Welcome back, son.'

Clive and Jody smiled at each other and as they turned to leave and push through a small circle of intrigued hotel guests and staff, Mr Smith called out, 'Please don't go, we want to thank you for finding our son.'

'It's fine. Glad to help', said Jody, turning towards the door.

'No, no, I want to show you how grateful we are, please take this,' said Tony's father with a folded wad of bank notes in his hand.

'No, honest we don't want it.' repeated Jody.

Tony interrupted, 'Take it Jody, use it for the animals.'

Jody looked at her partner Clive for his thoughts, but he merely shrugged his shoulders. 'OK, if you insist,' said Jody as Mr Smith eagerly pushed the money into her hands and instantly clasped them firmly between both his hands in a genuine gesture of relief. After saying their goodbyes, Clive and Jody turned towards the hotel entrance. Tony and his parents walked towards the hotel restaurant, and Jody distinctly heard Tony say, 'By the way mum, I'm a vegetarian now.'

*

The next morning at 7am, Angie's auntie Jean was preparing breakfast for everyone, and neatly wrapping food parcels and filling flasks for the day, as Robin, Caroline, Ron, Angie, Clive and Jody, sleepily arranged themselves around the kitchen table. Henry the Labrador sat on the floor between Clive and Jody, his tail gently sweeping the floor as he anticipated a few treats off the table.

Clive looked around. 'Gary's late up.'

Jean turned towards the cooker to stir baked beans being heated in a saucepan. Over her shoulder, she said, 'Oh, he left at six…said he had to collect his gear and would catch up with you later.'

'He's so cloak and dagger!' laughed Ron. 'No doubt when we see him again, he will have a fifty pound rucksack on his back, three changes of clothes, a tool kit and half a dozen gadgets for his next project!'

By eight o'clock, the six activists had joined the bustle at the Milborne Park car park, coyly introduced themselves and were soon in earnest discussion with the RSPCA officials and volunteers – of whom a few recognised Robin and congratulated him on his performance on the Jeremy Bateson Show. Ever-present Press reporter Bob Rayburn also took the opportunity to conduct a quick interview with Robin who made it clear that their little band of activists were offering their full cooperation in assisting the RSPCA members and Ferne animal sanctuary manager Trevor James, in what was a really exciting experiment to discover whether Lady Patricia was consciously leading the herd to a destination in her mind.

The reporter quickly occupied the telephone box next to the car park, ringing the Press Association and a few other news outlets, having earlier been briefed by RSPCA team-leader Helen Watson and Trevor James on the plans for the day. Fortunately, the weather was set to remain fairly dry, with a chance of light drizzle as it had for the previous five days and with no sign of strong winds. Horses often become 'skitty' in gusty wind – the term 'got the wind under their tails' perfectly describes the sort of excitement in horses that could make travelling on roads difficult – even dangerous.

It had been decided that the horses would be shepherded out of the car park just after 9.15, when the school-run was mostly over. Meanwhile the straw was being swept up, buckets collected and a considerable amount of horse manure was being shovelled into wheel barrows, destined for local allotments.

Food for both horses and humans had been purchased and placed in the vehicles which consisted of a hired camper-van, an activists' transit van, Clive's window cleaning Vauxhall Viva, a couple of volunteer's cars, an RSPCA van and the Ferne Animal Sanctuary's vehicle. The caravan, hired as a temporary mini-headquarters, had been collected earlier by the hire company.

The horses were alert, ears twitching, eyes wide-open and nervously moving around the car park. At exactly 9.15 a.m the car park barrier was suddenly raised – briefly alarming the nearest couple of horses.

Helen Watson and Trevor James had worked out a route from the car park with the local police. It meant a brief excursion onto the A30 with the police temporarily halting the traffic, then escorting the horses onto the minor roads south of the village of Henstridge

LADY PATRICIA

and Henstridge Marsh (the original meaning of Henstridge is 'the ridge where stallions were kept') and thence onto the tiny village of Todber which is only five miles from Shaftesbury.

The minor roads run virtually parallel with the A30 and the hope was, that if Patricia was still leading the herd by the time they reached Todber, six miles or so from Milborne Port, it would give the unique convoy greater hope that she was indeed instinctively heading for her birthplace - the Ferne estate.

On the other hand, if Patricia changed direction, started to wander seemingly aimlessly or brought her herd to a full stop, then the game would be up and the only solution would be to try to hold them in a field, find transport for the herd back to Chard, and for Patricia, an inevitable date with a tranquilliser dart.

Trevor's sanctuary van and a police car moved a few yards away from the car park entrance and stopped side by side. Behind them, but leaving the car park entrance clear for the horses to exit onto the road, was another police car, followed by the two vans used by activists, the RSPCA van and a couple of volunteers' cars.

Except for the drivers of the convoy, all the other people involved had been told to move forward on foot as soon as Lady Patricia and her herd had exited the car park, and walk up on either side of the road to produce what could be described as a rolling human pedestrian escort.

The leading vehicles began to move forward slowly. Trevor's daughter Rebecca had been calling the herd out of the car park and she quickly ran to the sanctuary van and jumped into the passenger seat next to her father as Lady Patricia walked out past the car park barrier and into the road. The herd leader began to follow the front police car and the sanctuary van, and in a few seconds all fifteen horses were on the road. The vehicles behind them then moved slowly forward as the escorting pedestrians walked up on either side of the horses.

Helen Watson was alone driving the RSPCA van immediately behind the horses and within five minutes the entire convoy was on the A30 which had been closed to traffic by the police. 'Wow, that went well,' she said out-loud. The next stage was only a few minutes away – a right hand turn off the A30 into a narrow road. This involved the front police car stopping on the main road a few yards past the junction and four officers jumping out and unravelling a white plastic tape and spreading it across the road as a barrier.

Trevor had turned the sanctuary van off the A30 into the minor road and stopped 30 yards from the junction. Patricia had halted at white tape and turned her head to look into the narrow road where she could see the rear of the stationary sanctuary van. Trevor and Rebecca climbed out of the van and called to her. 'Come on Patsy, come on girl.' Patricia recognised their voices and after a brief hesitation began to lead the herd towards them.

Rebecca said, 'Dad, you drive off slowly and I'll walk with them.'

'Good idea Becky,' responded Trevor, climbing back into the van. 'I'll keep going slowly enough to bunch 'em up. If you want to get back in the van, you can catch me up.'

As he began to move off again he saw in his side mirrors that the whole herd had exited the main road, and the pedestrian teams were now lining both sides of the new narrower road. As the last horse's tail was off the A30, and Helen's RSPCA van had moved into the lane, in a flash the police reopened the main road and streams of vehicles were immediately zooming by.

In the quiet lane, with the sound of the A30 traffic fading, activists Ron and Angela trotted up to the front of the herd and joined Rebecca. 'Hi, Becky,' said Angela breezily. Rebecca recognised the two activists and frowned. 'I hope you aren't going to start chanting or waving banners,' said Rebecca snappily.

'No, no', said Angela quickly. 'And we're sorry about what was said when we first met. We felt bad about it afterwards – it was rude and uncalled for.'

Ron added, 'Yeah, all we want to do now is to help you get the horses to wherever they want to go.'

'OK,' said Rebecca, as she turned to walk backwards viewing the front row of the horses which were seemingly contentedly walking towards them a few yards away.

The convoy moved steadily along to the muffled clip-clops of sixty unshod hooves and the quiet conversations of the walking human chaperones. Trevor was delighted that all seemed to be going well as his daughter jogged up to his passenger door, neatly opened it and jumped in.

The village of Todber was less than six miles away. Trevor turned to Rebecca who was peering into the left-hand side mirror to view the horses. 'Becky I don't want to tempt fate, but we should be at Todber by lunchtime. I know they are not exactly galloping, but they will need a rest – and some food and water, before we try to calculate the best route from there to Ferne. Maybe a lay-by or something.'

'OK, dad,' responded Rebecca. 'Shall I jump out and warn the walkers and drivers of course, especially Helen, that we will be looking for a resting place, either near or just after the village.'

'I think that's right, don't you? asked Trevor.

'Absolutely, dad. See you later,' his daughter yelled as she climbed out of the van.

The morning went pretty well. There were a few hairy moments when vehicles including noisy farm tractors came in the opposite direction, but their drivers managed to pull close into the verges and gateways, switch off their engines and allow the procession to pass. A worse problem was excited horses and cattle in the fields either side of the lanes, charging along the fences and hedges, transmitting their excitement to Patricia's herd.

At one stage Trevor speculated with Rebecca that they might arrive at their destination with a dozen more horses than they left Milborne Port with, and even a few cows!

A couple of hours passed and the procession was nearing Todber. Out in front Trevor and Rebecca peered ahead hoping to see somewhere the herd could stop. 'Doesn't look good for a stopping place, Becky,' said Trevor. 'I think we should keep going through the village and see whether there's somewhere on the other side.'

Todber is a small village and the convoy was through it in no time, and attracting the attention of only a handful of locals. As they left the village, Rebecca shouted, 'There,' pointing ahead at a layby on the right hand side of the road, adjoining a very wide grass area separated from a field by a thick blackthorn hedgerow. 'Perfect,' responded her father, slowing almost to a halt. 'Out you go Becky. We can park all the vehicles in the layby and use them as a barrier to keep the horses on the grass verge.'

Rebecca leapt out and called to the pedestrians on the right hand side to stop walking and encourage the horses to move into the layby and the grass verge. Lady Patricia obliged and soon all the horses were neatly penned in by the vehicles with the escorting people filling the gaps between the vehicles.

Helen Watson came running up to Trevor. 'Trevor, I can't believe it is going so well.'

The sound of vehicle made them turn round as a Landrover pulled up next to them and a grinning, ruddy faced man stuck his elbow out of the driver's window. 'Heard you were coming this way,' he said. 'Do you need a hand with anything? That's my field just the other side of the hedge. There's a water trough there if you need it, if you're stopping here for a while?'

Trevor said, 'Oh terrific, thanks, Mr...?

'Just call me Danny, I've been fascinated with your story since you left Chard. I know the old Ferne and it was such a shame when the sanctuary had to shut down and move.

Trevor turned to his daughter. 'Becky, can you get the buckets out of the vans and organise some water from Danny's trough?' As his daughter walked off he shouted after her, 'Oh and find someone to help you break out a bale of hay too.'

As his daughter trotted off, Trevor clambered out of his seat and walked round to the Landrover driver's window and introduced himself and Helen to Danny, who climbed out and enthusiastically shook hands with both of them.

Trevor explained, 'Well, to answer your question, we really had no idea if we could get this far from Milborne Port without a problem, so we didn't dare think about getting through Shaftesbury. But now, I reckon we do have a good chance of getting to Berwick St John.'

'The police won't let you take this lot through Shaftesbury,' said Danny sweeping his arm to emphasise to size of the convoy.'

'We decided not to think about that in advance just in case the herd refused to cooperate, and we might have had to forget the entire idea,' explained Trevor.

Danny frowning, said, 'The roads up into Shaftesbury are steep, and traffic can be a nightmare. The police would probably want you to go south around the town to avoid the steep roads and the traffic.'

Helen put her hand on Trevor's arm. 'Trevor, we need to get a call into the police to see if they can escort us from here to Berwick St John.'

Danny spoke, 'Don't worry, look I'll nip home and telephone Shaftesbury police and tell them where you are and that you need to get to the other side of Shaftesbury.'

'Danny, you're a star,' said Helen, giving the farmer a gorgeous smile and squeezing his arm.

To his surprise Trevor felt a brief twinge of jealousy at the gesture.

'Will you be coming back?' Trevor asked Danny.

'No, I've got a few urgent jobs at the farm,' Danny replied. 'But I will call the police, and I wish you good luck.'

'Thanks Danny. We really appreciate your help,' said Trevor.

'No problem at all,' said the farmer, as he swung open his Landrover door and climbed in. As Danny drove off with a wave, Trevor and Helen wandered round the strange encampment. The RSPCA staff and volunteers, had been joined by the animal rights activists in carrying buckets of water from the trough in the field behind the hedge, and a bale of hay had been broken open and shaken out onto the grass verge.

Lady Patricia and her herd were calmly grazing as their human 'escorts' opened packets of sandwiches and flasks of tea and coffee and chatted amongst themselves. Trevor and Helen passed on the contents of the conversation with local farmer Danny who had offered to ring Shaftesbury police station and suggest the 'convoy' would need police assistance to get beyond Shaftesbury.

Forty minutes after Danny had left, a police panda car arrived at the scene from the direction of Shaftesbury. Sergeant Dennis Fletcher introduced himself and explained that local farmer Danny had suggested that the convoy of horses and vehicles would need police assistance. The Sergeant opened up a map and spread it on the warm bonnet of his Panda car as Trevor introduced him to RSPCA team manager Helen.

The policeman said, 'If you want to be sure to get to Berwick St John well before dark, you would need the shortest route and that would be through Shaftesbury itself, but that won't be possible I'm afraid, and anyway it would involve steep hills. I suggest that you go round the south of Shaftesbury and get moving as soon as possible.'

He pointed to a spot on the map and continued talking. 'The best way would be to go straight on through Stour Row…it's only a tiny place and it's only a couple of miles to the B3901 which goes to Shaftesbury. We can accompany you through the outskirts of the town and down to Cann and then onto Cann Common. Depending on how things go, you might find a place to hold your ponies for the night, and then it's only a couple of miles in the morning past Ludwell to the A30. We would have to close the main road briefly, but you would be on it for a few minutes and then you turn off onto the Berwick St John road. Ferne is only a few minutes down that road.'

Trevor and Helen had carefully followed the sergeant's finger all the way along the map. And they rose from leaning on the police car bonnet. 'That looks good,' said Helen.

'It all depends on the time,' replied Trevor. 'I think we should get back on the move as soon as possible. Even if we can get no further than Cann Common today, it would be good to get to Ferne tomorrow morning. It will mean sleeping in our vehicles, and setting up teams to watch the horses during the night. It wouldn't be funny if they disappeared overnight!'

Helen held up both hands in mock alarm and said, 'Oh Trevor, please don't say that – even in jest!'

'Sorry', grinned Trevor as Helen mischievously waved her fist at him.

Helen asked him, 'How many people have we got? There's me you and Becky, two of my inspectors, and our vet, there are half a dozen animal rights folk and probably a dozen RSPCA volunteers – that's if they don't go home later. Let's say twenty people and seven or eight vehicles. So we should be able to have at least three teams of half a dozen people to take it in turns during the night to watch the horses.'

'That should be enough,' said Trevor. 'We will have to sleep in our vehicles. But we should enquire now whether any of the volunteers are planning to go home this evening. Becky, do you want to run round and tell everybody the plan and see if we are going to lose any volunteers this evening. I'll start picking up the buckets and checking the horses.'

He turned to Sergeant Fletcher who had been listening to the conversation and taking a few notes. 'Sorry sergeant. Does all that sound all OK to you?'

The policeman replied, 'Yes, I'm off back to the station. Just keep going straight and we will be waiting to clear your way around the outskirts of Shaftesbury and down to Cann Common. We should also be able to call in a couple of times during the night to see whether everything is OK. You're wise not to try and get all the way to Ferne today.'

He glanced at his watch, and said, 'If you can get on the way soon, you have a good chance of you being at Cann Common by four o'clock. There won't be much daylight left on a dull day like this.'

'Thanks Sergeant,' chorused Trevor and Helen, as the policeman climbed into his Panda Minii-Minor, waved, swung round in the road and drove off towards Shaftesbury. Trevor looked at Helen, and muttered, 'So he reckons this is a dull day!'

*

The equine and human convoy was back on the road just before one thirty, with Rebecca calling forward herd leaders Patricia, Gregory and Lucky. Helen's RSPCA van and Trevor's Ferne van led the way, with the walking escorts either side of the horses and half a dozen vehicles at the back. There was also an old grey Renault a few yards behind the convoy with reporter Bob Rayburn looking out for any phone boxes from which he could relay regular up-to-date reports on the equine exodus to his media contacts.

Soon the convoy swept through the small village of Stour Row drawing a handful of villagers watching in silence. By 2.45pm the procession approached the junction with the B3091 where Sergeant Fletcher was waiting outside his Panda car with two policemen astride motorcycles. Trevor pulled up next to the Sergeant and wound down his window. The officer said, 'We've found you a field for the horses at Melbury Abbas. It's next to Cann Common, – where they have their village fete so there's also hard-standing for your vehicles. So follow us, and if you can keep the horses going, you should be there by half three.'

The Panda car and one of the two motor cycles pulled out thirty yards in front of the convoy while the second motorcycle waited for the procession to pass and then moved out into the centre of the road with its lights flashing to defend a space behind the last cars. There was a brief halt while the police held up traffic to allow the equine convoy safely onto the B3091 road, and another wait at a further roundabout to switch onto the neighbouring B3081 and on towards Cann Common.

After one and a half miles, the procession proceeded through Cann Common, and police Sergeant Fletcher stood in the centre of the road directing Trevor's and Helen's vans to turn right into a narrow village street. Ten minutes later they reached the village of Melbury Abbas, where two more police officers stood pointing to a field entrance with its gate wide open.

A couple of dozen residents had turned out to greet the procession, and a few of them signalled to Trevor and Helen to drive into the field and turn left to stop on some gravelled hard-standing. Trevor, Helen and Rebecca jumped out of their vehicles just in time to see a nervous-looking Patricia stop immediately in the gateway. Trevor and his daughter ran into the field and called to Patricia to follow them. The herd leader hesitated and faced the field suspiciously as Gregory and Lucky, being jostled by the bulk of horses behind them, joined Patricia in the gateway. With encouraging calls from Trevor and Rebecca, Patricia pursed her lips and nickered, and carefully trotted forward, the herd following her into the field. The drivers of the rest of convoy vehicles drove into the field and parked on the hard standing. The walking escorts hovered together in a bunch once the gate was closed, and stood chatting and congratulating each other on a successful day.

In the gathering gloom, Patricia trotted around the field boundary fence, followed by her herd. Activists Clive and Jody wandered over to their friends. 'What now, Ron?' asked Clive.

Ron shrugged, 'I don't know, but I think we should stay until the horses are at Ferne – assuming that is where they finish up.'

'Oh, I agree', said Caroline. 'Let's see this through. I've really enjoyed it – it's even been interesting talking to the RSPCA people. Not exactly animal rights pioneers, but pretty OK.'

'So are we staying here all night?' asked Robin. 'I'm bloody starving.' The other five activists grunted their agreement.

Robin spoke, 'Tell you what, let's join the others and see what they are going to do. Some might be going home, but hopefully most of them will stay to complete the journey tomorrow.'

As they mingled with the RSPCA officials and volunteers, they were joined by some of the villagers, who pointed out a water-tap fixed to a post near the entrance to the field. Suddenly a cheer came from some of the throng, as two men arrived pushing a large metal tea-urn, and two ladies carried trays of sandwiches and slices of cake. A table was produced and loaded with plastic cups, pots of milk and bowls of sugar.

Angela whispered to Robin, 'This is when you wish you weren't a vegan.'

Robin leaned forward to check out the sandwiches. One of the ladies saw him peering, and assured him, 'Fresh ham and cheese sandwiches, and one of my jam and cream cakes.'

'Oh thank you, but we've brought our own food,' lied Robin. 'We'll just have a cup of tea with sugar, but no milk.'

'Help yourself', said the lady. 'This is the tea urn we use on our fete day – it really keeps the tea hot.'

'You didn't tell her you were vegan, did you?' whispered Angela.

'No, of course not,' answered Robin quietly, handing a plastic cup of hot tea to Angie. 'She probably wouldn't have a clue what a vegan is! It wouldn't be fair to make her feel awkward.'

'You're such a nice man Robin,' said Angie, giving him a peck on the cheek.

Jody joined them. 'There's bugger-all we can eat,' she complained quietly. 'I don't know whether there is a chippy in the village, but there will be in Shaftesbury. Why don't we ask the RSPCA people if they want some chips – our treat. We've got the hundred quid that Tony's dad gave us.'

'Problem is,' uttered Ron, 'what if they ask us to get fish or meat burgers. We'll have to explain that we are vegans. They are animal welfare people - they should know what vegan means.'

'What if one of them comes with us and buys their own fish or whatever?' asked Angie. Shaking his head, Ron said, 'But we will be carrying those animal products. Wouldn't a vegan be a hypocrite if he was a lorry-driver transporting livestock for slaughter?'

'Bloody hell,' said Jody, 'When you go vegan everything gets so sodding complicated.'

Ron replied, 'I vote we tell them we are going to town for chips and offer to pay for them. If they ask for fish or any other animal products, we will just have to explain why we can't do that. I mean they've got their own transport, and the village has given them sandwiches – which we can't eat!'

'I agree' said Robin. 'Let's play it that way. We'll offer to collect chips for everybody and pay for them. Jody, you've got the money. And Clive's van is nearest the gate.'

While these discussions were taking place, Trevor, Helen and a couple of RSPCA inspectors were filling buckets with water, and spreading a bale of hay along a fence. The RSPCA vet and Rebecca, were looking for any signs of injury or other health problems with the horses.

Clive and Jody rushed over to the RSPCA volunteers with an offer to pay for chips from town. This idea was very popular and Clive hastily scribbled down the orders in the note-book that he kept for his Dorchester window cleaning customers. A few volunteers asked for fish or burgers, but Clive and Jody stated that the money was donated by a man who was opposed to eating animal products, and quickly moved on ignoring those who offered to come with them and pay for fish or meat pies. Clive muttered that his van was not insured for passengers and he merely pretended not to hear people who offered him extra money for fish or meat pies.

As Jody opened the gate to allow Clive to drive out of the field, he was confronted by a tractor towing a trailer with three blue portable toilets strapped vertically on the back. The tractor stopped to let him out and as Clive drove off, the RSPCA's manager Helen Watson strode forward to the tractor cabin window. The driver shouted, 'We keep this for our summer fetes, but you might as well make use of them for a night.'

'Oh wow, thanks so much. What's your name?' asked Helen.

'I'm Tom,' he replied.

'We're very grateful, Tom. They'll be much appreciated I'm sure,' said Helen, having to shout over the sound of the tractor's diesel engine;

'It's OK', said the tractor driver, 'I'll drive in and maybe you can get a bit of help get 'em off the trailer. I'm only up the road, so I'll leave the tractor here.'

As soon as the blue toilets were wrestled onto the ground and erected along the fence, a queue began to form, but had to wait while a hose-pipe was attached to the tap near the gate, and the toilet reservoirs and cisterns primed for use. Several of the men had already sneaked off to the far end of the darkening field to relieve themselves, so Helen quickly labelled the nearest toilet, 'Ladies Only'.

An amused Trevor saw her pinning up the notice. She saw his

smirk and shouted, to cheers from the women, 'We know what poor aims you men have. We country ladies don't want to paddle about in your pee, thank you.'

An hour or so later Clive and Jody returned with a score of large portions of chips, double wrapped to stay warm. Tom's trailer freed of its blue toilets, was quickly covered with a large plastic sheet and became a large table for the assembly, which consisted of a unique collection of 'animal people' in a joint mission, with a wide variety of views on animal welfare and animal rights, plus a few interested residents of Melbury Abbas. As the sandwiches and chips disappeared, and the tea-urn remained fully employed, conversations rumbled well into the night.

Trevor and Helen had made sure that everybody knew that at 8.30 in the morning, the police would be arriving to prepare for the last leg of the journey to Lady Patricia's birthplace – the Ferne estate.

'I wonder what happened to Gary?' speculated Ron, sat in the driver's front seat of his Transit van.

Angie, sitting next to him, shrugged. 'He said he was collecting his gear from wherever he hid it. Maybe someone else found it.'

'I doubt it. I suspect he may have hitched back to Northampton to his sab group, after all, the fox hunting season has started.' said Ron.

In the back of the van on a double mattress, lay Robin and Caroline. Hearing the conversation in the front seats, Robin said, 'I reckon you're right Ron. Maybe he had organised a lift home with Iain Poller from Bristol.'

'I dare say he'll be giving some poor huntsman a bad time sooner or later,' added Caroline. She continued, 'Ron, what are we going to do if the horses do go back to the old Ferne place?' asked Robin.

'Well, if they go in there voluntarily.' Ron replied, 'by which I mean if the grey mare goes in voluntarily…'

Angela interrupted again, 'Her name is Lady Patricia, have a bit of respect.'

'Yes, I know.' said Ron, pretending to be a little irritated, 'As I was saying if Lady Patricia goes in there willingly I reckon we've done our bit. It's her choice.'

'But, I reckon they will eventually be taken back to the sanctuary at Chard,' said Robin.

'Maybe,' said Caroline. 'But I think we've done well. The experiment Robin talked about on the Bateson Show has been completed, showing that a leader of a herd of horses and ponies not only remembers where she was born, but instinctively knows how to get there. It's fantastic really, but I don't think we can do anything more.'

'On the other hand,' said Caroline. 'What if she refuses to follow the plan?'

'Oh you of little faith,' said Robin.

'We will soon find out,' said Ron. 'I vote we get some sleep and see how it goes tomorrow. The TV programme was fantastic publicity for us – we should be chuffed.'

Soon the van was silent except for Robin's snores.

*

Eight o'clock the next morning, the tea urn was being put to good use, as were the blue toilets. Two police motor-cycles and Sergeant Fletcher's Panda car had arrived.

The sergeant quickly found Trevor, Helen and Rebecca each clasping hot cups of tea. 'Morning sergeant,' said Helen. 'Want a cuppa?'

'No thanks. I'm fine. By the way, I've been to Ferne this morning and spoke to the guy in the gate house. I told him, that if all goes well, we will be there sometime between ten and eleven. He will be watching out, ready to open the main gates and then another gate into the first field on the right. He's going to park his car across the track that goes up to the old Ferne buildings just to be sure they go into the first field. There's plenty of grass and working water troughs.'

'That's great sergeant,' said Trevor. 'We're virtually ready to move off, and I've still got a couple of hay bales in my van.'

'That's good,' said the Sergeant, and continued, 'You have to go out through the village the way you came in, but you will have to turn right at the main road instead of left. From there it's not much more than a mile to a turning on the left marked Ludwell, which is then almost straight to Ferne.'

Trevor winced. 'If Patricia knows where she is going, as the crow flies, she might want to turn left. Turning right out of the village is going away from the A30. Patricia may refuse.'

'Don't worry, we will make sure they go right,' said the policeman. 'You've got enough people to make sure of that, and we have two men on bikes.'

Trevor's daughter Rebecca came trotting up, followed by RSPCA vet Roger Penman. 'All nags present and correct, Dad,' said Becky.

'Right,' said Trevor, as the members of the human escort gathered, wrestling with knapsacks, and dropping plastic cups and chip wrappings into a large litter bin which had magically appeared, near Tom's trailer.

'Please gather round,' called Trevor. 'The same process as before, people either side of the horses. My van and Helen's at the front, other vehicles at the back. The police will clear the way as they did yesterday. We are going back through Cann Common village and we are turning right onto the main road, but only for a mile and then first left towards towards Ludlow.'

Helen stepped forward and said loudly, 'Remember, if you think there may be something wrong with any of the horses, Roger, our RSPCA vet will be in his car at the back and Rebecca, Trevor's daughter, will be walking on the left. So is everybody ready?'

A muffled cheer emanated from the crowd. But as they turned away, Trevor, said, 'Before you go, please show your appreciation to Tom for his trailer and the toilets, and the ladies of the village for their tea and sandwiches. Without them it would have been a miserable night. And can I also say thank you to our young activists for supplying us with chips last night.'

As a short round of applause faded, Ron whispered to Angie, 'That's the first thing I've been applauded for in my life! Who'd have bloody thought it would be for sharing chips.'

*

Helen's RSPCA van and Trevor's sanctuary van, led the way as Rebecca called the horses to the gate. The escorts formed their lines either side of the road, and Patricia led the herd through the gate and trotted behind the two vans. The convoy slowed to a walk in the village and was stopped by the police at the junction with the main road.

'This is it,' thought Trevor as the police waved him and Helen into the junction turning right. Patricia hesitated and the herd bunched up behind her. Trevor could see in his wing mirror that his daughter was standing in the middle of the road to the right, calling the horses. To his relief he saw Patricia move into the right turn, waving her head and flicking her tail as she moved forward.

'Phew.' said Trevor, as he peered through his offside window to the left to see Helen grinning back at him through her wound-down window. She mockingly pretended to wipe the sweat off her brow in relief. At the walking pace of the horses of around four miles an hour, the convoy followed two police motorcyclists who stayed well ahead to warn approaching vehicles and direct them to pull in and stop until the procession passed.

In twenty minutes the convoy reached the left hand turn signposted Ludwell, and steadily moved into the narrow lane without any problems, soon passing to the west of the village and on towards a junction with the A30. The police had closed the road using plastic tapes and a couple of panda cars, but before the horses travelled the last hundred yards to the junction, the police drove out into the A30 and closed it in both directions

In a matter of yards, there was another junction immediately on the right and the convoy moved smoothly off the A30 and onto the road towards the village of Berwick St John. Behind the procession the police quickly re-opened the busy A30 as the front of the equine procession proceeded round a slow right-hand bend, with the RSPCA and Sanctuary vans leading the way.

As they approached the entrance to the Ferne estate, Trevor and Helen were amazed at the sight of a huge crowd of people blocking the road about thirty yards past the entrance to the Ferne parkland. A television camera crew filmed the convoy approaching and a smiling Joe and Clare stood by the open gate next to their gate lodge.

Helen and Trevor drove their vans slowly past the entrance and parked their vehicles in front of the crowd. They both quickly climbed out to stand together watching the herd approach. Lady Patricia trotted towards them, staring at the crowd beyond Helen and Trevor. Then the grey mare turned her head, surveyed the open gate to her birthplace, threw her head high and with a loud neigh, galloped through the gateway, with tail held high. She slowed to a trot as she approached Joe's car parked across the track, but then saw the wooden gate wide open to the field on the right hand side.

With another loud neigh she charged into the field and galloped chaotically up the inclined field, with her herd equally excited galloping after her. Patricia threw herself down and rolled on her back, first to the left and then to the right. She scrambled to her feet, shook herself and trotted further up the inclined field, followed by her herd.

The crowd had rushed from the road and into the track and stood fascinated at the sight of oddly matched highly excited horses. The television crew were quick to capture the antics of the horses and, pleased with the footage, carried their camera back to where Trevor and Helen stood leaning on the post and rail fence, with their arms around the shoulders of a beaming Rebecca.

Gate lodge residents Joe and Clare Turner joined them – all smiles. Joe was wiping his eyes. 'You OK, Joe?' queried Helen.

'Silly old bugger,' said Clare grinning. 'Soft as putty he is.'

'Oh Joe,' said Helen, putting her arm affectionately round his shoulder.

'It's just that I never thought I'd see them again,' said Joe blinking furiously. 'My favourite was Patrick – gentle giant. And look at Patsy there, happy as Larry she is. When they tried to get her into a lorry to take them all down to Chard, I had to walk away.

She fought like a tiger and the loaders were not very pleasant. I couldn't watch it. It was horrible.'

Helen gave Joe another hug and asked him, 'Joe, we were surprised to see that huge crowd at the gate when we arrived. I assume they are local folks.'

Joe replied, 'Yes, they're from the village. The fact is, the folk round here worshipped the Duchess. She used to invite everybody to visit the sanctuary whenever they wanted. When she died, everybody assumed that the Animal Defence Society would keep the sanctuary going, but they couldn't keep all the Duchess's gardeners, her housekeepers and handymen, butler and all. And then the death duties and the courts got involved – the big house was demolished, and the whole estate just rotted. So the animals were gradually rehomed, until the Sanctuary went to Chard with the horses and a handful of cats that could not be homed.'

'All very sad,' said Joe. 'And we still don't know what Animal Defence is going to do with the estate. Probably finish up with developers fighting over it.'

'Shame,' said Helen. 'Such a beautiful place.'

'Come in and have a cup of tea,' said Clare. 'And after, we'll take you up the track and you can have a look round. You'll be able to visualise what the place was like in its heyday.'

'OK' replied Trevor. 'But we must move our vans off the road and thank everybody who helped us get the horses here. It was a pretty remarkable journey! You coming Helen?'

'Too true Trevor. I've got to thank my RSPCA people for all their efforts… especially our volunteers from Milborne Port.'

The villagers of Berwick St John were beginning to walk back down the track to the main gate and make their way back to the village, most probably for a lunchtime drink or two at the Talbot Inn in the village to chat about the return of the horses and reminisce about the Duchess of Hamilton's wartime sanctuary.

The six animal rights activists wandered down the track to the road amongst the local villagers and the RSPCA crowd. Robin muttered, 'Does anyone else feel a sense of anti-climax?'

'I know what you mean,' Ron answered, 'It's because we know

the horses will almost certainly go back to Chard, and that probably their leader won't cooperate and will be knocked out with an anaesthetic dart.'

'Oh come on,' Angela said, 'We originally got involved to make people think about animal liberation, and it was our involvement that got Robin on national TV to explain animal rights.'

'Angie's right,' said Caroline. 'The problem is that when we sabotage hunts, we can sometimes save the life of an animal. We know they will be after it again, but we go home knowing satisfied that it was not caught that day and that hunters were pissed off with us. This operation was different – we got involved to promote animal liberation for domestic animals – and again we succeeded for a while.'

The group got back to Ron's Ford transit van, parked parallel next to Clive's Vauxhall Viva van - his window-cleaning ladders still fixed on the roof. The activists executed a group hug, climbed into their respective vehicles and solemnly waving to the RSPCA folk, they set off.

The RSPCA volunteers who had walked all the way from Milborne Port to Lady Patricia's birth-place were invited to cram in the various vehicles for lifts home. The police motor-cyclists kicked their bikes into action and waved as they sped off back towards the A30 and Shaftesbury.

Only the RSPCA van and Trevor's Ferne Sanctuary van were left in sudden silence in the Ferne estate lay-by area. Trevor, Rebecca and Helen were invited into the Gate Lodge by Clare while her husband Joe padlocked the front gate. The three guests flopped silently and exhausted onto the sofa.

Clare emerged from her kitchen with a huge fruit cake, and placed it on the table. As Joe came in and hung the main gate key on a hook on the back of the lounge door. Clare handed out plates to everyone, bearing large chunks of sliced fruit cake. 'Tea's brewing,' she said, and the trio at last broke the silence with a chorus of grateful sighs.

'Wow, lovely cake!' said Helen sinking her teeth into a slice held in her right hand, and using her left hand as an extra plate to catch the crumbs. 'You'll have to give me the recipe, Clare.'

'Of course', replied Clare. 'It was Joe's mother who gave it to me – she was worried that I'd starve him', she chuckled.

*

Twenty minutes later all five of them walked up the track, watched suspiciously for a few seconds by the horses, before returning to grazing

'My favourite was Big Patrick,' said Joe. 'Let's see if he remembers me,' he added, cupping his hands around his mouth, and calling slowly, 'Hey Patrick, hey Patrick, hey Patrick.'

Patrick raised his head with a tuft of grass in his motionless jaws. Turning his head towards the group of humans leaning on the fence, he allowed the tuft of grass to drop and plodded towards the five.

'Oh bugger', said Joe, 'I used to give him a carrot every day – I hope he doesn't take offence.'

'How long ago was it that the horses were moved from here', asked Helen.

'When was it, Clare?' asked Joe.

'It was 1974, three years ago,' she answered.

'Horses never fail to amaze me,' said Rebecca as Big Patrick came to the fence and nickered. 'He obviously remembers your voice, Joe.'

Joe reached up and stroked Patrick's head,

'Hello old boy. I'm sorry I forgot your carrot – I'll get you a couple later.'

'Silly old bugger,' tutted his wife..

The group left Patrick with his head over the top rail of the fence and walked on up to the end of the concrete track where the massive foundations of the old Duchess's stately home were all that remained of the house – and even they were covered in weeds.

'Blimey,' exclaimed Helen, 'It must have been huge – what a shame.'

They walked on into a large farm-yard surrounded with semi-derelict farm buildings and cottages, all gradually collapsing as nature was doing its best to replace them with trees, shrubs and ivy. They wandered a bit further and came to huge high barn, which had a four foot high brick wall all round, with a single iron gate.

'The Duchess had this built solely for the purpose of allowing all her livestock and the horses to shelter from the bad weather, whether rain, wind or hot sun and flies. The floor was always covered in a least a foot of straw and the troughs were self-filling,' explained Joe, pulling the gate open.

'And that building over there,' said Joe pointing to the right, 'was built as a cows' maternity unit. In the war the Duchess was ordered by the government to have a dairy herd for the war effort, so she had this built so that her cows could calve indoors.

'Over there,' said Joe turning, and pointed again to another brick building on the other side of the yard, but slightly laid back. That was the slaughter-house she had built, because she refused to allow any of her animals to be killed elsewhere.'

Clare said, 'Did you know that the National Farmers Union and young farmer groups used to come and see how she operated? And of course there was a huge walled market garden with lots of greenhouses built along one wall. She employed several gardeners and three or four women for the laundry house – all derelict now of course.'

'Shame, a real shame,' said Helen. 'I suppose with death duties so high after the war, there must be many such places around the country. Let's hope that whatever happens to the estate, it will reflect the Duchess's compassion, somehow.'

Trevor was looking around with his mind set on the security of the horses. He noticed another gate with an overgrown grassy track beyond it, leading in the opposite direction to the track they had walked from the Gate lodge.

'Oh, that's a back way into the estate,' said Joe. 'It goes round the south boundary to a road where there is a permanent gate. It was only used for bringing in supplies like animal feed and equipment, so as not to disturb the folk and their visitors in the big house.'

Trevor wandered over to the gate and tugged at the chain and rusty padlock. Satisfied that the lock was so old and rusted that it would never yield to a key, he strolled back to the others and they all made their way back out of the yard and back down the track to the Gate lodge.

Back at the gate lodge, Joe raced in grabbed a couple of carrots from the vegetable rack and ran puffing up the track to give them to Big Patrick, while Clare insisted on more tea and cake for Helen, Trevor and Rebecca.

Joe returned, happy that Patrick had taken his carrots and he and Trevor went outside to discuss the problem of getting the horses back to the sanctuary at Chard.

'I'll sort out transport,' said Trevor. 'I will have to bring a vet to dart Patricia and this time we won't have anybody interfering – I think the animal lib project is over.'

Joe said, 'Clare and me will keep an eye on the herd and call you if there are any problems. If you put your two hay bales inside the gate, I'll enjoy feeding them again – and they'll have access to the big barn up in the yard. Just let me know a day or so before you bring the lorries.'

'You're a star, Joe, and so is your wife. I'll just pull the hay bales out of my van and put them inside the gate. I'm hoping that we will get the horses home within the week, but I'll keep you informed.'

'Do you need a hand with the bales?' asked Joe.

'No, you go in and I'll do that.' A few minutes later Trevor had dragged the two hay bales out of the rear door of his van, and placed them next to the gate to the lodge. He dusted himself down and returned to the lounge. 'Right folks, he said, 'It's time we let these kind folks get on with their lives.'

'Your right Trevor, said Helen. 'We should be on our way'.

Joe and Clare stood up and Clare said. 'Well it's been lovely to meet you – it's a day we won't forget in a hurry.'

Helen pecked Joe and Clare on their cheeks, 'And we won't forget that cake in a hurry. And thanks for the recipe Clare,' she added, patting her pocket.

The five of them exchanged hugs and emerged from the lodge.

Trevor, Helen and Rebecca walked to the two vans and Helen hesitated at the rear of her RSPCA van.

'Well it's been great working with you two. I hope you manage to get the horses home.'

'Yes, we couldn't have got here without your help, Helen,' said Trevor, extending his hand to shake Helen's.

'Glad to help. Let me know if we can help you with anything,' replied Helen, a little pensively. She turned to Rebecca and gave her a brief hug. 'You've been terrific Becky, it's been a pleasure. OK, I'm off back to work,' she said opening her van door.

'See you,' breezed Trevor, opening his van door and climbing in.

His daughter Rebecca looked furious as she opened the passenger door and leaned in.

'Dad, what the hell are you doing?' she said in a hoarse whisper.

Trevor looked at her in surprise.

'What's the matter?' he asked.

'What's the matter? What's the matter? Quick, get out and invite her down to the sanctuary for a few days.'

'Oh, I don't know,' said her father.

'Dad, if you let her drive off without asking her to visit us, I will get out and walk back to Chard. I mean it.'

Trevor knew full well from the look on his daughter's face that he had no choice.

'OK! OK!', he said, opening his door just as Helen started her engine.

He waved a hand and ran the few steps to the RSPCA van. Helen wound down the window and said, 'Problem, Trevor?'

'Er no, we just wondered whether you fancy coming down to the sanctuary for a couple of days. We've got plenty of room.....it's Becky's idea,' he blurted - slightly blushing.

'I'd love to, Trevor. I've got a few days leave to fit in. I'll call you...and thank Becky for me!' she added knowingly.

'That's good. I'll let you know when we've got the horses home.' said Trevor, stepping away from Helen's van.

As Helen put her van in gear and moved slowly off, she waved to Rebecca – both of them with big grins on their faces.

Trevor put his van in gear and pulled out onto the road. He turned to look at his daughter, who stared ahead expressionless – while out of the corner of her eye she saw her father wagging his finger at her.

Chapter 11

Gary Rorke awoke with a start and instantly turned on his torch just in time to see a rat scamper away from his rucksack. 'Find your own bloody food, Ratty,' he called as the rodent vanished through a hole at the bottom of the door. Except for his thick coat he had used as a pillow, he emerged from his sleeping-bag fully clothed, pulled on his boots and checked his watch. The luminous dial revealed that it was 7.30am.

With his torch still piercing the darkness, he took two steps to the door of the old shed and pulled it open. The shed was attached to a crumbling single-storey cottage, the walls of which were almost completely covered in ivy, and which had a roof which was full of gaping holes pierced through the tiles by fallen branches. One huge branch had smashed through the roof and stood at an angle on the stone floor of the cottage.

He had arrived at the estate at 11am the previous day, and from the foundations of the former mansion he watched through his binoculars as the horses filed through the main gate and into the field alongside the track. He had entered from the opposite side of the estate, following a grassy track that led to the yard and the large field shelter at the centre of the estate. He was amused to see that the crowd that greeted the return of the horses, included his activist friends and the RSPCA and Ferne Animal Sanctuary contingents.

He watched as the horses were shepherded from the road onto the sloping track, and then through a gate into the adjacent field. He continued to watch as the crowds dispersed, and a little later as he saw his friends drive away in their vans – no doubt back to Milborne Port and 'Auntie Jean' - their mission accomplished. Then he saw the gate-keeper and his wife, walking up the track with Trevor, Rebecca and Helen, so before they entered the central yard he slipped into the bushes behind the large barn where he was close enough to hear their conversation.

When the five of them returned to the gate lodge, Gary waited until he saw the Ferne and RSPCA vans leave and the gate-keeper finish putting out hay for the horses. 'Maybe it's time to go home to my long-suffering wife,' he thought to himself guiltily, but he had been intrigued by some of the conversation he'd overheard as he hid behind the barn, while Joe and Clare, explained the sad history of the estate to Trevor, Rebecca and Helen.

What he heard decided him to spend half an hour or so to explore the estate a bit more deeply. He found his way through a collapsed section of an eight foot high brick wall which he found was the boundary wall of the vast original kitchen gardens – now an impenetrable jungle of waist-high grass, nettles, saplings and shrubs. Along one wall were several huge decomposing greenhouses full of weeds and saplings. There wasn't a single pane of glass still intact in any of them.

Clambering back out through the gap in the garden wall, he found what appeared to be a row of workshops next to another crumbling cottage with green mouldy windows. Plunging back into the trees he found another three wrecked cottages and a trace of an old path leading to a low stone pillared doorway into what appeared to be a cave. After ducking his head in the low entrance, he flashed his torch around the walls and roof of the cave. The cave was dome-shaped and brick-lined. He suddenly remembered from somewhere in the back of his mind, that from the 1600s many members of the aristocracy had built 'ice caves' to store ice for preserving perishable food and drink. Ice would have been collected in the winter and stored in the 'ice-houses' for the summer. Even without the ice, the cave was incredibly cold and Gary was pleased to get back into the open.

He made his way back to the derelict cottage and the rotting shed that he had shared with a rat the previous night. He collected his rucksack, carried it into the yard and opened it on a low wall. He took out a plastic box holding half-a-dozen muesli bars and a small bottle of fruit juice. He grabbed three of the bars, stripped off the packaging and munched as he wandered into the central yard. He peeped round the edge of a building to look down the track to see if anyone was about, and saw that the horses were spread out and peacefully grazing in the long field that reached from the main gate to the yard at the centre of the estate.

While he ate, he tried to imagine the estate in its heyday – it was obviously a thriving concern for many generations. As a socialist, he didn't have much time for the privileged aristocracy, mainly because of their bloodsports, but what he'd learned of the Duchess of Hamilton was impressive – certainly her instant decision to offer her home, as a sanctuary for the animals of Londoners at the outbreak of war.

What Gary didn't know was that when the Duchess died early in 1951 she had left the estate in perpetuity to the Animal Defence Society which she had founded, and wanted the estate to remain as an animal sanctuary. She realised that her mansion would have to be sold, but unfortunately the severe restrictions she placed on the use of the house ended with courts deciding that the estate, buildings and land should become the property of the Animal Defence Society and that the Ferne Animal Sanctuary was a separate body occupying the estate.

Gary looked around at the tragic state of the buildings estate. 'So,' Gary spoke to himself as he often did, 'The dreaded aristocracy creates a wonderful compassionate thriving place during a world war, and afterwards it's handed over to animal welfare people, and they turn it into a derelict dump....very sad!'

He closed his plastic food box, pushed it into his rucksack and fastened the straps. 'Well Gary, I think it's time we went home,' he said, lifting the rucksack with his right arm and swinging it onto his shoulder. Suddenly from behind him he heard a snort. He spun round to see Lady Patricia standing alone and staring at him in the wide entrance to the yard.

'Hello, old girl,' Gary said, moving towards the grey mare. Patricia nickered at him, as he ran his hand down her neck. She had recognised the scent of the man who had appeared in her herd's exodus. 'Well, you got here girl…quite an adventure. You've got your way and you've got your herd. Be happy.'

He patted her neck, walked quickly past her to the metal gate, climbed it, paused on top of the gate to look back at the horse, and dropped to the ground. As he began to walk down the grassy track beyond the gate by which he entered the estate the previous day, he heard a clanging noise and turned.

Patricia was pawing the gate with her right hoof. She then leaned on the gate with her chest, and pawed it again.

'Oh bloody hell,' he muttered. 'No, you can't come with me,' he said firmly, turned and marched off down the track.

Behind him he heard Patricia whinny loudly - twice. He turned back and saw her staring at him and continuing to kick at the bottom metal bar of the gate.

'Oh shit,' said Gary walking back to the gate and examining the chain and old rusty padlock. 'No way,' he said to the horse over the gate. He moved to the hinge-end of the gate and saw that the metal hinges were welded to the gate and hung on spigots which were not only welded to the metal gate posts, but also had nuts screwed on top of the spigots to prevent the gate being lifted from the hinge end. 'No way,' he said again.

'Right, you stay,' he shouted at the grey mare, and turned again, adjusted his rucksack and walked down the track. After thirty yards he could still hear her battering the gate. He stopped, bent forward with his hands on his knees. He stared at the ground and muttered, 'Shit, shit, shit!'

He turned and walked back towards the gate where Patricia was stood weaving her head from side to side. 'Right!' he said impatiently, climbing back over the gate into the yard. He trotted out to the edge of the yard and peeped round the wall of a farm building to see where the rest of the horses were. They were still peacefully grazing spread out all over the field.

He scratched his head and pondered, 'What's she up to?' He didn't know that in the very yard he and she were standing in, less than three years previously, Patricia had fought for an hour against several men using ropes, sticks and shouts to force her up a ramp into a lorry to take her away from her birthplace, westwards to the new Ferne sanctuary at Chard.

Gary took off his rucksack and hid it in a corner of the field shelter. 'Stay right there,' he said to Patricia. He trotted off towards the row of old workshops he'd found earlier. He barged open a door hanging on one rusty hinge. It was quite dark inside and as his eyes adjusted to the dim building he saw a couple of old wooden boxes under a bench. He pulled out one box and wiped off the thick spider webs. There were a few old rusty tools in the box, but nothing that looked useful. He was looking for a spanner that might fit the nuts on the spigots of the yard gate.

He yanked out a second wooden box and found three old rusty spanners. He wasn't sure if any would fit, so he grabbed all three and trotted back to the yard. The grey mare wasn't there. 'Well bugger me,' he said. 'After all that, she's changed her bloody mind.'

He was just about to sling the old spanners into the trees, when Patricia snorted and came out of the barn where Gary had hidden his rucksack. Gary ran to the gate, and tried one of the spanners on the rusty nuts. They were all too big, but he found that using the thickness of one of the spanner's prongs wedged in jaws of a larger spanner, the combination gripped the nuts tightly. The first nut was so rusted that when he gave a strong tug on the bigger spanner, the nut disintegrated. The second nut moved and he wound it off the spigot.

He threw the spanners and the nuts into the trees and tried to lift the hinge end of the heavy metal gate off the spigots. It was too heavy. Watched by the grey mare, he looked around for something like a strong piece of wood or a branch to use as a lever under the gate. He found a likely joist from the wrecked roof of the cottage next to the shed he had slept in. He ran back to the gate and using the joist as a lever he succeeded in lifting the gate off its spigots. 'Happy now?' he said to the horse as he pulled the gate open.

He ran to the barn to retrieve his rucksack, and returned to the open gate to find that Patricia had walked through and was twenty yards along the grassy track. He pushed the gate shut and sweating from his activity, trotted after Patricia.

'Right you,' Gary shouted at Patricia as they trotted along the track together. 'When we get to the end of this track there's the last gate I'm ever going to open for you. All that way, all that hassle to get here, and you don't want to stay. So you go your way, and I'll go mine!' The mare merely snorted in response.

They reached the end of the track after a few minutes and stood together at a wooden gate which Gary easily lifted off its hinges and pushed open. The horse stepped through and onto the tarmac of a minor road, while Gary pushed the gate back into position and lifted it back on its hinges. He hesitated. The mare didn't. She trotted off along the right hand side of the narrow tarmac road. There was nobody around and Gary decided to follow her.

She cantered on for a couple of hundred yards when suddenly Gary heard what sounded like a tractor coming from behind him. He turned to see the tractor and its trailer just passing the gate that he and the horse had just left. He turned to look ahead to see how far Patricia was ahead, but she had disappeared!

As the tractor noisily passed him, the driver waved. Gary waved back and quickly looked ahead for the horse. The tractor was soon out of sight, and Gary continued briskly along the road to see a gap in the hedge on the right with a footpath sign which read, Winklebury Hill. There was no gate or stile – just an opening into a field rising steeply up hill. Gary stepped into the field, and saw Patricia two hundred yards away – making her way up the hill which was clearly too steep for him to do anything more than walk.

He cupped his hands and called twice, as loudly as he could, 'Patsy, whoa!' She did turn her head, but continued her slow gait up the hill until she disappeared. He knew there was no way of catching her, particularly, with his heavy rucksack. He stood in deep thought for several minutes. Had he made a mistake in releasing the horse? Why did she go on a journey with such determination with her herd, and then leave them? What is going to happen to her? Should he try to follow? She clearly heard his shout, but continued up the hill. 'What if she gets killed on a road? She won't have the security of a dozen people and several police vehicles. What if people get hurt or killed if she causes a road accident?'

He continued to argue with himself quietly. 'She chose freedom, time after time after time, but with freedom comes risks.' 'She doesn't know that, but you do!'

'Well, I can't do bugger-all about it now,' he said out loud. 'If it goes wrong, I will just have to accept that it was my fault.' He watched as the mare disappeared over the hill and as he walked further along the road towards the village of Berwick St John, Patricia was passing through the ancient remains of an iron-age promontory hill-fort on the crest of Winklebury Hill.

She then moved down hill, crossing the Cranborne Chase which had been reserved as a royal hunting ground after the Norman conquest and was the UK's sixth-largest Area of Outstanding beauty, overlapping the boundaries of Dorset, Wiltshire, Hampshire and Somerset, covering 380 square miles of woodlands, chalk grasslands and escarpments, hillsides and river valleys.

Gary strode into the village of Berwick St John and found a phone box. 'Hello, Liz, it's me," he responded to his wife's voice. 'Where the hell are you?' came the reply, quickly followed by, 'No, don't tell me.'

Gary smiled. Many years ago, he had suggested to his wife that it would be better if she didn't know too much about his animal rights activities.

'I'm on my way home – hopefully tomorrow sometime, if not I'll call you again,' said Gary.

'OK then,' said his long-suffering wife. 'Take care.'

'I will,' said Gary. 'Love you.'.

'Love you too,' she said, somewhat unconvincingly.

Gary replaced the receiver, stepped out of the telephone box and decided to take a quick look around the village. The attractive Talbot Inn included a small village shop and he needed to replenish his fruit drinks. He also bought a couple of apples, a banana, and a packet of biscuits and sat on a wooden bench outside the pub and ate his lunch, but still feeling uneasy about his role in Patricia's final bid for freedom.

Satisfied with his meal, he rose, adjusted his rucksack on his back, dumped his apple core and banana skin in a waste bin and set off towards the A30 where he hoped to hitch home to Northampton.

He had to pass the gated entrance to the Ferne Estate and he halted briefly to look at the gate lodge and the sprawling pastures either side of the track. He counted the horses grazing in the right-hand field - only fourteen. He wondered when Patricia's disappearance would be discovered.

He noted that there was a car parked next to the lodge and deduced that meant there was someone was at home. He didn't want to get into a conversation with anyone, so he marched the few hundred yards to meet the A30, crossed over the road and started thumbing for a lift.

*

Minutes after Gary had walked past the Ferne gate, Joe the gate-keeper emerged from his home to check the horses. With a handful of carrots in his jacket pocket, he checked the water trough nearest the lodge and strolled up the field. He counted ten horses in the field, which meant that there must be five in the yard or large barn.

He strolled into the yard where Big Patrick and Beadle were standing in the doorway of the large barn. Gregory and Lucky were silently staring over the gate which separated them from the grassy track. He gave each of the four a carrot and peered around looking for Patricia. 'Where the hell is Patricia?' he muttered

She was not in the yard or the barn, so he surmised she must be still in the field and may have been standing hidden behind one of the other horses as he walked through them in the field.

Joe trotted as quickly as he could back into the field. No Patricia. Panting, he returned to the yard for a further check, but there was no doubt, the grey mare had disappeared. Big Patrick followed him as he walked to the heavy iron-gate which was fixed between two pillars. The gate, its chain and rusty padlock were still in place. Joe looked over the gate and was joined by Big Patrick and they both stared along the lane. Joe saw that the long grass in the lane had been trampled. He glanced at the hinge-end of the gate, which appeared to be normal, just as he turned away, something made him take a closer look, and he saw that at the top of one of the spigots that supported the hinges, there was a glint of bare metal amongst the years of rust. He realised that both nuts were missing from the spigots.

He climbed over the gate and followed the trampled hoof-prints and human boot prints along the lane. He half- expected to find Patricia somewhere, but the further he went along the track, the more he knew in his mind that he would not find the horse. Eventually he reached the wooden gate at the southern edge of the estate. It was still closed with a chain and padlock, but it was easy to see that it had been lifted off its hinges and dragged open, because the bottom of the hinge-end gate post had left a curved scrape on the ground.

He looked in vain for any signs of a vehicle being involved, but only found some hoof prints along the grass verge of the road. Joe retraced his steps along the grassy track, through the big yard and down the track to the Lodge. It took him a full fifteen minutes, his face was flushed and he was having trouble getting his breath as he pushed open the door to the Lodge. He rushed to the telephone, without a word to his wife, but she could see that he was distressed. 'What on earth is the matter, Joe?' she asked.

Joe lifted the handset and reached for the note-book containing telephone numbers, the latest being the Ferne Animal Sanctuary's number at Chard. He started dialling but was so breathless he had to put the phone back down.

'Sit down Joe and get your breath back, before you fall over,' said Clare. Her husband accepted the advice and sat down, still wheezing. Clare waited patiently for Joe to recover his breath. Eventually he took a deep breath, pursed his lips and blew out a long puff. He dialled the Ferne Animal Sanctuary's number and held the phone to his ear, waiting for a response. He placed his hand over the mouth-piece and turned to Clare and said, 'Patricia has disappeared.'

'What do you mean, disappeared?' asked his wife.

Still listening to the ringing tone, he snapped at Clare, 'Disappeared – vanished - gone!'

He was immediately sorry for his ill-temper and raised his hand in regret. 'Sorry, love, I didn't mean to snap. Oh… damn.' he moaned in frustration as he listened to Trevor James' brief answer-phone message, waited for the tone, then said as calmly as he could, 'I'm sorry, Trevor. It's Joe. I have bad news. Patricia has disappeared. She was here this morning, but this afternoon I couldn't find her. It looks like someone has opened the big iron-gate in the yard and let her out into the track on the other side of the estate. The gate at the end of the track has also been opened. Please call me back. I'm just about to call the police and tell them what's happened. All the other horses are OK.'

Joe replaced the phone and immediately picked it up again to call Shaftesbury police. He explained that a white mare had disappeared, possibly stolen or set free by someone who opened two gates to the east of the Ferne estate. He gave the police his telephone number and that of Trevor James at the new Ferne Animal Sanctuary. Joe was exhausted. He slowly put the phone down and slumped wearily onto the settee. Clare was already pouring out two strong cups of tea as she asked, 'Do you really think someone opened the two gates?'

'Positive. Both gates have been lifted off their hinges and then put back. In fact, I remember reading or hearing that's what happened when Trevor was trying to shut the horses in fields after they escaped from the sanctuary. Someone kept letting them out. I don't understand it.'

He paused to pick up his cup, but the phone rang and Joe grabbed it. "Hello, Ferne Lodge.'

'Joe, it's Trevor. What's happened?'

"Oh Trevor. I've went out an hour ago to check the horses, and I couldn't find Patricia. Do you remember the big metal gate in the yard by the horse shelter?'

Trevor responded, 'Yes, I know where you mean.'

'Well I didn't notice at first because it was still padlocked, but then I saw that it had been lifted off the hinges and dragged open and apparently hung back on the hinges. Do you remember the grass track beyond that gate?'

'Yes, you said it goes to the rear entrance to the estate,' replied Trevor.

'Yes, there is another gate at the end of the grass track, and that gate had also been lifted off, and then put back, just like the one at the yard.'

Trevor was incredulous. 'I don't understand it. The animal activist crowd helped us get the herd to you. We saw them leave once all the horses were safely with you. I can't believe that they would have hung around all night and this morning, to open gates to allow just one horse to escape. I wonder whether it's something to do with the original incident at our place – you know, where a guy was found dead in our field. The gate that the horses escaped out of had also been lifted off its hinges, although it was well smashed by the horses anyway. Were they just after Patricia? Why would anybody go to so much trouble to steal a nine-yea-old unbroken horse? It doesn't make any sense.'

'Beats me, Trevor,' replied Joe.

'Well, Joe, I was going to ring you today to tell you that I've organised transport to collect the herd - four lorries and a single trailer for Patricia I've got a vet on standby to tranquillise her – I guess I'll have to tell him we don't need him for the moment! We were all ready for the day after tomorrow. Will that be OK with you Joe?'

'Sure,' said Joe, 'That's fine. Just let us know when you are on your way so we can get everything ready. I will open the main gate so the lorries can drive all the way up the drive to the yard. We can shut the horses into the yard for loading. Should be OK. By the way I've given the police your number and ours in case anyone rings in to report a stray white horse."

Trevor agreed the plan and told Joe not to worry about Patricia for now, and added, 'Thanks for alerting the police Joe. I'm going to call the press as well – maybe offer a reward for information resulting in Patricia being recovered.'

'By the way', said Joe. I couldn't find any sign of a vehicle stopping at the last gate to the road.'

'Well I can't imagine Patricia simply walking into a trailer, and even more unlikely to be led away on a rope and halter. It's got to be an animal liberation stunt. I'll ask the police to contact the activists that were involved so far. I'm so sorry you have had all this bother Joe. How's Clare?'

'She's fine. Takes everything in her stride,' said Joe, smiling at his wife. 'See you soon Trevor. I'll let you know if there are any developments this end.'

'Thanks Joe. Give Clare my best wishes,' said Trevor.

Trevor replaced the phone and looked at the list of numbers on the wall. Finding the number for local press reporter Bob Rayburn, he quickly alerted him to the latest situation, including the offer of a financial reward for information leading to the whereabouts of the missing herd leader Lady Patricia. He added, 'Oh, Bob, and no more killer horses, please'.

'I'll do my best, Trevor,' said the reporter, with as much sincerity as he could muster. 'Have you alerted the Wiltshire press and local radio?'

'No, just the police,' Trevor replied.

'Don't worry, leave it to me. Oh, how much is the reward?'

'Can't say yet,' said Trevor, 'I'll have to talk to our trustees – just say "substantial".'

'That's fine Trevor, leave it to me,' said the reporter.

By five o'clock, Gary Rorke was on his second lift along the A30. It was late in the afternoon, and he realised he would be lucky to get anywhere near his Northampton home until the next day, and, he would need to find an evening meal and somewhere to bed down for the night.

Meanwhile, Lady Patricia had dropped down the south side of Winkelbury Hill in the failing light, and was nearing the quaint village of Sixpenny Handley. She passed behind the village unnoticed, crossed the A354 road by way of a roundabout on the B3981, and set off up the 160 feet-high Pentridge Hill, which like Winkelbury Hill was topped by a prehistoric hill fort. She continued moving south until she stopped to rest in an outcrop of pine trees.

Chapter 12

Late afternoon in 'Auntie' Jean's terraced cottage in Milborne Port, her niece Angela, and five fellow campaigners had greedily tucked into Jean's best vegan effort – beans and chips – and were now checking they'd not left anything behind as they prepared to go their various ways home.

Their two transit vans and Clive's Viva van, still with his ladders strapped onto the roof, were parked on the other side of the road opposite to house. There was the sound of a vehicle outside and being closest to the window, Caroline tugged the curtain back a few inches. 'Uh oh', she muttered. 'We got visitors – old bill!'

Two uniformed officers emerged from the police panda car. The door-bell rang and Henry the Labrador barked, hauled himself off the carpet and walked to the door, his tail wagging.

'I'll go,' said Angie and she crossed the room, took hold of Henry's collar and opened the door.

'Do you mind if we come in,' said the male officer identifying himself as Sergeant Ray Kelly and his colleague as WPC Maureen Hodges. Jean joined her niece in the hall and said, 'Yes, come on in.'

With everyone in the lounge, Sergeant Kelly looked around at the group.

'I'm sorry to bother you, but I understand that you folks have had some involvement with the horses which escaped from Chard and are now at Berwick St John.'

'Yes, we helped escort them there,' said Ron.

'Yes, so I understand,' said the sergeant quietly, 'and I also understand from Yeovil police, that you, and some others, shall I say, exploited the situation to raise the issue of animal rights. Is that a fair description?'

Caroline interrupted. 'As far as we know, someone broke into the Chard sanctuary in the night and a man finished up dead. He was certainly not there to give carrots to the horses, was he? When the horses refused to be escorted back to Chard we felt that it would be wrong to force them....'

Caroline was interrupted by Robin, 'And we were only trying to give the horses some time to experience a bit of freedom to choose where they wanted to go. Oh, and 44% of the audience on the Jeremy Bateson show agreed with us by the way.'

'That's right,' said Angie, preparing to join in the argument, but Sergeant Kelly raised his hand. 'Look, I've not come here to get into a debate. I've come to find out if you know anything about the fact that one of the horses has disappeared from the Ferne estate at Berwick St John.'

'What, which one?' asked Ron, rising from his chair.

WPC Hodges flipped open her notebook, 'It's a grey mare called Patricia – which we've been told was the leader of the herd. She disappeared this morning.'

'And,' said Sergeant Kelly, 'Somebody went to a lot of trouble opening two gates, and she hasn't been seen since.' As he said it, he registered an almost imperceptible glance between Ron and Robin.

The sergeant said quickly, 'Do you know someone called Gary Rorke?'

In an instant Angie answered, 'Yes, he's a hunt sab in Northampton.'

'Has he been working with you in your campaign with the horses?' asked the Sergeant.

'No, he will be sabbing his local fox hunts, because it's the start of the hunting season.' replied Angie.

'So you don't know anything about the disappearance of this grey mare?' said the policeman.

'No. Maybe it's something to do with the people who raided the Chard sanctuary,' suggested Robin. 'Why would we help escort the horses all the way from Chard to Wiltshire – where they clearly wanted to be? As far as we're concerned it's all over.'

'OK,' said Sergeant Kelly. 'If you have any ideas, or if you hear anything, can I rely on you to call Shaftesbury police? And meanwhile, if you don't mind I'd like to make a note of your names.'

'What for?' said Ron.

The policeman shrugged his shoulders. 'You don't have to,' he said. 'I've noted your van registration numbers, so it won't be difficult to find out who and where you are.'

'Well, you do that sergeant,' said Angie. 'We are about to go home.'

Sergeant Kelly motioned to WPC Hodge. 'Let's go, constable,' he said, and led her into the hall. As he opened the front door, he turned to Angie's aunt, and said, 'Thanks very much Mrs....' (clearly hoping the pause would result in her giving her name), but Jean smiled and replied, 'That's OK sergeant.'

Outside in their police Panda the sergeant started the engine. Checking his mirror he asked his partner, 'What do you make of that, constable?'

'I don't think they knew anything about the horse disappearing, but when you mentioned, what's his name'...

'Gary Rorke,' he reminded her,

'Yes, Gary Rorke, there seemed to be a brief moment of tension.'

'Oh you noticed that did you Maureen? We'll make a policeman of you yet!' he smirked.

'I bloody hope not, sarge!' she chuckled as they pulled away.

There was consternation in Auntie Jean's lounge. 'I don't understand this,' said Ron. 'It sounds like Rorke's tactics, but what's the point?'

Angela frowned, and suggested, 'Maybe, the people who broke into the Chard sanctuary still have some reason for taking the horse. Maybe they managed to tranquilise her.'

Robin shook his head, 'The only thing that makes sense would be if the sanctuary put up big reward to get her back. That might have been the original motive, but knowing how wild she is, why take the most difficult animal?'

Jody turned to her partner. 'Clive, do you remember last year around Dorchester, there was a spate of pedigree dogs being stolen from their gardens and even from outside shops. It turned out that they were being snatched by people who waited for the dogs' owners to post rewards in local newspapers. The thieves would then contact the owners and say they have found the dogs. The owners were so relieved that they agreed to pay up, and didn't dare report it to the police in case they didn't get their dogs back. Maybe, this is the same scam, but with horses.'

'Yes, but why the most difficult horse?' asked Clive. 'It doesn't add up. And anyway, would the sanctuary, a registered charity, pay criminals to get a horse back.'

The room fell quiet until Robin stood up and lifted his rucksack, saying,

'Come on Caroline, we need to get home.'

'You're right,' said Angie. 'There's nothing we can do. In fact we've been bloody brilliant. We... well Robin, has promoted animal rights on TV, we've re-united young Tony with his folks, we've helped escort of herd of horses for miles....' (and pausing for thought) added, 'And most of all my Auntie Jean has been fabulous.'

'Here, here,' chorused the group loudly, followed by laughter as Henry the black lab jumped off the settee, and with his tail lashing, happily launched into a series of loud barks until Jean told him off.

As the group continued to pack, Ron tried to push £20 into Jean's hand. 'No, no, I don't want it,' said Jean, holding up her open palms.

'But Jean, you've fed us for days, we've all had baths, and you've even had a couple of coppers in your lounge because of us,' said Ron, 'Please take it.'

'No', said Jean firmly.

'We'll make it up to you one way or another,' promised Ron, 'We are really grateful for your hospitality.'

Caroline rose and hugged Jean saying, 'You're a star, Jean.'

'Nonsense,' replied Jean.

Jean stood at her front gate with Henry, and waved off the six young activists in their two transit vans and Clive's Viva van.

As they vanished along the road, she turned and walked back to her open front door. 'Come on Henry', she said and he followed her into a startlingly quiet house. 'We could do with a couple of teenagers, students perhaps, Henry,' she said to the dog that was looking up at her and slowly waving his tail.

'It's too quiet, this house,' she said, 'Although you do your best, don't you Henry?' as he pushed his nose into her hand.

*

The next morning, Dorset and Wiltshire local radio and newspapers reported the mystery disappearance of grey mare Patricia, together with a brief summary of the herd's equine exodus from the Ferne Animal Sanctuary and their escorted journey by the RSPCA and animal rights volunteers some 35 miles to their previous home.

The bulletins mentioned that the Ferne Animal Sanctuary was offering a financial reward for information leading to the recovery of the missing horse. People were urged to call Shaftesbury police or the sanctuary with any sightings, and reported the news that the rest of the herd were being collected the next day and returned to the sanctuary by livestock transport.

Trevor was busy confirming the arrangements and phoned Joe at Ferne Lodge to make sure all was well with the horses. He was relieved to learn that the loss of Patricia did not seem to have upset them at all. Two horses seemed to have assumed leadership, and from Joe's description it seemed likely they were Gregory and Lucky.

Trevor's daughter Rebecca had been helping clean out the goats' night-time pen and she came into the kitchen to wash her hands. Her father emerged from his office and joined her. He filled a kettle with water and placed it on the Aga. With his back to Rebecca he told her of Joe's report that all was well with the herd and that it sounded like Gregory and Lucky had taken over the herd's leadership.

'That's good, Dad,' she responded, 'but I was thinking that when we go to collect the horses tomorrow maybe we should ask Helen at the RSPCA to see whether she can find a couple of her inspectors to help us out.'

Her father instantly knew what she was up to. Without turning round, and with a smile on his face, he said, 'Oh I don't think we need to bother the RSPCA. We'll have the drivers and their assistants, and Joe and Clare will be there of course.'

'Yes,' said Rebecca, 'But sometimes drivers can be quite impatient and hard – you heard what Joe said about the problems they had to get Patricia into a lorry to come down here. I just think that it would be good to have the RSPCA there.'

As the kettle began to boil and with Trevor still hiding a smile, he said, 'Well she might be away – you know how busy she is.'

'Yes, but I'm sure she would want to see the whole job wrapped up. And what if Patricia is found nearby over there? I just think it would be good to have some experienced animal people around. Who knows, the animal rights group might turn up again.'

'All right, I'll give her a ring', he said as he poured boiling water into a tea-pot.

'It's alright, I'll call her,' said his daughter as she practically skipped out of the kitchen, through the hall, and into the sanctuary office.

'Her number's on the wall by the phone,' Trevor shouted.

'I know,' she shouted back, closing the office door.

'Don't forget your tea,' he shouted after her, chuckling at his daughter's not very subtle attempt at match-making. She opened the office door by a few inches, shouted back, 'OK', closed the door again and within seconds was engrossed in a half-hour call to RSPCA manager Helen Watson, her cup of tea forgotten.

*

The next day was wet with a heavy drizzle. After an early breakfast, Trevor rang the horse transporters and confirmed the meeting at the Ferne estate would be at midday. He then rang the Shaftesbury police to enquire whether there had been any reports of sightings of Patricia.

A female officer responded and said that it was a bit unfortunate that the newspaper and radio reports referred to the missing animal as a 'white horse' rather than a grey mare. Trevor was intrigued, and the officer explained that the only calls so far were from hoaxers from public telephone boxes. The callers were saying things like, 'I've just seen a white horse on a hill near Westbury,' and then ringing off. Further pranksters called to report sightings of 'white horses' on hills at Cherhill, Marlborough and Alton Barnes.

'These chalk hill carvings of white horses are all over Wiltshire,' explained the officer. 'At one time there used to be more than a dozen carved on Wiltshire's hills.'

'No genuine calls at all?' asked Trevor.

'I'm afraid not,' she said. 'In fact, the latest idiot called to tell us that there was a huge naked man near Cerne Abbas with a big club and an even bigger penis.'

'Oh I get it,' said Trevor, 'That's the Cerne Abbas giant, isn't it?'

'Yes, just another chalk hill carving,' replied the officer.

Trevor sighed, 'Oh well, we've just got to hope that no news is good news.' The officer replied, 'Yes, we'll let you know if we get a genuine call. The jokers will soon forget about it.' She paused and added, 'I have to say though, it is possible the animal was stolen, or has been found and hidden, and someone will want the reward. If so, they won't call us. It will be direct to you.'

'Yes, we are aware of that scenario, that's why we haven't given a reward figure,' said Trevor. 'Presumably, you will want to know if we get a call like that,' he added.

'Well that will be up to you,' answered the officer.

'The problem is,' said Trevor, 'If the animal has been stolen or hidden for a ransom, and we pay a fee to get her back, we are encouraging crime. But on the other hand, we are responsible for that horse's life. If we refuse to pay, she could end up shot and turned into dog food.'.

'That's why I said it's up to you,' said the officer. 'We recognise the dilemma.'

'Oh well,' sighed Trevor. 'We just have to hope. Thanks, a lot. By the way, we are collecting the rest of the herd tomorrow.'

'Good luck – hope it goes well,' said the officer, sympathetically.

*

The following morning, at the Ferne Animal Sanctuary, there was low cloud and more drizzle. At 10am, Trevor called his six staff into the warm kitchen after their morning rounds and invited them to dry off near the Aga cooker. Rebecca had piled up a stack of toast and a large jar of blackberry jam on the table and invited the staff to help themselves.

Trevor asked, 'Anyone with any problems this morning?' As the staff shook their heads and crunched their toast, he continued, 'I'm afraid there is no news of Patricia. Becky and me are meeting the horse transporters at midday at Berwick St John . There will be four lorries, so be ready to open the main gate. We'll have to open each lorry in turn, and let the first batch of horses into the stable field. I'm sure they will be only too happy to be back, but maybe you can make sure there is a line of feed buckets on the stable hard-standing. That will settle them down after their big adventure,' he added with a smile. 'Apparently it sounds like Gregory and Lucky have taken over the leadership.'

Trevor looked at his watch, and announced, 'It's ten to eleven. We should be there within an hour - another hour to load them, and maybe an hour and a half to get back. With any luck we will be back by three o'clock.'

As the sanctuary staff chatted over the tea and toast. Trevor and Becky climbed into the sanctuary van. In the back were a couple of waterproof coats, rubber boots and two dozen head collars and ropes for leading the horses into the lorries. They left the sanctuary, drove through Chard and sped off east along the A30.

*

LADY PATRICIA

The erstwhile herd leader Lady Patricia had kept near the top of Pentridge Hill as she continued moving south west, but eventually she descended into the valley where she found herself near the tiny villages of Daggons and Alderholt.

She continued to the tiny village of Harbridge on the banks of the river Avon, and crossed a small bridge over the river to pass through another small village of Ibsley where Royal Mail delivery driver Bert Harvey's red van was parked outside a cottage. He had just delivered a parcel to an elderly lady resident, and was checking his list for the next delivery.

Suddenly he was aware of the sound of dull hoof-beats and he glanced through his side window as a white horse trotted confidently past him. He peered into his wing mirror, expecting to see someone following the animal, but there was no-one about. Then he recalled that the previous day there was a local radio appeal asking people in Wiltshire and Dorset to keep a look-out for a white horse that had disappeared from Berwick St John.. He also recalled there was a mention of a financial reward for information which led to recovery of the horse. He jumped out of his van and knocked on the door of the cottage as he watched the hind-quarters of the horse gradually disappearing up the lane.

The door slowly opened as the elderly lady peeped through the gap. Bert said, 'Sorry missus, but there's a horse loose on the road. There was a radio appeal yesterday for local people to look out for a white pony and inform the police. Can I use your phone?'

The grey-haired lady frowned, opened the door a little more widely and peered up and down the lane. 'I don't see a horse,' she muttered suspiciously.

'It's out of sight now,' said Bert. 'But if I tell the police it was here just now, they may be able to track it.'

The lady relented, saying, 'I don't generally let people in unless I know them, but you can come in, provided you wipe your shoes.'

Bert wiped his shoes vigorously on the door mat and stepped inside. The lady pointed to the phone on her sideboard. 'I'll have to phone 999', said Bert. 'After all it is a horse on a road – could be a danger.' His call was answered almost immediately, and Bert asked for the police. Within seconds he was quickly explaining the reason for ringing – describing the horse and its location. The male operator thanked him and said he would report it to Shaftesbury and Fordingbridge police. Feeling a bit embarrassed, Bert mentioned the reward and persuaded the operator to record his name and address and pass it to Shaftesbury police.

Smiling, Bert replaced the phone and turned to his host. 'Thanks missus. I tell you what, if they find the horse as a result of the call, there is a reward. I don't know how much, but I'll make sure you get some of it. What's your name – I should have noted it when I delivered your parcel.'

'It's Mrs Curtis.'

Bert leaned to look at the label on the phone saddle, and he pulled a small note-book from his breast pocket. 'I'll make a note of your telephone number and I'll keep you informed.'

Mrs Curtis chuckled, and said, 'It would be nice to have a little windfall – my pension doesn't go very far.'

'I'm sure,' said the postman pushing his note-book back into his pocket. 'I'll be off now. I'm Bert by the way. I'll let myself out,' he said, reaching for the door handle.

'It's all right, I'll see you out,' she said rising from her chair, and stood in the doorway as Bert walked around his van, she asked, 'Which way did it go?'

Bert pointed up the road as he opened his van door and climbed in.

Mrs Curtis watched the post van move off. As she stepped back into the house, she said to herself, 'You'll be lucky Bert, you've got more chance of finding a needle in a haystack than a single horse in the New Forest.'

*

Trevor and his daughter Rebecca arrived at noon to find the Ferne estate gate open and four Bedford lorries on the track. The four drivers and their assistants, two of them women, were chatting to Joe and Clare at the gate of the Lodge.

LADY PATRICIA

Trevor and Rebecca joined the group as Joe was explaining that he had herded the horses into the gated yard at the top of the track and that they were happily munching hay in the field shelter racks.

The group turned at the noise of another vehicle arriving in the lay-by - an RSPCA van. 'It's Helen,' said Rebecca excitedly. The RSPCA manager and a young man climbed out of the vehicle and Rebecca ran to greet them and walked back with them to join the group.

'Hello Trevor,' said Helen, smiling as she squeezed his arm (to Rebecca's delight). 'Hi Helen,' responded Trevor feeling slightly embarrassed. Helen introduced her companion. 'This is Brian Stevens. He works voluntarily at our West Hatch wildlife hospital. He lives in Taunton and has some experience in stables. So I thought he might be useful. And, I've got some news Trevor. The police contacted me to say that there has been report of an unaccompanied white horse.'

'Oh wow,' said Rebecca. 'Where was this?'

'A little village called Ibsley between Fordingbridge and Ringwood, just over the river Avon,' said Helen. 'It was phoned in this morning by a postman.'

'How far is that from here?' asked Trevor. 'Do you know it Joe?'

'Well, probably only 15 miles as the crow flies,' answered Joe, and added, 'But they are only B roads – so more like 20 - 25.'

Trevor thought for a moment. 'We have to get the herd back to Chard. We can't spend the day looking for Patricia.'

Helen said, 'Trevor, look. Why don't I leave Brian with you? I'll take Rebecca with me to the village where the horse was spotted. What worries me is that she could soon be in the New Forest – that's well over 200 square miles of woodland. I think it's worth trying to find her today.'

'I agree', said Trevor. 'Becky, get a head collar out of our van and a rope, just in case you find her and she's happy to hear a familiar voice. You never know, she might let you get a collar on her. You may even be able to find a farm who will take her in. It's a long shot, but worth a try.'

'Come on then, Becky,' said Helen. 'I'll look after her, Trevor. You should be back at the sanctuary with the horses this afternoon. We'll find a phone and leave you a message.'

An excited Rebecca ran to the Ferne Sanctuary vehicle, pulled out a head collar and a long rope and quickly slipped into the front passenger seat of the RSPCA van where Helen was snatching a look at a road map. As Rebecca clipped on her seat belt, Helen slapped the map into Becky's lap, started the engine and said, 'You're navigator.'

'You're taking a chance,' laughed Becky. 'We could finish up in Cornwall.'

'I quite like Cornwall,' said her companion. 'Nice beaches.'

As the RSPCA van moved off, Trevor welcomed the young RSPCA volunteer. 'You up for this Brian?'

'Yes, sir,' said the handsome, dark-haired teenager.

*

The operation to retrieve the sanctuary's fourteen equines worked like clockwork. The drivers and assistants were clearly experienced and patient, and the horses totally compliant. All the horses were loaded within forty minutes, and the convoy of lorries took just an hour and three-quarters to arrive at the Ferne Animal Sanctuary and park neatly in line in the road alongside the sanctuary boundary hedge. One lorry at a time, reversed into the sanctuary's main entrance. When the rear ramps were lowered, the sanctuary staff encouraged the slightly nervous horses to walk down the ramp and quickly through the gate into the sanctuary's field.

One at a time, the lorries were emptied, the ramps pushed back to vertical and the empty vehicles driven out into the road and away. It took only half an hour for all the horses to be back in the fields they knew. The sanctuary staff escorted the horses through the gates and down the sloping field to the stables where, by four o'clock, the horses were lined up, heads down in buckets of warm bran and flaked maize along the concrete apron of the stables. All the stables and the field shelter were open with lights on, and with fresh bedding of shredded paper.

The sanctuary staff then began the late afternoon feeds and health checks of the dogs, cats, goats, pigs, donkeys, rabbits and guinea-pigs. The ducks and poultry were already rounded up and herded into their fox-proof huts. Trevor was eager to get back to his office phone for news of the search for Patricia by Helen and Rebecca. He invited RSPCA recruit Brian Stevens to accompany him back to the house kitchen to warm up with a hot drink.

As Brian sat down at the kitchen table with a hot drink and the sandwiches his mother had made for him early that day, Trevor slipped into the office and saw that there had been three recorded messages. The first two were enquiries for cat adoption which Trevor scribbled down. The last message was from his daughter.

'Hi Dad, it's me. I'm in a phone box in Ringwood. We're on our way home. It's half past four and we've knocked on doors in all the little villages after Ibsley which is where the police said the postman saw a white horse. We've asked at a big school called Moyles Court, knocked on doors in another place called South Gorley and in a village called Lindwood. Nobody's seen any sign of a stray horse. Some people knew about Patricia from the local news, but nobody's spotted her. I hope everything went all right with the horses. Helen reckons we should be back something like six to six thirty. See you soon, bye Dad'.

Trevor put down the phone and walked back to the kitchen, where RSPCA recruit Brian was hugging a large mug of coffee.

'They're on their way back,' said Trevor. 'Probably be gone six by the time they get back. You all right?'

Brian nodded. 'Yep, I'm OK, I've not got to be anywhere. Can I call my mum and let her know I'll be late home?'

'Tell her you can crash here if it comes to it,' offered Trevor. 'Phone's through there in the office.'

*

In fact it was nearly 7pm before Helen's RSPCA vehicle arrived back in the Ferne Animal Sanctuary's yard. The 'living-in' Ferne staff were all back in their accommodation – a large three-bedroomed bungalow. The two married staff members who lived in Chard had been picked up by their partners.

Trevor prepared a quick meal for four (with a little coaching from his daughter) and soon the four were flaked out in the large lounge on two settees in front of a log fire. Trevor had invited Helen and Brian to stay the night. 'We've got plenty of rooms. This house was once a rectory and has four bedrooms. It won't take a minute to make up a couple of beds. You can have breakfast in the morning and you can have a look around. The horses seem totally unperturbed about their adventure, but we'll check them more carefully in the morning for any feet problems.'

'Great,' said Helen. 'You all right with that Brian?'

'Yes, my mum knows where I am. It would be good to have a good look round tomorrow. It's all a bit different than our RSPCA places,' said Brian.

Helen said, 'Well to be fair Brian, our RSPCA kennels, catteries, and stables are mainly for temporary accommodation. And of course West Hatch is our main wildlife facility – especially seabirds caught up in oil spills. Ferne often keep animals for the rest of their lives, don't you, Trevor?'

'Well,' said Trevor, 'We do try to find homes for the cats and dogs, though some of the older ones stay here for ever. Our farm livestock like goats, pigs, and poultry stay here for life – just the same with the donkeys and horses – we don't let them go.'

'Really, Trevor?' commented Helen mischievously, winking at Rebecca.

'Well, not deliberately, anyway', said Trevor, accepting his error.

The four sat smiling, gazing into the dancing fire, but deep in thought. Rebecca broke the silence. 'The fact that Patricia has been seen so long after she disappeared, surely means that she was not stolen for a reward.'

Trevor nodded, 'That's true Becky, assuming it was Patricia that was sighted. I don't believe any stranger could capture her anyway…unless of course she was tranquilised.'

Helen joined in. 'If she is in the New Forest, which seems likely, she has more than 200 square miles to hide in. She'll have plenty of company, because there are around 3,000 New Forest ponies wandering free. If you include donkeys and cattle it could be nearer 6,000. They're all owned by commoners - local people who have a right to graze animals in the forest. The owners are paid so much for each pony they allow in the forest and every now and again the ponies are rounded up and checked. The round-up is called a 'drift' – not sure why! A lot of the foals are sold for riding, though we suspect that some go into the meat trade. We've also complained about the fact that the ponies are branded with hot irons to identify who owns them.'

Young RSPCA recruit Brian frowned. 'That's dreadful! Branding is horrific. I stopped watching western films because there always seemed to be scenes of cattle being branded with red-hot irons. Surely there's got to be something better than that.'

Trevor said, 'You'd think so, wouldn't you? I saw something in a paper recently about freeze-branding in America. Instead of burning the skin with heat, they are using a freezing iron which is so cold it kills the animal's hair roots in the owner's pattern on the iron. The problem is that the freezing iron has to be held on the hide for longer than the hot iron. The commoners say that the hot-iron is quicker and therefore, they say, less distressing.'

Helen joined in. 'The commoners have ancient rights to allow their livestock to roam the forest rather than having to keep them in stables and fields. The problem is, a lot get injured and killed on the forest roads. And of course, there are three packs of hounds hunting in the forest – Buck Hounds hunting Fallow deer, Beagles hunting hares and a pack of Foxhounds. It's estimated that there are more than a thousand deer in the forest.'

'I'm surprised that they are not crashing into each other,' said Rebecca. 'I don't understand why hunting has not been banned.'

Helen stood up, stretched and said, 'All the 400 odd Hunts in England have long traditions stretching back into history. Lots of MPs support it, particularly Tories, and of course the New Forest has been a royal hunting forest for donkeys' years. It was only last year that our RSPCA Council finally approved a policy calling for a ban on all hunting wild animals with dogs.'

She stretched again, and in a tired voice, said, 'Trevor, do you mind if I get to bed. It's been a long day?'

'Oh of course', said Trevor. 'Becky, can you show Helen and Brian their rooms? 'I'll just have a quick check around the stables,' he added, dragging his coat off the back of a chair.

Chapter 13

Sir Hector Randall was having a bad week. On the previous Tuesday three of his fox hounds had to be euthanized after being hit by a car. The driver was outraged and demanded that the police be called to witness the damage to his car. The Hunt Master had no choice but to listen to a rant by the driver's wife. As Master and Huntsman of the New Forest Foxhounds, he carried a pistol in case a fox had to be dug out of its earth and shot. With the three injured hounds whining and shaking under blankets, he reluctantly decided that he should shoot the hounds rather than wait for a vet. After the first shot, the woman in the car screamed at him. 'You're a monster! It's you who should be shot.' He was relieved when the police arrived to record the incident and assure her that the Hunt would accept liability.

Now at the Saturday meet, despite horrific rain, the Hunt had been followed by four members of the New Forest Animal Protection Society. They didn't interfere with the Hunt, but everyone involved in the hunt knew that the protestors were armed with video-cameras.

The hounds had been in full cry and had 'marked' a fox at the entrance of drain-pipe in a flooded ditch. By the time the riders caught up to scene, huntsman Randall had already called the hounds away and motioned to the Hunt's terrier-man to take his dog down into the ditch. Producing a torch and kneeling in several inches of muddy water, the terrier-man peered into the pipe.

A foot-follower shouted and pointed out that the other end of the pipe was only about few yards away. He picked up a stick and waded in the muddy water and started prodding it into the pipe while the terrier-man was still peering in with his torch at the other end while desperately wrestling with his squirming dog.

Frankie Jones, founder member of the New Forest Protection Society, shouted at the Huntsman Randall. 'Why don't you give him best, Hector?'

Her husband Ken, added, 'Yeah, come on Hector you can leave that one - it gave you a good run.' Their shouts immediately prompted several hunt supporters to give voice, with shouts of, 'Bugger off,' 'If you don't like it why don't you piss off home,' and 'What are you doing here anyway, you twats?'

Meanwhile, the hunt supporter abandoned the stick and at the terrier-man's suggestion, began to block the opening of the pipe at his end with a few large stones. This caused the water level in the ditch to rapidly rise. After a couple of minutes the terrier-man shouted, 'Open it up!'

The backed-up water flooded into the pipe, and in seconds the head of the fox appeared at the other end of the pipe and an excited hunt supporter shouted loudly, 'Here he comes', which promptly caused the fox to quickly back up. The terrier had seen the fox and frantically wriggled out his owner's hold and dashed into the pipe.

There were ten seconds of dreadful snarling, barking and whining of dog and fox fighting in four or five inches of mud and water inside the pipe. It then went quiet. The dog's owner jumped into the ditch and knelt down in the muddy water to peer into the pipe. He reached in with his right hand and grasped his dog's docked tail. He put his boot onto the end of the pipe and hauled the dog outwards. As the two soaking combatants slowly emerged, each animal had its teeth clamped into the face of its enemy.

Hunt master and huntsman Hector Randall realised that the hunt monitors had all moved in with their cameras fixed on the dreadful scene. He took his humane-killer pistol out of holster and loaded it with a single bullet. He stepped down into the muddy ditch, and handed the gun to the terrier man who was still desperately hanging onto his terrier's tail.

'Shoot it in the head,' he shouted, and turning round virtually screamed at the watching hunt followers, 'Get these ghouls out of here. Get in front of their cameras.'

A dull thud of the humane-killer was heard and the terrier-man hauled his soaking wet dog up the bank of the ditch with the dead fox still hanging from the terrier's bloody face. He threw the empty gun to the huntsman, and prized open the fox's jaws to release his dog.

Someone threw him a sack into which he hurriedly bundled the dead fox. He chucked the sack back to a hunt supporter and clutching his dog ran off to his quad-bike to check the terrier's injuries.

Sir Hector Randall decided not to have the dead fox thrown to the hounds. He knew that the film of the squalid battle between the terrier and fox would be more than enough to damage his sport.

'I'm stupid,' he muttered to himself. 'I should have called it a day when the fox went into the drain.'

Feeling miserable and with his face like thunder, he called his ten couple of hounds on his horn and began to move off through the trees to make his way back to the road where the hound van was parked. The mounted hunt members and foot-followers had already dispersed and left for home, and only his whipper-in Harvey Crompton rode with him, silently, knowing exactly why his boss was in a bad mood.

Walking their horses through a clearing in the dripping trees, Hector twisted in the saddle to speak to Harvey. 'Take my reins Harvey. I need a piss.' The whipper-in moved closer as Hector slipped out of his saddle and handed over his reins. He walked to a large oak tree and fiddled with his fly-buttons and started peeing on the bark of the tree. He frowned as he heard a rumbling noise – like the sound of thunder.

While he was doing up his buttons, he noticed his hounds where becoming agitated. The rumbling became louder and he realised that the 'thunder' was the sound of galloping horses. 'What's going on Harvey?' he shouted as he ran back to his horse, snatched the reins and swung up into the saddle. Both horses started fidgeting, making small agitated steps sideways, ears twitching, eyes rolling, as suddenly a dozen ponies crashed into the clearing, scattering the hounds in all directions.

Hector and Harvey had to use all their riding skills to hold on to their seats, but suddenly it was all over and the thundering herd had vanished as quickly as they had burst into the clearing. Hector pulled his hunting horn out of his jacket to call his hounds back. As the hounds slunk back into the clearing the two men mentally counted them and watched for any injuries.

'What the hell was that, Harvey – someone moved the bloody Grand National?'

'God knows,' responded Harry. 'They were all local ponies, except for a grey at the front.'

As they made their way back through the drizzle and gloom towards the road where the hound van and horse trailer were parked, Harvey turned to Hector and said, 'You know what? Did you hear about the sanctuary ponies that escaped from Chard in Somerset and travelled to the old Hamilton estate near Shaftesbury. They've been taken back, except one grey Connemara grey mare that disappeared. The Chard sanctuary has offered a reward for getting the pony back, but I heard that it was last seen near Fordingbridge – that must be two weeks ago. From there it could easily have reached the Forest.'

'Yes, I think I heard something about it, replied the Huntsman. There was some sort of TV debate. I'll call the police tomorrow just to tell them what's happened, and we ought to alert the other local Hunts'.

They reached the hound van without further incident. One of the hunt kennel staff was waiting in the cab, and the hounds were quickly boxed. Hector and Harvey loaded their two mounts into a double trailer and followed the hound van back to the hunt kennels at Minstead.

*

When the hunt ended with the drain and terrier incident, and the scowling Hunt members dispersed, Frankie and Ken Jones and their friends Rachel and Peter of the New Forest Animal Protection

Group, had picked their way back to Ken's car and drove back to Ken's house in Burley. The four were cold and wet and still stunned by the distressing and scenes they had witnessed.

Within an hour they had enjoyed hot showers and Frankie dug out a couple of spare dressing gowns for their friends. The four sat deep in thought with hot drinks and toast as they stared into the crackling wood fire in the Jones's front room – their wet clothes hanging on either side of the hearth.

The silence was broken by Frankie. 'Horrible people,' she suddenly exclaimed. 'They could have left that fox.'

'They wouldn't let a fox go free in front of us. That would have been a victory for us,' said Rachel, rubbing her damp blond hair with a towel.

'That's true,' said Ken. 'Well, shall we see what we've got on film?'

'Not for me,' answered Rachel. 'I don't think I can bear to see it at the moment.'

'Nor me, Ken,' said Peter, reaching out to touch his girlfriend's hand.

'Let's leave it tonight, Ken,' agreed Frankie.

'I'll tell you what I'll do', ventured Ken, 'I'll look at it tomorrow morning, and if it's really good,' ('You mean really bad!' said Rachel), 'Quite!' agreed Ken and added, 'If it's really bad, I'll call you to discuss whether we send it the media, or to the League Against Cruel Sports, or both.'

'And the hunt sabs,' added Peter.

'Right, more tea and toast for everybody?' said Frankie, thankful that they were putting off reviewing the disturbing images of the day.

At ten o'clock the next morning Ken phoned the League Against Cruel Sports and described the grim end of the hunt. 'We filmed the whole thing,' said Ken. 'Do you want a copy?'

'Yes, we do,' replied the League's press officer. 'It sounds dreadful. In fact it's very timely because we are just starting to put together a film entitled, 'The Things They Do To Foxes', which we want to show to MPs and the media. From the sound of it your film would shock a lot of MPs. Many of them think that Hunts hardly ever catch a fox, so if your film shows what happens when a fox beats the hounds and gets down a hole, it will be a real eye-opener for a lot of people.'

At the same time that Ken was talking to the League Against Cruel Sports, Sir Hector Randall, Master of the New Forest Fox Hounds, was on the phone to the secretary of the New Forest's Verderer's Court, complaining about the interference with the Hunt's activities by the four 'antis' whom he described as 'hunt saboteurs'.

He also reported the stampede of a herd of New Forest ponies led by a grey mare. He complained that if the white horse was the one lost by the Ferne Animal Sanctuary, they should find it and take it home as it had no right to be on the forest, because its owners were not New Forest 'commoners.'

Sir Hector had earlier phoned the Masters of both the New Forest Buck Hunt and the New Forest Beagles to urge them to support his call for the verderers to take action against 'antis' disrupting their legal activities.

Later, Sir Hector received a call from Linda Philips, the secretary of the verderers' court, advising him that there was a meeting of the Court already scheduled for two weeks hence and she would suggest to the chairman that the two issues that he had raised should be featured on the agenda.

Her next call was to Trevor James, the manager of Ferne Animal Sanctuary, to report the complaints about the grey mare. Trevor explained the circumstances of the disappearance of Lady Patricia and that a substantial reward for information was still on offer for information leading to recovery of the mare.

He explained that the RSPCA and his daughter Rebecca had already made visits to the New Forest as the result of possible sightings of the horse, and that hours of searching had come to nothing. The verderers' court secretary was sympathetic, and suggested that Trevor attend the meeting of the court where the complaints from the local Hunts and some of the commoners would be raised.

When the conversation with the manager of the Ferne Animal Sanctuary ended, Linda found the telephone number for the New Forest Animal Protection Group and left a message asking for someone to ring back 'on an important' issue. Later that afternoon, Ken returned the secretary's call.

'The thing is', said Linda, 'the Master of the New Forest Fox hounds and the Chairman of the Buck Hounds have both complained about your group harassing their members and disrupting their sport.'

Ken put his hand over the phone mouthpiece, and repeated the words of the secretary to Frankie, who exploded. 'Bloody cheek! What sport? Setting dogs onto foxes for fun, tell him that's not sport…..' as Ken, with his hand still firmly covering the mouthpiece, whispered, 'It's not a him it's a her.'

Putting his finger to his lips, he removed his hand from the mouthpiece and spoke quietly, 'We don't harass anybody nor disrupt anything. We just watch and film. We are not saboteurs, we are witnesses to the evil torture of the forest's wildlife.'

'Between you and me,' said the voice at the other end, 'Don't tell anybody, but I hate hunting. But unfortunately it is a legal activity. The issue will be raised at the next verderers court. The hunt is alleging that you are disrupting their sport, so you will be able to have your say. The court session is two weeks today. Can I say you will attend?'

'You certainly can,' said Ken, 'And thank you very much.'

'No problem,' said the secretary.

'Oh, before you go,' Ken blurted, 'Will we be able to show the court the film we got yesterday?'

'That, I can't say. I can only ask the chairman.'

'Fair enough,' said Ken.

Frankie stood with arms folded as her husband carefully placed the phone back in its cradles. 'So what's happening?' asked Frankie.

'The hunt are complaining that we harass and disrupt their sport and they want the verderers' court to hear their complaint,' said Ken.

'Cheeky buggers,' bristled Frankie..

'She's on our side,' said her husband, 'She suggested we defend ourselves at the court. It's a fortnight tomorrow. She's going to ask the chairman if we can show the footage we got yesterday.'

*

Two and a half weeks had passed since the Ferne herd of equines had returned to their Chard sanctuary. To Rebecca's delight, Helen had not only visited the sanctuary and stayed the night twice at weekends, but had also brought Brian with her in her private car. Indeed, at Helen's suggestion the four of them visited an Indian restaurant in Yeovil on Saturday night.

After the end of the meal, they left the restaurant and found a quiet corner in a nearby pub. After Trevor had brought back a tray of soft drinks they began to discuss the problem of Lady Patricia's presence in the New Forest.

'Sounds like she's having a good time,' said Helen.

'If we can't catch her, she's going to be in danger, 'specially if she is setting up her own herd,' replied Trevor.

'Maybe', said Helen, 'if she's still at large by the day of the court hearing, I can make it clear to the court that the RSPCA would take action if anyone harms the animal. I assume that the chairman of the court would endorse that, and we could say that if the presence of this one horse results in serious problems, we, as the RSPCA and Ferne, will create a plan to track her down and capture her – probably using a tranquiliser dart gun.'

'It's a shame, though,' said Rebecca. 'She has complete freedom and it seems as if she's got plenty of horsey company. I mean, if we do bring her back to Chard, will she be miserable?'

There was a pause in the conversation, and Helen turned to Brian and asked him, 'Do you have any thoughts, Brian?'

Brian hesitated and puffed out his cheeks. 'Well, as I understand it,' he said, looking down at the table, 'Patricia led the herd away from Ferne, probably because of the incident with people who may have tried to steal her, or maybe another of the herd, and it all went wrong. I don't think it was anybody like some of these monsters you hear about who stab horses. Somebody like that would not have brought a horse box with them. Then she kept the herd going away from the sanctuary until she got back to the old sanctuary, where you would think she would be content. Next, somebody let her go or took her from there, leaving the herd that she knew so well.'

Looking up for a moment and seeing that the three others were surprised at his unexpected verbosity, Brian continued. 'From what you have all told me, there is no evidence that she was kidnapped, and yet clearly someone helped her escape by opening two gates. And yet they closed the gates behind her. Why did that person close the gates? It must have been because they did not want the rest of the horses to follow. I reckon it must have been someone who recognised she still wanted freedom, maybe one of the animal activists, or someone completely new who supports animal liberation. The thing is, assuming the white horse seen in the New Forest is Patricia, I don't think she will be happy to return, either to the new Ferne, or the old one.'

Brian reached for his half glass of orange squash, took a mouthful and set it down on the table. Nobody said a word. Rebecca stared at him, her wide-eyes shining.

'Well, well,' said Helen. 'Where's shy Brian gone?'

'Hear, hear!' said Trevor. 'That's brilliant Brian. That's a totally believable synopsis. I think you've nailed it!'

Brian felt his face warming, and he quickly drained his glass.

After another ten minutes, the four stepped out into the poorly lit pub car park and clambered into Helen's private car. As Trevor shuffled into the front passenger seat, Helen twisted sideways to fasten her seat belt and glimpsed Rebecca reaching for Brian's hand in the darkness of the back seat. Helen said nothing, but had a smile on her face all the way back to the Chard sanctuary.

Chapter 14

The New Forest Verderer's Court dates from the 13th century and is based in the Verderer's Hall, next to the Queen's House at the top of Lyndurst High Street. It was originally a court to hear cases of offences within the Sovereign's forest.

By the 20th century the Verderer's Court's purpose was to protect and administer the forest's practices, conserve the landscape and wildlife, and safeguard the future of 'commoning' - the right for local folk to graze their horses, cattle, donkeys, sheep, and pigs in the forest.

The Official Verderers of the New Forest consist of a chairman, who is appointed by 'the Crown', five elected local verderers and another four representing the Forestry Commission, Ministry of Agriculture, English Nature and the National Park.

As a reflection of the original purpose of the court, the large hall has a rough-hewn 'dock' which stands between the Verderer's seats and half a dozen long wooden pews for the public. Hung on the walls are the mounted heads of deer – including two fallow deer heads found with their antlers totally tangled – the result of a fight in the 'rut' of 1905. Apparently they fell into a ditch where one was smothered by the other that had died of a broken neck.

Another pair of antlers hanging on the wall marked a similar tragedy that occurred in 1967 when two rutting roebucks died because they couldn't break free from each other's antlers.

Also on display is a gruesome reminder of times past when only the sovereign could hunt deer in the forest. In Tudor times a large iron stirrup known as Rufus's Stirrup was used to measure local dogs. Those small enough to pass through the stirrup were considered not to be a danger to the monarch's deer, but larger dogs had their paws painfully mutilated to prevent them chasing deer.

*

On the last Thursday of November there was an unusually large crowd of people standing outside the Verderers' Court waiting for it to open at 11am. The increased interest was partly because of the two issues raised by Sir Hector Randall, Master of the New Forest Foxhounds, firstly the fact that an unruly runaway grey Connamara pony was present in the forest, but was not the property of a New Forest commoner, and secondly that members of the New Forest Animal Protection Group were disrupting hunting in the forest.

The two issues had been listed in the local newspapers, attracting some intense discussion in the town community. The number of visitors was also swollen by ten members of the New Forest Animal Protection Group, and Trevor, Rebecca and Helen.

As the doors opened and the crowd noisily rumbled into the hall, another group of six non-local visitors joined the line. They were hunt saboteurs Robin Chamberlain, Angie Wright, Ron Walters, Carol Dickinson, Clive Thomson and Jody Small. The activists had been alerted to the event by members of the New Forest Animal Protection Group and a hasty ring round had resulted in the sabs decision to visit the New Forest – particularly because that week's Horse and Hound magazine page of hunt fixtures showed that the New Forest Fox Hounds were hunting on the same Thursday – whereas their usual hunting days were Tuesdays and Saturdays.

The court attendant closed the heavy door and walked a few paces towards a chair located against the rear wall a few paces away. Before he reached his seat there was a rattle at the door. Shaking his head, he spun on his heel and returned to the door and half-opened it inwards. Two men were heard quietly apologising for their lateness. The attendant said, 'There are no seats available, so you will have to stand against the back wall.'

Angie casually turned her head to see who had entered.

Surprised, she whispered to Ron, 'It's Rorke! He's got Tony with him.'

Ron turned and his rustling coat attracted the attention of the other activists who also craned their necks to see who had arrived. They exchanged meaningful glances and whispers, but were quickly brought to attention by a strong male voice from the front of the hall.

A tall, white-haired man, in his fifties, wearing a dark green jacket and grey trousers was stood at a desk. He smiled and said, 'Good morning everyone. I notice we have quite a few new visitors and I welcome you all to the Verderers' Court. My name is Jonathan Robertson and I am the Official Verderer - a sort of chairman of the court. Today, I will start as usual with complaints received at my office. The first is from the Master of the New Forest Fox Hounds.'

Angie whispered to Ron, 'Should we boo or hiss?' Ron grinned

The chairman looked around the hall and said, 'I don't see Sir Hector here today. Has he deputed anybody to speak on his behalf?'

A hand went up, and an elderly man spoke from his chair. 'Mr chairman, they are hunting today.'

'I thought they hunted Tuesdays and Saturdays,' said the chairman.

The elderly man said, 'And occasionally, Thursdays, sir.'

'Well, I'm afraid unless there is someone here to represent the Hunt, their complaint will have to wait until January. The court does not sit in December.'

Ken Jones put his hand up. The chairman pointed to him and Ken rose, 'Good morning sir. My name is Ken Jones and this lady next to me is my partner Frankie. We are members of the New Forest Animal Protection Group. I understand that the Hunt Master has accused our group of disrupting their hunting, but it is not true. All we do is bear witness to their cruel activities which we believe should be banned by law. We attempt to film their cruelty and show it to the public and Members of Parliament in the hope that one day hunting wild animals with dogs will be banned.'

A brief ripple of applause emanated from Ken's fellow members

LADY PATRICIA

and the activists. The court chairman raised his hand and shook his head. 'May I remind everyone that this is a court, not Hyde Park corner. Mr Jones, I hear what you say, but the hunt officials have not come forward today to pursue their complaint. If they do wish to do so at next January's court, we may well want to see examples of your films, so we will give you fair notice of any such event.'

As Ken sat down, the chairman looked around the hall, and continued, 'On another issue, Sir Hector has also made a complaint that a stray grey horse that apparently does not belong to any of the commoners, is charging around the forest, frightening his hounds and almost caused him to fall off his horse.'

To chuckles from the public pews and a few grins from the other verderers, the chairman continued. 'Again, is there anyone else who has had contact or has even seen this animal. I understand that it may be one of the horses that escaped from an animal sanctuary in Somerset, and finished up on the original site of the sanctuary at Berwick St John. I'm told that all the horses have been returned to Somerset, except the one grey mare, which has disappeared.'

Trevor James raised his hand and rose. With a gesture of his open palm the chairman invited him to speak. 'Good morning Chairman. I am Trevor James, the manager of the Ferne Animal Sanctuary. Yes, we believe that the grey mare may well be our stray horse. She is a nine-year-old Connemara pony named Lady Patricia, and she was born at the late Duchess of Hamilton's Ferne animal sanctuary at Berwick St John. She is somewhat unique because she has never been ridden, never had any saddles, reins, bits or halters fitted on to her, and possibly because of that she has always been the leader of Ferne's herd of horses, both at Berwick St John and at the new sanctuary at Chard.'

Chairman Robertson interrupted the sanctuary manager. 'Mr James, you have heard the opinion of Hunt Master Sir Hector Randall, that your errant mare, assuming for the moment that it is she, has gathered a new herd and is perhaps a danger to horse riders.'

'All I can say, Mr Chairman, is that in my time she has never caused us any problems – except possibly when my daughter

Rebecca here, picks up Patricia's feet to pick out stones and check for injuries. If Patricia thinks Rebecca is taking too long, Patricia just walks away. She refuses to be tied up, often refuses to be groomed and insists on having her own way – albeit never hostile.'

'And are you referring now to your daughter or the horse, Mr Jones?' asked the smiling Chairman, beaming a huge smile at Trevor's blushing daughter, while laughter fluttered amongst some of the court's occupants.

'Sorry, Miss James – couldn't help it! Please forgive me,' said the Chairman, as he adjusted his glasses looked down at his notes, and continued, 'The problem with this horse, is that it is not owned by any residents of the New Forest. The only people who have complained about its presence so far, are the Master of the New Forest Fox Hounds and the chairman of the New Forest Beagles - who admitted to me on the phone that he has not seen any trace of the animal. It may be that the mare can be captured before the next session of the court in January, so I suggest that anyone who sees the animal makes a note of where and when, and contact the Ferne Animal Sanctuary, the RSPCA or the police.'

'Now we have other issues on the agenda…,' he paused because Helen Watson raised her hand and stood.

'I'm sorry Mr Chairman, my name is Helen Watson and I am the manager of the RSPCA's branch affairs in the south west. As there seems to be some concern about the nature of the horse, the fact is, it has an owner – the Ferne Animal Sanctuary – and is fully protected against cruelty under the 1911 Protection of Animals Act. If anyone has any concerns about people who might endanger the horse, the RSPCA or police should be notified immediately. Thank you Mr Chairman. That's all I have to say.'

As Helen sat down, and before the Chairman had time to speak, there was a shout of 'Wait a minute,' from a thickset, elderly man who rose from his seat at the end of the middle row of the public pews.

Without waiting for the Chairman's invitation, the man looked over to Helen and shouted, 'It's all very well you RSPCA people worrying about this horse, but don't forget someone was killed at the Chard sanctuary and a lot of people reckoned it was probably the white horse that killed the man who went into the field. The police said the guy was kicked in the head and died from a broken neck. What if somebody in the forest approaches this horse and gets kicked and suffers a terrible injury or worse?'

The Chairman was visibly irritated at the intervention. Staring at the man, he said, 'I have a message for you and everybody in this hall. I'm trying to be as accommodating as I can be, particularly as we have many visitors today. If anyone else wishes to speak on this or any other issue, they must raise their hand and wait for me to acknowledge them.'

Continuing to look at the man, he said, 'You are not a stranger to this court and therefore you should know full well that you cannot just jump up whenever you feel like it. However, you have raised the issue of health and safety surrounding this stray horse. We have heard from the manager of the Animal Sanctuary, that whilst not exactly a pussy-cat, the horse has never shown any violent tendencies. However, according to reports, apparently, in the dead of night some people entered the field – probably to steal a horse. Somehow one of those people ended up being killed and his accomplices fled the scene. The dead man has been identified, but nobody has been arrested in connection with the case, and therefore there is no-one who can tell us what happened. Clearly, if there was evidence that this white horse is dangerous and may attack anyone at any time, the court may have to insist that it is located, captured and if necessary, euthanised. We are not at that stage, because we do not even know whether any horse was responsible the man's unfortunate death, because there is no known eyewitness to the event.'

The chairman eyed a hand raised by one of the two late-comers standing at the back wall of the hall. 'Yes, young man. Do you have a point to make about this issue?'

The young man spoke while keeping his hand in the air, 'Yes sir, my name is Tony Smith, and I live in Oxfordshire.'

'You don't need to keep your arm in the air, Mr Smith,' said the chairman with a smile.

'Oh, yes, sorry sir,' said Tony, lowering his hand self-consciously.

'What is it you wish to say to us, Mr Smith?'

Tony took a deep breath and blurted out, 'I was one of the people involved in trying to steal the white horse from the Chard sanctuary.'

There was a gasp from the crowd and the noise of shoes scraping the wooden floor as the people in the public pews turned to look at the young man. Tony continued, pushed his hair away from over his right eye, conscious that everyone in the court was staring at him. He kept his eyes steadily on the chairman's face and continued, 'It was my friend who was killed. He said he only wanted the white pony, because it would fetch four hundred pounds. He was expert at handling horses and he said he would go in and put on a head-collar, and bring her out through a gate. Two of us waited at the gate and then we heard him shouting and the horse neighing, and the other horses charging around, so we knew something had gone wrong. We ran into the field and my friend was lying in the mud and he wasn't breathing. His head was bleeding and sort of twisted - the other horses were still charging around, but the white one, the one called Patricia, was just standing staring at us a few yards away.'

The court was in a shocked silence. Tony felt a tear run down his face and he fiddled for a tissue in his jacket pocket. He dabbed his eyes and took a deep breath, but before he could continue, the chairman of the court intervened. 'Mr Smith, before you say anything more, can I ask how old you are?'

'I'm seventeen, sir,' replied Tony.

'Mr Smith, I advise you to find a solicitor before you say another word,' said the chairman.

Pushing the damp tissue back in his pocket, Tony replied, 'My father is coming with me to Yeovil police station tomorrow, so I can tell them what happened.'

'Make sure that your father insists on a duty solicitor being present, before you say anything,' said the chairman.

'Thank you sir,' said Tony, and added, 'I just want to say that I hated that horse, but I now see that she was only protecting herself. Since then I've got new friends who campaign against cruelty to animals and that is what I want to do from now on.'

The chairman said, 'I wish you well young man. Your testimony today has been vital, because we can send out the word that no-one should attempt to capture or handle this white horse without involving the owners, the Ferne Animal Sanctuary. No doubt this issue will figure in our next court session in January, so I think we should now adjourn the court for lunch. I suspect that there will be far fewer folk coming back to court after lunch, and that we can get on with more conventional forest issues.'

*

Outside the court, the hunt saboteurs were in a huddle. Ron Walters was furious and rounded on Gary Rorke.

'What the hell's going on, Gary. Did you know Tony was involved with horse thieves?'

'No, of course not,' snapped Gary. 'When we found out from his parents' leaflet that he was lying, I challenged him and everything came out. He had run away from home and he teamed up with a couple of travellers who let him share their caravan. He looked upon one of them as a hero, but reading between the lines, the guy was just trying to get him involved in his dodgy activities. When the guy was killed trying to steal the horse, Tony took the guy's knife and wanted to get revenge. That's when he decided to hang around with us, because we were close to the horses. At Auntie Jean's he started to change his views. Do you remember how he reacted to the Bateson TV programme and Robin's speech? He was choked. Before he ran away from home, he was miserable at school, he had no friends and when his parents bollocked him for sniffing glue, he ran away. He thought the guy who was killed was his hero, but he now realises that the bloke was just a petty criminal.'

Angie said, 'OK Gary, but you've got to admit it's a hell of a change. From wanting to stab a horse to death one day, and the next being a fully-fledged animal rights activist. Has he still got the knife?'

Gary said, 'No, he gave it to me and I chucked it down a drain.'

'That's a relief!' said Angie.

'On the other hand,' said Robin, 'It took some bottle to stand up in that court, especially when he could be charged with conspiracy to steal a horse.'

'Where is he now?' asked Ron.

Gary said, 'His dad was waiting for him. He couldn't face you all. That's why we came in late,' said Gary. 'I've spoken to his mum and dad, and they've given me their home number. I'm going to call them over the weekend to see how they got on with the Yeovil police.'

'Right, come on then,' said Ron impatiently. 'Are we going to sab Hector's Hunt or not? They're meet is at Brockenhurst, it's only just down the road. We should be able to find em.'

A shout from behind them emanated from a group of members of the New Forest Animal Protection Group. 'Ron, are you going to the Hunt?' Frankie asked. 'We're behind your vans in the car park. Follow us if you like. We know where the Hunt is likely to be.'

'Great! Let's go folks,' said Ron, and both groups of activists quickly made their way to the car park.

As the hunt sabs, followed by hunt monitors, drove out of Lyndhurst to seek out the New Forest Foxhounds, in a nearby café, newspaper reporter Bob Rayburn from Chard quietly sat alone at a corner table with a cup of coffee and buttered toasted currant bun. He had joined other local reporters in the Verderers Court, having followed the equine exodus from day one - his name appearing under reports in numerous national and local newspapers. He realised that the story may still not have ended, but he had excited himself with the idea of cashing in on the unique story of a horse which having violently avoided capture by a horse thief, had taken her herd of disparate rescued horses and ponies on an epic journey to her birthplace, and then travelled on alone to the New Forest.

He had laid an ordnance survey map on the unoccupied table next to him. Referring frequently to his note book he was tracing a bright blue line of Patricia's journey from the Ferne Animal Sanctuary at Chard to her birth place at the original Duchess of Hamilton's animal sanctuary near Berwick St John.

The reporter had been baffled by the horse's next behaviour in deserting the herd, evidently with the assistance of persons unknown. According to sparse sightings, some of which had been reported sometime after the 'missing white horse' story had been publicised, Lady Patricia had climbed the hills, crossed the valleys of the Cranborne Chase, bridged the river Avon and disappeared into the massive area of Hampshire's New Forest.

With a yellow marker, Bob noted each town, village and hamlet community that Lady Patricia, with or without her companions, had passed through or near to during the epic route through the four counties of Somerset, Dorset, Wiltshire and Hampshire. He visualised thousands of fold-up leaflets mapping the route, and which would be funded by adverts of restaurants, garages, pubs, shops, hotels and 'bed and breakfasts' in the towns, villages and hamlets on or near the horse's route. He visualised the leaflets standing in cardboard holders on the counters at all traders along the horse's route, and possibly inserted in newspapers.

With a title of 'Lady Patricia's Journey,' he felt uniquely qualified to write the story, beginning with the dramatic death of a horse thief at the Ferne Animal Sanctuary and including all the events that ended with Patricia taking up residence in the New Forest.

Bob was convinced that Patricia's story could become a new exciting tourist attraction for people to begin at the Ferne Animal Sanctuary in Chard and then trace the route via Lady Patricia's birth-place at the original Ferne estate where she eventually deserted her herd to travel on alone to the New Forest in Hampshire and where her fate would be decided in Lyndhurst's historic Verderers' Hall.

Having completed the blue route and 'yellow-inked' features, Bob folded up his map, finished his last drop of coffee and carried the cup and empty plate to the counter. He knew exactly what he would be doing over the coming months - following Patricia's route, taking notes on attractions, visiting businesses and witnesses along the way, and writing the tale of the legendary white horse of the New Forest who chose freedom.

LADY PATRICIA

NO MORE SLAVES!

We want Freedom for our Brothers,
We want Freedom for our Friends,
Liberation for all Creatures in the World.
We want Rights to Dignity,
We want Rights to Liberty,
For all Creatures under Man, Suffering
Pain and Misery.

Every Cow robbed of her young,
Pigs lying in their dung,
Rats poisoned in a drain,
Lying silent in their pain.
Sperm whales diving in their blood,
Horses crashing in the mud,
Pheasants blasted from the sky

Do you hear all Nature sigh?
Horses whipped to die for bets,
Badgers drowned deep in their setts
Bulls tortured for human fun
Bile bears never see the sun.
A fox writhing in a snare,
Set by one who does not care.